ELLA

escape west by wagon train series

two part series

Copyright © 2018 Sadie Conall

Sadie Conall's website
www.sadieconall.com

Books by Sadie Conall

Madeleine (seven-part series)
historical romance fantasy
When the Wolf Loves *(Ryder: a boy alone now a free short story added to When the Wolf Loves)*
When the Wolf Hunts *(previously published as When the Wolf Bites: Part I)*
When the Wolf Bites *(previously published as When the Wolf Bites: Part II)*
When the Wolf Dreams
When the Wolf Breathes

Escape west by wagon train (two-part series)
historical western romance adventure set around mid-1840's
Ella
Ruby

This book is dedicated to

my readers
and those who support me, you know who you are
and to my sister Susan

And a big thanks to Charlene Raddon who designed my
cover. You can find her at:
www.silversagebookcovers.com

Author's Note

I'm dedicating this book as a thank you to all those readers who have stayed with me over the past four years, for your kind words, your reviews on Amazon and Goodreads, your emails, your follows, likes and messages on Facebook and Twitter and to those who follow my newsletter.

Also a special thanks to those readers who suggested names for the heroine of this story (which I asked for in my newsletter). To Robin for her suggestion of Ella which I love and to Karen and Linda for their suggestion of Constance and Julie for her suggestion of Martha.

This story, unlike the *Madeleine* series, has no fantasy in it. It's an historical western romance which begins near St Louis, Missouri in the year 1846, an exciting time in the young and rapidly expanding America, with steamboats and wagon trains struggling to cope with the influx of immigrants pouring into the territory.

The lucrative fur trade is almost at an end and fur trappers are finding employment elsewhere, some as scouts on wagon trains. It has been almost sixteen years since President Jackson signed the Indian Removal Act, where many tribes east of the Mississippi River were relocated west of it so settlers could farm their lands. By 1846 wagon trains had been rolling across their lands for almost ten years with an estimated half a million settlers heading to California, Oregon and Utah between the years 1843-1849 alone. And within a few short decades from the time this story is written, Native Americans living on their own lands will come to a bloody end as they are moved onto reservations, their land sold to settlers and railroad companies, with railway tracks eventually laid from coast to coast, opening the west to millions.

But this story isn't about the bloody wars which loom ahead for young America. It's simply a love story which begins when fate crosses a young woman's path and whether she decides to reach out to take the chance offered.

I hope you enjoy it.
Love Sadie x

St Louis territory, Missouri
April 1846

1

Marrok Gauvain crouched on a hill, looking through binoculars to the land which swept away beneath him. To the south and east lay woodlands along with levees which ran down to meet the Mississippi River, north of him and across the river lay the bustling city of St Louis. He glanced back towards the river, because even at this late hour large steamboats, keelboats and paddle-steamers were making their way towards St Louis, eager to berth for the night and allow their passengers to disembark.

He put the binoculars aside, squinting against the glitter of the setting sun on the water, watching as smaller vessels kept close to the banks, allowing right of way to the massive steamboats and paddle-steamers heading for the wharves of St Louis.

Marrok grunted as he watched them, wishing as he sometimes did that this territory was as he remembered it when he first came here ten years ago as a youth of nineteen. Back then, St Louis had outgrown itself as a frontier town and had settled into a bustling community with Indians coming to trade along with mountain men, French fur traders and settlers.

But it wasn't like that now. With the pressure to handle the hundreds of thousands of immigrants arriving each year with dreams of settling in Colorado, Oregon, California and Santa Fe, St Louis had become a boom town. But Marrok knew better than anyone that progress was inevitable and with money to be made off those settlers, only a fool would dare try and stop it.

A man once remarked to him that it had taken several hundred years to settle all that land east of the Mississippi River, therefore it was likely to take several hundred years to settle all that territory west of the Mississippi River.

But from what Marrok had seen in the past few years, if the numbers of people pouring into the territory were any indication of it, that land west of the Mississippi would take less than a hundred years to colonize.

Because it wasn't just Americans arriving in their thousands with hopes of settling in the west, but people from all over the world. Miners, blacksmiths and farmers, wealthy businessmen, doctors and lawyers all following a dream of owning land, of building empires.

Marrok was also one of them, so even though he might wish to turn the clock back to how this territory used to be, he'd also been seduced by the charms of the west. Indeed, he wished he were there now, in that fertile valley in northern Oregon with a river rich with salmon and forests teeming with elk and white-tailed deer.

Ten months at the most, that was all, and he'd be back there, carving out his own piece of paradise from the wilderness, this job done and forgotten.

He watched as the boats berthed below the town and knew if he were a betting man, there would be one wager he'd win. Almost none of those passengers would get a bed in St Louis tonight, not for a king's ransom, because such a thing was almost impossible in these bustling times. Marrok knew it because he'd spent hours walking the streets trying to get two rooms. In the end he'd paid almost double the usual going rate for two tiny attic bedrooms with single cots in a boarding house way at the back of town. But at least the place was clean, which almost guaranteed it was also free of bedbugs.

He sighed with fatigue and ran a hand over his face, feeling the dust and grim of the day's travel along with the day old stubble on his unshaven jaw. But shaving was the least of his worries. He had no time for such luxuries.

He put the binoculars to his eyes once more and swept the land around him, then confident he was alone and there was no-one to cause him trouble, Marrok packed the binoculars away in his saddlebags before checking his weapons.

One large knife hung in a leather sheath on his left hip. Another lay in a sheath on his right moccasin. A shotgun lay in a sheath by his saddle and a pistol lay in a leather sheath on his right hip. Another knife lay hidden within a leather bag which he carried over his shoulder, for Marrok trusted no-one these days, because along with the settlors pouring into St Louis came vagabonds, opportunists and thieves.

He reached for the wide brimmed leather hat which lay across his saddle horn but before he put it on and mounted his horse, he turned once more to look out across the country around him, squinting in the glow of the setting sun, wishing he didn't have to make the journey ahead of him. But he'd agreed to it and he wouldn't go back on his word. Besides, he was halfway there and he'd been paid well enough to do it.

He put on his hat and mounted his horse, but turned when he heard the sudden, distant sound of men's voices raised in alarm. He pulled at the rim of his hat to shield his eyes against the glare of sunset and saw a paddle-steamer bearing down on a large keelboat.

The men in the smaller boat raised their fists in anger, as the bigger vessel came in too close to the bank. The paddle-steamer sounded its horn and bells, warning the keelboat to steer clear, its massive paddle to the rear of the boat churning furiously, allowing the vessel to move away just in time to avoid a nasty collision.

Marrok felt the frustration of the men on the keelboat, because he'd been on flatboats taking wagons across the Mississippi and Missouri Rivers when those massive boats came in too close. They dominated the river, able to carry hundreds of passengers and livestock, but they also brought chaos with them. The smoke from their chimney stacks lingered long after they'd gone and the wake left behind damaged the levees. But they would keep coming upriver as long as there was money to be made off the people they carried. This morning alone, Marrok had counted twenty big vessels berthed below the town, both paddle-steamers and steamboats.

He kicked his horse on down the hill towards a small woodland which lay a few miles in the distance, planning to set up camp there for the night and even as he thought on it, Marrok felt the hunger pull at his belly. He'd eaten several hours ago in his favorite eating house in St Louis, after leaving his horse in a friend's livery to be brushed down and watered. The middle-aged couple who owned the eating house never served up anything fancy, but Marrok had never once been ill from their food and their premises were always clean. Nor did he mind the eating house was in one of St Louis's back alleys, well away from the hustle of the main streets, for Marrok liked the quiet there. And the couple always made him feel welcome, they didn't care who he was or where he came from, as long as he caused no trouble and had money to pay for his meal.

But it wasn't just food that Marrok wanted now, as twilight began shifting into grey shadows, it was the comfort of a warm fire and a good night's sleep. He was tired, but he'd been travelling now for over a week for a job he should never have accepted, but he'd been paid beyond what the job was worth and at the time, Marrok thought he could squeeze it into all his other commitments.

But he was pushing himself too hard, because tomorrow he must be on the road well before dawn if he had any hope of reaching the homestead before breakfast. By mid-morning at the latest, he must leave the homestead and heard north again, if he had any chance of making it back to St Louis by tomorrow night, otherwise he'd struggle to meet his own obligations.

He thought of the supplies he'd purchased that afternoon and decided to chance his luck and cut off some of the cured bacon to cook for himself, and take a few of the sweet bread rolls, because he had no desire to go to bed on an empty belly.

But he wouldn't touch the eggs. He only had six and he might need them to sweeten the deal tomorrow morning. Because if she didn't agree to return to Independence with him, this job would have been a waste of time for him and a waste of money for the man who'd paid him so much to ride all this way to get her.

2

Ella stood in the kitchen as Martha walked slowly around her, admiring the dress. "You make sure your hands are free of baking now, Martha," she scolded. "I won't get the stains out of it if you get something on it."

"Oh hush girl. You know full well I wouldn't dare get this thing all dirty, for I do declare it's the loveliest wedding dress I ever saw." Martha stood back to admire the satin and silk creation.

The dress was a perfect fit, hugging Ella's body in all the right places with the deep rich cream complimenting her skin tones and dark hair, while the satin and lace gloves reached up past her wrists covering her work-worn hands.

Ella lifted the satin skirt, feeling the weight of the half-dozen petticoats beneath it, then she dropped it, allowing the material to fan out around her.

"Oh Martha, I do love it," she said, a longing to her voice. "But you know as well as I do that I'll never wear it, for how can I marry such a man?"

"Because you've no choice," a spiteful male's voice came from the hallway.

The two women swung around to see Milton, older brother to Quentin Torray, Ella's late father, standing in the doorway. Ella felt disgusted to think he'd been standing there in the shadows watching her and wondered how long he'd been there.

He stepped into the room, a sneer on his weak mouth as he admired the dress, making her skin crawl as he looked her up and down. When he raised his eyes to meet her own, Ella recognized his self-satisfied grin for what it was. An entitlement that embodied all his power and none of her own. He knew it and she knew it. But as he grinned, a vicious spitefulness to it, Ella felt that now familiar rage, a thing unknown to her before her father's death. She felt it rise and take possession of her and before she could think on the wisdom of it, she leaned towards her uncle and when she spoke, her voice was low and full of venom.

"I will *not* marry Jebediah Crawley. I would rather rot in hell than allow you to sell me off to that old leech. You have no authority over me, you're not my guardian. And I'm telling you now Milton, the marriage to Jebediah will *not* take place."

She stepped back as her uncle took a deep breath, his face turning an angry red but before he could curse her and raise his fist, Ella turned on her heel, opened the kitchen door and stepped outside, slamming the door behind her.

Milton followed her, wrenching the door open, even as Martha fled the kitchen to the safety of her own room at the back of the house. Yet she heard Milton's rage, his voice booming out across the porch.

"You damn well *will* marry Jebediah," he bellowed, slamming his fist against the door frame. "The Church is booked for Saturday week. The Banns will be read out this Sunday."

He slammed the door so hard the frame around it rattled. Then Martha heard him stomp out of the kitchen and back down the hallway to the small study at the front of the house. It was a room which Quentin, her brother-in-law, had always used as his own. She heard Milton slam the door behind him, then there was nothing but blessed silence.

*

Milton sat down in the worn leather chair behind the old desk, his breath ragged with anger. He should be used to this defiance of his niece, but even after all these months he was still astonished by it, but the girl had fought him every step of the way since his arrival here some six months ago.

If he thought on it long enough, Milton knew the war between them had started on the reading of Quentin's Will, read aloud by an attorney in Illinois Town, which bequeathed that all of Quentin's belongings were to be shared between Ella, his only child and Milton, his only sibling. *Partners*, the Will had stated.

Except neither of them wanted a partner. Certainly not Milton. Especially not a defiant young woman of twenty-five who should already be married with several children hanging off her skirts and living in her husband's house far removed from this one.

Within days of the Will being read, Milton had insisted the ranch be put up for sale so he could get his half of the money out of it, because he'd no interest in making a life here. He wanted to go back to New York. He wasn't a rancher and never would be.

But it was then, on his insistence that the ranch be sold, that the war between his niece and himself evolved into a full on battle. Because she didn't want it sold and as if the good folk in this godforsaken place took her side, no-one came forward to buy the place, except one man.

Jebediah Crawley, the richest man in the territory. But along with his offer to buy the ranch, came one condition. Ella was to be included in the deal as his bride and to get the deal done, Jebediah had offered Milton an extra bit of cash, which Ella knew nothing about.

Milton had seen little harm in it, indeed he thought it was a good arrangement for all of them. He would walk away with a sizeable sum for his share of the ranch, plus a large amount of extra cash for making the sale happen.

Ella would get her share of the ranch, plus a rich husband.

Jebediah would get the ranch along with a young bride more than half his age who would give him sons and ensure his legacy lived on in this territory.

Milton grunted as he thought on it. Ella should be grateful to him for setting her up for life, because Jebediah could afford to give her whatever her silly female heart desired.

Except she wasn't grateful. And she was determined not to marry Jebediah, even though the marriage was to take place by end of April, or the deal was off. To make things worse, well aware the girl had no desire to marry him, Jebediah was now forcing Ella's hand, determined to have her as his bride by whatever means it took to get her to the alter.

Even starve her out, if necessary.

And the end of April was only two weeks away.

Milton reached for the bill of debt sitting before

him. It was a debt he owed from gambling, but it was way beyond his means. Yet it must be paid, otherwise the professional card player, who had arrived in the county upriver from New Orleans, would hurt him badly. Milton didn't doubt the threat because he'd seen the knives the brute carried.

He tossed the piece of paper across the desk in anger, thinking of the game of jeopardy he was playing. He knew his involvement in getting the girl to marry Jebediah was a low blow, but in fact he didn't really care too much. All he wanted was to clear his debt and move on back to the east coast with a wallet full of cash.

He turned and reached for the unwashed glass behind him and poured himself a generous shot of malt whisky. He had paid a fortune for the bottle to celebrate his good fortune after receiving the letter informing him he was to be a beneficiary of his late brother's estate.

But that good fortune turned to horror when he arrived here to discover the estate was nothing more than a small holding of less than four hundred acres. Worse than that, he had to share the pitiable ranch with his niece, a girl who was strong-minded, fiercely independent and given to fighting back.

Milton frowned as he sipped the liquor, trying to ignore that unease in his belly as he thought on Jebediah. The man was all fired up with the thought of marrying Ella, although in truth Jebediah's interest in the girl repulsed Milton. But he'd heard enough rumors circulating around town about the old man, with even the girls in the saloons in town staying well clear of him except one, and she was so scarred from burns suffered when young that she would take on the devil himself to keep herself fed and clothed.

Well to hell with them all, Milton thought as he sipped his liquor. He would be gone from here soon enough and never have to think of Jebediah Crawley or his niece again. Let them make their marriage bed and lie on it. He didn't really care one way or the other.

3

Jasper was shoveling the last of their hay when Ella stormed into the barn. And when she saw the tall, gangly black man of thirty-five, still working hard even though the ranch was falling to ruin around them, she felt her rage die away.

She loved Jasper, had loved him since she first met him along with Violet all those years ago, but since her father's death Ella noticed Jasper's dark hair had become flecked with grey and deep lines now framed his mouth. She knew it was the worry of what lay ahead of him, along with the grief of losing a man he'd loved, because Quentin and Jasper had been the best of friends.

He turned to look at Ella in astonishment as she came striding towards him in the bridal gown. "Lord above, Miss Ella. You do look a picture."

Ella lifted the skirt and petticoats high to avoid getting them soiled. "It's a gift from Jebediah, to bribe me into marrying him. Betsy told me it came upriver from New Orleans but it must have cost a fortune as the box it arrived in said it came from Paris, France."

Jasper leaned on the rake. He knew Betsy well enough because he talked to her once a month when he took the wagon into town with Ella and Martha to get supplies. Betsy and her husband owned one of the bigger mercantile stores in town and the bridal gown had arrived there, with a note for the box to be delivered to Miss Ella Torray.

"Well, I know nothin' about Paris Miss Ella, but I did hear folk talkin' on your upcoming nuptials when we was in town last, but I reckon that's between you and Mr Crawley."

Ella walked across to Bear, to pet him. Purchased years ago as a plough horse, Bear had been a big brute of a horse in his younger days and it had been Violet who named him Bear in jest, yet the name had stuck. Now he was old and plain worn out and like her father and Violet, his days were coming to an end.

"Well Jasper, I figure you and Martha have heard enough fights between me and Milton over the past few months to know my feelings on the matter. I refuse to marry that degenerate and I'm not being mean by saying it because everyone knows what sort of man he is," she paused to look down at the dress.

"Since I received it all those weeks ago I've refused to put it on, but Martha insisted this morning that I do so, just once. Unfortunately, Milton saw me in it and now thinks me agreeable to the marriage, so I let him know my thoughts on the matter and now he's in another filthy mood," she turned to look out through the barn doors, back towards the house.

Everything needed work. Rotten boards on the porch needed replacing. The gutter was leaking above the kitchen and more boards near Martha's room were rotting away. But there was never enough money to fix anything these days, let alone feed themselves or the horses. The chickens, pigs and cattle were long gone, all sold off to try and make ends meet or butchered to fill their own larder.

But as money slowly ran out as the months passed and the wedding to Jebediah loomed closer, Ella couldn't see a way out of it. In all truth, she'd begun to lose hope for her future because the decline in their affairs hadn't started with the arrival of Milton, it had started long before then, with the decline of her father's health. When his death came, it had been a blessing, his suffering over. But what little they'd had then had slowly been pilfered away in the months after Milton's arrival, as he helped himself to what he saw as his own.

She turned back to Jasper and found the former slave watching her, a look of concern on his worn, gentle face. But Ella was well aware that the arguments between her and Milton were a source of unhappiness for all of them yet like Martha, Jasper was powerless to help her.

She nodded towards the hay. "That's the last of it?" she asked, frowning. "Then from tomorrow the horses will have to make do with grazing in the fields although Lord knows there's little enough out there after the drought last summer."

Jasper frowned and glanced at the two horses. "I do despair Miss Ella, but what can be done? Ain't nothing's been right since Mr Quinton gone and gone sick."

Jasper still spoke in his Creole accent after all the years he'd lived here and usually his pleasant soft voice and gentle manner brought comfort to Ella. But not today. Their situation was now dire and she knew there was a chance they would lose the ranch without Jebediah having to buy it, because as it deteriorated, so did its value. Soon it would be worth next to nothing.

She felt the quiet of the barn and allowed it to embrace her, feeling her father all around for this was his place, where he'd worked alongside Jasper for so many years. She turned as old Bear whickered and as she moved once more to pet him, Billy reached out to nudge her from his stall. Billy was her father's horse and had cost a small fortune to buy, but Quentin had needed a good road horse to get to town while Jasper was ploughing the fields with Bear. Ella reached out to pet him, but Billy reared at her touch. He was jittery these days, but only since Milton started riding him, because he wasn't much of a rider and Ella had scolded him more than once for mistreating Billy.

"You alright, Miss Ella?" Jasper asked softly, seeing the unhappiness on the girl's lovely face but as Ella turned to answer him, the front door of the house opened and Milton stepped out onto the porch. Ella could see that he wore his coat and wide brimmed hat. He was leaving for the day. Probably going up to town again, to spend what little remained of her father's hard-earned cash in the saloons there.

"Oh Jasper, don't tell him I'm here, for pity's sake," she whispered and ran to the back of the barn to hide behind one of the empty stalls, the voluminous bridal skirt with its petticoats bunched within her hands, held up around her knees.

Jasper saw Milton step off the porch and hurry towards the barn and he turned back to his task of shoveling hay. "Doan't you worry none, Miss Ella," he whispered, hearing the rustle of her dress as she crouched down out of sight. He didn't look up as Milton stormed into the barn, slashing the air with his whip in frustration.

"Make yourself useful boy and saddle up that horse," he spat.

Mindful of Ella hiding not ten feet away, without a word Jasper turned and reached for Billy's blanket and saddle. But Ella clenched her hands in anger, because Jasper didn't have to be spoken to like that, nor do anything he didn't want to, because he was a free man. Her father had issued his former slave his manumission papers just before he died, allowing Jasper to go and do whatever he wanted. But out of loyalty to Ella and Martha he had stayed on at the ranch, despite the pittance in wages Ella could afford to give him.

"Hurry up boy, I don't have all day," Milton yelled, as Jasper finished tightening the cinch.

Unable to stand this abuse of a man who had been part of her family since she was five years old, Ella made a move to stand, but froze on hearing Milton's next words.

"Shame my brother set you free, boy. I could make good use of you down in New Orleans once that arrogant little madam is married off. Two more weeks to go, that's all, then I'm set up for life. So if you have any ideas about heading south, you think about coming with me, I'll make sure you do alright. But don't you go repeating this. You keep your mouth shut about my plans."

Jasper said not a word and in the silence that followed Ella heard leather and stirrups being pulled and stretched followed by the soft neigh of her father's horse as Milton pulled hard on Billy's mouth, then the sound of hooves on the hard-packed earth and then once again, silence. She stepped out from behind the stall and saw Jasper standing very still, looking out towards the barn doors. But there was something in the slump of his shoulders and his hands curled into fists by his sides that made her suddenly wary of him. Ella had never seen Jasper angry, not once in all these years. He didn't move as she came up behind him, not until she put a hand on his shoulder, then he turned to face her.

"You take no mind of him, Jasper. That vile way of talking is just the way he is. He talks like that all the time to me and Martha because he believes no-one in the world is as important as him. So don't you go thinking on heading south with him, because that man will take you to hell and back before he's done."

But there was a hard look in Jasper's eyes, which Ella had never seen before. "But where's I meant to go Miss Ella? When this place is all sold off, where's I meant to go? With you livin' across the way with Jebediah and Martha off somewhere's else, where's I meant to go. Who's goin' to take in an old man like me? I ain't hardly good for nothin' these days."

"Don't you go speaking like that Jasper," Ella scolded. "You're still young enough to work with horses and till the land, so don't you go worrying about what lies ahead. Besides, if I leave, you and Martha are coming with me. I won't let you down Jasper, I swear it and somehow we'll get by."

She moved to undo Bear's rope while Jasper turned to watch her, incredulous. "Miss Ella, surely you ain't takin' old Bear out for a run dressed like that?"

She paused for a moment, aware she still wore the wedding gown, but not knowing until that moment that she was indeed taking Bear for a run.

All she knew was that she suddenly wanted to ruin the dress, along with all of Milton and Jeremiah's plans for the wedding. She felt rebellious and Ella had never been rebellious in her life. She turned to Jasper and when she spoke, her voice was low and dull with anger. "I do believe I am," she said, leading Bear out of his stall.

Jasper shook his head at such recklessness even as he turned to reach for Bear's blanket and saddle and as Ella waited for him to saddle the horse, a thought struck her.

"Jasper, you keep those manumissions papers safe, don't you?"

"I sure do Miss Ella. After Mr Quentin done told me how valuable they were just before he passed away, I put them in a box under my bed."

Ella nodded. "Then you make sure you mind them well, Jasper."

She turned to mount the horse but Jasper stepped forward to give her a lift up, using his hands, allowing her to lift the dress so that it sat bunched around her knees, then she kicked Bear out of the barn. Jasper's face was grim as he watched her leave then he turned and strode to the door at the rear of the building and opened it. It led into a small room. His cot lay up against the far wall and there was a wood burning stove opposite to keep him warm on winter nights. He had a few clothes, a couple of muslin shirts and woolen pants and a pair of leather boots and a wide brimmed hat he wore against the hot summer sun, but not much else.

He went to the wooden box under his bed and pulled it out. There was a simple brooch inside, made with pins, even though Jasper had no memory of Violet ever wearing it. As far as he knew, it was the only possession she'd ever owned. He touched it briefly, thinking of the big, kindhearted woman he had loved liked a mother before putting the gem aside and reaching for the envelope that lay beneath it. He glanced inside and saw the precious papers lying within. His manumission papers. Signed by Quentin just weeks before he died, papers that made Jasper a free man and no longer a slave. He couldn't read or write, but he knew what the letters said as Quentin had read them out to him several times. Thinking of his old friend, Jasper carefully put the envelope back and slid the box under his bed and sat there for a long time, wondering what lay ahead.

He wouldn't think twice about leaving with Ella but he would have been happy to stay on this ranch for the rest of his days, buried up near Violet in the top field behind the house when his time came. But if Ella said it was time to go, he only had to pick up this box and his few clothes and he'd be ready to leave. Jasper frowned as he thought of Ella. She might talk all fancy and tell him not to worry, but how did someone like her escape marrying a powerful man like Jebediah Crawley?

4

Ella pushed Bear into a gentle canter, riding over land she had worked on alongside her father and Jasper since she was a young girl.

But those days were over. The decline had started when her father began having pains in his belly, followed by a diagnosis of an illness that Quentin had no hope of beating. When he went behind her back and bequeathed half the ranch to his brother, a no-hoper he'd been estranged from for decades, her father had not only signed away her future but the future of the ranch.

All those years they had talked about the ranch being hers one day, had been nothing but a lie. Yet Ella discovered what her father had done just days after his death, when the lawyer in town told her about the other beneficiary. It had been a devastating blow, dealt by her father's own hand and the final nail in the coffin of all her hopes and dreams of staying on the ranch, of getting married here and raising a family of her own, died on meeting Milton and understanding he wanted the ranch sold as soon as possible.

Now Ella's focus was on what to do and where to go and make haste about it while she still had some money, before Milton cheated her out of anything else. But whatever she decided, Martha and Jasper would go with her, because Ella wouldn't leave them behind. She'd also have to find work somewhere, because the money she gained from her share of the ranch wouldn't last forever.

She thought of New Orleans but then dismissed it, remembering Milton telling Jasper he had plans to head that way. Ella had no desire to see him once she left here. Besides, Jasper wouldn't be safe in the south.

Perhaps north, then. Or to one of the big cities on the eastern seaboard. Or west. She had heard enough stories to tempt her to go west, but to do that would take a lot of money. She remembered someone in town once saying that to make such a journey, a man needed $1,000 to set himself up with animals and a good wagon.

She reined the horse into a walk to rest him and gazed out over the land she loved with a passion. It had never brought in a lot of money, but she would have stayed and worked her fingers to the bone to make it profitable.

She wiped the tears from her face, staining the lace and satin gloves a little, not even realizing until then that she was crying. Which surprised her, because she wasn't an emotional sort of woman. She was more practical, a realist, able to see things as they were and she knew it was time to let go of this place and make some decisions, which she should have done months ago, but she hadn't had the courage. Now she did, because she was filled with rage at the unfairness of it all. Had she been born male, her father wouldn't have hesitated to leave his entire estate to her.

Ella thought of her upcoming nuptials to Jebediah Crawley. It loomed like some dark cloud above her, filling her with dread, but she also knew that if she agreed to the marriage, money would never again be a problem and she could give Martha and Jasper a home.

If Jebediah allowed it. Indeed, he might agree

to it now, but sometime in the future he might demand they leave, because that was the sort of man he was. Or he might use them as a bargaining tool in the years ahead, to get what he wanted from her.

And then Ella thought of Jebediah's men. A crude, brutal bunch, men who weren't born around here but came from other places, men who wouldn't treat an older woman or a black man with kindness.

She thought suddenly of the tin of money which Quentin had always put aside to pay for emergency repairs to the ranch and housekeeping. It was Martha who had urged her to hide it away. It held less than fifty dollars, but that was a small fortune to Ella and as Martha had said, "better for you to have it girl, then have Milton spend it on cards, drink and women."

Ella had hidden the tin and its precious contents in her room but when Milton came home late one night swearing and belligerent with drink, tearing the house apart looking for money, Ella spent the better part of the following morning sewing the money into the hem of her best jacket.

She often wished she'd stood up to him when he first arrived. She also wished she'd challenged his right to be a beneficiary of her father's estate. But when she'd asked her father's lawyer if he would take the case on, his reply had been devastating.

"There's little chance of you winning Ella. Your father willed his brother a share in the ranch when he was of sound mind. Which makes the document legal and binding. Besides, I'd be careful what you start, because your uncle could override *your* share in the ranch. As your father's closest male relative, Milton could by law challenge your right as a woman to have ownership of the property."

When the lawyer advised her to go home and obey her father's wishes, Ella gave up, defeated, accepting her fate.

She kicked Bear into a harder run, swearing softly at the unfairness of her sex and as she pushed Bear on, the silk and satin wedding dress billowed out behind her even as she tried to keep it bunched tight around her knees in an effort to stop the mud splattering the expensive material. She tried to grab the pins as they came loose in her hair, before they were lost in the earth below the horse's pounding hooves because she didn't have the money to replace them.

As she turned south, as Bear snorted from the effort of the hard run, Ella didn't see the man on horseback half a mile behind her, riding along the rutted road which led to the house. Nor did she see him stop to watch her as she kicked Bear on, pushing the old horse even harder.

5

Ella heard Martha talking to someone as she approached the open kitchen door and then the smell of hot sweet biscuits straight out of the oven wafted out to meet her, along with the sound of bacon sizzling in a pan. Yet they had no money for such luxuries, so where had Martha got the money for this treat?

She stepped up on the porch but stopped when she heard Martha laughing, a rare sound in the house these days, followed by the sound of a man's voice. He spoke too quietly for Ella to hear what he said, but of one thing she was sure. This was no-one she knew. This voice owned none of the angry tones which belonged to Milton, nor the thick lechery treacle which lay embedded in Jedediah's voice.

No, this man's voice was young, a sound as lush as velvet, a thing as pure as a caress on hot skin. This was a voice of beauty. This was a voice a woman could fall in love with.

She took a step forward but again stopped, unsure whether she should disturb Martha when once again, the older woman laughed. Curious now, Ella stepped into the kitchen.

Martha turned to stare at her in horror. She wasn't aware Ella had taken Bear for a run and now the girl stood with her hair hanging long and loose to her waist, most of her pins lost within the fields, her boots muddy, the silk and lace gloves ripped and stained, the exquisite wedding dress and petticoats hanging in untidy folds about Ella's long legs, the material covered in splatters of mud. Even Ella's flawless complexion was smeared with mud, where she had wiped the satin gloves across her face, to clear away the tears. But as Ella's hazel green eyes turned to the man sitting at the kitchen table, Martha thought the girl had never looked so lovely, nor so vulnerable, as she stood there in the doorway in that wedding dress.

The man stumbled to his feet, knocking the table in his haste, his eyes wide with astonishment at the vision of her, yet as she held his dark eyes set within a face that was young, yet worn, yet utterly beautiful, something about him made her stop and be still. Then she took a step towards him, drawn to him, before Martha stepped in front of her, coming between them, scolding her for her untidy appearance and for wearing the expensive dress in such a reckless manner.

Yet Ella barely heard Martha's words. Indeed, she couldn't take her eyes off the stranger. He seemed only a few years older than herself, more than a foot taller, as dark as she was pale, with several day's growth of beard claiming a strong square jaw. He owned an olive complexion with black eyes framed by dark lashes and his mouth, half hidden by the beard, suggested strength. She stared at him in confusion, then felt Martha's hand on her arm, an unusual hardness to her touch as she pulled the girl towards her.

"Ella, look at you girl, you are a sight! And in your wedding dress! What were you thinking! Goodness, whatever will Milton say, let alone Jebediah!" She pushed Ella towards the hallway door. "Go on, off with you! Get out of that dress before you do more damage to it. And clean yourself up before you come back down and join us for breakfast," she turned and nodded towards the bacon frying in the pan, along with the fresh bread buns and the muslin and calico bags of flour, salt and coffee beans, all sitting on the bench. "Lord knows we have enough of it."

Ella glanced back at the man who was still watching her, his huge frame seeming to fill the kitchen, even as Martha pushed her into the darkened hallway.

"Off with you girl, you look half wild. For pity's sake get out of that dress! Jebediah would have your head were he to see you now. Go! Clean yourself up then come back down and hear our news!"

"I'll need your help in getting out of this, Martha! I can't undo all these buttons by myself!"

Sighing, Martha hurried after her, pulling her into the study at the front of the house. Her hands moved quickly, undoing the satin covered buttons that reached from the neck all the way down the back of the dress. It was a stunning creation.

"Who is he, Martha? Why is he here?"

"Oh, I can't speak about it now, just hurry and get changed Ella. Oh, I can smell the bacon. Hurry, girl. Off with you."

But as Martha rushed back to the kitchen, she found the young man turning the bacon for her. He smiled and stepped back as Martha took over and as she thanked him, she heard Ella running up the stairs to her small room at the top of the landing.

Martha felt obligated to apologize for Ella's appearance, but she didn't have to, not after the conversation she'd just shared with this young man, not after telling him of Quentin's death and Milton's arrival here, along with the impending nuptials between Ella and Jebediah Crawley. She'd explained that despite Ella's wish that the marriage didn't go ahead, the girl had little chance of stopping it, otherwise she'd be going against her uncle's wishes and the most powerful man in the county and Martha was sure that one way or the other, either by blackmail or by threats, Milton and Jebediah would have their way and Ella would do exactly as they bid.

Martha offered the stranger another glass of water which he took with gratitude. She glanced at him and almost smiled as his big hand gently took the glass from her. She might very well be a woman in her early fifties and a widow these past seventeen years with her days of lusting after handsome young men well and truly behind her, but this young fellow was indeed a sight to behold.

He was tall and lean yet with a muscular body, and there was something about him that drew her to him. She had felt it the moment she opened the door to him less than an hour before and she'd just seen it in Ella, when the girl stepped into the kitchen. Perhaps it was his eyes, dark and full of fire, giving the hint of a man who would stand on the side of all that was right.

"I'm guessing that's her?" he asked, his voice causing Martha to think of maple syrup on pancakes on a warm spring day, for there was nothing hard about that voice.

Martha turned as he sat back down at the table, his tall hard body seeming to fold into the chair with an easy grace. Yes, he was a sight to behold alright, yet she had a feeling he wasn't aware of it as there was nothing overtly charming or seductive about him. Indeed, if anything, there was a hardness to him and Martha wondered what had happened in his life for this young man to own such strength, for she doubted he had yet turned thirty. She nodded and turned back to the bacon.

"Yes, that's her and like I said, I won't leave her, regardless of what you're offering me. I've been taking care of her and her daddy for more than fifteen years and I'm not about to walk out on her now, not when she's being bullied into marrying a man she wants no part of. I reckon that girl needs me now more than ever," she paused, but the stranger said nothing, just sat quietly watching her. Martha decided she liked that about him, that he didn't offer his opinion. She liked that a lot.

"And I can't change the fact that I'm her Aunt, so even though I'm tempted by your offer, I won't leave her behind. As for my son, if what you're saying is true and I got no reason to believe you're lying, not after reading that letter you brought me, well, in all truth I don't rightly know him anymore. I certainly can't imagine him a grown man. Willard left these parts when he was a lad of eighteen, some fourteen years ago, but I don't begrudge him that as a man's got to make his own way in the world, away from his Mama's apron strings. Besides, he was never a man to tend the land. He always aimed for city life, so he was here less than a year before he hightailed it out. But just so you know my feelings on the matter, my son is a stranger to me. You telling me he's a fancy bookkeeping man is a surprise, as is his offer. As to the letter you say he sent me a year or so ago? Well, I never received it. To be honest, I can't really say what I would have done had I read it. Anyway, here I am in these awful times and here you are. But I'll tell you again, I won't leave her."

She glanced once more at the young man but still he said nothing, so she turned back to take the cooked bacon out of the pan and lay it on a plate. She heard him get up from the table and go and stand in the doorway, looking out over the ranch. Then he turned to her.

"I understand your reasons for not leaving and under the circumstances, I do admire you for it. But this offer is not negotiable. It's either a yes, or a no, agreed on this morning as like I said before, I can't wait on your decision as I've commitments of my own and I'm under some considerable pressure to fulfil them," he paused, turning once more to look out across the ranch.

"So if agreeable to you, once breakfast is done, I'll be on my way as it seems likely I'll be returning to Independence alone. But I'll pass on to your son your reasons for not joining him, you can rest assured of that."

Martha paused in dishing out the bacon, feeling his words hit her like a blow. She hadn't thought it would be over so quickly, but this young man clearly wasn't one to waste his time.

"But I do think it's a shame you can't join Willard and his family. They were looking forward to seeing you."

Again, Martha felt a keen sense of loss at his words. For a moment she couldn't speak, knowing the opportunity to be with her son after all these years was slipping out of her grasp and would soon be lost forever. But Martha also knew she would never forgive herself if she left Ella here alone, to be bullied by two mean spirited men. She glanced over at the young man as he leaned against the door frame.

"I thank you for your concern," she said, taking a breath. "I think you know I'd dearly love to accept what you're offering, but I can't leave Ella to fight this battle alone. She'll either end up with nothing, with Milton taking it all, or she'll marry Jebediah and live a life of misery until his death and just to spite her, the man would probably leave her a pauper. No, I can't do it. I'm sorry."

He nodded, satisfied the decision had been made, yet he noticed Martha's hands tremble a little as she turned to pick up the eggs he'd brought with him. He realized then that she might act tough, that she believed she'd made the right decision, but Marrok could see she was unhappy about it. He watched as the eggs broke cleanly against the side of the pan, before dropping into the hot fat.

"These sure are a luxury," she said, glancing over at him, as he stood quietly watching her. She might have felt intimidated by another man standing so close yet strangely, Martha didn't feel threatened by him for even though he watched her, his mind seemed focused on something else.

"Our ranch chickens stopped laying months ago, so we had no choice but to make better use of them not long after my brother-in-law's death which a dreadful time, believe me. I didn't think Ella and Jasper would come out of their grief. But then Milton showed up and things got worse, with Ella and him fighting over something almost every day. Just shows the strength of that girl's character for she don't hesitate to pull him up on all his lazy, selfish ways. But if truth be truth, I know she ain't got no hope of winning against him and Jebediah. Not one hope."

Martha heard the stranger move and glanced up as he stepped out onto the porch and looked across the yard to the barn. Even from here Martha could just make out the farm wagon inside the big double doors. They hardly used it these days, only to get supplies once a month in town but even those days were coming to an end as their money ran out. Times were changing and changing fast.

She used a big flat spoon to scoop the fried eggs out of the pan fat, as the young man stepped back into the kitchen and came to stand in the doorway which led into the hall so he could face her. Martha glanced up at him, the bulk of him filling the doorway, blocking out the light.

"As I understand it," he said, speaking slowly as if deep in thought, "the girl has no obligation to stay here and marry this neighbor. She's only staying because she has no money or prospects and nowhere else to go. Am I right in that?" he asked.

Martha looked up at him as he towered above her. And somewhere between the smell of bacon and fried eggs she caught the scent of horse and man along with something like jasmine or honeysuckle. Had he bathed with herbs? She found the thought of that pleasing.

"No, she has no obligation to stay. No-one can legally drag her back here if she were to leave. But until someone agrees on a price for this place, she can't leave. She might as well have a rock tied around her ankle keeping her here, as Jebediah is the only one willing to buy the ranch on the condition she marries him and she'll marry him just to keep us all from starving," she shook her head in anger. "There's hardly any money left and what there is, Milton takes into town and spends it in one of the saloons and there ain't nothing we can do to stop him as he sees that money as legally half his. Too bad if we see nothing of it. So yes, Ella will do it. She'll marry the old leech just to give me and Jasper a home, along with Bear and Billy. Anyway, once those Banns are read in Church this Saturday, she's as good as gone," she began pulling pieces of bread apart before lathering them with hot bacon grease.

The young man frowned as he leaned against the door frame. "So why can't she re-negotiate the sale of the ranch herself? If she can sell it out from under her uncle, then why can't she come with us?" he glanced out the door towards the barn. "I can see a decent looking wagon out there and that will get her to California easily enough. So what's to stop her coming with us?"

6

Ella heard his voice as she came down the stairs and then paused as Martha began speaking rapidly, her voice high pitched and full of excitement.

Frowning, Ella hurried down the rest of the stairs and into the hallway but found the door into the kitchen blocked by the stranger. She reached up and tapped him on the shoulder to get him to move, but he jumped as though touched with a hot iron. Her first thought was that he moved well for a big man, her second thought was astonishment that she could spook him so easily. She laughed, seeing the funny side of it as he continued to back away towards the table. Clearly he wasn't amused and clearly, he wasn't a man made for fun.

She glanced across at Martha who was wiping her eyes on the apron she wore to protect the front of her dress. Then Martha surprised her by reaching out and taking her hand, pulling her close, before turning to the stranger.

"Ella honey, let me introduce Mr Marrok Gauvain. Mr Gauvain, my niece Ella Torray."

Ella reached out and took his hand, immediately aware of the strength of the man as he grasped her hand within his own and then she felt the heat of him. Startled, she let his hand go, yet held his gaze for a moment longer, surprised by how dark his eyes were. There was something hard in his face, but Ella saw a beauty there as well and felt that this was a man she could trust. She turned back to Martha, aware she could still feel the man's touch on her hand.

"What's this all about Martha? Why are you upset?"

"I'm not upset, honey. In fact Mr Gauvain is here on behalf of my son, Willard. But we'll talk on it later after breakfast as I don't want all this good food getting cold. Now go ring for Jasper so we can sit down." She was pleased to see Ella's hair pinned up, her face cleaned of mud, the wedding dress gone and her usual muslin dress back on, along with polished boots.

Ella stepped past Marrok, unaware he was as surprised by her as she was of him for he'd expected to meet a spoiled brat, not this rebellious wild creature who rode a horse in an elegant wedding dress. Willard had explained to Marrok who might be living here with his mother, yet the young girl Willard remembered from fourteen years ago had clearly grown into a young woman who knew her own mind.

Yet Marrok could see that Ella had suffered. It was there, in her eyes, a depth of grief someone only knows when they've buried someone they miss every day.

"Oh Ella, do hurry and ring the bell for Jasper. Lord knows I can't think at the moment. But Mr Gauvain will explain everything once breakfast is done. And the sooner the better, for we've all got some big decisions to make."

Ella stepped out onto the porch and swung a piece of tattered rope tied to an old brass bell. She wasn't aware of the man's eyes following her, but they were, as she pulled on the rope allowing the bell to echo out across the front yard and into the fields. Jasper heard it from inside the barn and came running, holding his own plate and mug, his gait slow and a little awkward as though his knee joints pained him.

He called out a hearty good morning then moved to sit on the top stoop. In the winter he ate with the family at the kitchen table, but the rest of the year he preferred to sit outside in the fresh air.

Ella took his plate and mug and handed both to Martha, who filled his mug with coffee and a good helping of the hot bread, bacon and eggs. Ella left the kitchen door open and if Marrok thought it unusual to have a ranch hand listen in on their conversation, he said nothing. He moved to sit at the table as Martha dished up a plate of food for him, passing it to Ella to serve him.

Then Ella joined him at the end of the table, as Martha sat opposite. They talked of little things while they ate, of the ranch, of the weather, of the changes in the territory. But most of the time the stranger kept his head down, eating with a man's appetite. Ella watched discreetly as he pulled a piece of hot bread apart then dipped it in the soft egg yolk before eating it. It was the same way she liked to eat her eggs. She thought his hands like her father's, and she'd loved her father's hands. Big and burned brown from outdoor living, she also knew there were calluses on this man's palms because she'd felt them when she'd held his hand in her own.

It was obvious he was in a hurry. The way he ate, his occasional glance out the door to where his horse grazed in a field near the barn, as if his mind were elsewhere. He also watched Jasper, clearly curious about him, but Marrok made no mention of the lean, black man who sat quietly eating his food.

When Ella finished her meal, enjoying every delicious mouthful of the feast, she reached for her mug of coffee and glanced once again at the stranger. He would be gone soon enough, for this was obviously not a courtesy call. His clothes intrigued her, for he wore buckskin pants and shirt along with soft moccasins, suggesting a man more familiar with living in the wild.

"Martha said you're here on behalf of Willard, yet why buy all these supplies for us?" she asked, bewildered by his generosity.

Marrok sat back, reaching for his own mug of coffee before turning to look at her. Ella almost flinched from the intense look in those coal black eyes and for a brief moment thought his eyes like those of a hawk. Gloriously dark, aware of everything, seeing it all.

"Willard actually paid for them," he said, his voice soft, yet that same deep baritone. "He obviously didn't know about your father's death, or Violet, who Martha mentioned had also passed away and he thought you might have a family of your own living here so I figured if I bought enough for eight people, I'd have plenty to share," he paused before adding the real reason he was here.

"I also reckoned on Martha returning with me to Independence. I was hoping we could take one of the steamboats up the Missouri River from St Louis, which would get us back to Independence in just over a week and for that, we'll need supplies."

Ella glanced across at Jasper and saw the look of shock on his face. She knew her own face must surely look the same. "I don't understand," she said, her voice sounding weak with dismay and she hated that.

Martha leaned towards her. "The long and short of it is Ella, that Willard and his family are heading west to California and he wants me to go with them. But as I've said to Mr Gauvain, I've no intention of doing any such thing, especially not now when everything here is such a mess."

She paused, thinking Ella suddenly very pale. "Mr Gauvain said that Willard sent me a letter a year ago, but I never received it. It was about his plans to head west to California with his young family and his hope I'd join them. I was supposed to meet them in a place called Independence but when Willard and his family arrived and I wasn't there to meet them, Willard thought I must have died or moved on. All he had was this address, so he sent Mr Gauvain to find out what had happened to me and I'm mighty glad he did."

Ella glanced at Jasper as he moved to stand up to look at Martha. But Willard's name was a familiar one to Jasper, as they had worked together on the ranch alongside Quentin when Ella had been a child of ten.

"Independence?" Ella asked looking back at Martha. "But I've heard of it! Everyone has. It's a town on the Missouri River, where people gather before heading out west in wagon trains for California or Oregon."

Marrok nodded. "Which is where Willard and his family are waiting on Martha at this very moment," he said. "Perhaps it might help if you understand my own role in this. The wagon train company which Willard and his family have paid to take them west to California, employs me as their scout. The company aims to leave Independence in the last week of May and as I've three wagons of my own in that company, I'm eager to get back as soon as possible.. And make no mistake about the urgency because when I left just over a week ago, there were already hundreds camped out ready to roll and when those wagons start to move out they won't wait for anyone, certainly not me, nor any of you."

Ella turned to Martha. "Of course you must go Aunt! You know it'll break my heart to see you leave, but you must go!"

Marrok saw the emotions flicker across Ella's face. She was clearly devastated by this news, but she wouldn't hold Martha back. He admired her for it, especially under the circumstances. She would stand here and fight alone with Jasper, although Marrok knew the girl would likely be married to her neighbor within weeks. There was no way out for her.

"Honey, I've no intention of leaving you here alone!" Martha said with some heat to her words. "Anyway, there might be a better way around our problems."

"There can't be Aunt. We've been through it all over the past six months. There is no other way."

Marrok was shocked to see the spirit go out of the girl so quickly, like a flame had been doused and wondered what else she had endured in this house since her father's death. He hated to see that girl who strode so defiantly into this kitchen in her wedding dress less than an hour ago looking so defeated. So before Martha could reply, Marrok found himself answering her.

"There is a way, but you and Jasper must agree to come with us to California," he said.

Ella heard Jasper's sharp intake of breath, but she couldn't look away from Marrok. "How can I possibly go west? I have no money and no prospects until I sell this ranch and there's little chance of that happening unless I marry a man old enough to be my grandfather."

And there it was, the fire back in her eyes. Marrok almost smiled. He thought she would do just fine on the trail west.

"I'm inclined to disagree with you, Miss Torray," he said, then nodded towards the yard outside and the barn beyond. "I saw a decent looking wagon out there. There's no reason why you can't take it west."

Ella stared at him in confusion before turning to Martha, her eyes wide. "Go west to California? But how is that possible when I have to sell this place? And I won't walk away from it. I can't. It's all I have. It might be all I ever have."

Martha reached across the table to take her hands in her own. "I know that well enough girl, but Mr Gauvain thinks there might be another way around this, one that doesn't involve your uncle."

Ella felt ill. Her mouth was suddenly so dry she couldn't speak. She reached for her cup of coffee but found it empty, so reached for Marrok's half empty glass of water instead and took a sip, unaware of the look of surprise which passed over his face.

"California!" she said again, her hands trembling as she set Marrok's glass down on the table. "Yet

California's on the edge of the world. Whatever will I do out there?"

Marrok leaned towards her. "May I make a suggestion?" He paused, wondering why he'd even considered this, because having her and Jasper along would give him a whole lot of work on top of the load he was already carrying.

But he couldn't think on that now. The words were out there, the plan in motion and he wasn't a man to take back what he'd started.

"From what I understand, from what Martha's told me, you have a half share in this ranch. It has to be sold and preferably today, because I can't wait around. So instead of waiting on your uncle to make the rules and the decisions on your future, what's stopping you negotiating the sale with your neighbor instead? Do the deal behind your uncle's back if you must, for I understand he hasn't honored you. With the money you get from the sale, you and Jasper can join Martha and her family, because from the little I've seen while I've been here, I think you've got enough to make the journey west on your own, with your own wagon. But you'll need six oxen to pull it and at least three men as your teamsters and the wagon will have to be caulked to make it waterproof and framed with hoops and canvas, but I can help once we reach St Louis. What we don't get done there, we can finish off in Independence before the wagon train rolls out in seven weeks."

He looked around the kitchen and what lay before them on the table, then waved his hand around the room. "You'll need to take all of this. Kitchen utensils, plates, cups, kettle, bread pan, frying pan and a dutch oven if you have one. All your candles, candle holders and candle molds," he nodded towards the bottled preserves of onions, pickles and tomatoes, alongside the dried fruit of apples and peaches on the shelves above the bench.

"All of those, including any other food you have along with needles, sewing thread and material to make clothes. Indeed, everything you use here, you take with you except heavy furniture. You'll also need your mattresses and pillows, as well as blankets."

He pushed his chair away from the table and stood up. "I'll give you a moment to talk it over. Then you either ride to your neighbor and negotiate a sale, or I ride out of here alone. But if you do decide to come with us, then Martha and Jasper can start packing while we ride over to see this Jebediah Crawley." He moved towards the kitchen door and looked at Jasper.

"I'll come with you to see what you've got. You'll need tools, water barrels, bridles, reins." He glanced back at the women still sitting at the kitchen table, staring at him. "I'll go and take a look at the wagon and see what condition it's in, while you both think on what you want to do."

The women nodded but before he headed for the steps, Ella stood up from the table. "How long have I got?" she asked him. "To make up my mind?"

Marrok glanced back at her. "I had hoped you'd already made it," he said, then followed Jasper down the stairs and out into the yard, but as they headed for the barn, Marrok noticed again that odd way the man had of walking.

Jasper paused at the outdoor pump and quickly washed his plate and mug, glancing up at Marrok as he looked around the yard.

"That was a mighty fine thing you did for us this mornin'. We ain't had a meal like that for a long time, not since Ella's daddy passed away. As for the wagon, well, me and Mr Quentin always took real good care of it. We put it away in the barn most nights so even though it's a few years old, I reckon you'll like it just fine."

As they headed into the barn, Marrok watched the man walk, that strange gait where he swung his hips while his knees seemed to bend inwards, but if the man were in pain from his deformity, he didn't show it.

"How far away is this Jebediah Crawley?"

"Not five miles southwest of here."

Marrok nodded, cursing under his breathe. Even if they left now, they wouldn't be back before mid-afternoon which meant little hope of reaching Illinois Town and getting across the river to St Louis tonight. Unless of course the girl decided to stay. Which would mean Martha stayed as well. Marrok half wished it, for his own sake, but the thought was quickly followed by a curious feeling of disappointment, which surprised him.

*

Martha said nothing for a moment then pushed herself away from the table. "Well, before any discussion takes place on anything, this kitchen's got to be cleaned. So go grab some water Ella so we can start washing up."

But as Ella went to take a bucket to the pump outside, she turned to Martha. "If I decide not to go, I want you to leave with Mr Gauvain, because you'll never get another chance Martha and you know I'll be fine. Once I sell this ranch and leave with Jasper, we'll head north, maybe to Chicago. I heard it's a mighty fine place up there on the lake. So you don't need to worry about us. Jasper and I will look out for each other."

Martha frowned. "Chicago! You're talking about a place that's barely more than a frontier town and cold as hell I reckon. And I don't doubt you'll be fine Ella, but I ain't leaving you. My sister would turn over in her grave if I walked out on you now and although it's not for me to tell you what to do, I will ask you this. What have you got to lose?" She paused for a moment, then leaned towards her niece. "Think on it carefully Ella. For who knows what might lie ahead for you, when you take a chance."

For a moment there was only silence in the room, the dishes forgotten, then the girl shook her head. "But what do I say to Jebediah? How do I negotiate with a man like that?"

Martha shook her head. "I don't confess to being any kind of businesswoman, but I'm sure Mr Gauvain will help you figure it out. Now, go get some water. We got a lot of work to do, either way you look at it."

7

They rode hard without speaking until they came to the boundary where Quentin Torray's land stopped and Jebediah Crawley's began. Ella reined in Bear and as Marrok came up beside her, he leaned forward in his saddle.

"He has no railing up. How did your father keep his cattle off Jebediah's land?"

Ella shrugged. "We didn't bother about it too much. We never ran too many head anyway, so it worked more in Jebediah's favor than our own because his cattle were always grazing on our land." She nodded towards a large two-story house way in the distance.

"He runs an empire from there. Everyone who works for him, works from within that house. Some say even the county Sheriff is based out there when he's around. From what I heard, Jebediah only leaves the place once a month to visit the girls and saloons in town."

"Martha told me a little about him when I first arrived at your ranch. But what's your thinking on him?"

Ella frowned, then shrugged. "The same as everyone else, I guess. He's greedy, unkind and a bully. He's not popular in the territory, but people are inclined to bow and scape to him because he's so wealthy. He could do a lot of damage to someone if they made an enemy of him."

Marrok peered across the land to a dusty road, way in the distance. "Is that the only way in and out of his property?"

Ella raised herself slightly in the saddle and nodded. "Yes, that road takes him north into town but there's a crossroads not a mile from our gate. From there you can head in any direction you want."

"So the purchase of your ranch would obviously give him more land, but if he were to build a road through it, that would give him better access to anywhere in this county. Which would save him considerable travelling time."

Ella nodded. "Yes, of course. But my father would never have allowed Jebediah to build a road through our land."

Marrok said nothing for a moment, then he turned to Ella. "I would use that to bargain with him. And another thing you could use, tell him I'm a buyer. And tell him you've leaving today for Boston to live with Martha's family but you want to strike a better deal over what he offered Milton. If Jebediah's unwilling to meet your price, tell him you'll sell the land to me."

"But what if he doesn't care about my selling the land to you? What if he only wanted the deal so he could marry me?"

Marrok saw the stress on her face and found it disheartening to think that two grown men were manipulating this young woman into a life she wanted no part of. It made him angry.

"Then our bluff fails. But I doubt it will," he paused, looking back towards that distant house. "You know, a cattle man loathes the thought of sheep grazing anywhere near his cows so it wouldn't hurt to tell Jebediah I'm planning on running them, and not cattle."

Ella looked at him in bewilderment. "Sheep?"

Marrok laughed suddenly, a deep pleasant

sound. Then he shrugged. "Why not? Sheep eat a lot of grass and cattle men hate the idea of sheep scab. I would imagine the thought of sheep grazing anywhere near a man's cattle would keep him awake at night. Indeed, it might be an idea to tell him I plan to bring in five hundred ewes within the month," he paused and looked across at her. "Do you feel confident doing this?"

Ella shook her head. "No, but I'll do it. If I recall, Milton negotiated the sale of our ranch at $3 an acre which included the land, the buildings and the horses."

"And you," Marrok added. "Which was a bargain." He frowned and looked out across the ranch. "Milton was foolish. He should have asked for so much more. But a bare acre of land closer to St Louis sells for more than $2, so perhaps you could offer Jebediah $2.80 an acre which would include the land and the buildings, leaving you to claim ownership of everything else. Which is the two horses and the contents of both the barn and the house," he thought on it for a moment, as Ella also added up the sums before racing him to the total.

"Which comes to a total of around $1,120. Once I split the difference with Milton, I'll have nearly $600, including what's left of my father's housekeeping money. But will it be enough to get me to California?"

Marrok nodded. "It will be enough if you're careful. But I'm willing to help you in St Louis and Independence and make sure you pay a fair price for everything," he pulled on the reins and steadied the horse as the animal danced about nervously, eager for a run but as Marrok glanced back at Ella, he saw the fear on her face. He decided then that it wouldn't hurt to scare her a little, just in case she lost her nerve while negotiating with Crawley.

"The deal must be done today Ella, because I can't hang around. So if it all goes wrong here, if he decides not to buy it, then you could end up with nothing. Or a marriage you don't want. So you'll have to reel him in, make him think he's getting a bargain, that others want it, that once this chance is lost to him, he won't get it back." His tactic worked, for even though he saw Ella blanch with fear, he also saw the grim determination in her eyes.

"Once Jebediah signs the papers and gives you the cash, let him know you'll be gone by tomorrow even though I'm hopeful we can pack up the ranch and be gone by this afternoon."

"What if he doesn't have that much cash on him?"

"He'll have it. You said he has men working from the ranch, so I'm sure he'll have his lawyer there as well as a bookkeeper. Anyway, we'll know soon enough. If a small army rides out to greet us, we'll know Jebediah keeps that sort of cash in the house. Besides, a man as successful as Jebediah likes to do deals and I doubt he'd waste his time travelling into town every time he has to sign a contract or handle cash."

Ella thought of her father. Quentin would have been well pleased to know his ranch was worth $2.80 an acre.

"Come on, let's get this done," Marrok said, and kicked his horse on.

*

They were less than two miles from the house when fourteen riders appeared, coming in fast, spreading out to form a circle so they'd come in around the back of Marrok and Ella, leaving them no room to escape.

"Here's the army," Marrok grunted. "I bet they're heavily armed, which proves Jebediah carries a small fortune of cash inside the house."

Ella watched the men ride hard towards them and felt the fear take hold in the pit of her belly. Marrok saw it and was stunned to see how pale she suddenly looked and watched in dismay as she swallowed a few times as though trying not to be sick. And then she started to fidget with Bear's reins, her hands visibly shaking, causing the horse to move about with unease.

Desperate to calm her, Marrok nudged his horse closer to Bear and spoke rapidly, aware of the drumbeat of those fourteen horses' hooves coming closer.

"I can't speak for you Ella, not if I'm a potential buyer, so even if you don't feel like it, act with confidence. If you appear weak, Jebediah will win and you'll leave here with nothing." He paused as she turned to look at him, her lovely hazel green eyes wide and full of fear. It shocked Marrok.

"You don't know him like we all know him here in this county. He's a monster. Everyone is scared of him. And me more than anyone, because of what I have to lose."

"Ella, listen to me. You have to be strong. If

not for yourself, then for Martha and Jasper. Don't let Jebediah win. Don't let Milton win. Fight this battle if you must for your father, for all those years he worked hard," he glanced over at the riders who were less than half a mile away now. "I want you to tell these men you've come to do business with Jebediah and insist on seeing him. Tell them you won't speak to anyone but him. Talk with a strong voice and hold your hands together to stop them shaking."

Ella nodded, thinking suddenly of Quentin out in his fields for all those years, working long back backing days. And now she stood on the brink of terrible loss, seeing her father's years of hard work all come to nothing, for if she lost it all, so did Quentin. He would have ended up working hard all his life just to hand everything over to Jebediah and Milton. And worse of all, those two men would end up making her parents look like fools, because all those dreams her parents held between them when they came to the ranch as newlyweds would have meant nothing. Well, to hell with that.

Ella had no time to reply to Marrok before the riders were upon them, yelling and shouting as their horses thundered around them, their purpose to intimidate.

Ella straightened her back even as she felt the beginnings of that now familiar rage, yet that rage took away her fear and allowed her to focus. She steadied Bear, grateful Marrok was with her because she knew with a woman's intuition as she looked at the leering smiles on the men's faces surrounding them, that had she come here alone, she might never have left. Because Jebediah had

Milton's word that he could take her in wedlock and it wouldn't take much for Jebediah to keep her at this ranch until a preacher arrived to marry them.

She shuddered at the thought then took a deep breath as she raised herself in the saddle, appearing taller than her five feet six inches. Then she took Marrok's advice and allowed her voice to ring out, loud and strong.

"You all know who I am. I have business with Jebediah. I wish to see him urgently."

"Miss Ella," the head man said, glancing at Marrok before turning back to Ella, his face badly needing a wash and shave. "You know I can't let you through. No-one gets to see Mr Crawley unless they got an appointment."

Ella paused for only a moment, her mind racing, desperate to get this done and be gone from here. "Of course I'm going to see him! Don't be ridiculous! Jebediah and I are to be married within two weeks! If you don't let us through, I'll have you reprimanded."

The men glanced at each other, then the head man nodded towards Marrok. "Alright, we'll let you through, but not him. We got no idea who he is."

Ella closed her eyes and took a breath, giving the men the impression she was intensely aggravated when in fact she thought she was going to be sick.

Don't let Milton and Jebediah win

She heard the words that Marrok had spoken, but in fact she saw her father's face, worn from a day out in the fields with Jasper.

She opened her eyes and looked back at the lead

man.

"If he doesn't go through, I don't go through and I shall tell Jebediah why, for this is an important business meeting and I'm sure Jebediah won't want to miss it. Now, pull back and let us through."

There was an awkward stillness among the group of riders then the lead man nodded. "Very well Miss Ella. I won't be held responsible for stopping a man meeting with his future bride so you can both ride on, but we'll go along with you."

Ella nodded and kicked her horse forward. She didn't look at Marrok. But he glanced at her as she rode on ahead, surrounded by those fourteen men, and Marrok thought she appeared fearless in that moment. Like some dark-haired goddess of old.

8

Jebediah sat behind a huge carved wooden desk in a room the size of the entire ground floor of Ella's home. She'd heard plenty of rumors about the opulence of this place, but until now had never seen it for herself. Or truly believed it. But now she saw that every one of the rumors was true.

Yet the luxury and wealth on display left Ella cold, leaving her with no regrets about her decision to head west with Martha and her family.

As she walked into the room, Jebediah half rose from the massive wooden chair he was sitting on behind the desk, the chair padded in thick velvet for his comfort. He was a terrifying sight, a huge man standing close to six feet five inches tall, yet hideously obese. His dark eyes were half hidden within folds of fat, his lips bulbous and extruding over a recessed chin, his teeth badly decayed or missing. Yet as Ella watched him, as he allowed himself to fall back in the chair, his shoulders seeming to collapse on his great body, Ella suddenly saw him for what he was. A man who indulged his every whim, regardless of the expense or the consequences.

He was stunned to see her. "Miss Ella Torray!" he said, speaking slowly in that breathless slimy voice which made Ella's skin crawl, as though she sat before him naked and alone. "Good Lord, I never expected to see you here, especially at such an ungodly hour! Please, do sit down. May I offer you refreshment? Perhaps a coffee? For its rather early in the morning for an impromptu visit, don't you think? Indeed, you're coming here has taken me completely by surprise. Luckily you find me up, despite it being only an hour or so past dawn."

His scolding her for turning up unannounced did the opposite of what he intended, for Ella understood that Jebediah sought to take away her confidence. Instead his words made her feel stronger, even though her legs were shaking beneath her skirt. She sat down, glad to have the support of the chair beneath her before sitting up straight, her hands together to hide their trembling, for all she could hear were Marrok's words *if you appear weak, Jebediah will win*

She took a silent, deep breath as Jebediah watched her, his own hands clasped over his huge belly, looking at her with those tiny black eyes and Ella willed herself to hold his gaze. But when he smiled, licking his lips, as though she were a treat he was eager to devour, Ella realized in that moment that there was something wrong with this man. Something wrong in his nature, yet she didn't have the experience to understand it because she was unfamiliar with the ways of men. Yet all her instincts warned her never to be alone with him. He would easily overpower a smaller man with his size and strength, let alone a woman. As she thought on that, she despised Milton for his bargaining her away into a marriage with this loathsome creature.

"No, thank you, I'm afraid I have no time for such pleasantries," she said, forcing the words out, willing herself to sound in control.

"Indeed, I'm leaving the territory shortly to join Martha and her family back east." She paused at the look of shock which passed over Jebediah's face, shock that he was unable to hide. Then Ella carried on, choosing her words with care.

"So I've come to offer you a new deal on the ranch. A better deal than what Milton offered you."

"Does he know you're here?"

"No and I do realize he's my partner with equal shares in the ranch, but he negotiated the sale of it behind my back so I'm returning the courtesy."

Jebediah laughed softly. "How intriguing! That you've come to re-negotiate the deal I struck with Milton! Yet how could it possibly be better, when I have you to look forward to as my bride?"

"Come Jebediah. You know that was never going to happen, so I'm here to offer you another deal, but it comes with conditions."

"Which are?" Jebediah asked, eager to play this new game, as he once again licked his lips.

"First, we agree to a price and we sign a contract here, this morning. You can arrange for your lawyer to find Milton and have him sign the new contract. I believe he's currently in town in one of the saloons. The second condition is that I want the deal done in cash, this morning, but I want to personally give Milton his share." Ella paused, her mouth suddenly dry, but she didn't dare ask for a glass of water because her hands were shaking too much to hold it.

"If those conditions aren't met, I'll leave here and sell the ranch to the man I rode in with. He wants it, but I came here to give you first option. I think you deserve that after all these years of being our neighbor."

Ella saw Jebediah's eyes flicker to the window and she grasped at the thought that he might be nervous about losing the sale. It gave her hope.

"And the price?" he asked, his voice suddenly hard.

"My uncle offered you $3 an acre. I'm offering you $2.80, which includes the four hundred acres and all the buildings. But I keep the two horses and the contents of both the house and barn. If you're agreeable to it, I'm happy for you to have the papers drawn up now, otherwise I'll sell it to my other buyer."

"The other buyer being the halfbreed you rode in with?" Jebediah asked, a smirk on his bloated face.

Ella blinked. For a moment she said nothing, willing her face to remain blank, yet she was taken aback by Jebediah's words. Marrok a halfbreed? She tried to keep her mind on the negotiations, yet in truth she now struggled, even as she remembered those dark eyes that always seemed aware of every little thing. His buckskin clothing and moccasins instead of leather boots. The way he wore his hair long and tied back with a piece of knotted leather. Ella cleared her throat.

"It doesn't matter who he is," she said, fighting on. "What matters is setting myself up in Boston, so I'm going to accept the deal which gives me the best price. He intends to run sheep and says he can bring in five hundred ewes within the month."

Now Jebediah did flinch, his huge body seeming to shudder. "Sheep, you say? What joke is this, Ella! Your ranch isn't big enough to carry that many sheep and they'll graze over onto my land! This is nonsense!" He half raised himself off the chair to see better out the window. "What? Is he a

Navaho? Bringing in the Navaho *churros*? I grant
you they're strong hardy beasts but I'll tell you
now, I will *not* have them on land next to mine.
They'll bring in the sheep scab and graze me out."

Ella said nothing for a moment then leaned
towards him. "Do you really think I care whether
he brings in sheep scab or grazes you out?" She
shook her head. "Your cattle have grazed on our
land for decades, without my father giving you one
word of complaint, even when we didn't have
enough grazing for our own cattle!" She sat back,
willing herself to keep calm. "All I care about now
is leaving this territory in the next twenty-four
hours with cash taken from whoever gives me the
best deal. That's going to be you, or the sheep
farmer."

Jebediah said nothing, just glared at her. When
he spoke, all pleasantries were gone and she saw
the cruelty in his face. This was the Jebediah
Crawley everyone knew.

"Well, who would have thought such a beautiful
young woman could be so ruthless!" he hissed,
leaning towards her. "I've seriously misjudged you
Ella and I must admit, you now intrigue me a great
deal more than you did, so I urge you to think on
our original deal. We could make a great team in
this territory. Just think on all our sons owning all
of this one day. And more. For I intend pushing
more ranchers out between here and Illinois
Town." He paused and smiled, but there was a
viciousness to that smile. "By your coming here, I
imagine you're now aware of your uncle's debt?"

Ella felt her heart lurch at that. No, she knew
nothing of Milton's finances.

"Ah, perhaps not. Well, it probably doesn't matter too much now. You see, the whole point of the deal I made with Milton was to ensure you became my bride and for that privilege, your uncle and I agreed that he would be paid a substantial amount of money to make sure it happened. It was our secret, you see, between Milton and me, to secure your hand in marriage," he shrugged, as Ella struggled to keep the anger from showing on her face.

"However, if you're no longer part of the deal, I don't see the point in discussing this sale further as your hand in marriage was the only thing I truly wanted. You see, I need strong healthy sons Ella and I know you could give them to me, as I'm aware very few women in this territory will come near me. By securing you through a secret deal, I was happy to pay whatever sum Milton asked but without you, the purchase of your ranch holds little interest for me. The land is worthless, because there's little water. As for those two old horses you want excluded from the sale? You're welcome to them."

Ella felt the desperation claw at her and she thought suddenly of that winding road around her father's ranch which Marrok had pointed out to her. It made for a long route into town for Jebediah. So she tried to ignore the double hand her uncle had played by using her as a pawn, and instead played her own last card.

"So you plan to force other ranchers out, yet you'd forego the sale of my father's ranch to spite me? Is that what this is about, Jebediah?. Well, you do whatever you want, because I won't be around to see it. I shall sell my land to the halfbreed waiting out there and within the month you'll have hundreds of sheep grazing on your land while I'll be setting myself up in Boston. Oh, and that road that winds around our ranch that takes you several hours to get into town? I do believe the sheep farmer intends to buy the ranch opposite, which will completely close off your access to Illinois Town. So before I leave, be forewarned. That halfbreed out there has money and like you, he sees the value in being close to the Mississippi and St Louis. Who knows how many thousands of acres he'll buy up before year's end, or how big the flock he'll bring in."

"Old man Timmins wouldn't sell his land!" Jebediah roared. "That ranch has been in his family for decades!"

"Well Jebediah, you know better than anyone that everyone has a price."

The big man growled and used his legs to push his chair back from the table. Ella saw then that the chair was on wheels and as Jebediah cleared himself free of the desk, he used his arms to push himself to his feet. He towered above her, a behemoth of a man.

"I'll give you $1.20 an acre and nothing more. It isn't worth more to me than that."

Ella hardly dared breath. She watched as he made his way across the room to a table. He moved slowly, his great weight bearing down on massive legs. As he reached for a bell, Ella rose from her chair.

"I won't take $1.20. You know as well as I do that the land is worth more than that. The government is selling unbroken land to settlers for just over a dollar an acre. Our ranch is worth $2.80 an acre with the buildings."

Jebediah squinted at her, his hand on the bell. "$2.50 and that's my final offer. Take it or leave it."

Ella knew then that it wasn't the land he wanted, but what Marrok had so clearly seen. An access road built straight through her ranch.

Ella wondered how she could have missed it. Had her father known? He must have, yet he never spoke of it. But an access road would give Jebediah a quicker, easier route into town and that alone would be worth a fortune to him, both in time and money. The negotiating with Milton for her hand in marriage had been nothing but a game for this man, a game she could so easily have lost.

She stood up and walked around her chair, needing to move, and glanced out the window to see Marrok standing against the corral railing less than a quarter mile from the house. She saw him then, as Jebediah had seen him. A half-breed. Different in every way from Jebediah's men standing around guarding him. He looked at ease leaning against the corral, but Ella reckoned he was more like a tightly wound coil, ready to react to any threat. She saw his knife in its buckskin sheath on his belt and the other knife in the sheath on his right moccasin. His shotgun remained in the leather sheath by his saddle, yet she doubted he'd need it. She was quite sure this man could defend himself easily enough with just knives. As if aware she were watching him, Marrok suddenly turned and met her gaze through the window. Ella felt her breath catch in her throat. He had known she was there all this time, that's why he was standing there. This stranger, a man she had known for only a few short hours, had been listening out for her, keeping her in his sight.

She was aware that Jebediah still waited on her answer and Ella could almost hear him hold his breathe for the tension in the room was palpable. Now it was his turn to stand in fear.

"$2.60 and we have a deal," she said, her voice soft, the way a woman speaks when she sees a man she admires. Then she took a breath and closed her eyes, forcing herself to refocus, before turning back to Jebediah.

He was watching her, yet his eyes weren't on her face, but on her skirts, a lustful look to him. Ella decided then to end this.

"$2.60 an acre and the ranch is yours. Draw up the papers and I'll sign them here," she paused, almost challenging him. "But if you don't carry that kind of cash, we'll have a problem settling."

Jebediah shook his head, clearly irritated. "There won't be a problem."

He rang the bell and within moments a slim man of about forty entered the room. Well-groomed and dressed in an expensive suit, he glanced at Ella before looking across at Jebediah who waved his hand in a disrespectful way to introduce him. Red Nevons, his lawyer, a man who had an office here at the ranch, because Jebediah was his only client.

"Get some papers drawn up for the purchase of this woman's ranch," Jebediah muttered before stumbling back to his desk. "I believe the other party to the agreement can be found in one of the saloons in town, although we've agreed she'll take all the funds now. We've also agreed on $2.60 an acre. Get the paperwork done as soon as you can," he sat down at his desk and glanced once more at Ella before turning away. "Now, get her out of my sight."

*

Ella felt the weight of the money bag on her hip as they rode across Jebediah's land. Marrok rode just behind her, happy to play the part of the disgruntled buyer. They didn't speak until they were in sight of Ella's home, or what now belonged to Jebediah, when she finally reined her horse in. Marrok rode up beside her and she reached over to shake his hand, her face jubilant.

"We did it!" she yelled, ecstatic. "I'm free of both of them! Can you believe it? And the deal breaker was you moving sheep onto this land," she burst out laughing, overwhelmed. "However do I thank you, Marrok! I took Jebediah Crawley on and won! You were right, he wanted the land to build a road! How did I not see that? Lord above, I won't forget this day. At $2.60 an acre! My father would be overjoyed!"

Marrok smiled. "You did well Ella, you got the best possible price. You should be very proud. Now can we get moving? So you can start packing?"

They rode those last few miles and Ella allowed herself the luxury of looking back, of seeing the trees her father had planted when he came here as a young man, the fields where he had ploughed with Bear, before Jasper came to live here all those years ago. The barn he raised with the help of men from neighboring ranches, the shelter belts for cattle, the wells he'd dug which never gave enough water.

But there was something that played on Ella's mind and just before they pulled up at the house, she turned to Marrok. "Jebediah said you were a halfbreed."

Marrok shrugged. "Then clearly he's no fool. But the fact I'm a halfbreed might bother some people," he paused as he looked across at her. "Does it bother you?"

Ella thought about it, then shook her head. "No, I don't think so. But I've never met a halfbreed. Should it bother me?"

Marrok laughed, that lovely sound as lush and deep as his voice. "Well, I have no plans to cause you any worry."

They rode their horses on at a walk into the yard and Ella looked over at him. "I was raised to take people at face value, Marrok. If I didn't trust you, I would never have gone to Jebediah's with you. It was you who gave me the courage to negotiate with him and besides, I knew from the moment we all shared breakfast together this morning that you had our best interests at heart, for what man goes to the trouble of buying food to share with people he's never met, even though another man paid for it!"

She dismounted and stepped towards him. "I know you're in a desperate hurry to get back to Independence but I need to stop over in town and find Milton, to give him his share of the money. If I leave it here, one of Jebediah's men might find it and take it, and I don't want Milton coming after me saying he never received it and that I still owe him his share. Besides, I want to pack up his things and give them to him, so he never steps foot on this land again, even though I no longer own it," she paused before adding softly. "But more than anything, I want Billy, my father's horse."

Marrok dismounted and they both turned as Jasper come out of the barn, ready to take Bear from Ella like he'd always done.

"I'll go and help him pack up the barn," Marrok said. "As for going to town, of course I'd prefer it if we didn't have to go there, but I understand your reasoning for it. Besides, from what I understand of your uncle, he'll be easy enough to find."

"Thank you," she said, then turned to tell Martha the news that would change all their lives.

9

After watering the horses at the trough, Marrok and Jasper unsaddled them then left them to graze in the field behind the barn. Then Jasper showed Marrok how much he'd packed away. The wagon was half full. Marrok was impressed by how much the man had done in the few hours he and Ella had been at Jebediah's.

"Well, I ain't never seen the point in slackin' around," Jasper said. "If a job's got to be done, better it be done quick and as best you can."

The wagon contained three water barrels, a feedbox for the horses and a large chest of tools. Marrok lifted the lid on the toolbox and saw a couple of old hammers in there, a good hand saw, an axe and two shovels.

As he helped Jasper pull bridles and other horse tack off hooks and shelves, he asked him how he felt about heading out to California.

"Don't rightly know how I feel to be honest with you. I guess I'll know once we get there. But I got my manumission papers packed away, safe and sound." He paused when he saw the surprise on Marrok's face.

"You were a slave here?"

"Yessir. Mr Quentin done bought me and Violet down in New Orleans, a long time ago now but we was never treated as slaves here. Every month me and Violet got taken up to town where Mr Quentin spent money on us, not much for he never did have much, but it was somethin'. He never did that for Miss Martha."

"Where's Violet?" Marrok asked, unable to hide his shock that Ella's father had slaves.

"Oh, she's been dead a good many years. Buried up in the top field behind the house alongside Mr Quentin and Miss Adeline, Ella's mama. But Mr Quentin was as determined as any man can be about gettin' my papers sorted before he died. He always spoke about it, just never got around to it. So if Miss Ella changes her mind and doan't want me to go west with her, I guess I'll head north. But I ain't been nowhere but this ranch and into town since I was a boy of fifteen."

"Were you born in New Orleans?" Marrok asked, curious.

"Doan't rightly know where I's born. I reckon I's just blocked it out. If I chance to think on it at all, I reckon New Orleans might have been bad times for me. But I do remember Mr Quentin buyin' me and Violet. I do remember that, but even that time is a blur of nothing much at all."

Marrok glanced down at the man's left hand as Jasper packed an old saddle away in the back of the wagon. The little finger was gone, along with the two fingers next to it, leaving only the thumb and index finger. Yet the man used his hand easily enough as though born with this disfigurement. But Marrok knew he had not. The stumps were cut clean through for they had healed badly with some disfigurement. He would bet everything he owned that those fingers had been taken off by an axe. And that made Marrok wonder about Jasper's legs. Had they been broken during an act of violence and healed all wrong?

"Anyways, Miss Ella's been payin' me wages since her daddy passed on, so I's got a bit of savings tucked away. I'll be alright. No-one needs worry about me."

"Did you like living here?" Marrok asked, feeling some disloyalty towards Ella by asking the question, but he needed to know.

"Yessir, I reckon I mostly was. Mr Quentin and me worked together real well. He ain't never once treated me bad, even if I worked a bit slower than him. But I liked workin' the land. And I liked workin' with the horses. We had cattle and pigs for a long time, as long as I can remember, and a big old henhouse full of chickens but after Mr Quentin died and Mr Milton came along, Miss Ella started selling the stock off just to get by," he shook his head, frowning.

"Now I ain't sayin' nothin' to wrong anyone here, but I think things got a little tight for Miss Ella around that time. But I aren't complainin'. That girl always did right by me. And I like where I live. Out back there," he nodded his head towards the back of the barn.

"I's my own room. Nice and warm in the winter, nice and cool in the summer. And I's near the horses if they need me. I sing to them on the nights they doan't settle, durin' a storm or when we get high winds and after all these years, I reckon Bear and Billy are just as much a part of me as I am them."

Marrok said nothing for a moment, just watched the man work. Then he stepped towards him. "I like that you're an honest, hardworking man Jasper so if you decide not to join Ella and Martha in California, you're welcome to come and work for me. I'm heading to Oregon where I plan to build a ranch of my own breeding horses, but I'll need good men who aren't afraid of hard work. It'll be quite different to what you know here because the country is mountainous and a lot colder, but the land is rich and fertile. It'll be tough, can't say it won't be, but I'm a fair man and I'll give you a fair wage."

He paused as Jasper stared at him incredulous.

"I don't expect an answer now. Just think on it awhile, you've got months to decide," he paused, frowning. "Any chance you can cook?"

Jasper shook his head. "No sir, I doan't cook. That's always been Miss Martha's job. I can clean real good, but what I care about most is the horses and cattle and tillin' the land. I liked that just fine workin' alongside Mr Quentin. So if Miss Ella doan't want me, then I guess I'll accept your offer and be grateful for it."

Marrok smiled at him then reached out to shake the man's hand. For a moment, Jasper looked at him in bewilderment, then took his hand.

10

Ella stood at the door of her father's study, unwilling to enter. Because unlike when her father was alive, the room was now untidy, with the lingering stench of Milton and the tobacco he chewed leaving a rank staleness which seemed to hang in the air.

This room had been Quentin's sanctuary for as long as Ella could remember, even back to the days when her mother was alive. He would sit at that battered old desk every night and go over their accounts, trying to find different ways to make the ranch work. Or he'd come in here after supper and close the door and read a book, or a broadsheet from St Louis even if it were a few weeks old, just to get away from all the talking of the women in the kitchen.

So it was her memory of him and not her uncle which pushed Ella to step across the threshold and enter the room. She curled her lips in distaste when she saw the dirty glass sitting on her father's desk next to the empty bottle of whisky. She didn't bother to pick them up and take them back to the kitchen. Let Jebediah do what he wanted with them, although she doubted Jebediah would ever set foot in this house. He'd build his road through the property and graze his cattle here, but the buildings would probably be left to rot unless one of his foremen moved in and made the place his own.

She glanced up at the wooden shelf behind the desk and saw the half dozen books there which Quentin had owned. Ella took them down and glanced through the titles. Half of them were about farming, the others were short novels about the wild west. That made her smile, because if her father read these books, then perhaps he might agree with her decision to head west. She liked that idea and put the books aside, deciding to take them with her.

She moved to open the drawers in the desk, looking for anything of her father's that she might keep, as she had no desire to leave anything behind which might fall into the hands of Jebediah or his men.

She found a few letters written to her father from long ago friends, along with a poem by her mother. There was no date on the poem, but Ella thought it must have been written during their courting days. But then she found a legal document, an agreement for the purchase of the ranch dated almost thirty years ago. Ella thought her parents would be well pleased she'd got $2.60 an acre, which gave her a substantial inheritance, despite having to share it with Milton.

She knew her parents had been happy here and those memories would be what she took away with her when she left in a few hours. Even after her mother's death, when Violet and Jasper came to live here and then Martha and Willard, they had known a lot of happy times.

She put the agreement, the letters and the poem on top of the books then turned back to open the bottom drawer. She was startled to find a pistol in there. She reached down and picked it up. It was her father's gun, yet she'd rarely seen him use it. Ella knew all about guns because Quentin had wanted her to be competent with them. He had taught her how to fire, reload and clean them, so Ella had never been afraid of shotguns or pistols, but she was wary of them. She looked through another drawer and found several boxes of ammunition, but these weren't for the pistol. They were for the gun leaning up against the wall in the corner of the room.

It was a Colt 1839 shotgun, with a 24-inch barrel and six-shot cylinder, Quentin's pride and joy, a gun which had taken him more than a year to save for. Ella reached for it, deciding to take it with her, along with the pistol and all the ammunition.

Then she left the room and hurried upstairs to her parents' bedroom, but as she stepped inside she was reminded once again of Milton as the room smelled bad from tobacco and unwashed clothes. Ella looked with distaste at the unmade bed and the used chamber pot sitting in the corner of the room, which he'd left for her or Martha to clean up. She felt that unfamiliar rage threaten to overwhelm her when she saw that, a rage this selfish man had brought into her life over the past six months. Because of him she couldn't wait to be gone from here, a place she'd cared so deeply for all her life, just to be rid of him forever.

She quickly searched the dresser, ignoring Milton's few possessions. He owned a brush and comb set, a razor in a leather pouch, a few coins, but little else.

In the drawers she found some evidence of her parents. Her mother's corsets and petticoats and other undergarments. Her father's shirts. A few bits of cheap jewelry, including an inexpensive ring that might have belonged to one of her grandparents because she'd never seen her mother wear it. She tried it on and it fitted perfectly. Ella liked to think a woman close to her had worn and loved this ring. She took it off and put it aside so as not to damage it then reached for a tiny portrait of her parents on their wedding day, along with her mother's wedding ring, a brooch and a pair of cufflinks. In another drawer she found her father's harmonica but he'd rarely played it after her mother's death. In a bottom drawer were some of their clothes, neatly folded.

She found more letters and legal documents, including her parents' marriage certificate within a box tucked away inside a small chest. Milton had clearly gone through the chest hoping to find something of value, because the papers were scattered everywhere. Ella quickly bundled everything up she wanted to take, but as she turned to leave the room she heard someone working the pump in the yard below. She went across to the window and peered through the lace curtains.

It was Marrok. He had taken off his shirt and stood half naked, wearing only his moccasins and buckskin pants as he worked the pump and as the water came rushing through the pipe, he pulled the leather tie from his hair, allowing it to fall free, then ducked under the sprout of water. It wasn't much of a sprout because the water table beneath their land was so low. As he continued to work the pump to bring up more water, Ella saw the well-defined muscles on his arms and shoulders and back, as he washed dirt and debris from his body. Without doubt he was a fine looking man yet watching him under that spurt of water made her wonder about this strange day.

She had woken this morning wondering how to escape the grasp of Milton and Jebediah. Now she was packing to move to California.

Marrok had changed her life in a matter of hours, yet who was he? She knew nothing about him, other than he came here on behalf of Martha's son and that he worked as a scout for a wagon train company. Yet he must be exhausted, for not only had he been travelling for hours to get here by sun-up, but he'd also gone to Jebediah's with her and now he was helping them pack up the ranch.

She watched as he stepped away from the pump and shook his hair free of water, his body a powerful beautiful thing, then he turned and walked back across to the barn.

"Hurry up girl, there's work to be done down here!" Martha's voice came from the bottom of the stairs and Ella heard a touch of impatience in it, along with panic.

She stepped away from the window and hurried to her own room. She'd slept in here since she was a babe and even after all these years it was nothing fancy, just a single room that held a narrow bed, a wall of shelves and a bedside cabinet made by Quentin when she was a small girl and it had been enough, because she'd been happy here, until Milton arrived.

But she didn't want to think of him so she turned and reached for two old travelling cases off a high shelf and began to pack away her few worn dresses, stays, shifts, boots and stockings. She added a few little trinkets her father had made for her over the years, along with what she wanted to keep of her parents, then she closed the case and stepped back. She had everything she needed. Jasper and Marrok could help carry down her mattress before they left, along with Martha's, and put them in the wagon.

As she headed for the stairs Ella didn't dare look back at the rooms behind her. Because this part of her life was over and there was little point in lingering on the past, or what might have been.

Martha was waiting for her at the bottom of the stairs, holding something in her arms. Ella knew what it was. A crocheted blanket Martha had made with Ella's mother when they were just girls.

"I want you to have this. I've enough things of my own to pack away so it's time I passed it on and I think Adeline would want you to have it. You'll see it's been mended over the years, but it's kept me warm enough on cold nights, so I reckon it'll go some way to keeping you warm when you're sleeping in that wagon."

Ella set down the two travelling cases and held the blanket to her face, smelling the age of it. She didn't mean to cry again, but she did, and Martha took her in her arms, comforting her as she had done for the past fifteen years.

"I know this is hard for you girl, but I think your folks would be happy you're getting out of here. You know as well as I do that this ranch ain't worth much of anything now. Even your father was coming to the end of it. There's been too many droughts and never enough water."

Ella thought of her vegetable garden out back which she had tendered since she was a child.

"You're right, I know it," she said, wiping her face. "But everything's changed so fast since Marrok arrived here, I'm struggling to cope. And I'm terrified. What if I run out of money all alone out there?"

"Hush girl. You know full well you'll be with me and my family. We'll do this journey together every step of the way, so don't fret none about what lies ahead or for things that ain't yet happened. Thoughts like that will take away your courage. So wipe away those tears and pick up your cases. We've got a wagon to finish packing."

Illinois Town, Missouri
April 1846

1

It was almost full dark when they arrived in town.
Marrok sat on the buckboard beside Jasper and as
he reined the horses in outside a boarding house
which Ella had recommended, he was glad to be
here.

He pushed his wide brimmed hat off his face to
wipe the sweat from his brow, feeling hot and tired
and wishing he were across the river in St Louis
already. But he knew when he'd agreed to ride to
Jebediah's with Ella that was never going to
happen. By the time they'd finished packing up the
wagon, it had been well past mid-day. Not nearly
enough time to get back to St Louis.

He had allowed his own horse to be harnessed
with Bear to pull the wagon, but getting to town
had taken longer than planned, even though he'd
pushed the horses harder than he should have,
especially the old plough horse.

Martha and Ella had said very little since they
left the ranch. They had walked some of the way
but now sat in the back of the wagon looking as
exhausted as he felt. But Marrok was aware of the
emotional cost of packing up the ranch and leaving
it behind. Jasper and Ella had wept when they
finally rode out of the yard and even Martha had
glanced back towards those three graves on the hill
behind the house.

Marrok dismounted and helped the women
down from the wagon. As he placed his hands on
Ella's waist and swung her down, she almost fell

against him, she was that tired. She felt the strength of him as he lifted her as though she weighed nothing much at all and as he set her down on the boardwalk, she smelled the musky male scent of him, yet it wasn't offensive. She was also close enough to notice the stubble on his jaw against that otherwise flawless complexion.

Yet there seemed nothing tactile about this man. He was all highly strung energy, as if it pulsed off him like a living thing. Some might have called him handsome, indeed, Martha had said that very thing. But Ella wouldn't have called Marrok handsome, because his face held a rawness to it, a hardness that warned people to stand clear of him. She wasn't sure if that thrilled her, or terrified her. So no, she wouldn't have called him handsome. Perhaps striking, charismatic, even desirable.

He stepped away from her and she took her hands off his arms, aware of the hard band of muscle beneath the buckskin sleeve. She was also aware of the heat of him. It seemed to radiate off him like the fire in the hearth back at the ranch.

They booked four single rooms which were small, but clean. The elderly couple who owned the boarding house suggested a livery just a block away.

"You want good stables and an honest man? Take your horses and wagon around the block to Allan Endon. He'll look after them just fine. Won't find a better man. But get them horses and that wagon round there smart before he locks up and goes home for the night."

They left Martha behind to rest in her room but before Marrok and Jasper left for the livery, Marrok suggested Ella watch the main street in case Milton rode by on his way back to the ranch.

"It's getting late and I'd hate to miss him while we're at the livery," Marrok said. "And I don't fancy going back to the ranch tonight, or in the morning, when we don't need to."

Ella did as he asked and stepped inside the boarding house and waited by the front window, looking out onto the main street which led to the road back to the ranch.

But she didn't see Milton and within the hour Marrok and Jasper re-appeared with Milton's suitcases. She stepped outside to meet them.

"Are you ready for this?" Marrok asked.

Ella nodded, but he could tell by her face that she wasn't. She dreaded the thought of confronting her uncle. But what she was ready for, was for this to be over.

*

They found Billy first. Tethered to a post outside one of the towns saloons, the horse's head hung low in misery. When Ella went to pet him, Billy reared back.

"Oh, he's treated you bad," Jasper said softly, reaching out to gently take the horse's bridle. Billy snorted, then whickered as he recognized Jasper, moving his head to nudge him.

Marrok ran his hands over the horse's hind quarters, seeing the whip marks.

"Your uncle's left him out here in the heat all day without water and any man who treats a horse like this doesn't deserve to own one," he said angrily before turning to Jasper.

"You remember how to get back to the livery?"

Jasper nodded. "Yessir, I reckon I do."

"Then we'll see you back at the boarding house later."

Jasper nodded and walked off with Billy, heading for the livery where Endon was waiting for them. Once he'd helped feed and water the horse and settle him down, he'd make his way back to the boarding house.

Ella and Marrok stepped up to the saloon and peered through a window. Milton was sitting at a table on the far side of the room, playing cards with three other men.

"That's him. The man with thin grey hair sitting with his back to us."

Marrok heard her grunt with rage, but he understood well enough now to know that Milton would be gambling Quentin's hard earned savings. This was money put aside over the years for repairs to the ranch, along with feed for the animals and their own supplies. Ella moved to push open the swing doors, but Marrok quickly pulled her back.

"Ella, just stop for a moment," he said, an urgency to his voice. "If you go in there angry, this could all go wrong."

"Whatever do you mean?"

"Just calm down. You don't want to get on the wrong side of him and get him all fired up and then have him declare the sale of your ranch illegal, done without his approval. If that happens and the whole thing has to be renegotiated with Crawley, then you're on your own because I can't stay around and wait for that to settle," he paused and let her arm go. "So let me go in there. Besides, a saloon isn't any place for a woman and the men in there won't appreciate you storming in. I'll ask Milton to come and talk to you out here."

Ella glanced along the street which was mostly empty now with all the stores closed for the day. The only places open were the handful of saloons and those with working girls, which would stay open until late. She looked back at Marrok and nodded, knowing she could talk to her uncle out here in relative privacy, without being overheard.

"And just another suggestion," Marrok added after she agreed, his voice low and deep, soothing her frazzled nerves. "Offer him $80 for Billy, just to sweeten the deal. But no more. We all saw the state of Billy's mouth and the whip marks on him. The horse isn't worth more than $80. But that $80 brings Milton's share of your ranch up to $3 an acre, which he negotiated with Jebediah. That should make him happy."

Ella looked at Marrok, unable to tell him about the secret deal between Jebediah and Milton for her hand in marriage. She couldn't tell him. She wouldn't. Because it made her feel as if she had no more value than Bear or Billy. Because even had the ranch sold for $3 an acre, that still wouldn't have given Milton the deal he negotiated with Jebediah. It sickened Ella to think on it.

But she agreed that Marrok should go into the saloon alone. She watched over the top of the swing doors and saw the look of distaste on her uncle's face when Marrok approached him and asked him to step outside. When Milton turned and saw Ella's face at the top of the swing doors, he became belligerent.

You're angry because I've finally caught you out, she thought.

The barkeeper asked him to keep his voice down, but Milton refused to leave the table, saying he had a winning hand. When Ella saw Marrok's hand go to her uncle's collar, knowing he wouldn't think twice about hauling him outside, she decided she'd had enough of men telling her what to do. So she picked up Milton's bags, grunting with the weight of them, then pushed her way through the swing doors and entered the saloon.

She saw Marrok's hand drop away when he saw her, but she was glad it hadn't been him who resorted to violence. Let it be her, because this was her battle.

Every man in the room turned to look at her.

"Now Miss Ella," the barkeeper called out. "You should know better than coming in here. What would your daddy say if he saw you?"

"It's because of my daddy that I'm here," she replied, her voice hard. "Besides, this won't take long. My uncle and I have some business to attend to. Once he agrees to come outside with me, I'll leave."

Marrok watched her cross the room, the weight of Milton's bags causing her to stumble a little. He wished she had stayed outside, but he had to admire her courage. He was beginning to learn there was nothing soft about this girl. He almost smiled at the look of shock on Milton's face when Ella dumped the bags beside him. Clearly Jebediah's lawyer hadn't yet bothered to seek him out to get his signature on the sale agreement.

Marrok thought Milton very thin. Yet he was dressed immaculately, a contradiction of his real worth because even though he looked like he had money, he had none.

Marrok also saw in him something he'd seen in other men who believed the world owed them. It was never about what they could achieve themselves, it was always about what they could get from others and once he left Ella behind, this man would find someone else to leech off, because that was how men like this lived.

He uttered a foul oath as he looked down at his bags. "What the hell is all this about?"

"We can talk here in front of everyone and have them know your business, or we can talk outside in private."

Milton sneered at her in her plain homespun clothes and Ella did feel plain under his gaze, next to the one working girl in the saloon dressed in her brightly colored dress of silk and ribbons.

"I'll finish here first," he spat at her. "What you've got to tell me can wait till then."

She leaned towards him, her voice a whisper, yet full of rage. "You'll come with us now, or as God is my witness I'll ride out of here with it all."

He looked up at her then, a look of panic on his face but before he could speak the barman approached them. He nodded towards the door at the back of the room.

"Go use the private room Miss Ella. There's no-one in there," he turned to Milton. "Leave your hand where it is and go talk to your niece. These boys can take a break as well. I'll watch the cards and see no-one touches them."

Ella glanced over at Marrok. "I want you there as well," she said, then strode towards the door.

"What the hell is going on?" Milton yelled, pushing his chair away from the table.

He put his cards face down then spat at the men at the table who were also standing. "I'll be back. This won't take long."

But before he followed Ella and Marrok into the private room, he scooped up the money he'd placed on the table and picked up both his bags.

2

The room was used for those who could afford to pay for privacy, men with enough money to entertain women without the threat of gossip, or high-end card players passing through town. It had been in this room where Milton had incurred his debt with the professional card player from New Orleans. A man who was currently playing cards in another saloon, who wouldn't leave town until Milton paid him in full.

Milton shut the door behind him yet glared at Marrok as he took in his buckskin clothing. "And who the hell are you? You put her up to this? By God! You just wait until we get back to the ranch Ella! You'll damn well pay for embarrassing me like this."

Marrok ignored him and pulled out a chair for Ella. She sat down and reached for her purse, placing it on the table, yet Marrok noticed her hands were trembling. As if aware of it she quickly tucked them in her lap, so Milton couldn't see them under the table.

"All your belongings are in those two bags," Ella said, nodding towards the suitcases. "You should thank me for going to the trouble of packing them because it's going to save you a long walk back to the ranch tonight although I'd advise against it, as it now belongs to Jebediah Crawley."

"What the hell have you done?" Milton snarled, still standing.

Ella took a breath, willing her voice to be strong, remembering Marrok's words when they rode to see Jebediah.

If you appear weak, you'll leave here with nothing

She couldn't appear weak before Milton now, or all would be lost, so she ignored his question and turned to introduce Marrok. "He's here to escort me and Martha to Boston, to live with Martha's son and his family."

Milton suddenly looked pale and for a moment Ella thought he was going to be sick. "You can't leave, damn you. You're marrying Jebediah Crawley in a matter of weeks."

"No uncle, I'm not. In fact, I settled the sale of the ranch on Jebediah earlier this afternoon. As of now, he's the proud owner of everything my parents worked so hard for."

She paused as Milton almost choked, then she carried on. "I've taken what was mine from the ranch but if you want anything that's left, I suggest you get there before Jebediah's men arrive in the morning," she paused again as Milton's hands became tight fists.

"You've cheated me!" he spat viciously. "You've gone behind my back!"

"Just as you went behind mine and negotiated a marriage between me and Jebediah knowing full well what sort of man he is, just like everyone else in town," she paused again, willing herself to remain calm.

She didn't dare glance at Marrok, but she felt his strength as he stood silently, positioned between her and Milton. "So I decided to negotiate a better deal," she continued. "A deal which frees me from any obligation of marriage. The sale was effective this morning and I have the paperwork to prove it, along with this."

She reached to open her purse, revealing the

cash. "This is exactly half of my father's estate, as per his wishes. And where you negotiated an unrealistic $3 an acre with Jebediah, I negotiated $2.60 for the land and buildings and as no-one else has come forward, I do think we should be grateful to Jebediah that he accepted my offer at all."

"Damn you," Milton spluttered. "Damn your arrogant young hide."

Ella looked at him with dislike. "If you count the money you'll see I've given you an extra $80 for Billy which amounts to the original deal you struck with Jebediah for $3 an acre."

Milton reached for the money and counted it. Then he turned pale, his fingers trembling as he went through the money again. "There's not enough here. There's not enough!"

"No, there's not enough," Ella said, standing up, pushing her chair back from the table. She wished with all her heart she didn't have to say it, not in front of Marrok, but she couldn't *not* say it, such was her rage.

"Jebediah told me everything about the deal you made with him. About your plans to get me to the altar, to make sure I went ahead with the marriage. And for all your hard work in deceiving me, you were to be rewarded with a large sum of cash. He also told me about your debt to a card player, so I know full well that sum of money in your hand, money earned off the back of my father, will barely cover it."

She shook her head and looked at him with disgust. "I feel ashamed that the same blood runs in our veins."

"Go to hell," Milton yelled. "Damn you! I'll

leave here a pauper because of your meddling!"

He stuffed the cash in his pocket then stepped away from her, glanced back at Marrok then reached for his bags.

But he didn't return to the saloon. Instead, he opened the door into the darkened alley and slipped out into the night.

"He's leaving!" Ella said in astonishment, even as she leaned forward, holding onto her chair for support. "He can't leave! He needs to sign that sale agreement."

Marrok could see her trembling. "I wouldn't worry about him, Ella. He'll try and sneak out of town tonight, maybe pay a ferry man to get him across the river to St Louis but that professional card player will find him, because he'll want his money. As for Jebediah," he shrugged. "He's got the men and the resources to track him down to get his signature on that document so they'll find him, one way or the other. Jebediah will want that done sooner rather than later, you can be assured of that."

Ella looked at him, then nodded. "Is it over, do you think? Or will he come back and cause heartache for me all over again."

"It's over, Ella. Let him go. You've got a whole new life waiting for you in California. Let's go meet up with Jasper and Martha and have some supper."

Ella nodded then stepped towards him, placing a hand on his arm. "How do I ever thank you Marrok? I owe you everything."

He shook his head. "I only made suggestions, you did everything else, so take credit for it Ella.

Be proud of what you've done today. I certainly am."

Ella linked her arm through his because she didn't think she'd make it back through the saloon without his support. Marrok paused to tell the waiting card players that Milton had left, but the men didn't seem too bothered by it. They simply shrugged, then carried on another game without him.

3

Marrok lay abed that night in the narrow cot unable to sleep, not only because the bed was too small for him and the straw mattress not thick enough to stop the hard boards beneath pushing into him, but because he couldn't get rid of the image of Ella.

Of her storming into the kitchen back at the ranch in that extraordinary wedding gown, looking so vulnerable with tears smeared across her face, yet looking heartbreakingly beautiful at the same time.

Or when she faced Jebediah looking confident and strong even though Marrok knew she'd been shaking in her boots.

Or when she stormed into the saloon to confront her uncle.

The girl had courage that was for damn sure and it would help her over the coming week when she'd have to make some of the toughest decisions of her life. Buying oxen and employing men were tough choices for a man, let alone a woman, but now he was this far in, Marrok wouldn't abandon her, unless they ran out of time.

He pushed aside the sheets and sat on the edge of the bed, running his hands over his face. How the hell did he get her wagon caulked, framed, and ready to go within the week? Including buying the oxen, employing a team and buying supplies. But it had to be done, because he had to leave St Louis within seven days at the most, otherwise he'd have to leave her behind. If he left it any later to get back to Independence, he'd risk losing his job as scout along with a place in the wagon train.

And he couldn't do that. Nor could he let Artie

down, not after all these years of planning.

He thought of his three wagons and his own team of twelve men waiting for him in Independence. Marrok hadn't yet finished buying his own supplies, let alone sort out everything for this girl.

He stood up and paced the room. But it could be done. He could buy his supplies in St Louis at the same time as Ella and at least he'd have her wagon to transport them.

He thought of Homer. His old friend might be able to help, if his workload wasn't too heavy.

Marrok moved to sit back on the bed, wondering why he'd done it. Why had he invited some strange girl to change her whole life and accompany him and Martha west?

Had it been Martha's desperate words, shared with him just before Ella arrived home in that wedding dress? Was it because he'd felt sorry for the three of them? Or was it because he'd recognized in Jebediah and Milton the worst of men and knew that Ella didn't have a hope in hell of winning against them.

Marrok moved to open the window above his bed, finding the small room claustrophobic. He rarely slept indoors, preferring the clean fresh smells of the night around a campfire, to the feeling of having four walls crowding in on him.

He could hear Jasper snoring next door, because the man had his own window open to let in the cool spring night.

It struck Marrok then what a strange thing it was that he'd been sent to find one person and ended up with three. As for Ella, by inviting her to join them, for the first time in his life Marrok had allowed a woman to come between him and his plans and everything he'd worked so hard for over the past ten years now threatened to collapse around him.

He thought suddenly of the two rooms he'd booked in St Louis. One had been for Martha, the other for himself. But his room would now go to Ella, although he didn't care too much because he'd rather be bunking down in Homer's livery anyway. He hoped Jasper didn't mind joining him.

Willard had paid for the rooms, but that money was wasted on them tonight because they'd sit empty. Although in hindsight, Marrok was glad he'd paid for three nights in advance because at least the women had somewhere to stay while Ella's wagon was fitted out. He just needed to negotiate another few nights, which might prove difficult with St Louis being so busy.

.Meanwhile his own deadlines loomed, waiting for him in Independence, so instead of wasting time on sleeping, Marrok sat by the open window and began to make plans.

4

It was close to dusk when the flatboat nudged the west bank of the Mississippi River, causing Billy to rear in fright, his hooves stamping on the rough planks of the vessel, shaking his head, upsetting Bear in the traces beside him. Jasper moved quickly to calm him while Ella stood by Bear, as the flatboat once again nudged the bank.

"*Hey up, hey up,*" the ferryman yelled as he threw a rope to a man standing on the crude wharf waiting for them. The man caught it and tied it to a post, securing the flatboat, before moving to open the vessel's railings.

"*Ready now, move on, gently does it,*" called the ferry man, turning to Marrok who was sitting on the buckboard.

Marrok nodded towards Ruby and Jasper, encouraging the horses to move on, off the wooden platform and up onto the wharf. But Billy once again reared, trying to shake free of the harness, causing the flatboat to rock unsteadily. Aware of the weight of the wagon harnessed behind the two horses, Jasper did his best to sooth the distressed animal.

"*Move on, move on,*" the man on the wharf called and at last the horses stepped forward, lowering their heads against the weight behind them, their shoulder muscles straining until at last the wagon was off.

"Lord above, I do declare that's a sight to behold," Martha said softly, where she stood beside Ella.

But Ella barely heard her, she was focused on the horses and getting the wagon up the slight bank, away from the river and the flatboat behind them.

"*Hey up, hey up*," the ferry man called again, holding the bridle of Marrok's horse as he came up off the flatboat behind the wagon.

The horses strained to get the wagon up the slight bank, the smaller front wheels spinning for a moment in the damp earth, before settling in the rutted tracks made from countless other wagons that had come this way. Then they were above the river, with the wooden buildings of St Louis looming just before them.

The ferrymen called out, wishing them well, before heading back across the Mississippi to Illinois Town for the night.

Marrok checked the wagon's wheels and axles with Jasper, before looking over the three horses, but they all seemed just fine. He mounted his own horse as Jasper and Ella climbed up onto the buckboard, leaving Martha to sit on a mattress in the open back of the wagon. As Jasper flicked the reins and the horses moved on, Marrok stared at the town ahead of them, hoping those two rooms he'd paid for were still available, because the women were exhausted, along with Jasper.

They'd had to wait all day to get a vessel to take them across the river because there'd been a long line of settlers before them, some of them waiting for days to get their wagons and animals across. In the end, Ella had used some of her father's money to bribe two ferrymen to take them after their last run of the day, despite it being close to dusk.

As Marrok and Jasper spoke of the horses and the load they were pulling, Ella turned and looked back the way they'd come, back across the Mississippi River to Illinois Town. The river looked lovely in the glow of the setting sun and she could imagine how the ranch would look around about now. But she'd left it behind forever, along with three beloved graves and never again would she be able to place flowers there, nor pay her respects to her parents and Violet.

But she'd made her choice and with a deep ragged breath, she turned back to face west, looking at the town of St Louis as it loomed before them.

St Louis, Missouri
April 1846

1

The wharves had been built just below St Louis and during their visits to Illinois Town once a month, Ella and her father and Jasper had often stood and watched the big boats come up and down the river. Now she could almost touch them and by her reckoning, there had to be more than a dozen steamboats and paddle-streamers lying at anchor while others were tied up at the wharves. Nearby were dozens of pirogues, keelboats, flatboats and canoes.

South and west of St Louis lay open fields and woodlands, even as Marrok remembered those woodlands as dense forest when he first came here as a youth of nineteen. But over the years the trees had been felled to expand St Louis, including building more wharves to cope with the big boats now coming upriver daily as well as building more stores to cope with the influx of settlers along with saloons and liveries. Settlers also felled the trees for firewood and the evidence of that lay in the fields ahead of them, with hundreds of small campfires flickering in the early evening.

Ella had not expected to see so many settlers, yet the smells from their wood fires and cooking mingled with animal and human waste and unwashed bodies.

"Lord Almighty!" Martha said, looking over at the massive camp. "Why, there must be hundreds of people camped there! Whatever are they waiting for?"

"They're settlers, Martha," Marrok said. "All aiming to head west and all waiting on supplies, or for wagons to be fitted out, or for boats to take them up the Missouri River to Independence or St Joseph."

Yet Marrok was shocked by the numbers of people who had arrived here in the past two days, since he'd left to go and find Martha. He reckoned there might be more people camped here now than all the folk he'd taken west by wagon train over the past three years. He was suddenly reminded of a conversation he'd had with the captain of the steamboat which had brought him down from Independence last week.

"Four paddle-steamers came up from New Orleans yesterday with more than four hundred German immigrants aboard, with hardly a word of English between them," the captain had said, as dismayed as everyone else at the speed with which this territory was expanding. "They said there were another four ships behind them, all coming from Europe, full of people coming to settle in the west where they can buy land for $1 an acre."

But they would keep coming, everyone knew that, until the American government closed its western borders. Yet there was little chance of that happening, not with the money to be made off these settlers.

As they rolled on past the camp, Marrok pointed out the disassembled wagons waiting to be carried aboard a steamboat, piece by piece, to travel upriver to either St Joseph or Independence where they'd be reassembled. He didn't say it, but he wished Ella had the money to afford such luxury, because that journey would take just six days.

But that expense was beyond her, which left her no choice but walk her team to Independence, a distance of several hundred miles which would take at least another two weeks. Meanwhile Marrok was hoping to persuade Martha to take passage on a boat and go upriver to Independence by herself, to meet her son.

He glanced over at Ella as she sat beside Jasper on the buckboard and knew he'd have to do that slower journey with her. Because a black man with the use of one good hand and a young woman carrying money would be easy prey for the rogues and villains prowling around these days.

He moved his shoulders, trying to ease the tension in them, just as the setting sun sent a stunning splash of crimson light across the sky and in that moment, Ella seemed framed by fire. The sight of her in that light unnerved Marrok, more so because he knew he was drawn to her, even if he wasn't yet sure why, as he wasn't a man who paid much attention to women unless they were offering something he wanted.

"Look at the animals in the corrals over there!" Jasper exclaimed, pointing to the vast wooden pens which were holding hundreds of cattle, horses, donkeys, mules and oxen, all waiting to go west with their owners.

"Are we setting up camp here alongside these folks?" Martha asked.

Marrok heard the fatigue and dismay in her voice and shook his head before nodding towards town. "I've rented two rooms in a boarding house for you and Ella. Jasper and I can sleep in a friend's livery and keep an eye on the horses and wagon," he glanced back at Jasper. "You happy with that?"

"Yessir," Jasper said, smiling. "I don't mind where I sleep just so long as its dry."

"Come on then, let's get moving. I'd like to get you all indoors before full dark and get these horses brushed down and watered."

They passed more settlers camps and heard the different languages, the laughter, women scolding tired children and men loudly discussing something in a language that came from eastern Europe. Someone was playing a fiddle and nearby came the sound of a harmonica. It made Ella think of her father.

2

They pulled up outside a livery on the far side of town and a man in his mid-thirties stepped out of a log cabin next door. He laughed when he saw Marrok.

"Glad to see you, old friend! I was getting a big worried about you! I thought you'd be here yesterday!" he called, hurrying across to the wagon before looking up in surprise at Jasper and Ella sitting on the buckboard. "No wonder you're a day late! Looks like you got more than you bargained for!"

Marrok dismounted and turned to introduce everyone before turning back to the stocky built man standing beside him. "Homer Axton, a man I consider my brother and the man I'm hoping can sort out your wagon, Ella."

Homer shook his head. "Not sure I like the sound of that," before he reached out and hugged Marrok. "It's good to see you back safe and sound as we've got some real ruffians around town these days. And I reckon you were lucky you got those two rooms booked when you did because I doubt you'd get them now. The town's filled to the rafters, even worse than last year," he glanced up at Jasper and Ella, then turned back to Marrok. "Looks like you might need my loft. I'll charge you the usual."

"You know I'd be grateful for it." Marrok said then nodded towards Ella. "Miss Torray and Jasper have both decided to join Martha's family and go west."

"In that wagon?" Homer asked, curious.

Marrok nodded. "But we need it caulked and

framed. As soon as possible. I know your brother is booked ahead for weeks but we'll pay him extra, because you know the deadlines I've got waiting for me in Independence."

"Old friend, you ask too much! Did you not see the number of settlers camped on the outskirts of town? Every one of them wants the same thing and every blacksmith in St Louis is working around the clock to get folks up to St Joseph or Independence by end of May. There aren't enough hours in the day to get it all done. I already heard talk that some folks will be leaving later this year, but it can't be helped. Can only hope they get across the Rockies come winter, is all." He scratched his beard and shook his head. "But we owe you more than we can ever repay so I'll talk to Melvin tomorrow and see what we can do."

"I'd appreciate it," Marrok said, as Ella and Jasper climbed down off the buckboard.

Homer walked around the wagon, helping Martha climb down before he pushed aside belongings to test the strength of the wagon floor, banging hard on the sides before bending down to push and pull on the wheels.

"Well, it looks to be in pretty good shape. From the look of it I reckon it's been under cover most of its life." He kicked the wheels with the toe of his boot. "And someone's been keeping the wheels and axles oiled. Can't do more than that."

"Yessir, that would be me," Jasper said. "Me and Mr Quentin always put this wagon in the barn at night. Looked after it like a baby."

Homer nodded. "Well, it shows. Some folks go to the trouble and expense of strengthening the wheels with iron, but I don't think it makes much difference. Not with a good wagon like this. Besides, the extra weight only makes it harder for your animals to pull."

He nodded towards Billy and Bear, still in their harnesses. "You need at least four more of them, as that's a hell of a load for two horses to pull alone. You want to sell them to me and buy oxen? Aramis Stent's got the best damn oxen in the territory. But you know that better than anyone Marrok, but make sure you get six of them. Some folks can only afford to buy four, but it ain't enough. Oxen like to work in pairs so if one gets sick or dies off, it's partner ain't happy. And it's always better to have two spares. Tell Stent I sent you and he'll do you a good deal."

He moved to unlock the big double doors of the livery before turning back towards the wagon and horses, his hands gentle as he petted Bear.

"This here is an old fella. Not sure if I can give you a good price for him. And this other one's been badly used. You won't get much for them to be honest, not enough to buy oxen, so I reckon you should keep them. They'll both handle the long walk across country well enough, as long as there's enough feed and water out there."

He paused and turned to Marrok. "I heard there was a big buffalo run just inside Indian country last month. Some boys from Independence rode up and shot several hundred of the beasts before scattering the rest. Can't have those big buffalo herds eating the prairie grass before the wagon trains get through. If there's no feed, there's no chance of your animals making it.

Anyways, best get these horses inside so I can tend to them. And there's enough fresh straw in the loft for you both to be comfortable enough."

He pulled Bear's bridle and the horses followed him into the livery which was dark and hot and smelt of straw and animals. There were ten stalls, each one already occupied by a horse. A buggy sat up against a far wall and two wagons were at the rear of the building. Jasper helped unharness Billy and Bear while Marrok removed the saddle and blanket off his own horse. Then Homer turned to Ella.

"You want to unpack the wagon now? Or wait till morning? By the time I get Melvin around here in the morning to look at it, it'll be after 7am, so we can unpack it then. I reckon he'll do a good deal for you on white canvas as he's just brought a boatload of it up from New Orleans, already waterproofed with linseed oil. And what he don't use this year, he'll use next year. Anyways, if we leave the wagon 'till morning it'll be safe enough in here." He turned to Marrok and Jasper then nodded towards a side door. "I'll lock these big doors behind me, but if you go out later, just bolt that door behind you."

Marrok nodded. "Best we unpack the wagon in the morning. But if I can leave you and Jasper to tend the horses, I'll get the women settled in their rooms before it gets too late." He turned to Jasper. "You okay with that?"

"Yessir, I'll be just fine," Jasper said. "I'm happy tendin' Bear and Billy."

"Well, that's that then," Homer said. "I'll get my wife to bring you a plate of beans and rice for supper along with some biscuits and hot coffee. There won't be no charge for the food."

But while Jasper tended to the horses and left Ella and Martha to get their bags, Homer pulled Marrok aside. "You obviously got a ferry across the river alright, but you were lucky Marrok. Today I heard there's folk been waiting over in Illinois Town for a week to get across. And even with all those steamboats and paddle-steamers berthed down at the wharves, there's folk still having to wait more than two weeks to get a boat up the Missouri. So a word of advice, if you're heading up that way with the wagon and horses, you better get your name down on a list soon as you can, otherwise be prepared to pull some fancy strings. This boom on immigrants heading west is good business for men like me and my brother, but I guess you got to feel sorry for those folks who get left behind."

Marrok frowned. "I wish we were going up the Missouri, but unfortunately Ella's finances won't stretch that far. It'll be a long walk to Independence for her and her team."

Homer looked surprised by this. "Well that's a shame, because I heard from more than one person that it's chaos over in Independence. Sooner you get there, the better I reckon, as it's busier up there than it's ever been. Same thing over at St Jo. Some smaller operators have moved in selling places on their wagon trains, so you'll see plenty of smaller outfits heading out west around the same time as yours. I also heard some folks over in St Joseph got impatient waiting on companies to get up and go, so they set off alone," he shook his head, even as he saw the surprise on Marrok's face.

"They don't understand they got to let the prairie grass grow," Homer continued. "And you know what it's like out there. I don't fancy their chances myself, but some folks just don't think right. And another bit of news, you might hear talk of a high and mighty St Louis politician on a crusade to try and stop these big boats bringing all these settlers upriver, but I reckon he should be careful what he's preaching. He's just as likely to get his head blown off by such talk. There's too much money floating around these days off the back of those settlers and once spring and early summer is done and everyone's gone, things will quieten down for a little while before they all start coming again."

He stepped back as Martha and Ella came towards them with their bags.

"Anyway, enough said. Best get the women settled for there's enough freebooters and thieves around these days. Doesn't pay to be carrying bags and the like around at this hour of the night. Meanwhile I'll get my wife onto those beans and rice for you and Jasper."

*

They passed saloon bars and bowling lanes, pool halls and upmarket French restaurants and the cheaper American eating houses, all of them packed, the laughter and shouts echoing out into the night.

Marrok walked ahead with Martha, carrying the heavier of the women's bags while Ella trailed behind, glancing in the windows of restaurants and stores. She envied the women who passed them by wearing fancy clothes, or those who sat in flash restaurants wearing jewelry and dresses of silk and brocade, for her parents had never had the money for such luxuries, nor had the two young men who courted her.

"Oh do stop dragging your feet Ella," Martha scolded, turning around to hurry her along. "I'm bone tired and aching for a warm bed."

Marrok glanced back to see what had caused Martha's ill temper and saw the wistful look on Ella's face as she stepped away from the window of a French restaurant. He found her curiosity intriguing, but added nothing to stir up Martha's comment. They ended up on the other side of town, where a three-story boarding house stood wedged between a general store and a barber shop. The stores were both closed, but light poured from the windows of the boarding house. Marrok knocked on the door and a stout woman in her fifties answered it. She glanced at the two women in bewilderment before looking at Marrok.

"I had your rooms ready yesterday, but you never showed. Let me tell you young man, I could have rented them out for ten times what you paid for them but I didn't because I'm an honest woman and I run my business that way." She nodded towards Martha and Ella. "I understood one of the rooms was for your own use so unless you've got a wife here, you're sleeping somewhere else, for I won't have no hanky-panky in my house. I've got a good decent name in this town and if you want that sort of carry on, you'll find a room to rent above one of the saloons."

Ella glanced at Marrok, aware for the first time that she was taking his room. He didn't seem too upset about it as he stepped up onto the porch, towering over the woman.

"I understand your concern Mrs Blackwood, but my plans changed at the last minute and now these two women will take the rooms I paid for. But I take it you've got supper ready as we agreed?"

The woman nodded. "I have. But you only paid for two, so if you want extra, that'll cost you. I'm not in this game for charity or taking care of strays."

"I'll be eating elsewhere, so supper is for two, as agreed and paid for." He paused and hoped like hell that what he asked for next was not impossible. "These women will also need those two rooms for another five nights, as well as breakfast and supper. They'll pay for half of it now and half when they leave."

Mrs Blackwood stared at him and Marrok could see her mind ticking over, wondering how she could make more money on this. Willard would be paying the extra nights for Martha, but Marrok knew he'd have to pay for Ella. He couldn't ask her for more money. Not when he'd asked her to join them. Coming west had never been her idea.

"I got two older men who've booked those rooms, but they ain't eating here and if truth be told, I always prefer women staying in my house, they're less trouble and don't leave behind a mess. So you better make it worth my while so it don't cause me too much heartburn when I tell those gentlemen they're going to be sleeping in my basement on cots."

Marrok nodded. "I'll make it worth your while. But we'll discuss it tomorrow." He nodded towards the bags he was carrying. "Shall I carry these up to their rooms? It'll save you all the trouble."

The woman nodded and handed him the keys. As they headed up the stairs to the top floor, Mrs Blackwood called out behind them. "Breakfast is at 7am sharp. I won't keep it later. And make sure you lock the doors behind you as you never know who's prowling around these days. St Louis got a whole bunch of trouble camped out on the edge of town."

The rooms held a single bed in each, with a mattress of fresh straw, woolen blankets and cotton sheets. A pillow lay on each bed. Small nightstands held a candle and candlestick holder. Marrok placed the bags on one of the beds, leaving the women to choose which room they preferred.

"Don't worry about getting to the livery in the morning. I'd rather you stay here and think on what supplies you'll need to take west, so we can order them tomorrow. I can help Jasper and Homer unpack the wagon before Homer's brother arrives to take a look at it, because sooner we get the wagon fitted out, sooner we can leave St Louis. So try and get a good night's sleep. I'll be back mid-morning to sort out your rooms with Mrs Blackwood and go over what you need, before we head out to the mercantile stores and put in your orders."

But as he turned to go, Ella stopped him. "This room, I can pay my way. It's only fair."

Marrok nodded. "We can talk about it in the morning." Then he touched his hat, wished them a good night's sleep then he was gone.

3

Marrok walked quickly along the main street, his moccasins silent on the wooden boardwalk as he headed back to the livery on the far side of town. It was almost full dark now, yet the thought of rice and beans and trying to get some sleep were the last things on his mind. He felt restless, so he kept walking, his mind full of everything that Ella needed to get done.

He passed the alley where his favorite eating house was and thought about going in there for a meal. But then decided against it. He wasn't hungry, for his stomach felt all churned up from the events of the past two days.

The sound of laughter along with pianos being played echoed out onto the street but Marrok ignored them all and walked on, past saloons and pool halls, but just when he went to step down and enter an alley which would take him back to the livery, he heard a woman singing.

It came from a saloon just down from where he stood, the sound of her voice husky and deep yet utterly feminine, a sound that found its way deep into a man's thoughts and touched him where no-one had a right to go.

Instinctively Marrok moved towards the sound, drawn to it, stepping back into the dusty street to cross over to the opposite boardwalk, as the woman was singing in one of the less reputable saloons in town which surprised him. With that voice, she could have gone anywhere and named her price.

The saloon was crowded, with men standing out on the boardwalk looking through the open door

Sadie Conall

to get a glimpse of her. Marrok joined them, stunned by her voice. Only once before had he heard such talent and that was in a singing hall in New York many years ago. He had gone to the venue by mistake, thinking it a pool hall, but once he heard that woman sing he'd never forgotten it.

He was tall enough to peer over the men who stood before him and through the open doors he saw a curvy girl in her early twenties standing in the center of the room, singing a song he'd heard many times before, but never had he heard it sung like this. Her voice was full of emotion, tearing at your heartstrings.

She was about as tall as Ella, but perhaps a few years younger. Her complexion was flawless, framed by hair that was like a red-hot flame.

She came to the end of the song and bowed to the male audience as they clapped and cheered and when she turned and glanced across to the back of the saloon, Marrok saw her eyes were as grey as the slate found high in the mountains of the pacific northwest. And like every other man watching her, he was bewitched.

He expected her to speak in a voice from faraway lands owned by the Celts, for her coloring came from those distant lands of marshy bogs and misty mountains, of ancient folk songs accompanied with bodhráns or bagpipes and men who fought with axe, pike or sword. But when she spoke to thank her audience, her accent was American, suggesting roots in one of the east coast cities of New York or Boston.

Marrok went to walk on but paused when he noticed two men standing at the back of the room nudging each other and smirking as they watched the girl. He felt the hairs stand up on the back of his neck, feeling unnerved by their attention of her, for it wasn't admiration he saw in their faces, but cruelty. He paused for a moment, deciding whether sleep was more important than making sure the girl was safe, before he pushed through the crowd and stepped into the saloon.

4

Ella smelled of soap, but she had washed herself from head to foot from the bowl of hot soapy water supplied by the boarding house. When she crawled into bed, hoping there were no bedbugs, she held the crocheted blanket made by Martha and her mother close to her face, hoping to smell a lingering scent there of Adeline. But her mother's smell had left long ago, yet the blanket did what Martha hoped it would. It gave Ella some comfort, because now she was alone, with Martha gone to her bed in the room across the hall, she felt fearful and unsure of what she was doing without Marrok's energy to push her along.

She wished she were tired, she wished she could just roll over and go to sleep and she wished she had more money. If she had more money, she'd have so many more choices. Like take a steamboat up to Independence, rather than have to walk her team all that way.

The light from a half moon took away the shadows in her room but still, Ella felt as though she were standing on the edge of an abyss, a great dark chasm of darkness below her yet a whole new life waiting just beyond. She just had to find a way to get across that chasm.

She understood from the conversation between Homer and Marrok earlier that she had no choice but pay more to get her wagon outfitted quickly, otherwise she'd have to stay behind in St Louis and do it without Marrok's help. But that wasn't an option for Ella, because she knew she couldn't do it without him. She was strong, but not strong enough to cope with such a huge thing on her own with only Jasper to back her up. And if her wagon took longer to fit out, if she went to the back of the queue, she faced the very real possibility of missing a wagon train altogether and having to wait in St Louis or Independence another year.

She moved to sit up, feeling on edge, even as she went over everything again. He hadn't said anything, but Ella knew Marrok was also worried about her lack of funds. But then she thought of something else, something that made her more unsettled. Would Marrok expect payment for all his help? If he did, that made her money dwindle away even further.

She crawled across the bed and pushed aside the curtain to look out over the town, wondering where Milton was and if he'd managed to flee that card player. But she didn't want to think about him, because he'd never cared about her. Instead, Ella let her thoughts drift to Marrok. She doubted he'd be asleep. Not a man like that. He'd be out and about, watching and listening to what was happening in town before he went to his bed.

She thought of Jebediah calling Marrok a halfbreed. The tone of his voice had been derogatory, yet his comment meant nothing to Ella, as she'd never met a halfbreed. Anyway, she liked Marrok's character well enough and so far, he'd been nothing but generous to her.

She sighed and reached up to open the window, allowing fresh air to enter the room along with the sounds of the town and despite the late hour, the street below wasn't quiet. Ella could hear men talking loudly in a saloon just across the street and from somewhere else came the high-pitched sound of a woman's laughter. And from other saloons and restaurants came other voices and laughter as well as the sound of pianos being played.

Ella wondered if Martha were still awake. She hoped so, because she needed to talk. She crawled off the bed and moved across to the door before opening it carefully because one of the hinges squeaked, then hurried across the small landing to stand outside Martha's room. But as she went to knock, Ella heard the sound of the older woman snoring from behind the door.

Feeling a little lost, Ella returned to her room and crawled back on the bed, once again pushing aside the curtain to look out on the street. Suddenly she wanted more than anything to be outside, to be walking those streets, exploring this town she would never revisit.

But she couldn't because she was female, which was so unfair. She put her arms on the windowsill and thought of a world governed by men who declared all respectable women should be indoors come nightfall unless they were escorted out by a man. Ella wondered what men would say if women were to govern that all men must be indoors come nightfall, safe and sound, so women could go out and enjoy all the delights that St Louis had to offer, alone if they wished, without judgment or harassment.

She laughed at the thought and feeling empowered by it, she climbed off the bed and went to her bags. She rummaged through her clothes until she found what she was looking for. A pair of work pants she had sometimes worn while out riding Bear around the ranch. They were old now, but she'd packed them away in case she needed them on the trail.

She thought on what she was doing for just a moment before throwing off her shift and pulling on the pants, followed by an old shirt of her fathers, which she tucked tight into her pants. The shirt made her look big, but at least the curve of her hips and breasts were hidden. Then she tied her hair up under the wide brimmed hat she had always worn when out riding, before looking down at herself. She might just be able to pull it off. She was tall and slim enough, yet the curve of her hips might give her away. But she had something to hide those curves. Her father's jacket. She reached for it and held it out before her. He'd always worn it when going to Church, or into Illinois Town on business, or to a neighbor's wedding or county dance.

She pulled it on and in her bare feet she practiced striding out like a boy. It was difficult, and she concentrated hard on not swinging her hips, the usual gait of a woman. She laughed at how ridiculous she felt and went to take the jacket off when she saw her father's small pistol lying in her case. Ella paused for only a moment then shrugged the jacket back on before picking up the pistol and putting it in the pocket of the jacket. It wasn't loaded, but if she needed it, it would make a good weapon to intimidate or threaten. Then she opened her bedroom door and crept out into the hall, holding her boots in her hands so she didn't wake Martha before making her way down the stairs.

*

The sounds of the town erupted around Ella once she left the quiet of the boarding house. She walked quickly, keeping to the shadows and away from the light which spilled out onto the boardwalk from saloons and restaurants. She followed the sounds of pianos and harmonicas and the men and women laughing. She peered through saloon doors, looked into restaurants, nodded back when men nodded to her and Ella felt alive being out here amongst it all and as she walked on, she was delighted when no-one gave her a second glance, but she made sure her hat was pulled low over her face.

Through the windows of fancy French restaurants she saw the white linen tablecloths, the crystal glasses and expansive china and the women in their glorious dresses with their hair done up in elaborate curls sitting opposite men who had the money to pay for whatever they wanted. Ella couldn't help but wonder what it must be like to be such a woman.

When a group of men came around a corner further up town, talking loudly, making their way towards her, Ella ducked down an alleyway and waited for them to pass. Then she walked on, passing couples walking arm in arm or small groups of men but none of them bothered her.

She sauntered all the way to the far end of town, enjoying herself, when she saw a crowd of men gathered outside a saloon half a block away. Ella wondered what held their interest and hurried across to see for herself. She had barely reached them when she heard a woman sing, her voice so pure, with such perfect pitch, Ella wondered why more people hadn't gathered to listen.

She wanted to get closer, to see who this girl was, yet there were too many men standing outside on the boardwalk. Then she saw another alley which ran between a ladies' refreshment saloon and a general store, both closed for the night, their service alleys dark and empty. If she dared, she could cut down one of the alleys and walk around the back of the buildings and reach the saloon on the other side. She decided to go for it, not stopping to think that such places held danger.

She reached the alley without incident then stepped off the boardwalk and into the shadows, putting her hand out to touch the side of the ladies' refreshment saloon to guide her and only when she reached the end of the alley did she feel afraid as it was almost pitch black down there. Moving quickly, she came around the back of the building and suddenly the light from the saloon where the woman was singing blazed the way ahead. Ella hurried, swinging around into the alley which now ran the length of the saloon. She passed empty crates and wooden boxes then saw a set of stairs on the outside of the building which led to rooms above the saloon. And then she saw a ground floor window.

Ella dragged one of the crates forward, pulled herself up onto it, pushed aside the leaves of the vine which covered this side of the building and looked through the window. The panes of glass were dirty with years of dust and grease, so using the corner of her father's jacket, Ella wiped a small portion of the glass and as the dirt and grime came away, she saw a girl a bit younger than herself standing in the middle of the room, surrounded of men, her head slightly back and her eyes closed as she came to the end of a song.

Ella gaped at the girl's beauty, but it was her voice that held her enthralled, just like the men around her. Deep and husky, full of longing and anguish, it tugged at your heartstrings.

"One more," a man cried, followed by others clapping and cheering her on. The singer laughed then nodded, holding up one finger, teasing her audience with the promise of one more song. Ella listened spellbound as the girl began a well-known song of love and loss and as she came to the end of it, Ella glanced around the room.

She was stunned when she saw Marrok leaning against the bar, transfixed as every other man as he watched the girl. The look of yearning on his face made Ella feel incredibly stupid, standing there on a crate in a darkened alley. Because by comparison to that girl, Ella was just a simple girl off a ranch who wore plain homespun dresses and practical boots. Girls like Ella didn't belong out here in the night. Only beautiful women like that girl owned the night.

The euphoria of being out here alone was gone and Ella felt a sudden desperate need to get back to her small, rented bedroom, to get out of her worn farm clothes and forget about tonight. Yet as she went to climb down off the crate, she heard the men clapping and cheering as the singer thanked them for coming to hear her sing and Ella moved back to peer through the window. She saw the girl head towards the stage while Marrok remained where he was, standing alone at the bar yet strangely, Ella noticed the liquor in his glass remained untouched.

She climbed down off the crate and made a move towards the street, when a dozen or more men spilled out of the saloon. One of them slipped into the alley to urinate and Ella quickly pushed herself back under the stairs and into the vine, waiting for him to finish before he moved away with his friends. And then at last the crowd was gone, moving on to other saloons or gaming houses or to return to their homes or camps on the edge of town.

Ella took a step forward, trying to find that same confidence she'd felt when she left the boarding house but only managing to feel foolish, when a man suddenly burst into the alley from the street, running fast.

The stairs still concealed Ella's hiding place and the man ran on past her, yet he was close enough for her to smell the stench of his unwashed body and clothes, along with the reek of tobacco and whisky. And then she heard the thud of a door opening followed by a girl's cry of pain and two men swearing.

Startled, Ella stepped out of her hiding place, not sure what was going on when she turned and walked straight into the arms of another man. Their bodies collided and as her hands smacked up against the solid hardness of his chest, as he reached out to grab her arms in a vice like grip, Ella lost her balance and fell against him, the force of the impact knocking her hat off and allowing her hair to fall loose about her face.

"What the hell!" the man muttered in astonishment.

Ella knew that voice. She would know it anywhere. Startled, she looked up into the face of Marrok.

He let her go, swinging her gently back against the vine, under the stairs. "Stay here! Don't move!" he hissed at her, then took off down the alley.

Ella sank into a crouch, her legs trembling beneath her when once again she heard a woman's pitiful cry, followed by a man's coarse language. She waited only a moment before pushing her hair back under her hat then reached for her father's pistol and ran after Marrok.

5

She knew they would follow her once she left the stage and the only chance she had was to run, because their intention was clear in their smug faces and dirty grins. They couldn't believe they'd found her after all this time.

There was little point in calling for help, because no-one could help against these two men so she'd sung more songs than she was paid to do, to give herself time to think. She'd try and find somewhere to hide for a few hours, then she'd get back to her rooms, pack her bags then get out of town.

But she hadn't been quick enough. Because as she opened the door into the alley, she saw the other man racing towards her, a grin on his face, a look that told her they had finally won after all these years.

She cried aloud at the hopelessness of it, even as the other man came up behind her from inside the saloon and shoved her outside. She landed on her hands and knees and felt the first backhanded slap across her face, even as she put her hands up to protect herself. And then a kick to her ribs, not only to cause damage but to slow her down in case she got away, but the voluminous material in her dress stopped his boot from breaking any bones. But she felt it. She felt every bit of its violence.

And then the worst. The other man pushed her over onto her back and straddled her, reaching up with both hands to circle her throat. She only had time to cry out before those fingers began to crush, not to kill her, but to damage her vocal cords.

She kicked and squirmed, raking with her

fingernails at his face and hands as the second man lashed out and slapped her across the face for the second time.

But then suddenly someone else was there, pulling the men off. She heard his fists slam into their flesh and she curled into a tight ball, protecting her face and throat as the three men fought around her. Then the sound of someone shouting.

She looked up and saw a young man about her own age standing not ten feet away, holding a pistol in his hands, yelling at the men to stand back. And then there were angry oaths, followed by running steps and then silence.

She rolled away, her hands still in front of her face ready to deflect another punch when someone placed a hand on her shoulder, the touch gentle, asking if she was alright. But this wasn't the voice of a male.

She rolled over and looked up to see a girl about her own age kneeling beside her, holding a hat in her hands, allowing her long hair to tumble free.

6

Ella glanced at Marrok as he bent over, his hands on his knees, dry retching from a punch to his belly. She quickly put her father's pistol back in her pocket then pulled off her hat before bending towards the girl who lay curled like a child, her legs drawn up to her chest, her arms covering her face. Ella reached out to place a hand on her shoulder. "Are you alright? Do you need a doctor?" she asked.

The girl rolled over onto her back, holding her belly as though it pained her, then looked up at Ella in astonishment.

But Ella was equally shocked, because the girl lying beaten on the ground was the flame haired singer from the saloon. "Oh my," she whispered, as she saw the ugly bruises on the left side of the girl's face and around her throat. "Oh, you're hurt bad, you need a doctor."

The girl coughed and her hands went to her throat before she shook her head and pushed herself up onto her knees. "No doctor," she said, her voice hoarse and ragged, nothing like how she'd sounded only minutes before when singing to the crowd in the saloon.

And then Marrok was kneeling beside Ella, his hand on her back and the heat of him through her father's jacket was like a brand, burning her. They helped the girl to her feet but as Ella turned to meet Marrok's gaze, their faces only a heartbeat apart, she saw the bewilderment on his face as he looked down at her clothes.

"What the hell are you playing at?" he asked, his voice low.

"I wanted some fresh air," she answered.

"And the pistol?"

Ella took it from her pocket. "My father's. But it's not loaded."

Marrok shook his head then closed his eyes as though too exhausted to ask anything else. Then he looked back at the girl, as though forgetting Ella was even there, which only made her feel more stupid. When he asked the girl if she was alright, a softness to his voice, Ella was astounded by the jealousy which swept through her, an emotion unknown until now.

The girl nodded but groaned softly with pain, her hand going to her side where the man had kicked her. But as the lamp light from the saloon revealed the girl's bruised face, it also showed the dark bruising and swelling around her throat. "I don't know who you are," she said, her voice nothing more than a whisper now, "but thank you for coming to help me. You don't know what you've done."

"Do you know those men? Because they seemed to know you," Marrok said. "I saw them watching you from the back of the saloon and it looked like they meant you harm. When one of them followed you backstage and the other came out here, I knew you were in trouble. Yet why would they want to hurt you?"

The flamed-haired girl looked up at Marrok and saw his buckskin clothing, before glancing over at Ella, noticing again her worn pants and a shirt that seemed far too big for her. She frowned, bewildered by the two of them and although grateful for their help, she didn't want to talk to them about her problems. What she needed was to get back to her room and pack, then get out of town. She reached out her hand, first to Ella, then Marrok. "My name's Ruby Daegan," she said, her grip strong. "And I thank you again for your help tonight. Are you camped out in the fields along with all those other settlers?"

Ella was surprised by the soft touch of the girl's hand, as if she'd never known a hard physical day's work in her life. Her voice was soft, her words eloquent, suggesting she'd been educated well past childhood. Clearly, she had come from a privileged home.

"No," Ella answered. "We're staying in a boarding house on the other side of town just until we get the wagon fitted out, then we're leaving for Independence to join a wagon train west to California."

Ruby nodded, then suddenly reeled away as if to be sick. Marrok stepped forward and put a hand on her arm. "I think we'd better get you to a doctor, ma'am. Or get you home safe. Those men might still be about."

"No, I don't want a doctor. I'll be alright once I rest and my room is just upstairs." She reached up to touch the bruising on her face before touching her throat. Then she thanked them again before stepping back inside the saloon, the lock turning behind her.

7

Marrok looked down at Ella, his eyes lingering on her hair loose about her shoulders, before looking down at her clothes. Ella saw his puzzled look and went to explain, but without a word Marrok reached for her hat and suggested she put it on.

"I think it best you hide your hair under this. Otherwise we'll attract attention we don't want."

When Ella finished pushing her hair up under the hat, Marrok suddenly reached out and took her hand, pulling her along the alley and up onto the boardwalk. Then he spun around to face her.

"What the hell are you playing at Ella? Why are you out here all alone, dressed like that? That could have been you in that alley. It's dangerous enough for a man out here alone, let alone a young woman!" He paused, as though struggling to contain his frustration, yet Ella could see his exhaustion. "You've just seen the type of men walking around St Louis. This town isn't like it used to be. Why didn't you stay in your room where it's safe?"

"Because I didn't want to!" Ella yelled back at him. "Why *should* I stay in my room! I'm not the one causing trouble. Those men are! So why don't they stay in their rooms! And it was *you* who ended up throwing punches! Honestly! You're all hard edges, Marrok. I bet if I touched you, I'd cut myself."

Marrok stared at her, a little wide eyed, then he took a deep breath. "You held a pistol to those men so you weren't exactly acting like an angel, yet you did save me and that girl from getting a worse beating, so I thank you for that. But the only reason I asked you to stay in your room was to protect you. If you wanted to come out and see St Louis at night, you had only to ask and I would gladly have escorted you."

He paused as a group of men came towards them. Once they'd passed, Marrok took Ella's arm then gently pulled her along the boardwalk, back towards the boarding house. Ella could feel him trembling beside her but knew it was fatigue, along with having a few punches thrown at him, rather than the shock of seeing her out here. So she said nothing more, but as Marrok hurried through town, his big, callused hand slipped down her arm to hold her own hand as he pulled her along behind him, all the way back to the boarding house. It crossed her mind that she probably wouldn't get away from him if she tried and for the first time understood her vulnerability. It was his strength against her own. His hard, male body against her own soft female one and as she was dragged home, Ella had a feeling that if she stopped and pulled back, Marrok would simply lift her over his shoulder and carry her home and there wasn't a darn thing she could do about it. Scream and cry and shout and make a fuss, but he would win because he was bigger, stronger and a male looking out for her. Other men would applaud him for it.

Ella decided he was like an ox, all brawn, ready to push aside anyone who got in his way. She was determined not to apologize for leaving the safety of her bedroom. She wasn't a prisoner!

A block away from the boarding house, she decided she'd had enough so shook her hand free, not without some violence. He let her go, surprised by it, yet smart enough to recognize the frustration on her face.

"Can we just let up for a moment," she said, a little breathlessly, her hands on her hips, looking around the town. It was late now, the restaurants and eating houses closing and even the sounds of pianos becoming less frequent in the cool night air, along with the raucous laughter and shouts of men. "I need to take a breath," she said. "I haven't got your long legs."

He looked down at her legs and as his gaze lingered on them, barely concealed beneath the worn linen fabric, Ella felt the heat rise in her face.

"They look just fine to me," he said and Ella wanted to stamp in frustration.

She moved on past him, holding her hands in tight fists as she walked on ahead. She never saw the smile that broke across Marrok's face as he watched her walk off. He admired her spunk and yes, he could understand her frustration. She was young. She wanted some excitement and as he followed her, an idea began to form. Perhaps he could take her out for a meal before they left, to one of those fancy French restaurants he had seen her peering into through the open windows. Yet how did he find the time!

Ella stopped outside the door of the boarding house and turned back to look at him. He walked nice, she had to give him that. But everything about him was nice, although he didn't seem too bothered about how he looked, or what he said or what people thought of him which she liked about him. He stepped up to knock on the door, but Ella stopped him.

"You'll wake everyone if you do that," she said, scolding him, even as she reached for the doorknob. "I left it on the latch," she said, as the door opened beneath her touch.

Marrok took a breath, knowing how foolish it was to leave the door unlocked in these times, yet Ella seemed unaware of it. But he said nothing, even as she turned back to him. She was thinking of the consequences of tonight if Martha found out.

"Look, can we keep this between ourselves? You know Martha will only worry if she finds out. She doesn't need to know about any of this."

Marrok nodded. "I won't say a word. But try and get some sleep, Ella. We've all got another big day tomorrow."

He watched as she pushed open the door, stepped inside and locked the door behind her. He waited for a moment, then confident she had at last gone to her bed, he turned and made his way back to the livery, feeling his own bruises where one of the men had landed a couple of good punches. But it was nothing he wasn't used to.

He hurried on, feeling the chill as the night deepened towards midnight but as his own fatigue began to claim him and the hunger rolled in his belly, Marrok decided to take a detour home, back past the saloon, just to make sure that flame haired girl was alright.

8

Ruby sat fully dressed in a plain homespun dress as she peered out from behind the worn lace curtains in a bedroom that wasn't her own. She tried to stay calm, desperate to keep her hideaway a secret, until the morning at least.

She didn't think it possible to sleep, because of the adrenaline and fear still racing through her body which had started the moment she saw those two men step into the saloon. They had known she'd seen them and they'd enjoyed tormenting her, knowing there was nowhere for her to go.

Her escape into the alley had failed miserably and had that young couple not stepped in to help, Ruby would be on a boat right now, heading downriver to New Orleans and then on a ship back to New York.

She shuddered as she looked around the empty bedroom. She had come here after packing up her few belongings and creeping along the hallway to this temporary sanctuary, giving herself a few precious hours to think and plan.

But she had been sitting here in the dark for over an hour and still hadn't come up with any ideas, even as she watched the street below, looking out for those two men. It seemed they'd gone to lick their wounds for now, but they'd be back. Ruby had no doubts about that and there was no reason for them to hurry now they'd found her. They had all the time in the world to get her on a boat down to New Orleans. They would probably want to torment her a little, after everything she'd put them through.

Her face throbbed where they had hit her, and

her ribs were bruised but thankfully not broken. She touched her throat, her voice nothing more than a whisper now, but Ruby didn't think they'd had time to damage her vocal cords. Yet they would have, had that young couple not come by and if they'd succeeded in that, then after all these years, her father had finally won.

Her hands twisted anxiously within the fabric of the worn dress, which she had traded many months ago for the last of her own silks. The trade hadn't been a fair one, but at the time Ruby had placed more value on the plain homespun dress than her own expensive creation.

She wondered again who the young couple were who had come to her aid. The man had been dressed in buckskin, which suggested he was a woodsman or mountain man. But the girl had worn pants and a shirt, as though she had come off a ranch, or hill country, far from St Louis. Yet they weren't simple folk. Ruby could tell that by the way they spoke. She also envied them, because they had each other and she was alone.

She moved away from the window and began to pace the room, mindful to stay on the square patch of threadbare carpet so her boots didn't echo on the wooden floorboards and wake anyone. But it was almost midnight now and she could feel the silence in the big old building where fifteen other people slept.

She was frightened, unsure where to go or what to do, because there was no way out from here, other than go back down the Mississippi River to New Orleans. But she'd escaped New Orleans, she couldn't go back.

She closed her eyes, certain she'd be safe here, for a little while at least. But they'd found her, despite all her best efforts.

She'd fled New York more than four years ago, finding sanctuary in towns and cities along the east coast, but moving continuously, never staying for long in any one place, even though she'd come close to being caught twice before. But after all these years, they'd finally caught up with her and in St Louis of all places, where she'd been for less than two months.

But Ruby had a sickening feeling she knew how they'd found her. She had worked for almost six months singing in an exclusive brothel in New Orleans, where she'd made good money, especially in tips, singing to wealthy men. But one of the customers had known her father. As soon as he entered the room Ruby had recognized him, just as he recognized her. She had seen him many times at home in New York, when he'd come to do deals with her father and like her father, he was as mean and dirty as they came. She had left the brothel that night and hurried through the streets of New Orleans in the dark, until she found a room in a hovel way on the other side of town. The next day she'd caught a steamboat up the Mississippi River to St Louis, but in hindsight, she should have gone back east, back to the big cities on the eastern seaboard where it was easier to hide.

Ruby put her face in her hands, feeling the pain of the bruises, knowing she was fooling herself if she ever thought she could be free of him. Because he would never give up, not until she were back in New York. Not until he could punish her for running away.

She looked over at her few belongings packed away in a small travel bag, knowing she had to leave tonight. She couldn't stay here until morning, it was too dangerous now. The owner of the saloon would find her room empty tomorrow and be upset, because her singing had brought in the customers. But he'd take one look at her bruised face and tell her to get lost because Ruby had seen him do the same to one of the working girls who'd had a little too much to drink and fallen down the stairs.

"Do you think this is a charity house?" he had yelled at the desperate girl, in front of all the other staff. "Because I ain't running one, and I can't have you mixing with my customers looking like you got on the wrong side of someone's fist, just like I can't have you lying upstairs for two weeks while you heal, without making me any money."

Ruby didn't know where the girl had gone and it never crossed her mind that she might have needed help. But girls who lived this life were hard, well used to looking after themselves. It had probably never even occurred to the girl to ask anyone for help but she'd been replaced easily enough, because there were girls arriving in St Louis every day looking for work.

She thought of the other girls asleep in the building. She hadn't made friends with any of them, except one, because she mostly kept to herself. Three of the girls entertained customers and had bedrooms such as this one, large and luxurious on this floor, although the girl who had occupied this room had left suddenly the day before with a customer. But by midday tomorrow another girl would be living in this room, a girl with no fears about entertaining men in that bed.

Another woman slept in the attic, but she worked in the kitchen as cook and cleaner. Two barmen slept in tiny, cold rooms in the basement while the owner and his wife slept in a big room on the second floor next to the room occupied by their two young children. That room was above this one, which made Ruby keep her silence while she laid low here.

She would miss this place. She had been happy in this town. Employed as a singer on her first day here, she had been given a small box room on the first floor all to herself which had been luxury compared to what she had experienced in other places.

But now she had to leave. Because if those men returned in the morning or saw her in town, they would sweep her away before anyone could stop them.

She returned to the window and glanced down on the empty street. She might have nowhere to go and be running scared, but at least she had two things to be grateful for.

She had money, thanks to dear Papa.

And she had Clara, a friend Ruby trusted with her life.

She glanced across at the bed, thinking she might chance it and stay the night after all, yet she found the thought of sleeping in the bed distasteful.

She had spent days cleaning her room and paying for fresh straw when she first arrived here, to make sure the room and bed were free of bugs. But she doubted this mattress was free of anything.

She looked over at the battered chaise longue in the corner. She could drape a blanket over it. At least that would be cleaner than the bed.

Ruby felt her belly clench with hunger but ignored it for now, because hunger was the least of her problems. She thought again of Clara. Maybe her friend would help, not only with food but perhaps she'd hide her away somewhere, just until she could get out of town. Thinking on it, she went to move away from the window when she saw a big man stop on the other side of the street and glance across at the saloon. She stared at him in surprise because she'd recognize him anywhere.

It was the man who had come to her rescue earlier in the alley. Yet what was he doing here? Had he come to see if she was alright? That thought stunned Ruby, because no-one had bothered to see if she was alright for a very long time.

She remembered his wife saying they were going to California, they were just waiting for their wagon to be fitted out. Ruby wondered how long it took to outfit a wagon. As she was thinking on it, the man turned and walked away, heading for an alley which lead towards the back of town.

Ruby remained by the window looking down on the street and slowly an idea began to form.

What did she know of California?

Almost nothing, but she had vague memories of another singer in some other saloon she'd worked in speaking of the big singing halls out that way, in a place called San Francisco. The girl had said you could make in one night what it would take weeks to earn here. Ruby hadn't believed her, but she vividly remembered the girl saying it took more than a year to travel out there.

She would have to buy a horse, yet she knew very little about horses.

And supplies, because what was there to eat out there?

And what would she sleep in? A canvas shelter like the rest of those settlers camped out in the fields on the edge of town? Ruby didn't fancy that idea, but she would do it, if she had a chance of freedom. But she couldn't do it by herself. She had no idea where to go.

She stood up, pacing again, keeping her boots on the carpet as her mind reeled with the thought of all that travelling. It would be hard, but she had come this far. She went to the bigger of her two bags and opened it, reaching down into the bottom for a leather purse. It held all her savings, money she'd earned over the past four years singing across the country, as well as the money she'd taken from her father's safe.

Like father, like daughter. Take what you can, no matter the cost.

It never occurred to him that she'd go through his personal papers and find the code but then, a lot of things never occurred to him, like how unhappy she was. Yet would he have cared anyway?

But Ruby never saw it as stealing. She thought of it as a mere pittance of the eventual fortune she would have inherited one day, even though that day would never come now.

She counted it twice, just to make sure she had it right. A little over five thousand dollars. A fortune by anyone's reckoning, but her father could well afford the loss of it as this kind of money was just petty cash to him.

Ruby wondered as she often did, if she hadn't taken the money, would her father still have sent his thugs after her? She thought he would have, because getting her back to New York was never about the money. It was about control. Her father wanted her back for the sake of his vanity. He couldn't bear to think that his only child, his only daughter, had run away, humiliating him before his friends and business colleagues. To punish her, to teach her a lesson, to show her who was boss, he'd spend every last penny he had to get her back.

She put the money back in the bottom on her bag and thought once more of her plans. She didn't have much to take with her, only the two bags, both of them easy enough to carry.

The dresses she wore at night for her performances belonged to the saloon and in truth she would be glad to see the back of them. Every night she had to grit her teeth as she pulled them on as none had been washed well enough and the body odor and cheap perfume other girls had splashed over themselves lingered in the fabric.

She felt the hunger gnaw at her belly again and as she reached for a blanket off the bed, a wave of dizziness almost brought her to her knees. She gripped the side of the dresser to stop herself falling, but it wasn't just hunger which made her feel ill. It was fear, along with bitter disappointment. Because another town, a town she had grown to like in the short time she had been here, was now lost to her like so many other towns.

She sat down on the chaise longue until the dizziness passed and knew she couldn't leave until she'd rested and had a decent meal. So she took off her boots and crept across the wooden floorboards to jam a chair hard up beneath the doorknob. It was a trick she had learned from another girl in some other saloon somewhere else. No-one could get in with the door wedged like that.

Then she took the two blankets folded at the foot of the bed and held them to her face to smell them. She grimaced at the smell of tobacco and stale fabric. But it would get cold in the early hours of the morning and the blankets were better than nothing. She placed one over the chaise longue then lay down on it, covering herself with the other. And as she lay there in the dark, the beginnings of a plan took root and she went over it again and again, trying to find fault with it. wondering if she had the courage to pull it off.

9

Seven days later, Marrok and Ella were sitting in one of St Louis's finest French restaurants, each holding a glass of wine.

"Here's to your courage," he said, holding his glass out towards her.

Ella gently touched his glass with her own. "My courage?" she asked, feeling out of depth in this fancy place, along with the man sitting opposite her.

Neither of them had intended to come here alone, but Jasper had pulled out of this celebratory dinner first, followed by Martha.

"I got no hankerin' to set foot in a fancy place to eat, even though I know Miss Martha's got her heart set on takin' us out on our last night in St Louis. But the food I get from Homer's wife suits me just fine and I'm happy to stay with the horses."

Which meant Marrok had arrived at the boarding house alone, to walk Ella and Martha across town to the restaurant, only to find Martha feeling poorly with a headache. Mrs Blackwood gave her a potion which helped, but Martha insisted it was just rest she needed.

"It's just too much excitement over the past week, that's all it is. but I know I won't cope with all that fancy food and wine. My head will be out of sorts for days and I got to feel well for tomorrow for our big day so I'll just take Mrs Blackwood's potion and have a quiet night and go over all my purchases again and make sure I've got everything. Now, off you go Ella. You and Marrok go and enjoy your last night in St Louis."

Marrok and Ella had been upset that Martha

and Jasper wouldn't join them and although Marrok had thought on taking Ella out for dinner when they'd first arrived in town, he'd simply run out of time. It had been Martha who had suggested they celebrate, using funds provided her by Willard.

But Marrok had no intention of allowing another man to pay for the dinner he would now share with Ella alone. It would come out of his own money, whether he considered it an extravagance or not.

"Yes, your courage," he replied. "If you didn't have courage you would have taken the easy way out and married Jebediah, because you know he would have indulged your every whim. How happy you would have been with him is another matter," he smiled at the look of distaste on Ella's face.

"You also showed courage in negotiating the sale of your ranch, because not many women would have done that. You showed courage by deciding to come west, knowing full well you'll have to do most of it on your own, responsible for your own wagon and team. So, yes, I'd very much like to toast your courage."

Ella took another sip of her wine, allowing the rich drink to linger in her mouth before she swallowed, and as it hit the back of her throat she closed her eyes, feeling her senses reel from the high alcohol content. She'd never tasted anything so wonderful. When she opened her eyes, she found Marrok watching her.

"I've only ever drunk brandy wine or punch and both were at neighbors' weddings, or dances in town." She looked at him, thinking his face softer in the light of the candle which flickered on the table between them. "But here I am, sitting in this lovely place with you, yet I feel as if I'm all in a whirl, as if some part of me doesn't quite believe this is real. I have a wagon all rigged up ready to head west, along with oxen and teamsters. Who would have believed this eight days ago? And I have you to thank for it."

Marrok smiled and put down his glass of wine before leaning towards her. "No regrets?"

Ella shook her head. "None. But I am afraid of what waits for me in California. But I guess I'll deal with that when the time comes."

The waiter approached and spoke rapidly in French. Ella understood not one word of what he said but Marrok nodded and looked at his menu. Ella looked at her own, saw the French words but understood none of them. She glanced across at Marrok and found him watching her. He smiled and leaned towards her.

"Would you like me to order? I'm partial to beef myself, rather than fish, so I think I'll choose that."

Ella nodded. "That's fine with me."

She watched as he spoke to the waiter, who took their orders and menus, then left them alone.

"I can't speak French fluently, but I do understand a little," she said. "But not enough to get by in a fancy place like this."

Marrok laughed. "Well I rarely frequent such places myself, but tonight is special. It's a shame Martha and Jasper couldn't join us." He glanced around the restaurant and it was a lovely place, with expensive furniture, fancy lighting, linen tablecloths and fine china. He'd booked a table for four by a window so Ella could look out on the street, one of the very windows she'd stopped to peer into on her first night in St Louis.

He watched her discreetly as she took another sip of her wine, yet Marrok thought she looked vulnerable sitting opposite him in the candlelight. She hadn't been able to afford a new dress so had worn one of her cheaper new muslins instead, but the color suited her and Martha had pinned her hair up in curls. That she had bothered to look nice for him made Marrok glad he'd taken the time to bathe in one of the town's bathhouses and that he'd paid extra for soap. Even if the wool of his new pants were annoying against his legs, along with the new calico shirt, both purchased especially for tonight because the restaurant wouldn't have allowed him entry had he come in his buckskin. But Marrok didn't regret the purchases, because this special girl deserved this night.

"To us," he said softly, lifting his glass and gently tapping her own. "For doing the impossible and getting it done!"

Ella laughed and took another sip of her wine because they had done it, achieving the impossible in just one week.

"You did it," she said. "You organized to have my wagon fitted out and helped me get a team. We can head out for Independence tomorrow, all because of you Marrok."

He laughed. "Well, we did it with the help of Homer and Melvin. As well as Jasper. We couldn't have done it without them."

Ella nodded. "I'm so grateful. I don't know

how I can ever repay you all."

Marrok sat back and looked at her, smiling. "There's nothing to repay. You paid them well enough for what they did."

She looked at him for a moment, curious. "How do you know them? Homer and his brother?"

Marrok shrugged. "I've known them since we were boys. We grew up together because our fathers were best friends, both fur trappers. When Melvin and Homer arrived in St Louis eight years ago, they borrowed money off me to buy the land where Homer built his livery and log cabin. In those days Melvin worked as a blacksmith out back of the livery, until he could afford to move into that building where you met him, about five years ago."

Ella remembered the building. A large timber structure with a small log cabin built behind it where Melvin lived with his wife and two small children.

"I'll miss them when I leave," Marrok said. "They're like family to me and even though they paid me back what I loaned them years ago, they still think they owe me."

He took a sip of his wine and as he glanced around the room, Ella noticed the dark circles of fatigue under his eyes. But she knew just how hard he'd pushed himself this week, just for her.

She was ready to go. She had everything she could possibly want or need for that long haul west, even if she'd spent more than she'd wanted. But everything cost so much more than she'd budgeted for and as the money dwindled away on bills, Ella didn't tell anyone, certainly not Martha, about the sleepless nights she'd had, worrying about not having enough money to set herself up in California. She knew full well that Martha had nothing to share with her and Ella couldn't rely on Martha's family to help her out if she got into financial trouble.

"Are you excited about heading out tomorrow?" Marrok suddenly asked.

Ella nodded, thinking of the money she had tied up in the oxen and wagon. She could always sell them once she reached California, which would help set her up.

She'd paid market value for the six oxen, which she'd purchased from Homer's friend, Aramis Stent. Melvin had caulked her wagon and water barrels and put up the frame and canvas sheeting, doing it at night after he'd put in a full day working on other settler's wagons. Claire, Melvin's wife, had cut calico curtains to size and hung them at each end of the wagon, to keep dust and debris out once the wagon was on the trail. She didn't charge Ella for the curtains, but Ella was still dismayed by the bills that kept coming in, while her money went out.

Marrok also persuaded her to buy woolen coats for herself and Jasper, along with woolen gloves and socks to keep them warm against the biting cold which lay ahead of them in the north.

"And new blankets if you can, Ella," he'd said. "Those ones I've seen in your wagon are almost threadbare. They won't keep you warm when the heavy snows come."

But Ella didn't have enough money for such

luxuries and besides, once they reached California they wouldn't need heavy woolen blankets, if all the stories she'd heard about the mild climate out there were true.

Ella had employed two young brothers as her teamsters. Abe and Wilber Linwood came from a small town in Tennessee. They'd left behind their parents, four older brothers and three sisters for a new start in California. Abe was the eldest, with only eighteen months separating him from Wilber. They had no plans to start up on their own, all they wanted was an opportunity to better themselves as they hadn't had much schooling, with neither able to read or write well. Their father had wanted them working on the farm, rather than stuck in a classroom wasting time with books. In their early twenties, the brothers had arrived in St Louis only ten days earlier with the intention of finding work as teamsters. But with little money and desperate for work, they'd accepted a job offer from Aramis Stent to work on his ranch, until they got a job as teamsters on a wagon train.

Ella meet the brothers when she arrived at Stent's ranch with Marrok and Homer, to look over some oxen. It was Marrok who suggested she hire them, so she did and the brothers accepted.

When Ella purchased six of Stent's oxen, Stent suggested the brothers walk the animals into town on the morning Ella headed out for Independence. "Not much point taking them into St Louis until you're ready to go, not with all those other animals grazing out on those fields around town. Might as well leave them here where they'll get fed and watered before they start out on that long walk west. I ain't got no problem looking after them until then." Ella agreed and the date for departure was set.

But as she enjoyed her last night in St Louis with Marrok, feeling excited and nervous about their big day tomorrow, she realized she knew very little about him. "Marrok Gauvain," she said softly, teasing him a little. "What sort of name is that?"

Marrok was surprised by the question. "If you mean its origins, it's French," he said, smiling. "My grandfather was born in France. He was an officer in the French army and came to America as a young man to fight in the Indian-French wars around 1752. After the wars he headed north with friends to trap beaver. A man could make a fortune trapping furs back in those days."

He could see Ella's mind working, trying to work things out. So he helped her, so she didn't have to ask.

"My grandfather married a woman from the Ojibwe nation. You may have heard the French call them Chippewa, as they supported the French during the Indian-French wars. When my grandfather and his friends arrived in one of their villages up near Lower Canada one winter, they ended up staying until the spring which is where my grandfather, and then my father, met their wives."

Ella looked surprised. "Were you born there?"

"No, nor was my father. We were both born in the wild, wherever our camp happened to be. It might sound a lonely existence for a child, but in fact it was the opposite because we lived within a large community of other fur trappers and their families. But French and Ojibwe were my first languages. I was about ten or eleven when I learned to speak English."

"So you never went to school?"

Marrok smiled. "Not a school as you would know it. But I did have an education, except my teachers were my grandparents, my parents and all those others we lived with," he paused, thinking back to those days.

"My grandfather was an educated man. As an officer in the French army, he grew up with certain privileges and he loved books. He took whatever he could find to read on our travels, if that were an old newspaper, a broadsheet, a book someone had discarded in some frontier town. Even if they were all out of date or old news, he devoured them. I grew up listening to his stories of life in France and the battles he fought in the army. He had a fascination for any story involving European folklore so I heard stories about knights and kings of old, including the French martyr Joan of Arc and the English King Arthur. It was my grandfather who insisted on calling me Marrok after a knight who served in the court of King Arthur. I found out many years after his death that Marrok was the only knight known to be a werewolf. But let me assure you, I'm no werewolf!"

Ella laughed, delighted by this story. "I think I would have liked your grandfather," she said, before sitting back as the waiter approached with their meals. When he left them alone again, Ella looked back at Marrok. "Tell me something more about yourself."

Marrok smiled. "What do you want to know?"

Ella shrugged. "How old are you? Do you have brothers and sisters? Are you're married?" She smiled and leaned towards him. "Do you have a wife and children waiting for you in Independence?"

Marrok laughed and shook his head. "No, to all your questions. As for my age, I was born in November 1817 which makes me almost thirty." He paused as he watched her. "I guess that gives us something in common. Neither of us have siblings and neither of us are married, yet it puzzles me as to why you aren't married. Do you not like men?"

Ella choked on her food. She took a gulp of water, then looked at Marrok in astonishment. "Yes, I like men!" she spluttered. "I almost married twice. Both were boys I grew up with. I went to school with them, socialized with them and their families, but realized almost too late that I didn't really care for either one of them. Besides, I didn't want to live with their mothers and I had no choice until we could afford to build a place of our own," she shrugged. "Anyway, I was happy working on our ranch alongside my father and Jasper. And had he left the ranch to me, I might still be there. Indeed, I do believe I *would* still be there."

"So you lived your whole life on that ranch?"

Ella nodded. "My mother died when I was five but Jasper and Violet had been living with us for two years by then. Violet was like a mother to me. When she died some four years later, I was inconsolable. Which is when my father wrote to Martha and invited her to come live with us. She's my mother's older sister but had been widowed two years before, so the arrangement suited us all. Yet I barely remember Willard. I think I was about ten when he left us."

Marrok frowned. "What about Jasper?" he asked softly. "What happened to his hand and his legs?"

Ella shook her head. "We don't know. They were like that when he came to live with us. If you ask him about them, as we've all done over the years, he'll just say he can't remember," she paused for a moment, then looked across the table at Marrok. "You may think less of my father for buying slaves, but until Jasper and Violet came to live with us, we'd never owned slaves. My mother was horrified that Papa had purchased slaves and she insisted they be paid some sort of wage. My father couldn't afford that of course, as even Martha never earned a cent from my parents in all the years she lived with us, but once a month my father would buy them all something in town. It wasn't much, but it was something," she paused again, thinking back to those long ago days.

"Jasper was about fifteen when he came to live with us. Violet was well into her fifties. I don't know if my father had already seen that my mother wasn't coping, but she most certainly would never have coped without Violet towards the end of her life. Nor Papa without Jasper. Which is why Papa insisted on getting Jasper's manumission papers in order, when he knew he was dying." Ella took a mouthful of her wine, not wanting to think of her father on his deathbed, so asked Marrok what lay ahead for her on the trail.

"It can be hard, you should be prepared for that," he said. "Everything you can imagine, will happen, so it's better you be prepared as best you can." He turned as the waiter approached their table and asked if they wanted dessert.

Ella nodded, eager to stay a little longer in this lovely place with this man. After the waiter took their orders and refilled their wine glasses, she raised her glass. "I'd like to make a toast now, if I may. To you, Marrok, for your kindness in helping me. You didn't have to do it and I know you're now behind in making your own deadlines, so if I can help in any way once we reach Independence, you have only to ask. I was also thinking, if you'd prefer I pay you for everything you've done, I'll find a way."

Marrok looked at her in astonishment. "I don't expect payment, Ella. I was the one who asked you to come west, so the very least I can do is help," he smiled and shook his head. "As for you helping me out, well, I'll keep it in mind."

They finished their meal and as Marrok pulled out a leather wallet from inside his jacket pocket to pay for it, Ella saw a thick wad of cash in there. She figured there must be several hundred dollars, if not more. Then he was pushing his chair away from the table and moving to help Ella out of her own. But as they made their way out of the restaurant and down the steps to the boardwalk, the cool spring air after the warmth of the restaurant, along with too many glasses of wine caused Ella to stumble. Marrok reached out to steady her.

"Careful," he said, reaching out to thread his arm through her own. Then he walked on, keeping her close, moving with an easy stride.

They passed saloons and restaurants and listened to other men and women talking and laughing and Ella remembered that first night in St Louis, when she'd walked around town by herself in her father's jacket and an old pair of her work pants. All she'd wanted that night was to have some fun and here she was, a week later, out dining with Marrok in a fancy restaurant on what had to be the most wonderful night of her life. Was she in love with him? She didn't know, but she'd never met a man like him. She also knew if he touched her, he'd leave scars, for this man seemed to have set something afire inside her. A desire, a need for something, yet she wasn't experienced enough to know what it was.

When they stopped outside the boarding house Marrok gently disengaged his arm, but Ella wasn't ready for this magical night to end. He smiled as he casually wished her goodnight, as though his task were done and only then did Ella remember that it had been Martha who suggested this evening, not Marrok. But she pushed that thought aside and went to thank him anyway, unaware her words now sounded a little slurred from too much wine and fatigue. But Marrok heard them. He smiled and made a move towards the steps. "Come on, let's get you inside. It's late and it's cold and we've got a big day tomorrow."

But as Ella turned for the steps she stumbled and as her hand reached out to stop herself from falling she grabbed at his shirt, inadvertently pulling him towards her. Marrok froze, yet when he thought on it later, he should have known better, because once that step was crossed between them, there could be no going back. But he allowed it to happen, because wasn't this what he'd wanted the moment he'd first seen her, riding across her father's fields in that wedding dress? So he stopped thinking whether this was right or wrong. Instead, he reached out and pulled her into his arms and kissed her.

*

For a moment Ella didn't respond, then she felt the heat and strength of him as he swept her up against him, his arms like iron bands leaving her no chance of escape as his lips moved on her own, claiming her, and then she lost all reason while Marrok was aware of nothing else but her taste and smell and all of him was at once hard male to Ella's softness.

He'd never known a kiss like it. It was all hunger and desire and lust and as he succumbed to it, as he pulled her closer, her body soft and yielding in his arms, folding into him, offering no defense to his passion, the sudden coarseness of a crude comment from some man passing by brought Marrok to his senses. He reared back, holding Ella at arm's length.

"I'm sorry," he whispered, a desperate sound to his voice as he took another step back. "Forgive me, that shouldn't have happened, because I'll tell you now Ella, I'm not the marrying kind. I take from women what I need and then I move on. I like to be alone. I'm not looking for any kind of romantic involvement, not now, nor in the future, so I shouldn't have done that because I know you're an innocent and I wouldn't hurt you for the world."

Ella looked at him, stunned by what had just happened. He said he didn't want to hurt her, yet he *was* hurting her, his words were tearing her apart because she knew now that she had feelings for him. Feelings she had never felt for another man. As he took another step back, as if she repulsed him, Ella felt her defenses flare.

"Don't worry yourself too much over me, Marrok," she said, her words hard. "And I'm not so innocent. I have kissed other men, you're not the first."

Ella succeeded in making him think his dismissive words meant nothing to her, because she saw him flinch, even as she tried not to think of the fierce crush of his mouth against her own. She glanced towards the door, as though it offered her a refuge and as she stepped towards it, she looked back at him. "Thank you for tonight, it was very special. I know I'll remember it for the rest of my days," she paused, her hand on the door. "I'll see you at dawn."

And then she was gone, the door closing behind her. Marrok turned away, uncomfortably aware of the heat and pulse of his body in response to that kiss and the feel of her leaning up against him.

You're not the first

Those words seemed to echo through his mind, boring into him like some sharp pointed knife, twisting and turning until Marrok turned in frustration, not understanding any of this. How could a mere girl like Ella, make a man like him so weak?

Yet he knew Ella was no mere girl. Because in the past week he'd come to understand just how strong she was, and feisty, and unafraid of a challenge. She was honest, she didn't play games with men like a lot of women did.

Some might say he'd just been cruel to her, yet Marrok knew in his heart he was in fact protecting her, because he knew from past experiences that if he encouraged her now, both would pay the price for it once they were out on the trail. The last thing he wanted was unnecessary gossip following either of them and Ella didn't need gossip following her to California, not now, not after all she'd gone through to get here.

He thought again of that kiss and the way she'd looked at him, those lovely green hazel eyes lingering on his mouth. Just thinking on it, Marrok felt the lust rise in him again. Swearing softly he turned away from the boarding house and headed across town for the livery. His life had been just fine before he met Ella, yet these feelings he had for her left him baffled. He'd kissed a lot of women, but none like that. Ella's lips had seared him, the desire in that kiss leaving him reeling, wanting more.

But he didn't have time for romance and he certainly couldn't afford to get involved with anyone travelling on the same wagon train as him.

Yet the thought of her lingered and he found himself outside the saloon where he'd heard the flame-haired girl sing just over a week ago. He hadn't seen her since that night he and Ella had helped her in the alley. He tried to think of her name yet it escaped him, even as he heard another girl singing inside. He stepped through the swinging doors, eager for a drink, anything to take his mind off Ella.

The girl's voice in comparison was thin and reedy and perhaps because of it, the place was almost empty. But it was almost closing time, with only a handful of men still there, most playing their last card game before the doors closed for the night. Marrok ordered a glass of whisky. But as he stood at the bar, he suddenly felt the hairs on the back of his neck stand on end and he turned to see a middle-aged colored woman watching him, as if she knew him.

But Marrok knew he'd never seen her before in his life. She looked worn, with hair grey beneath a white cap, her face showing deep lines of what Marrok would call despair, but as he met her gaze, she turned and disappeared into a back room. Unsettled by her interest, he suddenly had no desire to stay there and threw the liquor back, allowing it to hit the back of his throat, the burn of it hard and raw, then he turned and left the building. He hurried through the dark streets back to the livery, thinking of the two men he'd fought earlier that week in the alley. He'd barely given them a thought since that night, so presumed they'd left town.

A block away from the livery, Marrok paused at a horse trough outside a dark, shuttered store. He thought on it a moment, then pulled off his jacket before rolling up his shirt sleeves and pumping the water, cupping his hands beneath the deluge and splashing his face before drinking his fill. The coldness of the water woke him up, took away the feeling of alcohol and settled his stomach. When he was done, he gathered his jacket and headed for the livery but as he stepped through the side door, he paused, aware of that same feeling he'd had in the saloon, that he was being watched. He stood there in the dark for long minutes, until he was sure there was nothing out there, then he stepped inside the livery and closed the door behind him.

Jasper's snoring came drifting down from the loft but Marrok had no care to wake the man so he went to the far wall where fresh straw had been laid earlier that afternoon, spread his jacket over it then lay down. He didn't remember falling asleep.

10

The soft creak of the side door opening woke him an hour before dawn. Instantly alert, Marrok reached for his pistol and knives which lay near his buckskin clothing, left behind in a folded heap when he dressed in his new clothes to take Ella to dinner last night.

He moved into a crouch and ran to the stall nearest the door as someone stepped into the livery. Marrok cursed softly realizing too late that he'd forgotten to lock the door behind him when he came in last night.

He saw a shadow as someone stepped towards him, followed by the sound of straw being crushed beneath boot heels and then the soft hiss of a whisper. Marrok glanced up at the loft but had no time to alert Jasper as a second shadow stepped into the livery less than ten feet from where he crouched.

But the furtive movements and whispers disturbed the horses and as they moved about their stalls, Bear whickered nervously, waking Jasper.

Marrok heard the rustle of straw in the loft above him as Jasper pushed aside his blankets and called out in a sleepy voice. "Who's down there? That you Mr Marrok? Lordy be, you sure are home late."

Marrok said nothing, unwilling to reveal where he was, even though he knew Jasper would start down the ladder soon if Marrok didn't answer him, because he'd want to check on the horses.

"Mr Marrok? Lord, who's down there? I's comin' for you, you better be leavin' now!" Jasper called as he began to crawl across the straw towards the ladder.

Marrok didn't wait any longer. He judged the distance between himself and the first moving shadow then sprinted forward, his arms gripping low about the person's hips with the intention of dragging him down and knocking him out before he dealt with the second person and any others coming behind them.

Marrok grunted as he hit the floor, stunned when it wasn't the hard muscle mass of a man beneath him, but the soft curves of a woman. And then she cried out in pain and fear. Startled, Marrok rolled away as Jasper came down the ladder, a piece of wood over his shoulder, ready to fight.

"It's me Jasper," Marrok shouted, even as another woman's voice cried out in the gloom.

"We ain't carryin' weapons! We's two women! We're not here to hurt no-one!"

"What the hell!" Marrok cursed, before moving to strike a flint, lighting one of the candles in the lamp nearest him, allowing light to flood the livery. Jasper came to stand beside him wearing only his britches, holding the piece of wood like a bat ready to fight, both staring in dismay at the woman lying in the dirt as another helped her up.

"Who they be, Mr Marrok? You reckon they come to steal?"

The woman on the floor turned to look at him in bewilderment as she dusted dirt and straw off her plain homespun dress and out of her hair. "No," she spluttered, wiping dirt away from her mouth. "Of course we didn't come here to steal! Quite the opposite in fact!"

Marrok stared at her in astonishment, recognizing her instantly. It was the flame-haired singer from the saloon, the same girl he and Ella had helped in the alley. Standing beside her was the colored woman who had been watching him in the saloon.

"I'm Ruby Daegan, but I can see by your face that you remember me," she said to Marrok, before turning to introduce the woman beside her. "This is Clara, my friend."

Marrok looked down at the bags they were carrying, just simple things revealing few possessions.

"What do you want here?" he asked. "And why come at such an ungodly hour?"

Ruby took a breath, even as her hands went to her hair, because she'd lost a few pins in Marrok's tackle. Then she glanced around the livery until she saw the wagon, all fitted out, packed and ready to go, standing at the rear of the building. She looked back at Marrok.

"Your wife told me you're heading for Independence. Clara and I need to get there. All we ask is to hide away in your wagon until we're well away from St Louis. Once we're in Independence, we can find a team who'll take us west."

Marrok said nothing, aware of the hour ticking by towards dawn, when Abe and Wilber would arrive with the six oxen. Ruby saw his hesitation and licked her lips, her mouth suddenly dry, but Marrok had already seen the fear in her eyes.

"Please help us," she said, a quiet desperation to her voice now. "We have to get out of town under cover of a wagon. I've had Clara follow you and your wife for days, after your wife told me in that alley that you're heading west. All we want is to hide away, nothing more," she glanced over at Jasper. "I'm sorry for causing you trouble, but we didn't know you were sleeping here." She looked back at Marrok. "And Clara thought you were sleeping at the boarding house with your wife and mother."

Marrok was aware of Jasper staring openmouthed at the women, yet he felt just as bewildered. Ruby glanced back towards the livery door and again, Marrok saw the fear in her eyes, along with the bruises on her face and around her throat which were only now beginning to heal.

"You might ask why we need to hide so I'll tell you," she said, once again licking her lips. "Those men who attacked me in the alley are still in town and still looking for me. I've also had Clara follow them and they've been down at the wharves all week, watching every boat that leaves, so they know I'm still here. If I can hide away with a family where they wouldn't think to look, I might just get away from them."

Marrok glanced at the tall, older woman and seeing his hesitation, Ruby took the woman's hand in her own. "You can trust Clara. She's been taking care of me for the past week, since you saved me from those men. I've been hiding out in her room in the attic of the saloon as she's the cook and cleaner there and when she can, she gives me food."

"But why would those men want to harm you?" Marrok asked.

Ruby paused, deciding how much to tell, but knew she had nothing to lose. "They're two of my father's men. They've been chasing me now for almost four years, all the way across country from New York. They won't stop until they get me home but I'd rather die than go back there." She reached for her bag and as she fumbled within its contents, Marrok saw her hands trembling as she brought out a large leather purse. When she opened it, he saw the money inside.

"Look, I can pay my way. And Clara can pay her way. We're not poor. And Clara can cook. And I can clean well enough and you know I can sing."

Marrok stared in disbelief. There was a fortune in the purse. Enough to buy a whole town, let alone the last of the supplies which Ella so desperately needed, along with warm blankets for the northern winters.

"Put the money away!" he growled. "It's a wonder you haven't had it stolen, showing it around like that," he paused and stepped towards her. "Yet if you have such funds, why don't you just outfit a wagon of your own?"

Ruby shook her head. "I don't show the money around! You're the first person I've shown it to in all these years, just to prove to you I can pay my way. But you don't understand. I can't be found. I can't be seen. If I have any hope of escape, I need to hide. And you and your wife are my only hope. When you helped me in that alley, I knew I could trust you." She turned to Clara. "She saw your wife and mother pick up a lot of supplies today and heard the store owner wish them good luck so I knew you must be leaving soon. We came here to hide in your wagon."

Marrok let out a long breath. He didn't need this added distraction. Besides, it wasn't his decision to make. That must come from Ella. It was her wagon and therefore her risk. He turned to Clara.

"So Ruby's a runaway, but what about you? Do you have people chasing you?"

The woman shook her head. "I ain't no runaway. What I am, is a forgotten slave."

Marrok shook his head. "I don't need to know about your past. All I need to know, is anyone chasing you?"

"No sir, they ain't."

Ruby put an arm around Clara's shoulders. "I trust her with my life and she's honest and hardworking so I won't be without her."

Marrok thought on the contents of Ruby's purse and the supplies which Ella so desperately needed but couldn't afford. She could do with a cook on that long trail west, to help feed the men. Meanwhile Ruby would be another pair of hands, or she could even be a paying passenger.

"That woman who was with me in the alley isn't my wife but she does own this wagon, yet I can't make that decision for her. All I can do is ask if she'll take you on." He paused, then introduced himself before turning to Jasper. "I'm scout on the wagon train which Ella will be travelling on. Jasper's a free man and has worked for Ella's family for a long time. He's part of her team heading west."

He walked over to the side door and locked it.

"But there's nothing we can do until sun-up, which is a good hour or so away. I reckon we all grab some rest while we can because it's going to be chaos here within a few hours."

11

Marrok hurried through the quiet town shrouded in shadows, its inhabitants still asleep as it was early yet, the night sky only just beginning to break apart with streaks of light coming from the east.

But there was a sense of urgency about Marrok as he made his way across town, for he barely glanced at the slight mist rising above the Mississippi River in the cool spring morning.

Indeed, he was trying not to panic, but he knew he was pushing against time now.

He had woken Jasper and the two women a short while ago, urging them to silence as he helped Ruby and Clara up into the wagon along with their few bags, before pulling the calico curtains closed behind them. He'd thought the women looked drained with both fear and anxiety and like him, they hadn't been able to go back to sleep. While they whispered now and again in the dark, Marrok had lain awake and planned the best way to get around this, while Jasper went back to sleep in the loft above them.

He knew the women must be hidden before the Linwood brothers and Aramis Stent arrived with the oxen.

Nor could Homer and Melvin see them, because like Stent, they both knew a lot of people in town and might mention in casual conversation about the two women travelling in the back of Ella's wagon without meaning to cause trouble.

Marrok frowned as he thought on all this secrecy, not liking it one bit and as he reached the boarding house, he paused before climbing stairs on the side of the building.

If Ella didn't agree to this, the women would have to find another way to get out of St Louis without being seen. But Marrok didn't fancy their chances.

He moved with stealth up the stairs, hoping no-one woke and looked out their windows. When he reached the balcony running around the second floor, he paused and looked around but the street lay empty, everyone still abed, their curtains drawn against the early morning.

He reached for the rungs to climb the ladder which led to the attic bedrooms and hoped he chose the right window.

If not, he would be speaking to Martha first.

Ella opened the window on his third *tap*. She pulled the curtain aside, her face puffy with sleep and looked at him in astonishment.

"What are you doing here?"

He was taken aback by the sight of her. Her hair was tied back in a plait which hung down her back and although it was obvious he had woken her, she was as desirable to him in that moment as she had been last night when he kissed her. His feelings shocked him, but he pushed them deep, burying them, because he didn't have time for a flirtation with this young woman.

"We have a situation," he whispered. "Can I come in?"

"No, you can't come in!" she hissed at him and went to close the window, denying him entry, when she saw the urgency in his face and noticed his hair hanging loose about his face. Marrok always tied his hair back. Something was wrong.

"What is it? What's happened?"

"I need to talk to you, Ella," he said again and before she could stop him, he'd pushed aside the curtain and climbed inside, stepping across her bed, feeling the warmth of the blankets where she'd lain just a few moments ago. "I'll be five minutes, then I'll be gone."

He spoke rapidly, telling her everything he knew about Ruby and Clara. Ella was too astonished to interrupt him.

"I think they could be a good fit for you," he said. "You'll have two women to help you carry the load, along with the three men. Clara can cook, while Ruby can help with the chores. You can pay them a small wage but Ruby is prepared to be a paying passenger. She has a great deal of money, Ella. You can buy all the supplies you need in Independence with whatever money you decide to charge her."

Ella remembered what he'd said before, about life on the trail being hard. Without Martha around to help her, Ella would have to do all the womanly chores herself.

She'd be expected to take care of all the supplies as well as the men.

She'd have to clean up after them, fetch water and firewood, cook their meals, make their coffee, mend their clothes and tend their cuts and bruises.

But Ella had never been domesticated. She'd always preferred to be outside than working indoors. Those duties had always been taken care of by Martha.

"They're in the back of your wagon now, hiding. No-one needs to know they're there, except you, me and Jasper. They'll stay hidden until we get away from St Louis and once we get them to Independence, they'll find another team to take them west. But think carefully on it, Ella. They could solve a whole lot of problems for you," he paused, running his hands through his loose hair.

"But if you decide not to take them, at least give them safe passage out of town to Independence. They won't cause you any trouble and they're both small enough that they won't create extra weight for your oxen."

Marrok did his best to keep his gaze on Ella's face yet he was well aware of her body beneath her shift. He clenched his fists, even as he remembered their kiss the night before, feeling the edge of the warm bed at the back of his knees. It took every bit of self-control he owned not to reach for her.

But Ella was also aware of her state of undress along with Marrok standing before her, his hair loose around his shoulders, still dressed in the clothes he'd worn to dinner the night before and as she held his gaze, she became aware of the sudden, palpable tension in the room.

She wasn't so innocent that she understood she had only to reach for him and they'd both be lost. She could see it in his eyes.

So she nodded, eager to get this done and for him to leave because every minute he remained in this room, looking like that, was dangerous for both of them.

But again, like last night, it was Marrok who broke the tension between them by glancing behind her and looking out the window. Ella didn't have to turn around to know that the shadows of the early morning were shifting as the sun began to rise.

"Very well. Tell them I agree," she said, her voice soft in that small room. "I'll take them on. Now please leave before someone sees you here."

Marrok nodded but paused for a moment longer, as though deep in thought, then without a word he turned, climbed back over her bed, out the window and was gone.

12

Ella watched him reach the safety of the street before he disappeared down an alley, hurrying back towards the livery. She was grateful the streets were still empty, with most people still abed, but she knew it wouldn't be like that for much longer.

She slowly sat down on the edge of her bed, feeling a little shaken up, remembering the look on Marrok's face as he stood before her. She didn't think she'd forget that look for the rest of her days, because not even the two young men she'd been engaged to had looked at her like that. She glanced down at her shift and knew the threadbare material hardly hid anything at all. Then she reached up to touch her hair, feeling the braid hanging down her back, the hair escaping from it after being in bed and Ella felt suddenly mortified that he'd seen her like this.

The crow of a nearby rooster stirred her, followed by a dog barking and she suddenly thought of the two women hiding in the back of her wagon. She stood up and went to the jug of fresh water and dipped a cloth in it to wash herself and by the time she'd combed her hair and finished dressing, she'd made the decision not to tell Martha about them. Her aunt would find out soon enough once they left St Louis behind but until then, Ella couldn't face an argument about it because she had enough to think on.

Besides, this wasn't Martha's journey, it was Ella's to take alone. Because once they reached Independence, Ella would be responsible for her own team, with Martha joining her son's team, along with his family. The way Ella saw it, there was little point in seeking Martha's approval, because if she couldn't stand on her own two feet now and make her own decisions, she wouldn't be strong when it counted in the months ahead. So she may as well toughen up now and get ready for anything that lay ahead, not only on the trail west, but when she reached California.

*

When Ella arrived at the livery with Martha along with a youth she had paid to help carry their bags, she saw there was little chance of meeting the two women stowed away in the back of her wagon because there were people everywhere, including a small crowd who'd gathered to see them off. She welcomed Abe and Wilber who were harnessing the oxen to the wagon with the help of Stent, while Jasper and Marrok organized the horses.

Then it was time to say goodbye. It was an emotional farewell for Marrok and his childhood friends, because the likelihood of him ever seeing Melvin and Homer again was unlikely.

Jasper helped Martha climb up onto the buckboard as Abe and Wilber took their place on each side of the lead oxen to begin their long walk west all the way to California. Ella mounted Billy as Marrok grasped Homer and Melvin one last time amid shouts of good luck.

"Write if you can," Homer said to Marrok. "Let us know you're safe."

Marrok nodded. "If you decide to follow me, ride for Oregon and seek the Chinook. They'll know where to find me."

Melvin grinned. "If we stop making money, you'll see us soon enough old friend."

Marrok laughed, knowing there was little chance of that while St Louis kept growing. He turned to shake Stent's hand for all his help then moved to mount his horse, riding up beside Ella.

"Boys, you make sure you treat those oxen gentle, you hear me!" Stent called to the Linwood brothers as Marrok waved the wagon on.

"Let's get them moving!" he yelled.

Abe and Wilber glanced back at Stent, both of them looking nervous yet excited, then they touched the lead oxen lightly with their switches as Jasper flicked the reins. The wagon lurched forward, one of the lead oxen bellowing and shaking his head at the load behind him. Then the team found their rhythm and walked on, with Bear following behind the wagon on a long lead.

Everyone walked alongside them, calling goodbyes, wishing them well, including strangers as the street who stopped to wave them off.

"I'll send you that letter!" Marrok called to his friends, then they turned a corner and Homer and Melvin were lost to him.

Marrok glanced over at Ella and she turned to him and smiled, as they headed for the main road west out of St Louis.

13

Clara watched Ruby crawl slowly to the back of the wagon, the younger woman careful how she moved because the wagon was swaying quite badly over the rutted tracks in the road. Clara hardly dared breath as she sat huddled within blankets between all the boxes and crates, hoping Ruby didn't dislodge something and let everyone know they were here.

She'd tried to persuade Ruby to stay with her, but she'd come to understand that this girl wasn't someone who did what others told her.

Ruby reached the back of the wagon and reached up to peer through the gap in the calico curtains. Clara knew full well what she was looking for. Those two men, the same ones Ruby had sent Clara out to spy on when she'd had time away from her cleaning and cooking, to see if they'd left town. But no, they were still prowling the streets, clearly believing that Ruby was still somewhere in St Louis hiding out.

"Now they've found me, they won't leave until they get me back to New York," she said to Clara, telling her a little about her childhood. "And they won't care how they do it."

Clara had been shocked when Ruby told her things about her life with her father and one night in her attic bedroom, long after Ruby fell asleep beside her on the straw mattress, Clara remembered a conversation she'd overhead many years ago. It had been between Ada, her long dead mistress and Esther, Ada's only daughter.

Esther had accepted a proposal of marriage from a young man in New York and she wanted her parents to go live there with her. But Ada had refused to leave New Orleans, having heard only bad things about New York.

"Everyone knows the gangs are notorious up there and if your young man hasn't yet shared that with you, I'm sure he soon will. You've got the Irish and Italian Mafias fighting among themselves, then there's the English pitted against the Scots and then the Jews. I want no part of it."

Esther went on to marry her New York fiancé and never saw her father again. She saw her mother only once and that was when she returned to New Orleans for her father's funeral many years later.

When Clara remembered that conversation, she wondered if Ruby's father were involved in one of those gangs because it would explain the control he exerted over her, forcing her to run away.

"The river!" Ruby suddenly whispered in excitement.

Unable to help herself, Clara pushed aside the blankets and followed Ruby to the back of the wagon. She peered out of that narrow gap between the calico curtains and as the wagon slowly wound its way out of St Louis, heading west, they could just make out the wharves a few miles below the town and beyond them, the wide stretch of the Mississippi River.

The river lay glittering in the early morning sun. River men starting their day called out to each other as they worked flatboats and keelboats, while others climbed into canoes or pirogues and made their way upriver, or across to Illinois Town. All were wary of the big paddle-steamers and steamboats still lying at anchor or berthed at the wharves, waiting for passengers. Then Clara stiffened, and pointed to two men making their way down to the river.

"There!" she whispered.

Ruby recognized her father's thugs, feeling ill as she realized they were heading for the wharves, despite the early hour, to get a prime vantage point so they could watch to see who boarded the boats.

She cowered down behind the curtain, while Clara continued to look out of that narrow gap, needing to know if those two men turned their attention this way.

It was only when the wagon turned out of the street and into another, obscuring the wharves completely, that Clara moved to sit beside Ruby, reaching out to put an arm about her shoulders.

"It's alright, child, you's safe now."

14

They were several hours west of St Louis, moving at a slow steady walk, when Marrok called a stop. As Jasper helped Martha down off the wagon, Marrok rode over to Ella. He could sense her anxiety about meeting the women. He hoped she liked them, because if not, if she decided they'd be better off travelling with another team, then she faced a hard six months ahead, looking after the three men alone.

"You ready to introduce everyone?" he asked.

Ella nodded and followed him to the back of the wagon. As they dismounted, Ella saw Martha approaching her, stretching her back, just as she heard Marrok talking to someone. Ella reached for her aunt's hand. "Come with me, there's something you need to see."

Martha looked puzzled. "What is this girl? You want me to open one of my jars of preserves? I reckon we could have some of my pickles with the cheese and fresh bread and dried beef you bought in St Louis."

Ella said nothing, but gently pulled Martha towards the back of the wagon.

"What is this, Ella?" Martha said with some impatience. "I must say, this is all very odd," then she stopped and stared in astonishment as Marrok reached up to help a middle-aged colored woman down from the wagon. "Oh my!" she said softly. "What's going on here!"

Ella didn't answer her, because she was too busy looking at her stowaways. Clara brushed down her skirts and looked at Ella and Martha nervously, as Marrok turned to help the younger girl out of the wagon. Ella recognized the singer from the saloon, but without her stage makeup and the glamorous dress she'd worn to perform in, she looked pale, with dark shadows under her eyes and thin enough that her muslin dress hung off her. Had the girl not looked so stressed, she would have been considered a beauty with her light colored grey eyes and coal red hair. She moved to stand beside the older woman, who Ella mistakenly thought in her late forties, ten years older than Clara's actual age as her hair was streaked with grey and her face deeply lined.

She stepped towards them and held out her hand. "I'm Ella Torray, this is my wagon and team. I hope the ride wasn't too uncomfortable for you."

The older woman stared at her hand in bewilderment, then timidly reached out to take it. Ella could feel the hard calluses there, proving this woman was well used to hard work. She turned to the singer, who stepped forward with confidence and held out her hand. Yet Ella was surprised to find her hand soft like that of a child, suggesting she wasn't familiar with physical work.

"I'm Ruby Daegan," she said, in that same husky voice that Ella remembered "And this is my friend, Clara."

The older woman nodded and bobbed down into a short curtsey. "Mighty pleased t'meet you ma'am."

She spoke with a strong southern accent and although Ella would bet this woman had never seen the inside of a classroom, there was something worldly about her, suggesting she'd seen a lot in her life. Ella stared at them, taking the measure of them, yet Ruby and Clara both saw the sudden doubt in her face. In truth, Ella had expected someone a lot younger than Clara. As for Ruby, without her fancy saloon clothes on, she looked different to how Ella remembered her, with her face and throat still showing the bruising from the beating she'd taken in that alley. Indeed, the two women looked like paupers, wearing clothes that were almost threadbare. Ruby looked like she hadn't a dollar to her name, even though Marrok had said she had money. Clara and Ruby glanced nervously at each other, then Ruby stepped forward.

"We won't let you down if you take us west with you," she said, a touch of urgency in her voice. "We'll work hard and never give you a chance to doubt your decision."

Clara stepped forward as well. "We won't never let you down, miss."

Abe and his brother suddenly appeared around the side of the wagon, followed by Jasper, wanting to see what all the fuss was about. This time it was Marrok who made the introductions, before Martha turned to Ella.

"Would you kindly explain what these two women are doing here and why I wasn't told about them?"

Ella nodded, glancing over at Marrok. "Because there wasn't time, Aunt. Everything was agreed on before dawn this morning. Indeed, this is the first time I've met them myself. I wanted to tell you when we arrived at the livery, but there were so many people around it was impossible," she paused and glanced back at the two women who stood in silence, watching her. "I've yet to decide if they'll join us, but if they do, Ruby would be a paying passenger while Clara will be my cook. If they're happy with that, of course."

She glanced at Marrok and he smiled, even as Ruby reached for Clara's hand.

"That seems like a fine arrangement to me. And I can vouch for Clara's cooking. Best cook I've met since I left New York four years ago."

Clara turned to her and smiled and Ella saw the warm relationship between the pair and just like that, she knew they'd be part of her team. They all needed each other and if she didn't take them on, someone in Independence might offer them a better deal.

"But why hide in the wagon for goodness sake?" Martha said, wanting to know. "Why all the secrecy? Why not get to know everyone before we left St Louis?"

It was Ruby who answered and everyone heard those crisp eloquent vowels, suggesting she'd come from a privileged home. "It was because of me, Martha. You see, my father has employed two men to find me and take me back to New York, but I can't go back. The only way to escape them and get out of St Louis was under cover and when I approached Mr Gauvain and asked for his help, he thought we might be a good fit for Miss Torray's team. She only heard about us early this morning," she turned to Ella, a look of desperation on her bruised face. "I hope you see your way clear to taking us on and like Clara said, we won't ever let you down."

Ella was grateful that Ruby didn't mention their

previous meeting in the alley a week ago, as Martha knew nothing about that. But it seemed Ruby wanted to keep that secret as well.

It was Wilber who broke the tension amongst the group by stepping forward to welcome them, holding out his hand. "I hope you both join us, more the merrier I reckon," he glanced at Clara. "I sure hope you make good biscuits. I ain't had a good biscuit since I left my mama's kitchen."

Martha shook her head. "Well I never," she said softly, before turning back to Ella. "It might be a good thing for you to have some help heading west, for you ain't never been one for cooking," she turned back to Ruby, seeing the bruising on her face and throat. "It might be an idea for you to buy a headscarf when we reach Independence, along with a wide brimmed bonnet because with coloring such as yours my girl, you'll be noticed all over town and if those men show up in Independence before we head on out, you'll be an easy find in a crowd."

Ella looked at her aunt in surprise. "I take it you approve of them, then?"

Martha shrugged. "Like I said, might be an idea for you to have some help."

Ella glanced back at Marrok who was standing off to one side, watching her and smiling. She turned back to Clara and Ruby. "We can talk on money later, but if you're willing, then I guess you're coming west with us to California."

15

During the weeks it took them to walk to Independence, Ella's team settled into a routine that would see them all the way west. By the end of the first week, Ella knew she wouldn't have coped without Clara's help. The older woman not only took on the role of team cook, but did more than her fair share of chores although Clara insisted the wage that Ella paid her was more than enough.

Ruby also helped out with chores even though she was travelling as a paying passenger, but doing chores made her feel better about the cost of her berth in Ella's wagon, which Ruby thought was a pittance. She would have paid double what Ella asked, but both Marrok and Ella insisted the fee was a fair one.

But with Ruby now sleeping in the wagon with Martha, Ella had no choice but to sleep outdoors with the rest of her team so with the help of Jasper, Marrok set up a waterproof shelter for her and Clara to share. Canvas sheets were nailed to each side of the wagon which dropped down at night, giving protection from the weather along with privacy.

Jasper and the brothers slept in canvas shelters of their own, bought and paid for by Ella in St Louis. Marrok preferred to sleep outdoors by the fire, unless it rained, and then he raised his own canvas shelter.

But Ella struggled sleeping on the hard ground beneath the wagon, despite the comfort of her mattress. One evening around the campfire she confessed she was having nightmares, waking during the night thinking someone was chasing her so she was surprised when Marrok joined her by the fire on their last night on the trail, after everyone else had gone to their beds. Tomorrow they would arrive in Independence and although Ella was tired, she lingered by the fire, unwilling to go to her shelter.

Marrok sat cross-legged beside her and when he pulled a small leather package from his buckskin shirt and opened it, Ella looked at it with surprise.

"What is it?" she asked, curious.

"It's called a dreamcatcher. My mother's people believe they stop nightmares, so I'm hoping this will stop yours."

He picked it up and held it out towards her. The whole thing was just a bit bigger than Marrok's hand. Made of willow and rawhide strips, the willow had been manipulated into a circle, with thin strips of rawhide wrapped around it to keep the shape taut. Plaited strips of rawhide had then been woven between the circle, which reminded Ella of a cobweb. At the bottom on the circle hung several feathers.

"I had one like it as a child and I do believe they work, but you must keep it by your bed. The leather strips between the circle will catch your nightmares. The feathers will let the good dreams in."

Ella reached out to take it off him, their fingers touching briefly, then she turned it over gently in her hands. It looked fragile, yet it was strongly made. She looked up and found him watching her.

"The Ojibwe also believe you should try and understand your dreams, to discover what it is that's frightening you."

"Thank you," Ella said, feeling overwhelmed by this. "I'll put it beside my pillow when I go to sleep tonight."

Marrok frowned, worried about her, because she should have been abed by now. "Ella, you've months of sleeping rough ahead of you, so if it'll help at all, you're welcome to some spare canvas I have in Independence. You can add it to the canvas you've already got beneath your mattress. It'll help with the damp and might make you sleep better. But just remember these cold nights are almost over. With spring and summer ahead of us, it will get easier."

Ella nodded. "I know. It's just taking me a while to settle, that's all. And thanks for the offer of the canvas Marrok, but you'll need it for yourself and besides, now I have Ruby's money I can buy everything I need," she paused and turned to look at him, aware of his beautiful dark eyes watching her.

"It's just everything's changed so quickly. Three weeks ago I was at home trying to get out of a marriage with Jebediah Crawley. Now here I am sleeping in the wild, responsible for a wagon and a team of people," she looked down at the dreamcatcher in her hand, her fingers tracing the leather cobweb.

"Ella," he said, leaning towards her. "I've got three wagons of my own waiting for me in Independence. You can claim one of them for your own, to sleep in, if that will make it easier. Or you and Clara can share one. Have a look when we get there and decide for yourself."

Ella looked at him with gratitude. "Are you sure? Oh thank you Marrok, I believe that might suit me just fine."

"Well then, that's settled. Now try and get some sleep because you can't do much on the morrow if you're tired."

Ella did sleep better than night. She placed the dreamcatcher beside her on the pillow and when she woke in the chill of the early morning, she was startled to find that sometime in the night, she'd reached for it to hold close to her heart.

Independence, Missouri
May 1846

1

The town of Independence lay on America's western border, just south of the Missouri River and twelve miles from Indian territory. Most knew it as a landing stage for settlers heading west, because from late winter to early summer, Independence became a thriving crowded place as men, women and children arrived to prepare wagons and buy the last of their supplies before they headed out in wagon trains.

They shared the space with hundreds of animals and Ella and her team became aware of the town long before they saw it, as the sounds and smells of all those people and the herds of cattle and horses, mules, oxen, dogs, chickens and goats drifted out across the prairie to mix with the distant bells and whistles of steamboats coming upriver to berth at the wharves.

Marrok and Ella rode up over a slight rise, just ahead of her wagon, to glance over at the Missouri River off to their right and the big paddleboats and steamers, all of them full of passengers, all hoping to join wagon trains in Independence.

They reined in their horses to look down on the town below and like St Louis, Marrok was surprised by how many people were now camped down there, compared to when he left here almost a month ago to find Martha. Indeed, he'd left his team and animals grazing near a thick stand of trees a good mile west of the town but there were so many wagons and camps down there now, he couldn't make out his own three wagons, nor his team.

He turned as Abe and Wilber approached, walking on either side of the lead oxen. Jasper sat alone on the buckboard, while the women walked together alongside the wagon.

"Maybe it's time Ruby climbed back into the wagon," Ella said softly, looking over that massive camp below them.

Marrok nodded but before he could say anything, the women came to stand beside them as Abe and Wilber brought the oxen to a stop. Jasper jumped down off the buckboard to stretch and as they all looked over that camp below, Ruby looked up at Marrok where he sat astride his horse.

"If they came upriver from St Louis, they'd be here by now, wouldn't they," she asked softly.

Marrok nodded. "It's probably best if you get back in the wagon."

Ruby agreed and after getting settled within her blankets to make the ride a little more comfortable, the wagon and oxen moved on. Marrok pointed to the stand of trees way over on the other side of the camp, showing Abe and Wilber where to go.

"We'll get as close to Willard's camp as we can," he said, glancing back at Martha. "He'll be desperate to see you."

Near the town itself, streets of canvas shelters and big Conestoga wagons had been set up by merchants that came here every spring to sell their goods. There were mercantile stores, blacksmiths and carpenters who did repairs on wagons and looked over animals and harnesses, there were bakers, butchers selling dried meat, women selling clothes and handwoven blankets, there was anything and everything that the settlers could want.

Ella took a breath and looked beyond the camp and away to the west. Twelve miles in that direction lay Indian territory, untold acres of wide open country inhabited by tribes who had called that land their own for centuries.

But other tribes had moved into that territory over the past sixteen years, after being forcibly removed from their ancestral lands east of the Mississippi River after President Jackson signed the Indian Removals Act of 1830. By removing Indians west beyond the Mississippi River, the way was free for settlers to purchase their lands for a pittance from the Government and farm it.

Ella couldn't begin to imagine the distance she must travel to reach California, but looking at that land which swept away to the west, she felt afraid. Because within weeks she would be crossing over into Indian country and like everyone else, she'd heard stories of the battles fought in the east for Indian land.

What lay ahead for her out there? Would her wagon come under attack? Would she have to take up her father's shotgun and fight Indians? She shuddered and kicked her horse on, riding up towards Marrok, keeping close to him. She felt safer when she was with him.

*

It was impossible to get anywhere near Willard's camp, so Marrok made the decision to ride on towards his own camp and have Ella's team set up close by.

"We'll get these animals watered and put them out to graze, then I'll ride out and find Willard and let him know you're here."

They managed to get Ella's wagon within a quarter mile of Marrok's team. Then he left them to get settled while he rode out to find Willard. Jasper tended to Bear and Billy while Abe and Wilber unharnessed the oxen, then hobbled them so they could graze on the open bit of land around their camp. Ella and Clara started sorting through supplies and making lists of what they needed after those weeks on the trail getting here, while Martha washed and changed into a clean dress and re-did her hair. It had been a long time since she'd seen her son. Not in her wildest dreams had she ever thought to see him again so the very least she could do while she waited for him, was to try and look her best.

After digging a firepit with Clara, she left her to make coffee and hot biscuits and hurried into town to put in an order for the supplies they needed and buy scarves and bonnets for both Ruby and Clara.

But as Ella weaved her way around wagons and animals and people sitting around their fires, she felt truly afraid for the first time since she'd left her father's ranch. But of course she knew why.

Things would change now they had arrived in Independence. Marrok would have his own team to look after, as well as his job as scout. And Martha would join her son's family. Ella would be alone, responsible for five people, a wagon, six oxen and two horses.

She stumbled a little with panic and to calm herself, feeling as if she were once again standing on the edge of an abyss, she made herself think on what she had to buy. She must remember to purchase more canvas sheeting to put under their mattresses to stop the damp, because she'd had to decline Marrok's offer of sleeping in one of his wagons after Martha advised her not to.

"Don't get folk gossiping about you Ella. You go sleep in a single man's wagon, believe me, you're asking for trouble."

She was thinking on that when she finally reached the town and entered Courthouse Square. A large group of men were voting on captains and officers for their individual wagon train companies but Ella wasn't interested in men's business and walked on, making her way through the crowds to join the queues outside one of the biggest mercantile stores. She wondered if she should try another store, but there were queues everywhere so she stayed where she was.

A woman stood in line before her with two teenage girls and asked Ella about her own family. She was astonished to hear Ella was driving her own team west.

"Lord almighty. I got these two girls who ain't much younger than you and I can't imagine them doing that. And I got three boys and a husband I been married to for the better part of twenty years and I'm still having nightmares about heading out, so I can't imagine you doing it alone." She persuaded Ella to put in an order for vegetables.

"They got potatoes and onions that just arrived off a boat from up north and I heard they're bringing in a boatload of carrots and beets in the next week. So get your order in. It'll keep you going for a while. I heard some folks say we can trade squash and pumpkins with the Indians, but I don't know how true that is."

"Would you recommend a dutch oven?" Ella asked, as the queue moved closer to the shop doors. "I've been advised to buy one."

The woman nodded. "Can't be without mine, like most women here. They heat up real quick and you can cook just about anything in them."

And then at last Ella was in the store. She ended up buying four straw bonnets, as she also purchased one for herself and Martha. All of them were made with a deep, wide brim which offered shade against the hot sun and prairie winds. She also bought three headscarves and put in an order for more cured bacon, coffee beans, rice, white beans, the dutch oven and a sack of potatoes.

"I got steamboats bringing in supplies over the next week, but if the boats are late or you head out before it arrives, come see me and I'll refund your money. I got no problem with that." The storekeeper said, a thin, busy sort of man in his fifties who spoke with a thick European accent. He worked alongside half a dozen family members, all of them busy dealing with customers queries, for Ella could hardly move the store was so packed.

She left with her bonnets and scarves and stepped outside to put on her new hat. The wide brim immediately threw shade on her face and stopped the glare in her eyes, a relief in the warmth of that spring day. Then she hurried back to her wagon, passing several canvas stores, and when she found one belonging to a French family who were selling fresh loaves of bread, Ella purchased three of them. She would keep one for her team, gift one to Marrok and give the other to Martha to give to Willard and his family.

*

Martha was still there when she returned to the wagon. She was sitting on a supply box by Clara, with Jasper and the Linwood boys sitting on the grass eating hot biscuits and drinking freshly brewed coffee. As Clara poured her a coffee, Ella showed the women the bonnets and both were well pleased with them.

"Why, they're just fine," Martha said, choosing one with a blue ribbon. "They'll be good on the trail to keep the sun off our faces but they sure ain't like the ones we wore back home. Those hats were pretty dainty things compared to these."

Clara loved her bonnet and scarf, and took the scarf and wrapped it around her head, tying it at the back of her neck. "I ain't never had anything so pretty."

Then Ella headed for the wagon. Ruby jumped up when she saw her, for she was desperate to get outside.

"Are you sure none of my hair can be seen?" she asked, as Ella tied one of the scarves tight at the back of her neck as Clara had done. "And that the bonnet hides my face?"

Ella nodded, holding up a small hand mirror as Ruby tied the ribbons of the bonnet under her chin. "You look just like every other woman here.

No-one will know who you are and the wide brim of the bonnet shades half your face."

Ruby laughed, well pleased. "You know, I doubt my own father would recognize me. Come on, let's go, I can smell Clara's biscuits," she said, moving to the back of the wagon just as two riders came towards them.

Ella recognized Marrok, but Willard was a stranger. He'd left the ranch as a youth of nineteen, when Ella was just a child, now he was a grown man, with a family. He still owned a good head of dark hair and he was tall and lean like Martha, but his face was aged. Ella saw Marrok nod towards Martha, who had stood up as the men rode in, then Willard paused for just a moment before dismounting and hurrying across to embrace his mother.

2

It was an emotional reunion and the first time Ella had ever seen Martha cry. That tough woman who had never cried when Quentin got sick or even when he died, because Martha had seen her brother-in-law's death as a blessing for him in the end after months of suffering, she almost collapsed on seeing Willard. It had been more than fifteen years since they'd last seen each other and she cried again when she learned she had three grandchildren with another on the way, with Willard's wife Constance almost four months along.

When Martha packed up her belongings to move to Willard's camp which was more than a mile away, it was Ella's turn to cry. She had expected to lose Martha to her son's family, but not have her move away entirely. So the men talked about bringing Willard's wagons over to this side of the settlers' camp but in the end decided it wasn't practical, not for the short time they'd be here.

"We've got two wagons, twelve oxen, nine men, three children and a couple of horses," Willard said, shaking his head at the idea of moving. "We've been settled for almost two months where we are and the way I see it, my animals have just got enough to graze on before we roll out. Besides, Constance is taking this pregnancy pretty hard and I don't want to put her through the stress of moving. Anyway, you've got enough people camped over this side. Hardly any room left for a man's wagons and animals!"

Willard was saddened to hear of his uncle's passing and gave his condolences to Ella and Jasper. "Uncle Quentin was always such a hard worker. I can't remember a day when he wasn't out there working in the fields."

A bookkeeper by trade, Willard had spent the past ten years working for a company in Boston, until a year ago he and Constance decided to leave it all behind and start afresh in California. Around that time, they'd sent the letter to Martha, asking her to join them.

"When we arrived here and there was no sign of you, I knew my letters had either gone missing or Uncle Quentin had sold the ranch and you'd all up and left. I never dared think you might have passed away, but I admit it did trouble me. When I spoke about it to Artie Dalbert, our wagon master, he introduced me to Marrok and said there was no better man to track you down, if you were still alive. Clearly he was right. I can't thank you enough," he said, looking over at Marrok.

The men talked about the changes in camp since Marrok had been gone. "I think it's almost double in size since you left a month ago. And during that time, people have started to form groups and organize their wagons into circles. You'll find friends travelling together, along with large family groups like our own. There's plenty of different nationalities here, with some folk not having one word of English, but so far everyone seems to get on alright," he paused, frowning.

"Last week there was some tension when supplies started running a bit low, when boats arrived here late. And then word came in that there was a small herd of buffalo grazing not two miles inside Indian territory so a few dozen men rode up there and shot several hundred of the beasts and scattered the rest in a bid to stop them eating the grass. They brought back a lot of meat, enough to feed everyone for a few weeks at least, and so far there's been no retaliation from the Indians. But a lot of people here wish they hadn't done it, because they don't want no trouble," he paused, missing the anger that crossed over Marrok's face.

"Then there's folk who've been camped here for months, since end of winter, who are getting mighty impatient. They want to get moving, but no matter how many times they've been told we have to wait for the prairie grasses to grow so there's enough feed for all these animals, they're foolish enough to want to take the chance and leave now. There's others who don't use their firewood wisely, they burn it recklessly which means folk have to walk for miles to find kindling and wood."

Marrok had explained these things to Ella and her team on that long walk to Independence from St Louis. "Without enough grass, all those animals travelling with the wagon train will starve. And without firewood you won't be able to cook or heat water. So make sure you pick up any kindling or piece of wood you see on the trail, because if you don't someone behind you will. On the prairies you'll find dried buffalo chips which you'll have to collect as well. But it burns good enough and you'll be grateful for it when there's no wood or kindling. And if you see herbs that you recognize that will flavor your cooking or help with illness, pick it, or your neighbor will."

Ella glanced across at Marrok now, as he

listened to Willard and she thought his face once again set in hard lines, the softness she had seen in him in St Louis gone.

"And last week word came that the company we've paid to take us west will be rolling out by week's end, with close to two hundred wagons," Willard continued. "Which someone reckons is the biggest wagon train yet to leave for the west."

Marrok questioned these figures, because Willard was talking about the company he worked for as scout, which would also be taking his wagons west. But he hadn't yet had a chance to talk to Artie and if this were true, then over one hundred wagons had joined them during the four weeks he'd been gone. He found the numbers staggering.

"But what about all these other folk camped here?" Martha asked. "There's more than two hundred wagons here, who takes them west?"

This time Marrok answered. "They'll have paid to leave with other companies, Martha. Indeed, I heard before I left for St Louis that there were half a dozen smaller companies selling places in their trains this year. Some will be heading to California and Oregon, others will be going south on the Santa Fe trial. People who arrive late in the season will buy places with them, but they'd better be careful. If they leave here too late, they'll get stuck this side of the Rockies over winter and no-one wants to do that."

With the biscuits eaten and the coffee going cold, Marrok rose and made his excuses to leave, eager to catch up with Artie and his own men. Then Willard and Martha were making plans to leave.

"We'll catch up tomorrow Aunt, when you come to collect the rest of your things," Ella said, wiping away her tears. "We'll need to find your camp anyway, so come and get us so we can meet your family."

Martha hugged her, wiping away her own tears. "I don't feel right about leaving you alone like this Ella," she said, reaching out to hug her, before turning to Ruby. "But at least you have the use of the wagon to yourself now and that's how it should be, considering you're paying for the privilege," she reached out to hug Jasper. "This don't feel right somehow Jasper, leaving the two of you alone. I've been with you both since Ella was a child and it sure feels strange leaving you now.

"We'll be alright," Ella said, putting an arm around Jasper's shoulders. "Besides, we're only a short walk away so we'll see you every day, even if we no longer share meals together. Just think on the new lives we're starting Aunt, we've got to remember that."

But as Marrok and Martha left, with Martha's possessions tied down on the back of Willard's horse, Ella sat down, feeling desolate. It was Ruby who reached out to put an arm about her shoulders.

"Come on girl, cheer up. You've got us now and Clara and I want to go for a walk into town so you must join us."

3

But Ella didn't feel like walking all that way back into Independence, so she remained by the fire, leaving her team to go off without her. Except she felt unbearably lonely listening to all the family groups laughing and talking around her so she got up and hurried after them, trying to suppress that feeling of panic which threatened to overwhelm her now that Marrok and Martha had gone.

She weaved around wagons and campfires and animals, hearing different languages being spoken along with American accents from the north and south and east coast. Ella glanced at them, wondering if they'd be travelling with her, even as she discreetly looked into the back of their wagons to see what they carried.

But there were few surprises. Most wagons were filled with the same sort of goods she had in her own wagon, either brought with her from the ranch or purchased in St Louis. But then she saw a wagon filled with heavy furniture. She couldn't help but stop and stare. A dresser of mahogany, a sideboard of oak. One piece almost reached to the very top of the canvas frame. She thought of the potholes in the road her own wagon had lurched over on its journey west from her father's ranch and thought this furniture was in for a beating before it reached its destination. She also felt sorry for the eight oxen which were grazing nearby, having to pull such a load.

"Ella!" a deep baritone called out and Ella turned to see Marrok striding towards her. "I can't find Artie, so I'm heading into town with a list of supplies my men need." He saw her looking at the overloaded wagon and shook his head.

"I hope they're not travelling with us, because that's a whole lot of problems right there. I'd imagine their wagon master has already asked them to get rid of it all, because once these wagons hit bad weather a wagon carrying a load like that will get bogged down in mud and hold the train up for days, while men try and dig it out," he shook his head.

"If they refuse to leave it here, then Artie would make them unpack it all and leave it on the side of the trail, first sign of trouble. It's happened with others and it will happen to them. But people won't listen, even when they're told they'll hold up the whole train. When their furniture is left behind to rot in the wild, making it good for nothing but fuel for someone's fire, they'll still argue they can take it west."

Ella glanced up at him in shock. "People use that for firewood?"

Marrok nodded. "Seen it happen before. And out there in the wild, unless those folk have a cabin to take it to, it's not much good for anything else." He turned and glanced towards town. "If you're heading that way, I'll walk with you."

"Don't know where I'm headed to be honest," she said. "All my team went into town but I didn't feel like walking back, yet I couldn't stand being alone, so here I am. I guess I'll get used to it, this being by myself, but it'll take some time not having Martha around. She's been like a mother to me. But I've just got to think of my team now and make sure they're okay and keep my mind on what lies ahead," she nodded towards the distant buildings of Independence. "Anyway, that's where my team were headed, so thought I may as well join them."

"Come on then, I'll walk with you," Marrok said and Ella felt better having him beside her.

But as they walked through camp, Ella became aware of people glancing at Marrok in his buckskin clothing and moccasins, but he did look out of place compared to the calico, linen and woolen clothes worn by most people here. Marrok didn't seem too bothered by the stares but Ella knew him well enough to know he was aware of every little thing going on around him. She thought him like one of those great prairie hawks they had seen on their journey west from St Louis.

"Willard purchased a wagon especially for Martha and his children to share," she said, curious as to what he thought about that.

Marrok shrugged, obviously having little opinion on the matter. "Then Martha should consider herself fortunate, for most women here will be sleeping rough for the remainder of the year." He glanced across at the mercantile stores ahead of them and even at this late hour people were queuing to place last minute orders, terrified of forgetting something before the wagons rolled out. "But I have the impression that money isn't a concern for Willard, unlike most people here, as many of them will struggle to pay for what they need."

Like me, Ella thought, because even with Ruby's money she still worried. But at least she could now afford to pay for supplies, along with wages.

"What happens when we run out of things on

the trail? What do we do then?"

Marrok turned to look at her, those dark eyes now focused on her, making her feel as though she were the only woman alive. "We'll pass a few trading posts and supply stations along the trail and Fort Hall is well stocked but had you set out ten years ago when the first wagon trains rolled out, things would have been very different. There were no trading posts or supply stations that far west, only a few French and Spanish forts with most of them deserted. So life would have been hard for those people, but we can thank them for laying the trail and some of them now own those supply stations and trading posts. But no-one will starve, unless we get caught in the Rockies over winter," he turned and glanced out over that massive camp and Ella thought again how striking he was.

Tall and dark with a strength to his face that showed he'd lived a full life, Ella wanted to hear him tell it, to find out more about him, although once the wagons rolled out, she knew she wouldn't get that chance. He would be busy with his own team or be gone for days at a time, scouting out the country ahead.

"Could that happen?" she asked. "That we get stuck in the Rockies over winter?"

He turned back to her and nodded. "Yes, of course, if we get delayed. But that's why most companies roll out of here by end of May. June at the latest. Which gives everyone four to five months to get over the mountains before the first snows come." He paused and glanced around at the sprawling camp.

"But this year things are a little different because

there's so many settlers here, more than I've ever seen before, although the smaller companies will take a few of those people. But that can also create problems. The other day I heard a man say he plans to take his wagon train through a shortcut he knows across the Rockies," he shook his head.

"I told him my thoughts on the matter because I've travelled that route myself with men from a Paiute tribe who live up that way. It's fine for a man on horseback, but not for a team of mules or oxen pulling a heavy wagon. It's rough, hard country with a lot of the trails narrow and steep," Marrok paused, frowning with frustration.

"I heard another couple of scouts from other companies advising him not to go that way, but he seems set on the idea. I hope he listens to us. The only safe way through the Rockies is using the same trails we've been using for the past ten years. The same trails the Indians have used for centuries. And if you hear anyone saying otherwise, then take them for the fool he is."

He turned and nodded towards a camp on the far side of town, quite a distance from everyone else. "And they'd agree with me, as will their wives. Most of those women come from tribes to the west, or up north, and they know that route better than any of us."

Ella followed his gaze and saw a large group of men and women sitting around a campfire, with small children playing near them.

"People know them as muleskinners, because most of them use big teams of mules to pull those wagons they have with them. But it's those men who carry your supplies west. Most of them used to be fur trappers or mountain men so they know this country pretty well," he paused, frowning.

"It's rare to see women and children travelling with them, because those men like to travel hard and fast, usually in small convoys. Likely they're moving their families west, or north, away from all these settlers."

Marrok turned back to Ella. "I've heard there's a big group of them due in later this week from Santa Fe, with some of them heading out to Fort Hall a few days before us. So if we end up sharing our campsite with them in the months ahead, even though they usually keep well ahead of us, just keep your distance from them Ella. They're hard men and even I would think twice before crossing one of them."

Ella glanced back at the group. Their wagons were corralled in a circle, with some oxen and mules grazing inside it. A couple of men walked among them, checking on the animals, while others sat with their wives, or leaned against the wheels of their wagons and smoked pipes.

The men seemed big and muscular. They wore buckskin clothing and moccasins like Marrok, with long hair worn well past their shoulders. Thick beards covered half their faces and the felt or fur hats they wore were pulled low over their foreheads taking the glare off their eyes.

The women seemed quite young, as were most of the children, although Ella saw a few teenage boys sitting with the men. A few of the women wore buckskin dresses with knee high moccasins while others wore muslin skirts and shirts. All wore their hair in long plaits and all wore delicate silver and beaded jewelry in their ears, around their necks and wrists. A few of the women wore hats. A couple wore bowler hats that were once fashionable in cities on the east coast, while others wore straw bonnets decorated with seed beads or animals furs.

"Don't worry Marrok. I've no intention of going anywhere near them," Ella said. "Even their women look terrifying to me."

Marrok smiled. "Their women are hard because most have had hard lives. But their knowledge of living in the wild is as good as my own so if you were to make friends with them, you could learn a lot. But stay away from their men."

They hurried on to Courtyard Square where another group of men were raising yet another ballot, voting for first officers for another wagon company.

"Why must they vote? Can't every wagon take care of themselves?" Ella asked.

"Once people start living on top of each other with little privacy, you'll eventually get conflicts of one sort or another, which you'll see for yourself soon enough," Marrok said softly. "I've seen enough petty arguments escalate to violence, especially when people are tired or stressed, or when a strong minded man or woman don't take too kindly to being told what to do. But when a wagon master and his officers get involved, men who are seen as the law out there on the trail, things can calm down real quick."

A shout made them turn and a tall, broadly built man in his early fifties hurried towards them, along with two men in their forties. The older man laughed as he came towards them, surprising Ella when he reached out to hug Marrok, slapping him on the back.

"Glad to see you back, son! We were getting worried about you! But you're here just in time, as looks like we'll be moving out by end of next week," he paused and glanced at Ella. "This can't be Martha, the gal you went looking for!"

Marrok laughed. "No, this is Ella, Martha's niece and Willard's cousin. But Martha is here, safe and sound with her son." He turned to Ella. "This is Artie Dalbert, my good friend and our wagon master. He'll be sheriff and judge, all the way to Fort Hall."

Ella reached out to shake Artie's hand, feeling the strength in his grip. Despite his good humor, Ella saw the hardness in his eyes and firm line of his mouth suggesting this was a man of conviction, who wouldn't take sides, or be unfair. His face was deeply lined and he looked older than what he was but Ella liked him straight off. She turned as Marrok introduced the other two men.

"Joe Bracedon and Miller Minson. First and second officers in our company."

Ella shook the men's hands then turned back to Artie. "You'll be leaving us at Fort Hall?"

"Yes, ma'am. From Fort Hall, Marrok and I will head on out to Oregon together and can't say I ain't looking forward to it. After working together for the past three years for the same wagon train company, I reckon it's time we chased our own dreams."

He looked at Marrok and laughed again and Ella could see the affection between the two men.

Then they turned as Joe Bracedon held a piece of paper out towards Marrok.

"We got our list almost done. We just about met everyone who's leaving with us next week." He glanced at Ella. "I guess I'll add your name to that list ma'am, along with those who'll be heading out with you."

"Thought I'd address everyone tonight after supper," Artie said to Marrok. "Just to introduce myself and let them know what's happening."

Marrok frowned. "Which leaves me a week to get myself sorted, before we head out."

"Less than a week," Artie said. "You think you can do it?"

"I'll do it."

Ella watched Marrok, aware of his tension and with it, her own guilt for making him late in getting back here. She wondered how she could repay him or help him, when Artie turned to her.

"Glad to have you with us, Ella," he said. "But would you mind if I steal him away from you? We got things to talk over."

She nodded and said goodbye and turned to head for the stores, but couldn't help but turn back as the men disappeared among the wagons and camp sites. And she knew then it had begun. Her journey west to a new life in California was only days away. There could be no going back now.

4

She found Ruby and Clara in another of the mercantile stores buying linen.

Ruby looked flushed with excitement when Ella approached them.

"We've had such fun. I've bought some linen for our beds and soft feather pillows and another bonnet each and I bought Jasper a hat. And I've ordered more blankets for us all, even though you've already ordered some. But I can't tolerate the cold, never have, not since I was a child and I've heard enough horror stories of the mountain country ahead of us," she shook her head as Ella began to protest at all the expense.

"I won't hear any complaints, Ella. And you know I can do this, for I've enough money to do what I like. And besides, this is the least I can do for you and Clara."

Ella gave up arguing, thinking how young Ruby looked in that moment, so different to that girl in the saloon who had worn rouge on her cheeks and black pencil under her eyes. Ruby had also put on a little weight during those weeks between St Louis and Independence, with most of the bruising slowly fading from her face and neck.

"Where's Jasper?" Ella asked.

Clara turned to her, smiling. "He gone off with Abe and Wilber to look at horses. There be some fine animals over there in them corrals Miss Ella."

"Come on Clara, do lift them high," Ruby scolded. "I must see how good the stitching is, for I won't pay for linen that isn't of good quality.

Ella stepped forward to help Clara lift several pieces of linen and suddenly felt something within her grow and flutter until it threatened to explode.

Happy and excited. That's how she felt.

For the first time since she left her father's ranch.

5

"I've been doing this a long time and I'll tell you now, the best way for all of us to get along is for you to do as I say and be happy about it," Artie called across the crowd.

He stood on a high wooden box, turning to look out at the men, women and children who faced him, shouting to allow his voice to carry across the camp so everyone could hear him.

"That way we won't have too many problems and no-one gets hurt and we don't lose no-one. And you better hear it from me now, but I got no time for moaners or whiners. You got a problem, you come and see me directly or one of my men here so we can sort it out," he turned and introduced his officers, along with Marrok. "I don't want any one of you whining or moaning around other folks' camps causing trouble."

He paused as he looked out over the crowd, at the hundreds of people who would look to him for leadership over the following five months. Yet Artie could point to the ones who would cause him grief, just from the arrogant way they were watching him, as if they already knew better. But Artie had been taking wagon trains west for three years and in that time he had seen and heard it all.

"Now, we have a list of where your wagon will be in the rollout. You stay behind the wagon in front and don't take your mules or oxen or horses off that single rutted track until I say. You hear that? Otherwise one of you will end up in a ditch or wedged in a hole and I don't want to stop the whole damn wagon train and lose hours of daylight digging you out. Once we reach the wide-open prairies you can spread out, that way the dust won't be too hard on the wagons at the back. At night I want up to fifty wagons forming a tight circle, just like a corral, and I want all your animals inside so we don't lose any to wolves or bears or hungry Indians. You can make your campfires outside of that circle as well as put up your canvas shelters, for we'll start a rotating list of men who'll be on watch from the first night out. Make sure your campfires are safe so no fires can spread and keep your children close to you. I don't want no child wandering off from the wagons for I've seen more than one lost in the wild. You got to remember it's dangerous country out there and if anyone forgets it, someone's going to get hurt."

Artie paused as a nervous murmur rose above the crowd. Marrok glanced up at his friend and almost smiled. Artie knew how to put the fear of God into people, but it didn't hurt for they had no idea what lay ahead. It was going to be tough out there and the more prepared they were for it, the better chance everyone had of arriving safely at Fort Hall. After that, they would no longer be Marrok or Artie's responsibility.

"On our first day we'll travel twelve miles, as far as Indian country," Artie continued. "That should get you all used to your wagons and your animals before we cross over the western border. From that point on, I don't want any one of you folks forgetting where we are, that we're travelling through Indian lands, that our animals are grazing on grass that their buffalo should be grazing on. And know this for a fact, that without buffalo to feed and clothe them, a lot of them folks will be going cold and hungry."

"Does that mean them Injuns will be making trouble for us?" one man called out.

Marrok saw Artie grimace with distaste before raising his hand to quieten the voices that rose up in fear all around them.

"First of all, they aren't called *Injuns*. Secondly, they got every right to make trouble if you all just think on it a moment. How'd you feel if close to a thousand of them suddenly rolled through this camp pulling wagons, along with several thousand head of cattle, horses and oxen, taking your water and letting their animals graze on this grass. The way I see it, they have a right to defend what is theirs. So treat them with respect and we'll all get along just fine. But if you go cause trouble for them, well, expect trouble back, for push anyone hard enough and they'll push back. So if you shoot first, these people will come after you and you'd better believe they'll get you, for they're the best damn trackers in the whole darn world and the best marksmen I ever saw. So be it on your head if any one of you starts up any kind of trouble," he paused as a ripple of fear once again travelled around the crowd. And again Artie raised a hand for silence.

"There'll be two bugle calls the morning we roll out. The first one will sound at 4am to wake you up. That gives you two hours to feed yourselves and get your children organized and your animals harnessed to your wagons. The second bugle call will come around 6am which is the call to roll out. And you'd better be ready to move, because I ain't waiting on no-one." He looked around the crowd.

"Let's all keep safe and let's get to Fort Hall in one piece. Good luck everyone. You got any questions, you come see me or my men here."

Ella watched as Artie climbed down off the box and as he turned and walked through the crowd beside Marrok and his two officers, people reached out to talk, to ask questions and Ella turned away. She wouldn't be seeing Marrok tonight. His role as scout had begun.

*

"Lord above," Martha exclaimed, as they walked back through camp to their wagons. "I do believe I shan't sleep the whole time we're out there. Not until we reach California."

Willard laughed. "As long as no-one sets out to cause trouble like Mr Dalbert says, everyone will get along just fine."

Ella glanced across at Constance and noticed the dark circles under her eyes along with her pale complexion, revealing the sickness Constance was battling with this fourth pregnancy. She was five years older than Ella and a pretty woman with strawberry blond hair and brown eyes. Her children, nine-year old Clarissa, seven-year old Eleanor and three-year old Archer all owned their father's dark hair and eyes along with their grandmother's tall, lean build.

As they walked through camp, someone brought out a fiddle and as the music drifted across to them, Ruby grabbed Ella and Clara and dragged them along with her, with Abe and Wilber following.

"Come on, let's dance!" she cried with excitement as other people started heading towards the music.

"Sorry," Constance said, shaking her head, looking exhausted. "I'm getting these children home to bed, it's getting late."

Willard turned to Ella. "We'll see you tomorrow?"

Ella nodded and hugged them all goodnight then watched as they headed home towards their wagons.

"Come on!" Ruby cried, as more men brought out their fiddles to accompany the first.

"Not me!" Jasper said, his hands in the air. "I's going back to camp to check on the animals and sleep!"

He watched as they made their way towards the music, then he turned towards Ella's wagon. He'd just brewed a pot of coffee when Marrok called out to him, passing by on his way to his own camp.

"Are you not joining in the dancing?"

"Doan't know how," Jasper replied, laughing as Marrok came towards him. "Just got the coffee goin' if you want to join me."

Marrok sat down and as Jasper poured the rich dark liquid into another cup, Marrok glanced around the camp. "Sure is quiet without anyone around."

Jasper nodded. "Better to sit and be quiet than try and dance. Besides," he reached down and touched his knees. "These ain't made for fancy dance steps. And I never had time for such things anyways, so I never learned how to move my feet the right way. Mostly I reckon I'd trip over."

Marrok smiled. "You ready to leave at the end of the week?"

"Yessir, I am. But to be honest with you, I's still gettin' my head around the fact we're not goin' back to the ranch," he tapped his head. "I've got my memories tucked away up here, if I ever need to think on them, especially those of Violet and Ella's folk. I won't never forget them."

Marrok watched him, intrigued by this gentle man and his past. "You were close to them?"

Jasper frowned as he thought back. "Yessir, I was. But I got no memory of Violet before I met her in that slave market where Mr Quentin done found us. Everythin' I knew 'afore that day is lost to me, my mind full of nothin' at all. Yet, I reckon I won't go searching for it. I'll leave whatever I knew back there in the dark, where I can't find it." He tapped his forehead again, watching the tall handsome man opposite him.

"What was Violet like?" Marrok asked.

Jasper smiled. "One of the sweetest women that ever did live. One memory I got real clear is her standin' next to me in that market, both of us all chained up with no-one wantin' us. Me a sickly boy and Violet old, until Mr Quentin done showed up and took us north to St Louis, up the Mississippi River on a keelboat, with no chains or ropes or nothin' else bindin' us. I doan't rightly remember he said much. But I do remember the angry words spoken a'tween him and Ella's mama when we showed up at the ranch. I'll tell you now, those words lasted for days. I guess she didn't want us there. But Mr Quentin wouldn't budge. And so we stayed. Ella was just a little bittie thing in those days. But her Mama gave Violet a room behind the kitchen and I got the room behind the stable. Ain't never been happier than I was livin' there, although things changed a bit when Violet died."

"What happened to her?"

Jasper frowned and shook his head. "Never seen nothin' like it. I saw her outside at the pump, gettin' water. She looked just fine to me. But when she was carryin' the bucket of water back to the house she stumbled. I called to her and started runnin', for it looked like she tripped on her skirts or somethin' then I heard her cry aloud 'afore droppin' like a stone, restin' on her hands and knees like she was prayin' to the Lord. Then she just fell down. Never made another noise, just died right there. Not long after, Miss Martha and Mr Willard came to live with us, but Mr Willard never did stay long."

Marrok said nothing for a long moment, then he leaned towards Jasper. "How do you feel about heading west?"

Jasper shrugged. "I got no feelings on it to be honest. I just content to be with Miss Ella and Miss Martha. They's my family. Been with them so long, those folks are all I rightly remember."

They talked a little of what lay ahead then Jasper threw the dregs of his coffee on the coals. Then he looked at Marrok. "Is it true those Indians might attack us? Take our scalps for riding over their lands? I been hearin' all sorts of stories walking around camp."

Marrok shrugged. "I won't deny there's some ill feeling out there among some tribes, while others just want to trade. Whether a war happens this summer or in the years ahead, I can't tell you. But I think a lot of stories you hear are just folk stirring up trouble, so I wouldn't take much notice if I were you."

Jasper nodded. "I reckon I can sleep good on that."

Marrok made a move to leave. "Once we roll out I won't see you for a few days, for I'll be heading out early to scout. So if I don't get a chance to speak to you before we leave, just remember to go easy on the reins. Those oxen are slow but they're placid enough and if you're gentle with them, they'll work hard for you."

"Yessir, Mr Marrok, I remember all you done told me. And I'm glad you stopped by. It sure was nice talkin' to you."

"Just call me Marrok, Jasper. There's no need for formality between us."

"Yessir," Jasper said as the younger man turned and disappeared into the night.

6

Ella lay awake in the dark, listening to the soft breathing of Clara. Above them she could hear Ruby toss and turn in the wagon, the girl clearly as restless as she was. Ella had a moment of envying Ruby the comfort of the wagon compared to the hard ground she was sleeping on, even though her mattress was soft enough and the double canvas sheeting underneath stopped the damp rising. And anything was better than being married to Jebediah Crawley.

Unnerved by that thought Ella sat up, careful not to wake Clara, wrapping her arms about her knees in an effort to keep warm against the chill of the spring night.

She thought over all her supplies again, confident she had everything she needed and was as prepared as she could be. Artie had organized it so that when the wagons rolled out, her wagon would follow Willard's team all the way to the prairies, until they spread out to avoid the worst of the dust. And there would be dust, as hundreds of animals and over two hundred wagons trampled over dry ground.

Ella pulled back the canvas to look outside. There were no clouds, the sky covered in stars, yet along with their beauty come the smell of the camp, the air thick with wood smoke, spicy cooking smells, animal waste and other things.

Ella shivered and closed the canvas opening, lying back under her blankets. It was impossible to sleep. She found herself thinking of Clarissa, the eldest of Willard's three children. For some reason, the nine-year old girl had taken a liking to Ruby, following her everywhere.

"It's your hair! She's never before seen a woman with her head aflame!" Wilber joked, after Ella and her team had walked over to see Martha one night after supper. Clarissa lay snuggled within Ruby's arms as they sat on canvas sheeting around the fire.

"And that's why they called you Ruby! Because of your hair!" said Abe, nudging Wilber. The two brothers broke into loud laughter.

"Oh hush! As if I didn't have enough stupid comments like that growing up without having to hear them again from the two of you!" Ruby scolded them. "Well, I shall tell you something! Ruby isn't even my real name. And Daegan is my mother's name, for I will not have my father's. And you were lucky you grew up with a mother, for I never knew mine. All I have is the Irish she gave me, her love of singing and her coloring and I'm grateful for both!" Ruby paused, aware of everyone looking at her, stunned by her outburst.

The brothers looked upset. "We're sorry Ruby," Abe said, shamefaced. "You know darn well none of us would change a thing about you."

Wilber nodded. "We didn't mean to cause offence. We were just having a laugh."

"Well in all truth I don't care overly much," Ruby said. "And since my own father took sport in teasing me since I was a little girl, I'm well used to people making fun of me."

As Ella thought back on that conversation, she realized that Ruby would never let anyone get the better of her. And Ella wished she were more like that. Strong and independent. Yet what had caused Ruby to leave a privileged home at eighteen years of age?

She turned as Elmer Weslock began to snore in the nearby wagon. Ella wondered how Nell could possibly sleep with such a racket beside her, although Nell seemed to be the sort of woman who could put up with a great deal. She was always putting others first, particularly her twenty-two year old grandson Moss.

The small family had come out from Virginia with the aim of settling in California but from the conversations she'd heard between them, Ella often wondered if Elmer and Nell would have preferred to stay in the small country town where they'd both been born. They had married and raised their two sons there, but with the death of both their boys and daughter-in-law in a carriage accident more than twelve years ago, they had been left to raise their only grandchild. When Moss began making plans to head west a year ago, Nell and Elmer, both in their early sixties and having no other family, agreed to put up the money to finance the move, until deciding to sell everything up and go with him.

Ella liked the family, they were always the first to help anyone. Some said that Elmer and Nell spoilt Moss rotten but she found him independent, a young man who hated fussing of any kind and clearly he adored his grandparents, along with Ruby. Had Ruby given him the smallest bit of encouragement, Moss would have had Artie marry them tomorrow.

Except Ruby wanted no part of Moss or any other man. Her dream lay not in being a wife and mother but singing.

The snoring suddenly stopped. Nell must have elbowed Elmer in the ribs, getting him to turn over. She wondered suddenly if Marrok snored and grinned at the thought, before peering out from her canvas shelter towards his camp. She could see the form of him as he slept near his fire, but it was too dark to see his face.

He would be gone soon to scout ahead. And as Ella lay back down and closed her eyes, knowing she'd miss him, she once again saw herself standing on the edge of that great dark abyss with no idea how to get to the other side. Except she had an idea that the only person alive who could get her across to safety, was Marrok.

7

The bugle call came rolling across the fields on that cold May morning, stirring every person in Independence. It startled Ella awake and she rolled off her mattress and quickly dressed, her mind foggy from lack of sleep, and as she crawled from the shelter leaving Clara to dress behind her, she took kindling from the pile they had collected and stored near their wagon to get a fire going to make coffee.

And then Clara was working beside her, efficient and silent, taking the bread she'd prepared the night before and placing it in the newly purchased dutch oven before stirring the oatmeal.

Abe, Wilber and Jasper started dismantling their canvas shelters, with Ella and Ruby hurrying to help carry mattresses and bed linen, supplies and clothes to the back of the wagon. Then the brothers left to harness the oxen, leaving Jasper to do a last minute check over the wagon before moving off to tend to the horses.

And as Ella turned back to help Clara, she felt the rise of panic sweep through camp in the shouts and urgent conversations and it suddenly seemed impossible to get everything done in two hours, as men and boys organized wagons and animals while women and girls tended to small children, lit fires and began breakfast. The distressed cries of babies and toddlers being woken at such an hour only added to the urgency, as mothers tended to soiled laundry and sought clean clothes along with everything else.

And then Artie and his officers were riding through camp urging people to get organized. And then breakfast was done and cleaned up, dishes and ovens were put away, small children placed into the back of wagons for safety while the last of the animals were harnessed. With the arrival of daylight, people from town started to gather along with settlers who would leave later with other companies, to wish them good luck and safe travels.

At then 6am came around and the second bugle call rang out and the energy levels around camp rose to another level as men shouted impatiently to their teams and women called for their families to get everything aboard the wagons. And then Artie's call came down the line.

Wagons ho!

Ella felt the tingle up her spine as he and his officers rode past her wagon, Artie's voice loud and clear in that cool morning. Jasper had tied Bear on his long lead behind the wagon, leaving Ella to mount Billy. And as Jasper settled on the buckboard, Ruby and Clara hurried to pull on another pair of stockings beneath their boots to protect their feet, for they would walk for most of the day, just like everyone else who was fit enough to walk. Abe and Wilber stood at the head of the oxen waiting for their turn to move on out, ready with their willow switches, ready to walk alongside the oxen all the way to California.

And then the wagons in front began to move. Slowly at first, the oxen stumbling with the weight behind them but then they were rolling out. Joe Bracedon called out for Ella's team to get ready to roll as Willard's team came towards her and then Abe and Wilber were touching the shoulders of the two lead oxen with their switches while Jasper flicked the reins and as Ella sat astride Billy, she watched as her wagon began to roll.

They were on their way. Come winter, she would be in a whole new world. And as two hundred wagons rolled out of Independence amid cries of farewell and good luck, Ella laughed and kicked Billy on to look for Martha.

Her aunt was sitting on the buckboard two wagons in front of Ella's, next to one of Willard's drivers, her eyes alight with the thrill of it all. And as Martha looked down at the young woman sitting astride her horse looking up at her laughing, she silently thanked Willard for sending Marrok to find her.

*

They set up camp on the border of Indian territory that first night and as wagons were pulled into circles to create corrals for the animals, Artie and his men shouted instructions and encouragement. And once animals were unharnessed and left to graze within those huge wagon corrals, women began lighting fires to prepare meals for their families.

Ella counted herself lucky as she heard the complaints of blisters and exhaustion, because she'd had Billy to ride for most of the way. She'd joined Ruby and Clara for a while as they walked with Martha and Constance and the children and as they walked, they picked up kindling and herbs.

But she knew like everyone else that tomorrow would be harder because Artie hoped to cover fifteen miles, three more than they had managed today. Yet the day had gone well enough, because after that second bugle call at 6am, the wagons had rolled on for two hours before Artie called for a stop, letting everyone rest along with the animals. Then they had moved on before stopping for lunch around mid-day and then another long walk of some three hours before Artie called a stop around 4pm.

"Four o'clock lets everyone rest up before bedtime, including the animals," he'd said.

But by nightfall, most people were abed, ready for that 4am bugle call the following morning.

Indian Territory
May 1846

1

They rolled across the border into lands held by
native tribes just after 6am the following morning.
The wagon train's arrival onto Indian lands was
met by silence. There were no attacks, no warnings
to turn around and go back, only the creak and
groan of ropes and axles as the wagons moved
across rutted tracks made by other wagons. But as
if all who travelled on that wagon train were afraid
of being found trespassing on land that wasn't
theirs, other than the neigh or blow of horses, or
the grunt or bellow of oxen, everyone on that
wagon train moved across the border in silence,
with hardly a child heard crying on that cold grey
morning. And as dawn came and went, as the
morning slowly moved towards midday, there was
nothing to show that anyone lived on this vast
open land other than a few hawks flying low over
the high prairie grass looking for voles and mice.

The company managed the fifteen miles that
day without complaint, even as Artie discussed the
possibility with his officers of pushing them harder,
closer to twenty miles a day, to keep ahead of the
wagon trains coming up behind them.

It had been Marrok who argued against it.
"Better to keep them moving at a good solid pace
each day than push them beyond their endurance.
You don't want folk getting sick or their animals
falling under the pressure."

When they reached a wide, shallow river close to
4pm that afternoon, Artie called a halt, ordering the

animals be watered before they were corralled and for everyone to get their shelters up, for the sky to the north bore heavy rain clouds.

The first drops of rain fell just after supper and as fires were extinguished by the rain, as clouds swept in to take away all light from the moon, the whispers of unease began to circulate around camp. And Ella heard those frightened whispers, of being in territory known to be hostile, and like everyone else she felt afraid.

But Artie and his officers also heard those rumbles of unease and to put a stop to it, they ordered more men to stand guard.

"Better to have a man stand guard with a loaded gun in his hand than ask him to try and sleep when he's convinced he'll wake to some Indian standing over him with an axe," Artie said to Miller. "And better than having a group of men used to wearing their wives' britches getting everyone riled up and scared. Can't do much with a mob of men who aren't thinking right because they're seeing things that aren't there. Better to get them moving. And doing something. Take their mind off their troubles. They'll be so tired in a few hours they won't care about nothing much, but crawling under the covers next to their wives and getting some sleep."

So the guard was doubled, with groups of men walking about camp in the rain with shotguns. But Ella also slept with her father's gun close that night, just as Wilber kept his father's old-fashioned pistol close by and Ruby slept with hers.

It was close to midnight when Ella heard them. A small group of men on guard, passing by the shelter she shared with Clara. The men weren't speaking kindly of Indians, for they felt Indians were depriving them of their warm beds, even though there'd been no sight or sound of an Indian the whole time they'd been on Indian land. And even though it had been Artie who'd asked them to stand extra guard, to their way of thinking, this inconvenience wasn't Artie's fault or their own fault for stirring up trouble, it was all down to Indians.

*

Ella was almost asleep when the wind started up. And as the canvas sheeting on either side of their shelter blew in and out with the wind, all Ella could hope for was that the extra sheeting she'd purchased in Independence and used for ground cover would keep her mattress dry.

And as she finally fell asleep, with her dreamcatcher on her pillow, she wondered where Marrok was and if he had a warm shelter of his own somewhere in this foul weather. She wished he were back. She felt the world a safer place when he was around.

2

When the storm arrived, Marrok was in a teepee smoking a pipe before a warm fire with a chief from the Otoe people. The Otoe were a Plains tribe who lived in earth lodges, but when hunting buffalo they lived in teepees. And as the chief discussed with Marrok the changes that were happening on his lands, speaking in Chiwere, a Sioux dialect, Marrok could hear the anger in his voice.

Marrok had come upon the Otoe as they rode across the vast grasslands looking for buffalo. But this year the buffalo had not come.

They had talked to Marrok out there on the vast plains for over an hour and when the storm clouds rolled in, the men had invited Marrok to stay the night with them. He'd helped them set up their teepees and as they sat around the central fire pit and smoked pipes, eating dried meat and corn bread as the storm lashed the hide walls, Marrok wondered how long it would be before there was bloodshed. Because as long as the settlers' animals continued to graze out the prairie grass, the buffalo would go elsewhere.

These people found fish in nearby streams and rivers with plenty of deer in the woods, but they needed the buffalo to feed and clothe them, to make teepees, moccasins and tools. Marrok saw their frustration in their lean bodies, in the too-thin children, in the worn clothes.

They owned guns, but they were mostly flintlock muskets and most of them had long ago run out of powder and shot. For unlike the French and Spanish fur trappers who had traded weapons with them in years gone by, the American and European settlers now passing through their country wouldn't trade the new carbine shotguns with them.

Marrok's gaze settled on the five children lying beneath furs and blankets opposite him. They were all asleep, except for one little boy. He was about seven years old and wide awake, watching him. Marrok thought the boy too thin, his face almost gaunt. Then he turned his attention back to the men who wanted to know about this latest wagon train rolling across their lands. And when they asked to see it, Marrok was loath to take them, but better to show them the truth of it than hide what was coming.

He turned as someone passed the pipe to him and after he took a puff of it and passed it on, Marrok took the beef jerky from his bag and tossed it to the boy. The child was welcome to it and had Marrok more to give, he would have given it.

*

They sat astride their horses on a slight rise less than three miles from the wagon train. Besides Marrok, there were fifteen men. They were dressed like him, in buckskin and knee-high moccasins, the only difference were the old muskets they carried, compared to Marrok's shotgun.

Marrok heard the distant cry go up from someone far below on the wagon train. It was a cry of warning. And Marrok knew that within minutes every man would be armed, with everyone looking their way.

"It's a monstrous thing," the chief said quietly, speaking in his Sioux dialect as he looked down on the hundreds of wagons and animals. "We have been patient, for we enjoy trading with these people, but this is too much. Look how they pollute our lands. Our buffalo should be here, but our lands lie empty. And if our buffalo were here, those men would shoot them for the meat, but leave everything else behind. And besides their own waste, they leave hundreds of blackened campfires behind, having used our wood, cutting down our trees, leaving little for us. The earth cannot give back as quickly as these people take from it. It cannot be done. Soon there will be nothing left for us. My people are already going hungry, and this winter some will die from the cold. See how those women and children collect kindling from our lands and the herbs that our women need for our own cooking and healing. Our rivers and streams grow sour from their animals, and the white froth their women leave behind in the water when they wash."

The wagon train made its way slowly towards them, yet it was so long Marrok couldn't see the end of it. The wagons still travelled in that deep rutted track and the train stretched back for miles, the canvas covers above each wagon looking like some great rolling wave as they headed for the open prairies, the dust rising like some brown, misty cloud which carried no moisture.

Marrok could see people pointing at them, he could see women picking up small children and running back to the safety of the wagons. He heard more urgent cries and shouts go up and he hoped no damn fool fired a shot.

It would only take one stupid mistake like that to start a war.

"My people call this territory *Nibrathka*," the chief said with frustration. "It means *flat river* in their English, yet what will become of our *Nibrathka* once these people are finished with it. And what do they bring to my country? All I see is waste left behind them."

Marrok said nothing more, because he had no words. All he had was the truth and he was well aware that his truth might do more harm than good between these people and those on the wagon train.

But he could sympathize with these people, as could Artie. He and Artie were employed by wealthy men in the east who owned the wagon train company, but Marrok still owned Ojibwe blood while Artie was married to a Chinook woman. They were in the unenviable position to see both sides and clearly, one side was losing.

"Do you want to come down and talk to them?" Marrok asked the chief.

"Will they give me cattle to replace my buffalo?"

Marrok shook his head. "No, I don't think they will."

"Then I see no need." He turned and kicked his horse away, disappearing down the side of the hill, his men following him.

Marrok felt the wretched taste of hopelessness crawl deep within his belly and he reached for his waterskin, rinsing his mouth and spitting before taking a long drink.

Then he kicked his horse on down towards the

wagon train, to let Artie know that discontent was rising among the tribes who lived in this territory. Yet was suddenly grateful that this would be his last job as scout, because he didn't want to be around when someone lit the fuse which would blow open the powder keg.

And it would happen.

Push someone hard enough and they'll fight back.

3

Like everyone else, Ella saw Artie ride out to meet Marrok. The two men talked together for a long time, sitting astride their horses a good couple of miles from the wagon train, knowing whatever they said in confidence between the two of them, couldn't be overheard. Yet Ella thought both men looked as though they bore the weight of the world on their shoulders.

Much later, as she sat alone by her fire darning a hole in Jasper's shirt and a rip in her stockings, Marrok walked by, but he paused when he saw her sitting by herself.

"Where's your team?" he asked, stepping towards her.

Ella offered him a coffee which he accepted and as he sat on Jasper's box by the fire she poured him a mug of the hot liquid, before nodding towards her wagon.

"Martha in there. She has some nasty blisters on her heels, so Ruby and Clara are binding them with witch hazel and chamomile. Poor Martha, she can't tolerate wearing boots at the moment."

She nodded back towards the wagon circle behind them. "And Abe and Wilber are courting two sisters. I don't know how serious those boys are but I hope they know what they're doing. The family are from South Carolina, but they're heading for the Willamette Valley."

"I thought Abe and Wilber had their sights set on California?" Marrok asked.

"I did too," Ella said. "But they seem smitten by the sisters."

Marrok laughed as Ella nodded towards the

canvas tents set up some way from the wagon. "Jasper's gone to bed. But he's always up before anyone else. He pushes himself to make sure everything gets done. I don't think my team would run so well if it weren't for Jasper and I'd be the first to admit he takes the load off me."

Marrok nodded. "I like him a lot," he paused, glancing at Ella, then added softly. "Perhaps it's a good time to mention I've offered him a job working with me up in Oregon, if he doesn't want to carry on with you to California."

He saw the surprise on Ella's face, and felt a moment of regret for approaching a member of her team. "I offered him the job when I first met him back on your ranch, when he thought you were going to marry Jebediah Crawley and he had no-where else to go. It was before you decided to come west with me and Martha. Anyway, I don't think he'll leave you, but he's got another option if things don't work out for him in California."

Ella wasn't sure to be angry or grateful to Marrok. In the end she shrugged off her annoyance. "He'll do what's best for him I hope, but I'd hate to lose him. He's part of the family."

"How's Martha coping with her new family?"

Ella smiled. "She's loving it. She won't say it, but I think she's exhausted by the little ones. They're all abed, so she hobbled over to join us for a coffee and a piece of blueberry cake. Clara made it earlier after we had a share of blueberries from a huge wild patch someone found yesterday. You've never tasted anything so delicious, Marrok."

She offered him a slice of the cake and as Marrok ate it, he glanced back at Willard's camp.

Only a couple of Willard's men were still up sitting around the fire. Everyone else had gone to bed. He turned back to Ella, licking his fingers.

"And how are you coping Ella? With the early morning starts and long walks?"

She shrugged. "I'm used to getting up early because of the ranch. And I'm lucky I have Billy or Bear to ride, so it hasn't been too hard. Which I'm grateful for, believe me."

They turned as they heard the women climbing out of Ella's wagon, holding up their long skirts and trying to be quiet, aware that a lot of people were asleep. Martha was limping, walking on her toes in her stocked feet. She grimaced in pain as she came and sat down beside him.

"My poor heels!" she said, showing him the wrappings on her feet where Clara and Ruby had bound them, hiding the raw wounds. "Mine are bad, but there's a lot of others suffering blisters worse than mine. Someone said witch hazel and chamomile are the best to treat them, so hopefully it works."

They talked for a little about their days, how they were finding life on the trail and after complimenting Clara on her cake Marrok finished his coffee and made a move to leave.

"I'd best get to bed myself. I've got another early start in the morning." He wished them goodnight, then he was gone.

When Clara and Ruby stood up to go to their beds, for the first time since they left St Louis, Ella and Martha found themselves alone. And as Martha threw her dregs of coffee in the fire, she saw Ella glance back towards Marrok's camp.

"Don't stare too hard, girl," Martha whispered. "There's a lot of folk on this train who'd like nothing better than a bit of gossip. Don't be the first to give it to them. If you want a man, keep away from Marrok, for one like that will bring you nothing but trouble. He's not a man to settle, just remember that. Look to Pierce Calderson or Moss Weslock if you want a good man. Both are hard workers and you wouldn't go far wrong with either of them."

Ella thought of Pierce Calderson. In his early thirties, a stocky thickset man, he was heading to the Willamette Valley to set up a blacksmith shop. He was decent enough, but Ella couldn't see herself settling with him. Besides, there was something about Pierce that made Ella think he wouldn't take too kindly to being tied down, or being scolded by a wife, or harassed by children. But if he was inclined to marry there were enough girls watching him because like Martha said, he was a hard worker and ambitious. It just wouldn't be with Ella.

"You're being ridiculous Aunt, if you think I'm interested in Marrok," she said, hurt by Martha's words. "He's my friend. I can never repay him for what he's done for me. As for Pierce and Moss, you're wasting your time if you think you can match me with them. Or anyone else for that matter. I just escaped a wedding. I've got no inclinations to get involved with anyone this early in the journey."

Martha shook her head in despair, then stood up to kiss Ella goodnight as Abe and Wilber arrived back in camp. The brothers took a slice of the blueberry cake then said goodnight and went to their beds. But as Martha limped back to the wagon she shared with her grandchildren, she looked over at Marrok's camp. She liked him well enough, indeed, she respected him for all he'd done for her and Ella. But she saw nothing but misery ahead if the girl became involved with him, yet how did she stop something that might have already started.

*

Ella remained by the fire, stung by her aunt's words when Ruby appeared in the glow of the dying coals. She moved to sit beside Ella, her face red from washing in cold water.

"I thought you'd gone to bed," Ella said softly, as the whole camp now settled for the night. Other than the men on guard duty, they were among the last to still be up.

"I heard what Martha said to you," Ruby said, her voice nothing more than a whisper. "And she has no right, Ella! For I know Marrok likes you, indeed everyone knows it, including Martha, but she's just worried she'll lose you, that you'll head off to Oregon with him and she'll never see you again. I can see it in her eyes when the two of you are together, because he singles you out over everyone else. I think if you were to invite him for supper every night, he'd come, I'm sure of it."

"Oh, hush now Ruby. You're being foolish to talk on such things. He's a good man, who saw I needed help. That's all. More than likely he feels sorry for me, for out of all these wagons I'm the only single woman taking a wagon west by myself. And I would imagine he feels some responsibility towards me, for it was Marrok who invited me along on this journey in the first place."

Ruby laughed, but it wasn't a laugh full of joy. Instead it was low, soft in the quiet of the night and Ella couldn't mistake the sarcasm.

"You cannot see it, but I saw it within hours of meeting you. Even then he had eyes only for you. But I'll say no more on the matter, for I see it upsets you." She patted Ella on the arm then left to go to bed.

Ella didn't believe what Ruby said, but as she reached over to stir the hot embers of the coals, she became aware that Jasper and the brothers lay less than fifteen feet from her in their shelters. And beyond them lay other shelters, where men and women slept. There was no privacy here, with whispers and gossip already spreading about the state of some folk's marriages, the single men and women falling in love, the misbehaved children.

But as she thought on Martha's words, Ella began to feel uneasy sitting there alone, so she damped down what remained of the fire then went to bed. But as she lay under her blankets unable to sleep, Marrok filled her thoughts and she couldn't help but reach out to pull back the canvas to look across to his camp.

He was damping down the coals of his own fire and Ella watched as he crawled under his blankets. But as he lay on his back, his arms behind his head, he glanced over towards her shelter.

He couldn't possibly see her, but instinctively Ella moved back, stunned that he should seek her out.

And all she could hear was Ruby's words. *He singles you out over everyone else.*

*

She was reminded of Ruby's words almost a week later when Marrok rode into camp late one afternoon. And as he rode along the length of the wagon train looking for Artie, he passed Ella.

"How are you?" he called, before riding across and reining in his horse.

She pulled Billy up, surprised by the beard on his jaw, but he'd been gone for almost five days and clearly hadn't bothered to shave. He asked after Martha. "Is she faring a little better with her blisters?"

Ella nodded. "She is. But she's been riding in the wagon most days to let them heal."

Marrok noticed the cloth tied around Ella's left hand and nodded towards it. "What happened to you?"

"I reached for the coffee pot this morning forgetting to use a cloth," she said, feeling the dull ache from the burn. "I broke the skin rather badly, but it's nothing that won't heal in time."

Marrok swerved his horse closer to her own and held out his hand. "It can be serious if an infection sets in. Let me see?"

She unraveled the cloth and showed him the angry red welt. He reached out to take her hand, even as Ella felt people watching them, as the wagons continued to roll on by. Yet she was also conscious of how small her hand was within his own and as Marrok ran his thumb gently around the burn, he whispered something in a language Ella didn't know, before abruptly letting her hand go.

"What did you say?" she asked in surprise, as she covered the wound with the cloth.

"I took the burn away."

Ella stared at him, even as Marrok smiled. "Some tribes believe in it. If someone takes away the burn, it stops the pain and starts the healing. I've just done that for you. But as it heals, don't pop the blister. Let your body take the fluid back into itself. It's all nourishment. And once the fluid is gone, rub some honey into the wound so it doesn't leave a scar."

"You don't use lard on the burn?" she asked, startled by his suggestion.

He smiled and shook his head. "Putting lard on the burn will feed it and leave an ugly scar."

Ella nodded, unnerved by his dark eyes. Then he nodded politely. "I'd best get moving. Please give Martha and your team my regards."

And then he rode off to find Artie. Ella flexed her hand, aware of the heat where his thumb had touched her. She blinked, sure that she was imagining it, but it seemed the hurt of the burn had dulled, just a little.

June 1846

1

A month into their journey they were hit with a storm that left the wagon train bogged down for days. When the rains finally stopped, men spent hours digging mud out from beneath wagon wheels while women tried to get bed linen and clothing dry, leaving everyone short tempered and tired. And even after all that hard work, the wagons only moved a few miles that day with animals and wagon wheels continuously getting bogged down in the wet ground.

It was during the storm that Ella and her team discovered Ruby was terrified of thunder and lightning. For as the thunder boomed overhead on that first night, with shafts of lightning illuminating the prairie as if it were day, Ruby burst into the shelter which Clara and Ella shared.

"What on earth's the matter?" Ella cried, as Ruby crawled between the canvas flaps.

"I loathe storms. I'm so afraid of them. Can I stay here with you for a little while? Just until the thunder stops?"

"What?" Clara asked, pulling her blankets back so Ruby could crawl in between her and Ella. "A child like you frightened of storms? But you ain't afraid of nothing! What's a little thunder to you girl?"

"And it's damp here," Ella said, as the water tracked beneath the canvas sheeting.

"Well, it damp inside the wagon as well," Ruby said, pulling their blankets over her. "Tell me something of yourselves, anything you like, just to take my mind off it." She cringed as another crack of thunder boomed overhead. "I don't even care if you make it up, just talk to me."

Ella glanced at Clara, but the older woman just shook her head then rolled over and went back to sleep. Ella paused, then began to speak of her childhood. She told Ruby about her mother's death from fever, of helping her father out in the fields alongside Jasper. She spoke a little of Quentin's illness and of Milton's arrival at the ranch. She told Ruby how much she'd hated her uncle and his plan to marry her off to Jebediah Crawley. And lastly, she spoke of Marrok and his sudden arrival at the ranch and her decision to leave with him and Martha for Independence.

Ruby listened in rapt silence until Ella finished. "I can't begin to imagine your childhood," she said. "It sounds idyllic. I never knew my mother. From what I've been told she died not long after I was born. I have nothing of hers, not even a small portrait, so I don't even know what she looked like. But when I was about thirteen, I found a letter in one of her drawers, which made me think she didn't die at all but ran off with another man. I didn't dare ask my father, but it would explain his bitterness and why there was nothing in the house which showed she'd ever lived there," she paused as the sky lit up with lightning and Ruby counted before the thunder boomed overhead. She cowered under the blankets, then looked over at Ella.

"Do you want me to keep talking or do you want to go to sleep," she asked, sounding like a child, her voice muffled by the blanket.

"You can keep talking. I'll never sleep in this storm," Ella said, shaking her head. "I don't know how Clara can."

Ruby nodded then reached out to take Ella's hand. "Like you, I grew up with my father, but I rarely saw him. He left the house early, came home very late, leaving me to be raised by nannies and governesses. I only saw him when he needed to parade me in front of his wealthy friends at supper parties. When you talk of your father, it sounds like you were loved. I never was. I was a possession, nothing more," Ruby cowered again as another shot of lightning lit the sky followed by more thunder. She waited for a few minutes, before continuing.

"My father never remarried after my mother's death, but he had other women. Sometimes they came to the house and stayed a few days, then I never saw them again. Just before I turned eighteen, he met with me in our grand dining room. It was all very formal. He suggested I marry the son of one of his friends, a family I wasn't particularly fond of. They were wealthy and powerful, but they weren't nice people. So I refused. Which is when the war between my father and I came out into the open. He no longer bothered to hide his loathing of me, saying I should have been born male and I should make myself useful for once in my life and marry this young man and give him a grandson. After that comment, I began to plan my escape. Better to leave with my dignity and some of my inheritance, than be thrown out on the street with nothing."

"Will he ever give up looking for you?"

Ruby shook her head. "I don't know."

That night was the only time Ruby ever spoke of her father or her privileged upbringing. She never mentioned him again, nor her life in New York. And in the days and months ahead when Ella saw her laughing, or dancing with someone, or singing before the whole wagon train when the fiddles were brought out, she understood that Ruby took pleasure in the simple things because she'd never had them and they might be gone on the morrow.

Sometimes Ella caught sight of Marrok watching Ruby when she sang and like every other man in the company there was a stillness about him as he listened to her. During these moments it could have been so easy to be jealous of Ruby because she seemed to have it all, even though Ella now knew differently. So when it seemed as if the girl demanded you like her, when she clamored for attention, for love, Ella didn't mind at all, because she was quickly coming to love this girl.

2

Ella thought the rain was the worst, while others argued it was the dust. With the rain came the damp, with wet and dirty laundry crowding the wagons and restless children kept inside an already overcrowded space and exhausted men digging for hours to try and free the wheels of mud.

But the dust seemed to get into everything. It left a fine film over food and supplies, over the wagons and animals and it got into people's ears, noses and mouths. On the worst days, before the wagons had a chance to spread out and get away from that cloying brown cloud, everyone would tie scarves around their mouths and noses to avoid breathing it in.

One night around Ella's campfire, a discussion started on which was worse. Several of her neighbors in the wagon circle she shared, began to argue over it in good humor. Most of the men decided the rain was the worst, because of the mud, when the wagons came to a standstill.

But the women agreed it was the dust, because the rain at least allowed them precious days of rest and gave them extra water to do washing and bath dirty children. Whereas the dust soiled everything, even getting into the pores of everyone's skin.

Ella watched Marrok as he sided with the men, deciding the rain was the worst. He'd arrived back in camp that afternoon, after being away for several days. He hadn't yet had time to shave and he looked rugged and wild, but as his wagons shared Ella's wagon circle along with Artie and Willard, he'd come over to join the group for a coffee and the discussion.

"Wait until you get up north where the rain holds a bite to it," he said, smiling at the women. "Then you'll wish for the dust."

There was a lot of good natured debate over this and Ella laughed as she listened, leaning into Ruby as she agreed with the women. The dust was definitely the worst.

August 1846

1

He reined in his horse and turned in the saddle, trying to hear them, to see how far behind they were. Two miles, perhaps a little more, but close enough to run him down. His horse stamped its hooves, nervously prancing about, but like Marrok he was well aware of the pack of wolves hunting them down.

Marrok kicked the horse on, knowing his only chance to lose them was to head for the prairies, to ride for open ground, because the wolves wouldn't venture out from under cover of the trees.

He rode the horse hard, hoping the animal didn't blow out, but they'd been running since they came across the pack high in the hills more than five miles back, with the pack's huge, black alpha male chasing him down with the others following close behind.

Marrok thought he'd lost them when he rode along the bed of a wide stream, but they'd once again picked up the horse's scent. But that half hour had given his horse a break and given Marrok a precious lead, but with the horse now tiring, they would be an easy kill.

He came upon a long deep gully with trees towering above him and lush green ferns covering the forest floor. Running through the gully was another stream. Marrok reined his horse in and looked east, back towards the prairie. He might not make it because it lay a good mile away, but if he could fool the wolves again and enter that water, he might have a chance.

He rode down into the gully, feeling the absolute stillness of the place until he entered the stream, then the splashing of the water around the horse's fetlocks seemed to echo in that silent world. When the gully widened, with the ferns less dense here, he saw a slope a quarter mile away that would take him back up into the woods. But as he rode on, a movement ahead of him made him look up, even as he reached for his shotgun. But it wasn't a wolf.

He thought he imagined it at first, not quite believing what he was seeing, but yes, there she was, standing on the edge of the stream, looking back at him. A little girl, no more than four years old. And then she uttered a soft cry of hopelessness.

Marrok reined the horse in, giving the animal precious moments to drink from the stream, while he searched the ancient trees surrounding him. If her family had been here, they weren't now. He turned and looked behind him, listening for the wolves, but for the moment, he'd lost them. But they would come, he knew it.

He looked back at the child, thinking how quiet it was in this place, as if time stood still, the little girl's soft whimpers almost otherworldly. But she was no ghost. She whimpered again, her small hand going to her dirty face, the tears leaving a clear path down her cheeks. Marrok kicked the horse on, calling to her in one of the local dialects, feeling the sweat dry on his shirt, aware he didn't have much time.

He'd almost reached her when he heard the haunting cry lift above the trees less than a mile behind him. It was the howl of a wolf and it sent shivers down his spine. He turned back to the little girl and saw she'd heard it too. Terrified, she stumbled instinctively towards him, but Marrok didn't dare dismount. Desperate now to get moving, he kicked the horse on towards her then reached down and grabbed the back of her shift and lifted her up. She screamed as he swung her towards him.

She was as light as a babe, yet he couldn't give her his saddle because he needed to ride hard and fast, so he held her high against his shoulder.

"You're safe now, little one. Can you be brave and hold on tight?" he asked.

She nodded, yet the tears coursed silently down her dirt covered face. Marrok took the reins in one hand, then yelled at his horse to move on, kicking him out of the stream towards the slope, then back into the woods before riding hard for the open prairie. The little girl made not a murmur, intuitively understanding the urgency as she folded into him, her small hands gripping his buckskin shirt as she curved into the hardness of his body, her limbs seeming boneless, which made it easier for Marrok to hold her.

And then the prairie was before them, even as Marrok saw the pack come up on his right, and then others racing alongside him on his left, snarling, lunging to bite at his horse's legs and then at last they were out of the trees and galloping across those vast grasslands.

Marrok only turned back to look behind him when the sweat ran off his horse and the animal blew with exhaustion. The pack stood less than half a mile behind him, more than fifteen of them, pacing restlessly, deciding whether to chase him down.

But the horse had had enough, so Marrok reined him in. It was time to take a stand and there was no better place to do it, than right here.

Without taking his eyes off the alpha wolf, Marrok dismounted with the girl in his arms, putting her gently on the ground before reaching for his shotgun. Then he put one foot on his reins to keep the spooked horse from running, before aiming the gun above the wolves' heads and firing.

His horse bucked wildly while the little girl screamed and curled into a tight ball, her arms over her head and her legs drawn up to her chest, but the wolves turned and fled back into the trees.

Marrok stood there for long minutes, watching the trees as he petted his horse to settle him down then he moved to crouch by the girl who looked up at him in terror, her dirty little face wet with tears.

"I'm a friend," he said softly. "You have no reason to fear me, little one."

2

Ella always remembered the moment Marrok rode in with the little girl, because it seemed that moment was the catalyst for everything that had gone wrong.

They had been travelling for over two months when they dug the first of several graves. They also had their first accidents, both caused by fatigue and carelessness.

Four babies had been born since they left Independence, all of them delivered successfully in the back of wagons with the help of two midwives who were travelling with the company.

But as another young woman of eighteen struggled in labor, a little boy standing too close to his parent's campfire tipped over a pot of boiling water, badly scalding his arm. A doctor travelling with the wagon train was treating the horrific injury and perhaps because of this, along with everyone's fatigue and the young woman's struggle to deliver her babe, a black cloud seemed to descend over camp.

By the second day of the teenage girl's labor, as the doctor and midwives agreed it would be a breech birth, it became clear to everyone who lived close enough to the girl's wagon and heard her low cries of distress, that this was not going to end well. As dawn broke on the third day, Artie asked the girl's young husband to leave their wagon where it was, to give her privacy, as the rest of the company moved on.

Artie and Miller stayed with the young husband that night, not only to stand guard for the wagon sat all alone out there on the prairie, but to offer him support as the two midwives and doctor attended the young mother.

The baby didn't survive the birth. Artie and Miller helped the grieving young father dig the little boy's grave beside the trail and when the wagon caught up to the company the following day, the young mother kept to her bed. But within days word spread around camp that she had a fever.

"That girl just pushed too long and too hard," Nell Weslock said to Martha and Ella around the campfire that night. "Now she's got rips and tears inside and out that ain't healing. She's got no hope of fighting infection like that."

"Well, don't know about that," Martha said. "She's young enough to fight it off. But I heard she's still bleeding bad, likely got some afterbirth left inside. And that's not going to help her, no matter which way you look at it."

Less than a week later the young mother died. Artie said some prayers over the grave as the whole company gathered, then a small wooden cross made by one of the carpenters was hammered into the hard earth. The young woman's name and age were scrawled on it in charcoal.

"Shame she couldn't be buried with her baby," one woman murmured beside Ella.

Ella wished she'd just kept quiet and said nothing.

Then Marrok rode in with the girl, the same day the company had their first wagon accident.

Ella had been walking with Ruby, Clara and Martha and her three grandchildren when they heard a man scream. Everyone turned as men shouted for wagons to stop, for less than half a mile back a wagon had pitched over onto its side, the four oxen bellowing with distress as they were pulled down, the harnesses around their necks twisting dangerously.

Abe and Wilber ran back to see if they could help while Jasper climbed down off the buckboard to join Ella.

"What on earth's happened?" Martha asked, pulling her bonnet down low over her eyes to shade them against the glare of the summer day.

"Looks like his front wheel's gone into a pothole," Jasper said. "Never saw it myself. But looks like the soil loosened from all the wagons gone on before. Now it's done gone and broke his front axle."

It could have happened to any one of the wagons before or after, but it had happened to a young couple already struggling. The husband was homesick for his family on the east coast and had never taken to life on the trail and to add to his misery, his wife and child had been sleeping in the back of the wagon as they tried to shake off a fever.

Ella never said it, but she wondered if he'd fallen asleep while holding the reins. Because what other reason was there for him not to see the hole opening up in the road ahead.

"I hope there's no broken bones," Ruby said, as they heard the mother and child screaming inside the wagon. "They must have taken a bad fall when that wagon went over."

"Oh, that poor family," Constance said, a hand on her belly, as she joined them to see what had happened.

"Lord above, I'd rather cook and clean than

have to deal with all that mess," Martha said, as the oxen were unharnessed and dozens of men pushed the wagon upright before taking the wheel off the broken axle.

The family had suffered nothing more than bruising and shock, but like Jasper had said, the front axle was broken. Artie made the decision to stop the wagon train there for the night, so wagons were moved into circles and animals unharnessed and left to graze while men returned to work on the damaged wagon.

But as late afternoon turned to dusk, as coffee beans were roasted and children settled for the night, Marrok rode in with the girl. He hadn't even reined his horse in before a crowd had gathered.

3

The child was sitting in his saddle, looking tiny before Marrok, who sat behind her on the rump of his horse. He held her close, one arm wrapped around her so she didn't fall off. He'd managed to wash away some of the grime covering her, but her buckskin shift and moccasins were still filthy and her arms and legs looked fragile as they poked out from beneath the shift.

Artie hurried towards them, pushing his way through the crowd and only then did Ella see fear cross the child's face. She leaned back instinctively into Marrok, seeking his protection and Ella watched as he put his other hand gently on the girl's shoulder to quiet her.

"Dear Lord, where on earth did he find her?" Martha murmured in astonishment.

"She looks half starved," Clara added.

"And no older than Archer," Constance said.

Marrok dismounted and as he reached up to lift the child down from his saddle, Ella heard her whimper, even as her little arms reached out to grab Marrok around his neck.

He spoke to her rapidly in a guttural language, holding her close, as Artie strode towards them. Ella watched along with everyone else as Marrok and Artie spoke together in low measured tones, until the two deputies approached.

Artie turned to look at the two men and Ella was shocked by the anger on his face.

Again he spoke urgently to Marrok and then Miller spoke, his voice raised, allowing everyone who stood nearby to hear his words.

"Arapaho? But you know as well as Artie how

they feel about us moving across their lands! Goddamit, you'll bring the whole darn nation down on our heads, Marrok. What the hell were you thinking? Damn it, this will start a war because you know they'll come looking for her and how do we explain it!"

"I couldn't leave her behind!" Marrok said, his voice raised in anger, allowing everyone who stood nearby to hear him. "She wouldn't have lasted another hour, not with that pack of wolves on my tail. She's damned lucky I saw her at all for another quarter mile in either direction and I would have missed her."

Clara moved towards Ella. "Poor little thing, she looks half starved. We got a little rice and beans left over from our meal if she wants some of it."

"Go on mother," Constance said, gently pushing Martha forward. "Bring her over here. She doesn't look like she's eaten in days."

"I'll come with you," Ella said.

They walked across to where the men now talked in lower tones, their anger gone, aware of the crowd around them.

Marrok still held the child in his arms, her face turned into his buckskin shirt so she couldn't see the people staring at her.

The men turned as Martha and Ella stepped forward.

"This isn't a good time, Mrs Wilbyrne." Artie said, a hardness to his words.

Martha nodded. "I can see that, I got eyes Mr Dalbert. What we came for is the girl. If you want, we'll take care of her until you work out what you're doing. Ella's got some supper left over if the girl wants beans and rice."

"Well, she can't stay with Marrok! Or me for that matter!" Artie let out a loud sigh. "Yes, please, that would be very kind of you."

He turned to the crowd, suddenly aware of the murmurs rising, some of which turned his blood to ice with the ugliness of them.

"Come on folks, move on, there's nothing more to see here."

He stood and watched as people drifted away then turned as Marrok put the child down and once again spoke to her in that guttural language, before pointing to Martha and Ella. The girl nodded, but continued to lean into him.

"Come on child, let's get you fed and settled for the night," Martha said, holding out her hand. "And give you a good hot wash because you sure ain't cuddling up to me in them dirty clothes."

Again those guttural words and then finally the child reached out to take Martha's hand. Ella left with them but as she glanced back at Marrok, as he turned to speak to Artie and the two deputies, she thought he looked beyond exhausted.

*

"So where'd you find her?" Artie asked, his hands on his hips.

"Up in the woods, about seventy miles to the north west. She said her family were hunting deer when they were attacked by Kiowa. When her mother sent her deeper into the woods to hide, it seems she got lost. She doesn't know if any of them survived. But we better go carefully Artie if the Kiowa are on the warpath. It won't take much to have others join them. You know how tribes are feeling these days. It isn't about trading with us anymore, because so many of them are going hungry and they got nothing to trade anyway," Marrok paused and ran his hands through his hair in frustration before looking back at his friend and the two deputies.

"I understand your anger," he said to Miller. "But I couldn't leave her there, not with that pack of wolves on my tail. One sniff of her and she'd have been torn to pieces right behind me. By the look of her, I reckon she's been alone for days although she had the sense to stay by the stream."

"If her family are still alive after that battle with the Kiowa, you know they'll come looking for her Marrok," Artie said, his anger gone. "You know that better than anyone, that most tribes go back for those left behind. Doesn't matter who it is, man, woman or child, they'll go looking for them."

Marrok nodded. "Well, we'll find out soon enough for we'll be passing by those woods within the week."

"What happens if they're all dead? What do you plan to do with her then?" Joe asked.

Marrok glanced at Artie, feeling his friend's grey eyes on him. "She'll got north with me to Oregon."

Artie said nothing for a moment, then he nodded. "Yes, I guess she will," he said, turning to look north. "And the Chinook will take her. They'll raise her as their own."

*

Ella discovered later that night that the child's name was Nigamo-nii'eihii, because she asked Marrok if he knew the girl's name when he came across to her camp to see how the child was doing.

"The closest meaning I can give you in English is *bird that sings*," Marrok said, watching as Clara rocked the child to sleep in her arms by the fire.

The little girl was wrapped in a blanket and wore a pair of Ella's thick winter socks, because Martha had insisted on washing the girl's filthy shift and moccasins.

"She seems to have taken to you Clara," Marrok said, watching as the little girl slept.

"Well, I's know how it feels to be left all alone, so this baby must have been right scared, poor child. I ain't never met any Indians 'afore this one but I think she's just fine, like any other baby lost without her mama. So doan't you worry none about her, Mr Marrok. She's safe here with us. Ain't no-one goin' to hurt this baby while I'm watchin' out for her."

Marrok looked across at Ella as she offered him a coffee, but he shook his head.

"I'd better go and see my men before they go to bed. I've hardly had a chance to talk to them since I got back," he paused then rubbed his eyes.

"Can you thank Martha for me as well? I know she's helped you both with the child," he paused to look at the little girl. "I found her by a stream. By the state of her, I reckon she'd been there for a few days, as you saw from the state of her clothes. But at least her instincts kept her by water, otherwise she might have died."

"Well, she's fine now," Clara said, bending down to kiss the sleeping child on the forehead.

Marrok thanked them again then left them to return to his own camp, suddenly thinking of Ella stepping into the kitchen back at her ranch in her wedding dress.

And Clara, looking worn out when he first saw her in the saloon back in St Louis.

Now here they were living together, taking care of a lost Indian child.

Fate was a strange thing, he thought.

4

Artie made the decision the following morning to leave the damaged wagon behind. The nearest woods were seventy miles to the north where Marrok had found the Arapaho girl and Artie wasn't sending men all that way to cut down a tree and bring it back to make an axle. That would hold the wagon train up for two weeks or more and by then other trains would be on their tail.

Friends of the young couple offered to carry their mattresses and supplies in their own wagons, while the damaged wagon was taken apart for parts and sold to whoever bid the highest price for them.

The wagon's canvas cover would be used as shelter for the young family, all the way to California. Four of their six oxen were sold off, and what remained of the couple's possessions after friends helped with the rest, were secured to the back of the two oxen they kept. Then they set off on foot.

The week rolled on by but as the wagon train headed closer to the woods where Marrok had found Nigamo-nii'eihii, allegations against him for bringing the child into camp grew louder and more vicious. Those careless, angry words spoken aloud by Miller had stirred up trouble, so that everyone felt the simmering undercurrent coming from one group of settlers.

To help settle folks down, Artie called a halt earlier than usual one afternoon and after supper, called on the fiddlers to play something lively. Abe and Wilber went off to dance, while Ruby got up to sing a few songs.

But Clara and Ella stayed by their campfire with

Jasper and Nigamo-nii'eihii. It was well after dark when Marrok appeared and asked if he could join them, accepting a cup of coffee and a hot biscuit not long out of the Dutch oven.

"Why aren't you dancing?" he asked Ella, surprised to see her there and not with Ruby.

"She's here because she doan't like what some folks are saying about you, that's the truth of it," said Clara.

Marrok looked at Clara in astonishment, taken aback by her honesty but Ella just shrugged.

"In all truth Marrok, I think people are being unreasonable," she said. "I would have done the same thing had I been you."

Jasper leaned towards him. "Go on now, you go dance with Miss Ella and show them folks that you did the right thing bringin' this child back here. You got nothin' to be ashamed of."

Marrok thought on it a moment then shook his head, turning to Ella. "I know you'd be up for the challenge, but I wouldn't put you through something like that. Taking sides with me might earn you a few enemies and you don't want that following you to California."

Ella laughed, suddenly seeing a way she could finally repay Marrok. "Well, what do I care about enemies! Don't you remember how I dealt with Jebediah Crawley and my uncle? You were right there beside me Marrok, encouraging me every step of the way. So!" she laughed again and stood up. "Let's go dance!"

Marrok looked at her in bewilderment for a moment then smiled and stood up. They made their way in silence past the wagons to where the dancing was taking place, aware of people watching them. Most folk smiled and nodded to them, others looked at them with curiosity to see Ella stepping out with the wagon train's scout, but a large group of people looked at Marrok with dislike.

But when Marrok pulled Ella into his arms, she forgot about everything but him. He was a good dancer. His large body moved easily with the rhythm and when the music came to an end, he stepped back, as Ella brushed hair off her face, feeling flushed as she met his gaze and again, as before, she felt drawn to him, as if something bound her to him. And then the music began again, a slower tune.

Marrok said not a word but simply held out his arms and stepped towards her. Ella didn't hesitate, but went to him. They didn't speak as they danced, but as he turned her around so that Ella walked under his raised arm, Ruby passed them on the arm of another man. And all Ella thought of then was what Ruby had said all those weeks ago. *He singles you out over everyone else.* Well in this case he hadn't, because it had been Jasper who'd urged them to dance.

When the music came to an end, Marrok took a step back and thanked her, then he laughed, speaking softly as he leaned towards her. "I think we might have done it. No-one's taking any notice of me."

They turned to leave the dancers but as they stepped out of the light of the lamps set on the side of the wagons, Ella saw Ruby get swept up to dance by another man.

"Look at her," she said with longing. "She does everything with an ease and grace. She's beautiful, has an easy laugh, dances like a dream, sings like an angel and has every woman wanting to be like her and every man wanting to be with her."

"Well, perhaps not every man," Marrok said, softly.

Ella turned to find him looking at her and as she held his gaze she felt a sudden, overwhelming urge to step forward and kiss him, as though it were the most natural thing in the world.

Except Marrok turned away from her, to look back at the people dancing, to watch Ruby. Ella felt crushed by that, by his turning away from her.

But then he spoke, his voice so low that Ella moved closer to hear him.

"I know very little about Ruby's past," he said, as Ruby took another man as her partner. "But from what she told me in St Louis, it seems she's quite alone in the world so compared to most women here, her life seems almost carefree. She has no money worries, she doesn't have to do chores if she doesn't want to and she has no-one to answer to."

Marrok paused and at last he turned back to Ella. But this time she saw something else in his eyes, something she didn't understand. She might have said it was a softness, but whatever it was, it took away some of that hardness he owned.

"But did you ever think that the reason she glows with happiness is that for the first time in a very long time, she feels safe? Which is all because of you, Ella. As for her looks and her dancing and everything else, other than her singing, I believe you her equal."

Ella said nothing, stunned by his words. Then Marrok glanced back towards their wagons way over in the other circle.

"Are you staying here to dance? Or may I walk you home?"

"You may walk me home," she said, feeling dazed by what he'd said.

Marrok smiled and held out his arm, allowing Ella to reach up and grasp it with her hand so she could lean into him, like she'd done in St Louis. And it felt so right to be like that, to be beside him, to feel his warmth and strength, that Ella didn't want to let him go. So she walked slower, making his long legs almost stumble as he changed his stride.

She glanced up at him and wished he would talk, because she wanted to know everything about him. But he remained silent. So she asked him about the Arapaho child.

"What's that language I hear you speaking with her?"

Marrok glanced at her, surprised she asked it. "It's an Algonquian dialect, similar to that spoken by my mother's people. Yet why do you ask, Ella?"

She shrugged, thinking she might be in love with him. "I'm interested, that's all," she said. "Just how many languages do you speak?"

Marrok thought on it a moment. "My mother's Ojibwe dialect of course, along with French and English. And enough Spanish to get by. I also speak three other Indian dialects fluently."

"Then you are an educated man," Ella said, teasing him. "The way you handled my business in

St Louis proves it, yet now I find you can speak several languages, when I know only one."

"Well, some might argue that point about me being an educated man, but my grandfather was certainly educated. He taught me how to read and write. I could hunt and track small animals when I was barely old enough to leave my mother's side. So I'm accomplished in a lot of things, but perhaps not educated as some here might think," he smiled and glanced down at her as they stepped into the shadows of their own wagon circle.

They made their way around the animals and headed for Ella's wagon, passing Artie's team, then Marrok's, then Moss and Nell's and finally Willard's camp. They saw Clara and Jasper talking together by the fire, with Nigamo-nii'eihii still asleep in Clara's arms.

Marrok stepped away, releasing Ella's hand. "I thank you again, not only for helping me out tonight but for taking care of the child. Indeed, I would suggest that all debts are paid in full." He smiled, his face once again becoming soft, and handsome. "Sleep well, Ella. I'll see you in the morning."

Ella was disappointed he didn't kiss her, but such an act would have caused gossip to swirl from one end of the wagon train to the other. She watched him disappear across the darkened circle towards his own wagons, but knew that her helping with the little girl and dancing with him tonight was a small price to pay for what he'd done for her.

5

In the following week Nigamo-nii'eihii settled into life with Ella's team well enough, but she uttered not one word to anyone but Marrok. Ella and Clara communicated with her by using a crude form of sign language and most of the time they got on well enough with that. But sometimes during the night when Nigamo-nii'eihii whimpered in her sleep, Ella or Clara would reach out and pull the child into their arms.

During the day she would walk hand in hand with Clara, or sometimes Clara would carry her on her back which made the little girl laugh. Some days the child would ride with Ella, sitting in the saddle as she had with Marrok while Ella sat on the rump of the horse, holding the child secure before her. On these days Ella would ride Bear, because he was older and more placid.

Most people on the wagon train accepted Nigamo-nii'eihii as part of their community, but a small group still harbored ill feelings about her being there. They wanted her gone. Because of it, tensions between Marrok and those families continued to escalate.

"Watch yourself, Marrok," Artie warned him one day. "I don't like the mood of those men. It's like they're taking their frustrations out on you and they're breeding a lot of unease among some folk and I'm not happy about it." He shook his head. "All this nonsense over a little girl! But I take some blame for that because I handled her arrival here badly, as did Miller, and I regret that, but I can't unchange what happened. All I'm saying is, you be darn careful, for the way I seen those boys look at you suggests they mean you violence. I don't like it, but until I got cause to tell them to back off, I can't say nothing."

But Artie was worried enough to start watching out for Marrok when he was in camp, because he knew feelings this strong could escalate into something ugly. He was almost relieved when Marrok rode off to scout.

Marrok had been gone for two days when the wagon train stopped and set up camp by a river. It was surrounded by deep woodland which swept away to the north to meet up with the forest where Marrok had found Nigamo-nii'eihii almost a week earlier.

When he rode back into camp that night, towards dusk, Ella was inside her wagon going through her supplies with Clara. She stopped to watch him through the raised calico curtain as he dismounted, then saw him glance over towards her wagon. She held his gaze, then he smiled and nodded before turning to acknowledge his men as they approached to talk to him.

"He's a mighty fine lookin' man, Miss Ella," Clara said softly. "And only interested in one gal, far as I can tell. But we ain't got time to stand and look on handsome men. At this rate, Ruby will want her bed before we's finished here."

But as Ella bent down to pick up a box and open it, to check on the state of the flour inside, she couldn't help but look back at Marrok. One of his men had taken his horse to water and brush down as Marrok headed for the river. Over his shoulder was a blanket, a clean shirt and pants.

But as Ella watched him, a movement on the

other side of the circle caught her attention and she saw a man moving into the shadows of his own wagon to watch Marrok. Ella recognized him as one of the men who had been causing trouble. When she saw him grin, before turning and hurrying off, she stood up, feeling the hairs raised on the back of her neck.

"They doan't like Mr Marrok much those folk," Clara said softly.

Ella turned and found Clara watching another group of men. They were standing some distance away in the wagon circle behind their own and when the man who Ella had been watching walked over to them and said something, the men all laughed before looking down towards the river.

"Can you finish this by yourself Clara? I have to go find Artie."

"Sure thing, Miss Ella. But you better hurry yourself about it. Those men out there are sure lookin' for trouble."

6

Marrok found a private area shaded by trees about half a mile downstream. Here the river separated, for a bank of silt had built up in the middle, leaving a deep pool before the river carried on. The pool was on the other side of the silt bank, away from where the animals were watered and where women did their washing.

He pulled off his travel stained buckskin clothes then knelt at the river's edge to scrub them with silt off the river bottom before throwing them over some brush to dry. Then he entered the water, feeling the coolness of it against his hot skin as he swam out to its center, swimming across the silt bank to enter the pool.

It wasn't deep, only as high as his waist but deep enough to let him dive below the surface, reaching for river grit to scrub himself even as he felt the current pull against him, driving him back towards the main river. He pushed himself towards the surface before once more scouring his body with silt, feeling the days of hard riding fall away. Then he scrubbed at his hair before once more diving under the water. But when he resurfaced, he was startled to see a group of men come out of the trees on the bank of the main river, close to where he'd left his clothes.

There were sixteen of them, watching him in silence, their shotguns held low by their hips. If their purpose were to intimidate, Marrok thought they'd certainly achieved that.

He knew them well enough, for these were the men who wanted the little girl left out in the wild. They wanted her gone. They didn't care what happened to her, as long as she didn't bring the wrath of her tribe down on their heads.

Bullies, Marrok thought. But also cowards, because men like this would never stand to protect an innocent, even though they had small children of their own, with nearly all of them having daughters.

They were aged from their mid-twenties to late sixties and when the oldest in the group, a loudmouth arrogant man called Milne Barden took a knife from a leather sheath on his belt, Marrok understood their aim wasn't just to intimate, but to do damage, one way or the other. And then Barden glanced over at Marrok's buckskin clothing, to the wet pair of pants and shirt, and the clean pair of pants and shirt.

Marrok felt a moment of despair, for these were all the clothes he had, other than the clothes he had worn out to dinner with Ella in St Louis.

He wondered how long these men had been watching him. Had they just arrived? Or taken pleasure in knowing he was naked, his weapons out of reach, his clothing lying there ready to be cut to shreds.

Yet what did they think they could do? Cut him up a little? Intimidate him into getting rid of the girl? Marrok almost laughed. As if anything they could do to him would make him change his mind.

He wondered if they planned to kill him. They could easily make it look like an accident because he'd met men like this before, men who'd lost control with their prejudice and hate. So until he saw their intent, Marrok remained where he was, refusing to be the first to initiate the assault.

Barden finally made the first move by stepping towards Marrok's clothes, the knife in his hand, his face full of spite when a voice rang out through the trees. They all turned to see Artie hurrying towards them along with Bracedon and Minson, their shotguns held out before them.

"You go on back now boys," Artie called out, his voice loud and clear. "You got chores to do with your families. We're leaving here at dawn, so get away with you."

"You know why we've come," Barden said, his eyes turning back to Marrok. "He needs to be taught a lesson. He should have known better than bringing that girl here. She ain't welcome. And we all heard you and Miller say she'll bring a war down on us. We got our own families to think on."

Artie remained where he was, yet he knew Marrok well enough to know he was impatient to get this done and get out of the water.

"Stay low, lad," Artie whispered, then turned to Barden, his voice once again loud with authority. "No-one needs to be taught any lesson here boys. We all know he did the right thing. Think on it, if one of your own were left behind, wouldn't you want someone picking them up and caring for them? Or would you rather they be left alone to die? Now, I say again, off with you and get on with your chores."

No-one moved. Then Barden bent his head to spit before putting his knife away. Then he pushed aside his own men to head back the way he'd come. His men turned to follow him, their voices raised in anger and frustration as they crashed their way through the woods. And then there was silence.

Marrok saw Artie turn to speak to Bracedon and Minson and then the two men left, leaving Marrok and Artie alone.

"You alright?" Artie called, walking down to the river's edge.

Marrok nodded as he swum across the silt bank and back into the river. As he waded ashore, Artie picked up the blanket and handed it to him.

"How did you know?" Marrok asked. "How'd you know they were following me?"

Artie stepped forward to stand on the very edge of the bank and looked out at the thick woods all around them as Marrok dried himself and dressed in the clean clothes.

"Ella and Clara saw them talking," he said softly. "Both of them gals got a bad feeling about it, so Ella ran to find me. You got them to thank, I reckon." He shook his head and stood back.

"I took my eyes of them boys for one minute and they set out to do you harm. I won't stand for it Marrok. And I don't like the way they treat the few slaves they got with them, but those boys be hanged before they take any notice of me. I'll tell you now, I won't have this behavior on my wagon train so if they persist they can break off and find their own way west. Every day I can feel the mood changing around camp because of their meanness and I reckon that soon enough they'll begin to target me, Joe and Miller, forcing us to leave while they take over the train. I won't let that happen."

He turned to find Marrok dressed and watching him and reached out to place a hand on the younger man's shoulder.

"I'll say to you again son, you watch your back.

We both know them boys for what they are. Some men just never grow out of short pants. They can't even target a man alone without going in as a mob." He nodded in the direction of the wagon train. "We'll walk back together, just in case one of them gets trigger happy."

But as Marrok walked in silence alongside his friend, he felt a rage begin inside himself. He had been born in this country, he knew it better than anyone else on this wagon train, including Artie, for Marrok had travelled the width and breathe of it for more than ten years. And despite riding out every day to scout ahead, to keep these folks safe from whatever might lie ahead, these few men, half of them not even born in America, made him feel as if he didn't belong here, that this was no longer his home. Yet men like this were swarming across the country spreading their hate. He felt sick to his stomach thinking on it, but he didn't know how to stop it.

*

The tension between Marrok and the men came to a violent end with the bruised and bloody face of Milne Barden's wife. Everyone had heard them arguing the night before, yet no-one had heard the blows. When Aubree appeared late the following morning, her bonnet tied close about her face, Artie issued the men with a choice.

"Stop with the hate and violence or ride out on your own."

By mid-day the group had decided to travel on their own. By late afternoon they'd taken their forty wagons out of Artie's wagon train with the intention of following behind, running their group by their rules, not Artie's.

Marrok couldn't believe it when the men pulled their wagons aside, choosing to go on alone. But then he saw Aubree's face and was amazed that any man could treat a woman like that. It was something he could never understand. He never used women badly and as far as he knew, there were no bitter ex-lovers in his past. The women he'd loved and left, knew him for what he was. A man eager to move on, a man who'd be gone by morning. He never sought a woman who had expectations of him, so never felt the need to hurt a woman, like Aubree Barden had been hurt.

That night the wagons formed three circles instead of four, having lost those forty wagons. Yet that night was a happy one as people got to know new neighbors and after supper, Artie encouraged the fiddlers to play and asked Ruby to get up and sing.

It was much later, well after children were put to bed and the singing and dancing done, that Ella found herself sitting around a campfire with a large group of people, some of them having just joined her circle, listening as they spoke of their experiences so far on the trail.

The men spoke of their hopes to better their lives in the west. Nearly all of them were happy enough with their life on the trail so far.

Most of the women agreed, but many revealed their struggle to sleep without the safety of four walls and a locked door between them and the dark at night. Others spoke of the daily grind of walking long distances, of cooking for large groups over a small open fire with only the use of a dutch oven and a few pans and the constant struggle to keep up the cleaning and washing of small children with little water.

Martha was one of those women who spoke of the hardship yet surprisingly, Constance said she was content with her lot, which surprised Ella.

"And what about you?" One of the women asked, leaning towards her.

Ella looked up as Marrok passed their group and saw him glance at her. "I wouldn't change a thing," she said, and as he walked on, Ella saw him smile.

*

He approached her later as everyone started drifting off to bed. Ella was rinsing the coffee pot, ready for the morning brew when Marrok asked if she had a moment.

"Artie told me what you and Clara did today. I want to thank you."

Ella frowned. "Those men made me and Clara feel uncomfortable the way they were watching you. You saw us in the back of my wagon when you rode in. We were going through our supplies. When you went down to the river, those men didn't realize we could also see them." Ella paused before she spoke, then she dared to say it. "I think you already know I'd do anything to help you Marrok, after all you've done for me. You have only to ask."

He paused, his gaze intent as he watched her.

Then he nodded, leaning towards her, his voice low. "You've already done more than I ever expected of you Ella," he paused then added softly. "You're helping to look after a child I brought into camp, you stood by me that night by dancing with me and now you've stopped me taking a beating," he took a breath and looked around the camp settling down for the night. "We'll reach the woods tomorrow where I found Nigamo-nii'eihii so I'm riding out first thing in the morning to take a look around, to see if I can find her family. I'm hoping they're still there somewhere."

"What about the wolves?"

Marrok glanced up towards the forest which loomed in the distance. "They would have returned to their dens high in the wooded hills long ago. Besides, they won't come anywhere near the wagon train." He nodded to her, then smiled. "Good night Ella. Sleep well."

Then he walked away, leaving her alone. Ella would have loved to go after him, but of course she didn't. Instead, aware of the glances her way, she moved to finish rinsing out the coffee pot, damped down the fire and went to bed. But she fell asleep holding the dreamcatcher.

7

They reached the woods early the following afternoon and Artie called a halt for the day. Through the trees was a wide shallow river which wound back through the woods to meet that silt pool where Marrok had bathed the day before. Artie ordered that the animals be watered first, before they were let out to graze within the wagon circles.

Around dusk, as families finished supper and started getting small children ready for bed, one of the men on guard duty began shouting, pointing north. Everyone turned, with men reaching for their shotguns as everyone stood up to see what the commotion was about. Then they all heard a high pitched cry coming from the trees.

Artie ordered everyone back behind the wagons, as that shrill cry echoed out again. Ella and her team moved quickly, crouching behind her wagon when the little Arapaho girl suddenly struggled to be free of Clara. Before anyone could stop her, she ran beneath the wagon then sprinted across the open field towards the trees. Ella stood up to go after her, shouting at her to come back, when Jasper grasped her arm.

"Look Miss Ella, just hold up!" he cried, pointing to a large group of riders coming out of the woods more than a mile away.

Ella watched in despair as the little girl ran away, but then a man riding at the head of the group suddenly kicked his horse into a gallop, heading straight towards the child.

Artie yelled at everyone to hold their fire, then he mounted his horse and rode out alongside Miller and Joe, even as a woman somewhere on the wagon train screamed in terror, because the rider galloping towards the girl could be plainly seen now and he was a terrifying sight, with slashes of black dye spread across his cheeks and forehead.

"Sweet Lord Almighty," Clara muttered, clutching Ella's arm.

But as Artie and his officers rode out, Ella could see that they were deliberately creating a barrier between the wagon train and the child and rider.

"What's they doing?" Clara asked, peering out from beneath the wagon in fear. "They's just goin' on out there to get themselves killed!"

Ruby watched in bewilderment, until she realized they were protecting the rider and child, from some nervous youth or man from taking a shot at them.

The rider reached the girl and once again let out that bone chilling cry, then almost threw himself off the horse as he ran towards her, sweeping her into his arms.

"Well, look at that why don't you! It's the girl's father!" Abe said, standing up. "And Marrok! Look!"

Ella looked back at the riders and saw Marrok riding alongside an older man at the head of the group. They reached the rider and the girl at the same time that Artie and his two officers got there.

"They sure doan't look like they want to go war with us," Jasper said.

Ella couldn't help but smile. Marrok had done it. He'd found the child's family.

There were about fifty people in the group and almost all of them wore that same black dye on their faces. The women and children rode double, with packhorses pulling travois behind them and Ella could see the great bundles of buckskin tied down on the back of them. They had been hunting deer.

The men were dressed in similar clothes to Marrok, except his were plain compared to their beautifully decorated garments, with leather fringe, beadwork and hand painted designs.

The women wore long shift dresses with ankle boots, all decorated with porcupine quills and dyed seed beads. Bead necklaces and bracelets adorned the women's necks and wrists.

And then a young woman riding bareback appeared from the back of the group. Ella heard her soft cry and watched her dismount before stumbling towards Nigamo-nii'eihii and the man holding her.

There was a lot of talking then. Ella could hear the muted sounds of that guttural dialect she'd heard Marrok speak so many times to Nigamo-nii'eihii, then Artie was pointing back towards the wagon train, while Marrok pointed to an area just north of it.

And then the group were on the move. Nigamo-nii'eihii was settled before her father on his horse, while her mother rode alongside them. They headed for a large flat piece of land just north of the wagon train and when they stopped, it was obvious to everyone on the wagon train that they intended camping here for the night.

Ella was surprised when Artie and his officers rode back to join the company, leaving Marrok with the Arapaho. But she watched intrigued, like everyone else, as he helped raise half a dozen teepees, hobbled the horses and carried belongings into the teepees. And later, as smoke drifted from the top of those massive hide shelters, Ella envied them their teepees. Just to be dry and warm and out of all weathers, close to a fire where you could cook hot meals even when it poured with rain seemed an out-of-reach luxury to her.

Marrok stayed with the family that night, with Artie riding up to join them later. But as Ella and everyone else settled for bed, they all heard the muted sounds of laughter and the dull beat of a drum.

September 1846

1

Four months after leaving Independence, they came upon their first trading post. It was no more than a large cabin, stocked with supplies of flour, salted bacon, corn and coffee.

Behind the building a group of men from the Gros Ventre tribe had set up camp the previous night. They had brought maize and tobacco with them to trade and in return they took away blankets, knives and axes. Within hours of the wagon train pulling in, the men completed their trade, packed up their camp and rode out.

Artie allowed a stop of two days at this post, giving everyone time to buy supplies and replenish their water barrels from the deep well nearby. Then they moved on, even though it had begun to rain, but it was nothing more than a soft drizzle, not enough to stop the wagons, but enough to cause tempers to flare.

The rain slowed them down enough to allow a convoy of four muleskinners to catch up. The men had come from Independence, their wagons full of supplies for Fort Hall and that night they camped a half mile east from the wagon train.

Artie and Marrok rode over to join them for a coffee.

"We saw you roll out of Independence all those months ago," one of them said. "We followed not a week after you, but we got hit hard by rain a few weeks back. Stopped us for a good while, but we've been moving hard ever since to make up time."

Artie asked if they'd seen the group of forty wagons behind them, all those people who had decided to go out on their own.

The muleskinners shook his heads. "You folks be the first we seen since we left Independence," one of the men said, spitting tobacco juice.

The news left Artie feeling uneasy, wondering what might have happened to those settlers. Because even with the rain it would have been impossible to miss the old, rutted wagon tracks ahead of them.

They should have been a few days behind, at the most.

"If they was following you, they ain't no more," another of the muleskinners said. "I guess they could've taken it into their minds to settle somewhere, but if they went out into the wild, well," he shook his head in dismay. "I reckon they'd be lost by now. Even taken by Indians. There's a lot of tribes goin' hungry with the loss of the buffalo and if that be the case, you won't hear nothin' from them folks again. Forty wagons you say? Well, forty wagons is easy pickings for a tribe of hungry men."

He offered a bottle of whisky to Artie and Marrok to take a swig of, but they declined the offer, even as the man held the bottle to his mouth.

Another of the muleskinners rolled tobacco in his stained fingers, but before he put the wad in his mouth to chew, he nodded back the way they'd come.

"Just so's you know, there's another big group of settlers comin' directly behind you, with a big team of muleskinners behind them. About four to six weeks away, I reckon. Settlers told us they left St Joseph end of May. About eighty wagons all up, but they're bringin' a lot of animals with them, a lot of cattle, so you better hope you reach Fort Hall before those folks catch you. One fellow alone is runnin' more than five hundred head of cows. They'll eat more grass than can fed the settlers' animals comin' after them," he shook his head and popped the wad of tobacco in his mouth.

"Big trouble ahead I reckon, and not just with the Indians. Take them forty wagons that pulled away from you. I reckon they'd have guns, which the Indians don't have. And just say they ain't dead and they found a place to settle and put down roots, well, them kind of single minded folk won't think twice about stopping others crossing through their lands. Yessir, trouble brewing ahead I reckon," he paused to spit a mouthful of tobacco juice.

"Politicians so busy selling this country out from under us, they ain't made no rules. I hope I ain't alive to see it but mark my words, there'll be wars fought over this land afore long."

There was silence for a long moment then Marrok leaned towards him.

"The muleskinners coming up behind us. How many?"

An older man answered, his teeth almost gone from a bad diet and tobacco chewing. "Eight wagons or thereabouts. Should catch up to you within the month."

Artie glanced at Marrok. Neither of them liked the idea of either the muleskinners or that big wagon train rolling over them, especially not with all those cattle. But they should be at Fort Hall within six weeks, sooner if they pushed their animals harder and if the weather held.

Marrok wondered if the muleskinners behind them were the same family group he and Ella had seen in Independence, but before he could say anything, Artie asked about other wagon trains.

"You see any smaller ones leaving Independence?"

The muleskinner chewing on the wad of tobacco reached out to touch the earth, feeling the grass beneath him. "What I seen is hundreds of thousands of buffalo grazing on these lands. Not once, but many times. And I'll tell you, it's a sight to behold. But I don't see those numbers no more."

He shook his head and looked over at Artie. "Some smaller companies were gettin' ready to leave after us, but I hope they stick together and not travel by themselves. I saw one man tellin' folk he knew of a shortcut through the Rockies. I went up to his face and told him he was a madman. Takin' settlers with oxen and mules and heavy wagons through those narrow mountain passes is askin' for trouble. Can snow up there real heavy, early as September. Snow twice as deep as a man's cabin. Ain't no way to dig yourself out of that kind of snow."

Marrok looked at him in dismay. He remembered that man and he remembered having the same conversation with him. He hoped no-one listened to him.

"I seen settlers shooting buffalo," the older man spoke up. "And not for their meat or nothin' else, just to get rid of them. To stop them eatin' the grass," he glanced over at the man chewing tobacco.

"I agree with my son here, this territory is changing real fast. The way of life on these here Plains is being lost and ain't no-one doing a darn thing to stop it. I reckon we'll come through this open country in a few years' time and there'll be railings up, with cattle and horses being bred, the buffalo long gone."

"Can't see it myself," the man drinking whisky added. "Can't see the Indians lettin' all this land get into the hands of settlers. They been roamin' and huntin' on these open lands for as long as my great-grandpappy can remember." He shook his head. "I don't reckon there'll be wars ahead. Folks will work it out, because no-one can stop the buffalo roamin' this territory."

They talked for a little while longer, then Artie and Marrok returned to the wagon train.

Yet both men were subdued, both thinking the same thing but neither saying it aloud, until Artie did.

"You and I, we're partly responsible for this," he said, looking out at the country around them. "We're helping to bring all these people through. And maybe we should have taken a stand before now and tried to stop it."

Marrok shook his head. "Stop what, Artie? Progress? The river of money crossing this country? For I'm darn sure if you or I or anyone else tried to stop it, we'd be dead men. Or we'd be the ones starting a war."

"But that war's coming, you know it as well as I

know it," Artie said. "Just like most of those muleskinners know it. They've been moving across this country trapping furs all their lives, just like your daddy and granddaddy. They've seen what we've seen. The people hungry for land, prepared to do anything to get it and you know as well as I know Marrok, that it might not be this year or the year after that, but war is coming."

Marrok said nothing, he simply nodded then joined Artie for another coffee as neither man felt like sleeping.

2

One month out of Fort Hall they veered off course for some four miles to camp on the edge of a river where they stayed for several days. But it wasn't to rest, it was to cope with the dysentery that had swept through the wagon train two days before. Some folks still lay abed and with children sick from it as well, tensions in camp were high with exhausted, sick women trying to cope yet running out of clean linen and clothes.

By the third day camping by the river, as the illness began to wear itself out, Artie made the decision to stay one more day, to give people time to recover before they made the final push to Fort Hall.

As he was discussing it with Marrok and his officers, eight wagons pulled by large teams of oxen suddenly appeared on a rise behind them. Artie and Marrok rode out to meet them, to find out their business, because this was not usually a place the wagon train stopped. The appearance of the muleskinners made Artie uneasy.

"We wondered if you folks were alright?" one of the men called out to them as Marrok and Artie reined in their horses close to the wagons, aware of the big shotguns the men carried. "Ain't used to seeing wagon trains come this far west, 'specially a big company like you got here, so we followed you to make sure you ain't in no trouble."

"We had a bout of illness," Artie said. "Came here to get water and let folk rest. Reckon we'll be on our way day after tomorrow." He told them about the dysentery bug, giving the muleskinners fair warning to stay clear.

"Four muleskinners passed us two weeks ago, told us a big group was coming up from St Joseph. I guess that would be you?" Marrok asked.

The man in the front wagon nodded. "That'll be us alright. We passed another big wagon train just behind yours and there's a few smaller ones coming up behind them. You sure got a lot of wagons here though, ain't seen nothin' like it."

"You staying here long?" Artie called out.

The man in front shook his head. "Leaving first thing in the mornin'. We need to get to Fort Hall before you, for I reckon you folks'll be needing these supplies we got packed away behind us."

He turned and glanced back at the wagons, where heavy canvas sheeting covered stacks of boxes and muslin sacks. Then he nodded towards two men sitting on an empty wagon at the back of the group.

"Those two ain't coming west with us. They've had enough. Emptied their wagon at that supply post back yonder and they're heading up to Lower Canada. Too many of us doing this run now, ain't enough money in it for some of us, so they're heading north to join the Hudson Bay Company. Heard a man can make a fortune up there, just like the old days of fur trapping. Seems Hudson Bay are running wagons all the way across Lower Canada to Fort Vancouver. But they got those Russians hunting fur seals up in the Bering Sea and they pay big money for supplies, once they get their ships berthed in Vancouver Bay. Anyways, we'll go set up camp now we know you folks are alright. But best kept clear of us. We don't want your illness."

"I thought I saw you back in Independence, I thought you had your families with you?" Marrok asked.

The man nodded. "But most of that group headed out along the Santa Fe trail, some time before we left." He wished them well again and moved the oxen on, to make camp some way from the wagon train. But as Marrok and Artie returned to camp, Artie was still uneasy.

"Not sure why," he said. "Muleskinners don't usually go out of their way to see if folks are alright. They're usually in too much of a hurry. But I guess I should be grateful. Just ain't used to it, I guess."

*

Later that night Marrok accepted an invitation from Willard to join them for supper, along with Ella's team, to celebrate being free of sickness. And later, while they were having coffee and talk turned to what they would do once they left the wagon train, a few people strolled over to join them, including Pierce Calderson and the Weslock family. Elmer Weslock coughed into a piece of linen and Marrok was shocked by how much worse his cough had got.

"Nothing contagious," Elmer said, hitting his chest. "Doc just says its congestive heart failure, but I've got to admit that some days I have to push myself, which isn't fair on Moss."

"Well, we all know you for the stubborn jackass you are, which only makes things worse," Nell said, yet there was a fondness to her voice as she scolded her husband. "I reckon you're pushing yourself into an early grave, but you won't listen to no-one, most of all me."

Elmer smiled. "Don't fuss so, woman. You know I'll be alright. I'm just getting older like everyone else and I got to understand I don't have the same energy I had as a young man," he glanced over at Ruby. "And what about you? I hope you got plans to use that voice! It'll be a sad day that's for sure, when we can't hear it no more."

Everyone turned to Ruby. She blushed, clearly not used to compliments given before a large group of people. "Don't worry Elmer, I'm heading for those big singing halls. That's my dream."

"Well good luck to you girl. I hope it's everything you want it to be," Elmer said.

Clarissa smiled and leaned against Ruby. "My dream is to become a ballerina. I want to dance on stage and wear one of those pretty dresses."

"Oh, Clarissa," Willard spluttered, scolding her. "Do get your head out of the clouds. I honestly don't know where you get these ideas. You have to train for years to be a ballerina."

Constance looked dismayed as Willard berated his eldest daughter in front of everyone. But Ruby just laughed and reached out to put an arm around Clarissa's shoulders.

"I saw a ballerina once. She was on stage dancing and I swear she was the most beautiful thing I ever saw. She stood up on her toes and spun around, just like she weighed nothing at all."

"Well I saw a toy ballerina once," Clarissa said. "She was tiny, inside a jewelry box. When you opened the lid of the box she popped up to spin on a mirror. I can't remember the tune she danced to, but I remember it was lovely. If I had some money, I'd buy a jewelry box just like that one with the ballerina and I'd put all my jewelry inside."

"You haven't got any jewelry," Willard said.

"Well, one day I will have. You just see if I don't," Clarissa answered back.

"No need to speak to your father like that girl. You show him some respect," Constance said softly.

"Well, all I know for sure is that everyone has to have a dream. Just like everyone here on this wagon train has one, by heading to California or Oregon." Ruby said, then bent down to kiss Clarissa on the forehead. "Now, I must away to my bed, otherwise I'll be good for nothing in the morning." She excused herself and left, followed by almost everyone else.

Ella watched her team walk back to her camp, but she wasn't ready to leave yet. But then the Weslocks were saying goodnight, along with Pierce.

Willard looked annoyed as he glanced across at his wife, who sat with a hand on her swollen belly looking pale and tired, then across to Martha, Ella and Marrok before turning his gaze back to his daughter.

"It's fine to have dreams as long as you've got money to pay for them," he said, his voice low, as Constance turned to Clarissa.

"Off to bed with you, young lady. And wash your face before you climb up into the wagon. And try not to wake your brother and sister."

Clarissa said goodnight and left them, as Martha shook her head. "I do declare, where do young people get these fancy ideas," she said. "I was happy if I received a rag doll. Whether it was made well or not was of little consequence to me. I was just grateful to have it."

Ella laughed and when she made her own excuses to leave, Marrok stood up and offered to walk her back to her wagon. Ella was surprised, because she didn't need an escort. But she liked to think he wanted to be with her, as much as she wanted to be with him.

"I never had dreams of my own," she said, looking up at him. "All I've ever done is work hard although if I think on it, I suppose working my family's ranch was my dream," she paused as they neared her wagon. "Do you have a dream Marrok? Is Oregon your dream?"

He shrugged, his eyes dark as he looked at her. "I suppose it might be, because I took one look at that valley in Oregon and knew I wanted to spend the rest of my life there. If someone were to take it away from me, I'd be devastated."

Ella went to answer him when they both saw Jasper and Clara sitting by the low coals of the fire. They were enjoying a coffee together after Willard's supper. It looked like they weren't ready for bed either.

"You'll want to join them, so I'll see you tomorrow Ella," Marrok said, then stepped out into the dark towards his own wagons. Ella was disappointed he'd left and as she watched him disappear among his wagons, she wished she had the courage to tell him that all she really wanted was to be with him.

3

Ella woke before dawn the following morning, feeling a desperate need to bathe. Everyone was still asleep and even though she knew she shouldn't leave the wagons without someone with her, she crawled out of the shelter feeling hot and sweaty and unclean after the dysentery bug.

Since Independence she'd washed herself in the privacy of the shelter she shared with Clara, by heating water in a pot by the fire and then wiping herself down with soap and hot water. But now she felt an urgency to put her head under water and scour herself, for the scent of illness seemed to linger in the air.

She looked around the dark circle of wagons and saw no-one, other than some men standing guard. But they were watching the muleskinners up on the hill who were getting ready to leave. Ella could see the hot coals of their fires as someone heated coffee and beans, while others harnessed oxen to the wagons.

Ella took advantage of the guards' being distracted and quickly reached back inside the shelter for a blanket, a clean dress, stay and petticoat. Then she stood very still in the shadows, making sure she was alone.

It was already warm. It was going to be another hot summer's day. But as she turned to run for the trees, she heard someone close by and saw Jasper crawling out of his shelter, rubbing his eyes.

"You up early, Miss Ella," he whispered.

"I'm just heading down to the river. I won't be long."

"I'll go with you, this ain't no place for you to

be walking out alone."

"I'll be back soon enough, Jasper. I just want some privacy for a little while."

"Well, it ain't for me to say you can't, but you be careful Miss Ella."

She left him and hurried down towards the trees, stepping under cover of those dense woods and immediately feeling their shadowy depths and smells embrace her. She made her way down to the river's edge, moving with care between stands of elm, dogwood and maple, so she didn't see the man lying near the river's edge wrapped in soiled blankets. Or the empty wagon behind him, or the other man lying wrapped in blankets inside it. Nor did she see their six oxen, hobbled just beyond the wagon deep in the woods.

But the man lying by the river's edge saw her. And he watched as Ella headed north along the river's edge, looking for a private place to bathe. He saw the dress and undergarments she carried, along with the blanket. When she disappeared behind a stand of thick pine he sat up, looking back the way she'd come before catching another glimpse of her, more than a quarter mile away now. She was still walking, leaving the wagon train and everyone in it far behind her.

The man rose slowly from his blankets and looked back at the trees, finding it incredulous that she was alone. Then he stumbled over to the wagon and shook his partner awake.

"Come on, we got to move!" he hissed.

The other man rubbed his face, then sat up. "You want to leave now? I thought we're leavin' later."

"No!" he hissed. "We're leavin' now. Come on, move! We got the chance to take someone real pretty north with us."

*

Ella stood for a moment at the river's edge, feeling the utter quiet of the morning, for not even the birds had begun to sing yet. But that silence made her feel uneasy and as she looked out across the river, still shrouded in shadows, she suddenly had doubts about bathing here. The water looked grey in the pre-dawn light and she could hear it tumbling over rocks somewhere downriver. She shivered, looking around at the dense woods. The trees seemed to crowd in on her and as she looked back at the river, the water appeared to be moving rapidly downstream, but it was too dark to see properly. She was sure it wasn't like this back where the wagons were camped and she wondered again if she'd made the wrong decision by coming here.

But she wouldn't go back now. And every minute she lingered, was a minute lost bathing. So she stepped back behind some thick shrubs and undressed, taking off her soiled dress, stay and woolen stockings but deciding to keep her shift on. Then she used some of her precious soap to scrub her clothes clean at the river's edge before throwing them over a bush to dry. She stepped into the water, gasping from the cold, and began to scrub herself. Careful not to drop the precious soap and lose it, when she was finished she placed it back near her wet clothes then waded out into the river to rinse the soap off.

She stopped when the water reached her thighs, too afraid to go further as the current was strong. She crouched down and lay back, feeling the water through her hair as it cleaned away months of dust of living on the trail and the cloying scent of illness, unaware a wagon and six oxen were making their way through the trees towards her. When she finally came up out of the water, running her fingers through her hair, only then did she hear the sound of wagons on the move. She knew it was the muleskinners, heading out for Fort Hall.

Ella dived back under the water, feeling her skin tingle with the coolness of it, loving the feeling of finally being clean, but as she broke the surface she turned suddenly, hearing the clink of metal on wood. Like a harness against the wood of a wagon. Yet the wagon train lay more than a mile behind her and she knew the muleskinners had left. Bewildered, thinking she imagined it, Ella looked back into the trees, but she could see nothing there but shadows.

She scolded herself for being foolish then once again ducked her head beneath the water, unaware the wagon and oxen had come to a stop a quarter mile above her in the woods. Nor did she see the youth on the opposite bank come running down to the river's edge, looking at Ella in dismay as he gripped the bow he carried. He was young, barely a teenager, and like Marrok he was dressed in buckskin and moccasins. He wore his hair long and loose to his waist and across his shoulders he wore a leather sheath that held almost a dozen arrows.

He crouched low as Ella came up out of the water and called to her in a guttural dialect she'd heard Marrok speak so many times. She turned on hearing his voice and gasped aloud in terror when she saw him, but the youth was pointing furiously to the bank behind her. Ella spun around and saw two muleskinners coming out of the trees. One carried a large buffalo knife, the other held a long, plaited piece of rawhide rope. Ella turned back to the Indian youth, but he was gone.

She began to wade back the way she had come, to try and get to her clothes. If she could at least try and get closer to the wagon train, someone might hear if she screamed. But before she even got halfway, she knew it was hopeless because the muleskinners were almost there, where she'd left her clothes. She turned back to the bank where she'd seen the boy, but there was no-one there.

She heard a vicious laugh behind her and turned to see the muleskinners step down towards the river's edge and only then did Ella realize her shift clung to her body, revealing everything she owned. She crouched down in the water in an effort to hide herself, knowing she couldn't fight these two men. And if she weren't killed in the attack that was coming, Ella knew she would return to the wagon train in tiny fragments of what she was. Yet even as she thought on it, she could almost hear the cries of scorn and the misery which lay ahead, because everyone would blame her, it would be her fault because she'd dared to come here alone.

She struck out, half swimming, half walking, heading for the middle of the river, reaching out to grip boulders or rocks to give her purchase against the current which threatened to sweep her downriver. Because as the sun rose, only now could Ella see how deadly her situation truly was.

The noise she'd heard when she'd come down here in the gloom of pre-dawn, of water tumbling over rocks, was in fact the river rushing towards a waterfall less than a mile away. She could see it clearly now, where the water fell away into a valley far below. She began to pant with fear, and in her fear she stumbled, her arm taking the brunt of the fall and as she saw the blood flow from the deep cut, it seemed suddenly as if her body didn't move as it should, as if her arms and legs were moving too slowly. But the water was now to her waist, swirling dangerously around her and she felt the pull of it dragging her downstream towards that fall. As she struggled against it, one of the muleskinners called out to her, his voice high pitched and gentle, as though he called to a child.

"Come on back, girlie. We're not gonna hurt you. You take no notice of this big ol' knife. Me and Cecil just want to have some fun. We're gonna take you north with us. The three of us will have a fine old life together up near the Hudson Bay."

Ella turned back to look at them, horrified, understanding at last what they wanted. This wasn't just about an assault. This was about taking her away, up into the wilds of Canada.

4

Marrok splashed his face with water, ridding himself of the stench of the camp. He couldn't wait to ride out of here, for the place reeked of the wagon train's illness. He hadn't been affected by it thankfully, nor had any of his men, but almost half of the company had come down with it.

Because of that and the extra day of rest which Artie had allowed, very few people were about. Yet as Marrok looked around at the three circles of wagons, he couldn't shake a feeling of unease. It had woken him a short time ago out a deep, dreamless sleep, making him toss restlessly, until at last he rose from his bed eager to get outside just in time to see the muleskinners leaving, heading north to Fort Hall.

He frowned as he watched them. There were only seven wagons. But then he remembered the two men heading for Canada. No doubt they'd left before dawn.

Yet Marrok couldn't shake that uneasy feeling and he took a walk around the three wagon circles, talking to the guards, making sure everything was alright. Everything seemed like it was, but the feeling remained.

He wondered if it were because they were due in Fort Hall within the month. He and Artie would leave this wagon train behind then, to start anew in Oregon. But Marrok wasn't upset about that. He was looking forward to finishing his job here, excited about the future that he and Artie had planned in the north. But he would miss certain people, especially one strong minded young woman.

Thinking of Ella, Marrok stepped between the wagons but found only one of his men up and about at this early hour. He wasn't concerned about that. These men had worked hard for him and he wouldn't begrudge them a day's rest.

A newborn baby was crying in one of the other circles and across from Marrok's wagon a man was coughing with heart disease. Marrok knew it was Elmer Weslock. In another wagon close to Ella's, he heard the brief whispered conversation between a man and woman, the woman's voice harsh in the quiet of the early morning.

He glanced over at the shelter that Ella shared with Clara, but there was no movement there. It looked like she was still abed and resting like everyone else.

He walked back to his water barrel and took another ladle of water, thinking of getting some coffee going when he had a sudden image of Ella walking about camp, her long skirts swishing about her shapely legs. He had grown to like watching her, for he could see her quite clearly in the soft glow of her campfire most nights. He liked the way the shadows of the night shaped and molded the contours of her face, making her appear quite beautiful. And when she ate food that stained her lips he had to look away, for it highlighted them, making them the perfect shape and ripe for kissing.

She was like a flame, yet Ella seem unaware of it. But Marrok had seen that fire in her the moment he met her, when she burst into the kitchen in that wedding dress and it was that flame which drew him in, for he knew if it were kindled and tended by the right hand, it would ignite, burning and branding the man who touched it, who made it flare.

Sometimes the color of her green hazel eyes seemed to deepen, reminding Marrok of the colors of autumn, or the moss which lay on stones at the bottom of a river, rich in color yet hidden beneath a flowing tide. Yet Marrok knew without any doubt, like those submerged stones, that if guided by the right man, or woman, Ella could rise into someone formidable because she was strong like those stones, even if she didn't yet know it.

But it was the constant memory of her slim yet curvaceous body, held within his arms while they danced, as she moved seductively against him, or when he kissed her in St Louis, the heat and pressure of her mouth against his own, stirring him like no other woman.

He moved his shoulders, agitated, unsure of these feelings and tried to shrug them off. What was it about her? Darned if he knew, because he wasn't a man who gave in easily to temptation, or emotion. Having lived alone now for the better part of ten years, he liked his life, he liked making his own decisions, going where he wanted.

Yet when Ella looked at him, trusting him completely, knowing she would do anything he asked because she had no reason not to trust him, that scared Marrok a little. How easy to manipulate someone who trusted so blindly.

"Damn it," he swore softly and shook his head to clear the image of her.

He should know better. Because there were always young women eager to fall in love, all finding him a challenge because he was so different to most men. Yet not one of them had held any interest for Marrok. Not until this one.

Those few times he'd hurt Ella's feelings, he'd done it for her benefit, to protect her. He cared nothing for his own reputation, or what people thought of him, but gossip spread quickly in a close community like this and if she were to start a new life in California, she didn't need to sully her own reputation because of him.

But Marrok found it increasingly hard to stay away from her. Once or twice he'd almost kissed her but there had always been someone watching.

He sighed with frustration. He didn't have time for romance and his future held no plans for marriage. Perhaps later, in the years ahead, but not now. Yet if that's what Ella wanted, if she sought marriage, there were enough eligible men on this wagon train who would marry her in a heartbeat if she were agreeable to it, because Marrok had seen them watching her, as they watched Ruby and other single young women. But the thought of Ella marrying some young buck here gnawed at him a little.

He turned and saw Jasper come out of his shelter, the older man looking down towards the river, rubbing his face as though upset. Marrok felt that same uneasiness surface and hurried across to speak to him.

"Are you unwell, Jasper? Have you got the belly ache back, for you don't look so good."

Jasper's face seemed to collapse into deep lines of worry as he turned to Marrok. "I's well enough, but I ain't feeling too good about Miss Ella. She left for the river some time ago to bathe, but she ain't back yet. I's just about to go down there and see where she is."

"She went to bathe alone? At this time of the morning?"

"Yessir, I done told her not to. But she insisted on it. She wanted to get clean after all the illness."

Marrok turned and looked down towards the river. It lay a good half mile away, yet it would have taken her a while to reach it, then find a private spot. He turned back to Jasper.

"Keep this to yourself, not even a word to Clara. If anyone asks where she is, tell them you think she's visiting with someone."

"Yessir Mr Marrok. Lord above, I do hope that girl ain't gone and drowned herself."

"I'll find her. But I'm trusting you to keep this quiet Jasper. We don't want a scandal."

Jasper nodded and watched as Marrok ran off. But as he passed his wagon, something made Marrok reach for the coil of rope attached to the side of it. Then he ran for his horse and as he rode off, he hoped no-one noticed he was riding bareback.

5

He crouched under cover of the trees, searching the river, but there was no sign of Ella. If she had been here, she'd left already, or gone upriver to bathe.

Marrok glanced downstream. Unless she'd gone down there. But surely she wouldn't have dared, for anyone could see the water swept away towards a waterfall, where it dropped into a densely wooded valley over a hundred feet below.

Marrok knew this river was treacherous and so did Artie, which was why no wagon trains ever came here. And that was probably the reason why the muleskinners had followed them here, to make sure they knew about this place. Everyone avoided it because it was so dangerous, a child easily swept away over that ledge.

But if Ella came down here in the gloom of early morning, she might not have seen the waterfall or the rush of water. Yet no-one on the wagon train ventured this far downriver, because those who weren't sick had kept upstream, close to the wagons.

Marrok moved to study the riverbank, looking for Ella's tracks in the damp earth when he caught a movement on the opposite bank through a thick stand of dogwood. He moved back under cover, all his instincts warning him that something was terribly wrong here. He wanted to believe it was some deer, something harmless, but he knew it wasn't.

He almost swore aloud when he saw the girl. She was no older than thirteen and moving silently through the trees, but what turned Marrok's blood to ice was seeing how she ran. Low and at a crouch, as though running from something, or trying to hide from something. Marrok watched her sprint through the woods, then she suddenly turned and disappeared within the trees.

He knew she would be aware of the wagon train camped just a mile away across the river, just as she would know that the muleskinners had left a short time ago. Yet who was she?

Marrok turned and ran back to his horse, fearing for Ella's safety. But at least now he knew which way to go, because the girl had been running away from something downstream. He kicked his horse in that direction and as he made his way along the bank, he saw slight prints made from a woman's shoe in the damp earth heading downriver. Marrok had no doubt that they belonged to Ella. Yet how far downstream had she gone?

He rode on, then came across the tracks of a wagon, pulled by oxen. Marrok dismounted and touched the tracks. They weren't deep, which suggested an empty wagon had come through here. Just ahead, he found the warm scat left by the animals.

Marrok swore again. This was the eighth wagon, missing when the muleskinners rode out earlier that morning. They had come through here because these tracks were fresh.

He suddenly cussed at Ella for being so foolish. There were almost one hundred men travelling on the wagon train, with almost half of them being single. And camped just upriver, had been a group of muleskinners. Any one of them might take advantage of a woman bathing alone if they stumbled upon her, and it would be her word against theirs if an attack happened. Marrok also knew that Ella would be judged for it, bringing it on herself for going out alone, because that's just the way it was.

He rode on, following the tracks but as he rounded a bend, he heard the soft, desperate cry of a woman, followed by a man's cruel laughter. He pushed his horse on through the trees and when he came out on the riverbank, he saw her at last.

*

She was in the river, struggling against the current as she tried to get to the opposite bank, even as the shift she wore for modesty clung to her body, making her appear as though she were naked.

Marrok looked on in horror as he saw two naked men following her, the water up to their knees as they taunted her, their crude words telling Ella in no uncertain terms what they planned to do to her, as well as their plans to take her north, up to Lower Canada. Marrok recognized them. They were two of the muleskinners he'd met yesterday, the two men heading north to Canada to make their fortune.

He looked back at Ella. She was well past the middle of the river now, with the current sweeping her up against the boulders and rocks, although mercifully, those boulders also stopped her drifting downstream towards that waterfall. But even from here Marrok could see the cuts on her arms, along with unbridled terror in those lovely eyes. He could also see she was getting tired. He felt desperation sweep over him, because once she stopped fighting, she'd be lost to that current.

He dismounted and tethered his horse but as he looked back at the men, for the first time he saw the machete that one of the men carried, because he suddenly held it aloft, like a trophy.

Marrok knew no-one could fight against a weapon like that. It was like a shortened sword which some men called a buffalo knife, commonly used to butcher buffalo.

Gripping the rope, he took off at a run, aware of those spiteful voices again, followed by laughter. And as he climbed a boulder, he began to make a loop and knot with his rope, his fingers shaking with urgency as he created a lasso, then he swung it out over the river towards the man closest to him. It fell about the man's shoulders and as Marrok tugged viciously on it, it fell away to tighten around the man's neck.

Marrok pulled again, causing the man to fall back into the water, his fingers clawing at the rope, even as he began to choke. His friend turned in surprise, then saw Marrok. He grunted with rage then rushed to help his friend, which gave Ella a few precious minutes to get away.

Marrok cursed for not bringing his shotgun, even as he pulled off his shirt and moccasins. He thought for a moment of running back into the trees to try and find the wagon, along with any guns these men might carry. But he knew he didn't have time. Besides, they probably hid their guns in the bushes, near their clothes, which would leave Marrok no chance at all, let alone Ella.

So he reached for the knife held in the sheath at

his waist, then entered the water, pulling again on the rope as the man holding the machete turned to cut it free, his frustration and rage turning him into a mad man. His scream of rage made Ella turn.

She stared in astonishment as Marrok headed towards that deadly knife and she went to scream a warning, to stay back, only to hear her voice came out thin and reedy, her lungs on fire as she struggled to breathe. She watched as the men lunged at each other, their knives held out before them, the water up to their thighs.

"You want her too?" she heard the man snarl at Marrok. "I don't think so. We saw her first. She comes with us to the north. You go on back now, let us have our fun."

Ella stumbled back and felt the bank rise suddenly beneath her feet. She fell forward, crouching on her hands and knees in the water, watching in horror as the muleskinner slashed at Marrok. But he stepped away just in time before ducking down into a low crouch, even as the other muleskinner groaned, a low half-conscious gargle as he struggled hopelessly to free himself from the rope as the water washed over his face.

But Ella wasn't watching him. She was watching Marrok. "Oh God, no," she whispered, as that terrible knife thrust towards Marrok again.

But again Marrok reared back and as he did, he pulled with all his weight on the rope, pulling the other man up and out of the water just as that deadly machete slashed down low. The movement of the machete had the power of rage and hate behind it and even as the muleskinner swung it, even as he saw the arc of the blade heading towards his friend, he couldn't stop the momentum and watched in horror as he sliced his friend a deadly blow beneath his jaw.

Marrok took advantage of the muleskinner's grunts of disbelief and reached down and cut the rope, allowing the man to drift away. Then he wound the remains of the rope around his other hand, wrist and arm, in an attempt to protect himself against that machete.

"Damn you to hell!" the muleskinner raged, but as he lunged back with the machete, Marrok swept in low, bringing his knife up under the man's arm. He felt the knife slice deep and when the machete swung back, there wasn't a lot of power in it. But still, that sharp blade bit into Marrok's shoulder.

He instinctively rolled away, pushing with his legs on the river bottom as the muleskinner lunged towards him, seeing the blood pouring down Marrok's shoulder. Marrok took another step away, seeing the blood lust in the man's eyes and his low primal grunting as he lunged again, the buffalo knife sweeping closer and closer when Marrok heard the *swish* of something pass mere inches from his face. And then a cry of pain. The muleskinner went down, splashing frantically in the water.

Marrok stared at him in bewilderment, then dared to glance back at Ella. She was still crouched at the water's edge, but she was no longer looking at him. She was staring wide eyed at a youth standing not six feet away from her, an arrow to his bow, held close to his face, judging the distance. Marrok couldn't know that it was the same youth who had come out of the woods earlier, but he watched in disbelief as the boy released the arrow, hearing that same *swish* as it flew just inches past his face before thudding into the other shoulder of the muleskinner, followed by another anguished cry. And then a third arrow, this time into that fragile spot between the shoulder blades.

The muleskinner dropped the machete as he struggled to pull the arrows free, but his arms were useless. Marrok moved quickly to retrieve the buffalo knife before it was lost, then pushed the man away, out into the current. The muleskinner groaned as he drifted towards the waterfall, then he was gone, death coming quickly before he went over the edge, following his friend.

Marrok turned to the boy and called to him in that guttural dialect. The youth lowered his bow, just as a large group of men, twenty or more, came running out of the trees. They moved in silence, yet every one of them held a bow with a sheath of arrows on their backs.

Marrok hurried across to Ella, pushing through the current as one of the men called out to the youth in that same guttural dialect. Marrok heard the words, as the youth spoke rapidly, pointing at Ella then Marrok, then towards the waterfall.

Marrok reached out to touch Ella on her lower back, needing to know that she wasn't hurt. She turned to him, her face so pale he was shocked by it, before she nodded towards the boy. "He saved your life."

Marrok nodded, then pushed himself out of the water, feeling the painful wrench in his shoulder. He stepped up onto the bank and approached the youth. Ella heard them speak rapidly and then one of the men was talking to Marrok. She watched as Marrok turned to the boy and grasped him by the forearm, clearly thanking him, before handing him the buffalo knife.

Ella couldn't move. She felt as if she were in a dream and soon she would wake, but when a group of women suddenly appeared, including a girl of about twelve, she knew it was no dream. One of the women approached her and draped a blanket around her shoulders, covering her, before helping her to her feet. Ella tried to thank her as she pulled the blanket close, aware of its warmth, even as she trembled violently. She noticed Marrok talking to the young girl who nodded, before pointing towards her, but Ella turned away, feeling as though she were floating.

She noticed every man in the group carried shotguns in sheaths on their backs, while others carried old flintlock muskets. They also carried bows slung over their shoulders as well as a leather pouch of arrows, yet Ella now understood why they carried such weapons. She had just seen the reason why. Bows and arrows killed in silence.

Another man approached Marrok to look at the wound on his shoulder which was bleeding badly. Another conversation, then Marrok turned to her.

"They'll help us. Please don't argue about it or make a scene. Please just follow me." He didn't take her hand, but trusted her to follow him. And she did.

6

Ella sipped a herbal drink from a cup made of clay and watched as two women tended Marrok. He also drank something from a clay cup as the women applied a poultice to his wound before binding it with strips of rawhide. They worked efficiently yet in silence, aware of the men sitting in a circle close by, waiting to talk to Marrok.

When the dressing was done, Marrok got up and joined the men while the two women joined Ella, where she sat with three young mothers, four teenage girls and two toddlers, both boys.

Three other woman offered the men some smoked meat along with fried bread before turning to Ella and offering her the same. She took it with gratitude, suddenly ravenous and ate it in silence while the women sat and talked around her. She understood nothing of the conversation, but she was aware of the men talking in anger, with an older man pointing upriver towards the wagon train.

She jumped with nerves as a woman reached over to gently prod her, before trying to communicate using her hands. Ella knew this was plains sign talk, as she'd spoken of it with Marrok one night.

"There are many dialects between the Plains nations, so they communicate with hand signals. They call it plains sign talk. Children learn it when they're just toddlers."

The woman now touched her belly, swollen with pregnancy and then pointed at Ella, and then Marrok. Ella smiled, then shook her head, but she couldn't help but glance over at Marrok. He sat cross-legged within that circle of men, his wet buckskin pants clinging to him as her own shift clung to her. She pulled the blanket closer, yet these people didn't seem to notice she was undressed, not like the people on the wagon train would notice.

Then the talking was done and the men stood up, grasping Marrok by the forearms and again those guttural words. The women moved also, packing away their belongings onto the six travois behind them, including leather bags, clay mugs and the buffalo robes they had been sitting on. Ella saw several teepees folded across those travois.

She gave the blanket back to the woman who had draped it around her shoulders. Ella felt vulnerable without it and even though the shift had mostly dried, she crossed her arms before her in an instinctive bid to cover herself.

As the family group mounted their horses ready to leave, Marrok walked towards her and Ella gaped at him, seeing for the first time how closely those damp buckskin pants hugged his long legs. He was as exposed as she was and now understood why the women smiled when they looked at him. If he were aware of it, Marrok didn't seem to care.

They watched as the family group rode off and Ella had a moment of thinking how extraordinary this was. That they were here, that they had shared all this, yet had remained invisible to everyone on the wagon train.

The Indians left nothing behind, other than the scat of their horses. No-one would ever know that a large group of people had camped here overnight. There were no fire pits, no shrill cries of farewell, because their being here had been one of secrecy, with the family well aware that several hundred people were camped on the other side of the river.

And with two muleskinners now lying dead at the bottom of a waterfall, the family wanted no trace of ever having been here.

*

Ella walked back through the woods behind Marrok, following him through the dense shrubs and undergrowth, aware of the power of his body, seeing the way he moved as he pushed branches aside and stepped lightly over debris on the ground.

She was also aware that if ever there was a time for her to trust a man, it was now. They were alone, no-one knew they were together and neither one of them wore much clothing.

She could feel the heat coming of him even though she walked some four feet behind him and when they came to the river, he moved to crouch behind some trees, urging her to do the same. But there was no-one around, despite it now being mid-morning.

"We can't be seen like this, so you go on alone," he said softly. "I'll stay here, just to make sure you get across the river safely."

When Marrok turned to meet her gaze, at her hair long and loose which had dried in curls, her skin white as alabaster where her dress and shawl had stopped the sun tanning it, he felt his body stir with lust and knowing he was unable to hide it dressed the way he was, he turned away from her, wishing she would leave, for the temptation to take her in his arms was too much.

But Ella wanted to know what happened.

Who was that boy who'd saved his life? And how did Marrok know to come here?

"Jasper told me," he answered, with some harshness in his words as he moved to kneel.

"Jasper?"

Marrok nodded and looked out across the water and up towards the wagon train. "I had the strangest feeling something wasn't right when I woke this morning. I saw Jasper standing by your wagon, clearly distressed, and when he told me you'd left some time ago to come down here alone to bathe, I came to find you. When I saw the girl running through the woods, that young girl who was sitting next to you, I knew then something was wrong. She was the boy's sister, the one who killed the muleskinner and you were lucky they saw you, because that family group planned to leave at dawn."

Ella remembered the child sitting next to her, the girl who had silently watched her all morning. She wished she'd known it was her who had run to get help.

"I saw the boy before I saw the muleskinners," she said softy. "He came down to the water's edge and was pointing behind me, towards the trees, to warn me. I can't believe he killed that man to save our lives. He was a child."

"He was fourteen," Marrok said, glancing at her. "He was old enough."

"They've gone," she said, her voice breaking into a sob as she looked out towards the waterfall. "The muleskinners. They've gone over the waterfall."

She covered her face with her hands and cried then, sobbing quietly. Marrok moved to put an arm around her, grimacing at the pain in his shoulder and Ella surprised him by leaning into him. He took a breath, trying not to think that she wore only a shift.

She could smell his musky maleness along with the scent of herbs, packed into the wound beneath the hide dressings on his shoulder.

"At least there'll be no trace of them," he said softly. "And that family group will send some men back in the next few days, once the wagon train has gone, to dismantle the wagon and take the oxen. Both will be a tradeoff for the buffalo they've missed this year."

"But what if someone comes looking for those muleskinners?" Ella said, wiping her face on the hem of her shift.

Marrok shook his head. "No-one will. They had planned to head out this morning for Lower Canada. And the other group has already gone, they left for Fort Hall around dawn."

Ella shuddered, then turned to meet his gaze. "Who were they? That family group? What name do they go by?"

"Cheyenne. They've been out for weeks trading with other tribes and were on their way back to their village when they stopped here. They told me their tribe has been coming to this river for generations, but they no longer linger here as they did in the past. They say other men now camp here, men they don't like, men like those muleskinners." Marrok moved away from Ella to sit cross-legged, his naked upper body a thing of raw beauty as he stretched out.

"Yet they move like ghosts," Ella said, trying not to look at his wide shoulders, his hard muscular chest and belly. "No-one on that wagon train would even know they were here."

"You're right of course," Marrok said softly, "but those Cheyenne knew everything about that wagon train. How many people are on it, how many animals we have. They even knew we've been camped here for days because of that sickness. But that youth and others like him were watching the wagons all night, along with those of the muleskinners, which is why he saw you," he paused and looked at her.

"People on wagon trains think there's no-one around when they see no sign of life, but people like those Cheyenne are always around, watching from the woods, or up in the hills. Believe me, they know everything that's going on in their lands," he paused and looked out over the river.

"You say they're like ghosts, but they've known enough harassment from settlers to be wary of them. They've also heard stories about tribes being moved off their lands in the east, to make way for settlers, so for now, they just watch. But there'll come a day when they'll have no choice but to fight back, to keep safe what is theirs. But the day they fight back, I believe that will be the end of the wild as they know it, for how can it ever be what it was?"

"Is that what you see ahead for this country?" Ella asked in dismay. "Bloodshed?"

Marrok nodded. "Yes. Because I've seen it in

the east. It's inevitable, because no-one is stopping the tide of humanity pouring into this country and until the Government closes the borders to the west, they'll keep coming. But what man alive wouldn't want this country for his own? To be able to fish from its clean rich waters, or hunt in forests teaming with great herds of deer, moose and bear." He shook his head and looked at her, his eyes lingering on her mouth.

"All I hope is that I'm an old man, or long gone, before they find my valley and take it for themselves. I hope I'm not alive to see that."

For a moment all was still between them as Ella held his gaze, then Marrok moved, lifting his hand as though to reach for her, but instead he pulled back.

But not before he saw the disappointment in her lovely eyes. And as he tried to dismiss the ache in his body for her, he knew it was time for the truth.

"Ella, if I touch you I'm lost, for I couldn't stop myself if I took you in my arms. Lord knows I'm as red-blooded as the next man and I've been doing my darndest to hold back since I first met you, yet when you look at me like that, how can I possibly keep my distance? Yet I must, for we're different people, heading for different lives and if I allowed myself to love you, the bravest woman I've ever met, I know you'll haunt me for the rest of my days. And I won't live like that."

Ella felt the tears on her cheeks as she heard his words. This is what Ruby had seen, and Martha, and why Martha had warned Ella to stay away from him. Marrok was not a man to commit to any woman.

But Ella couldn't stay away. It was asking the impossible. She didn't care about the consequences.

She shook her head, even as she reached out to take his hand within her own and this time Marrok didn't move away. He sat utterly still, his breath shallow as she turned his hand over in her own, tracing the scars and calluses she found there. Yet she could feel the power of that hand within her own and knew well enough what Marrok was capable of doing with it. But he sat quietly, as she raised his hand to her face and held it there.

"Marrok," she whispered. "Can you not see my own feelings? Everyone else thinks them so transparent!" She moved to kiss each finger. "I loved you from the moment I saw you sitting at the table in my father's kitchen, when you stood up so suddenly on seeing me that you almost knocked it over. And when you helped me in my hopeless fight against Milton and Jebediah and again, here today, when you saved me from being brutalized," she shook her head, the tears falling freely.

"You think me brave my love, yet I am not so brave. I would have married Jebediah, for I saw no way out of it. So if anyone is to speak of courage here, it is I who must speak of your own. And that boy, for he saved your life and with it, my own."

She moved his hand to her heart as Marrok took a deep breath before moving to kneel before her, reaching up with his other hand to wipe away her tears.

But as he went to speak, a shout suddenly came from somewhere upriver.

"Miss Ella? You here girl? I's been worried about you all morning. Where are you, girl? You alive down here or you done gone and drowned?"

It was Jasper.

Marrok spun away from Ella as though touched by a hot poker and he groaned, not only from the wound on his shoulder.

"You can't be seen with me. Go now Ella. I beg you." He looked tortured as he spoke and hearing the urgency in his voice Ella moved, running down to the river and pushing herself once more through that current.

She reached the other side, turned back once, even though the wet material hugged her legs and thighs, then ran into the trees, back towards her clothes.

7

Marrok crouched there for long moments, hearing the distant muted sounds of oxen bellowing, a horse neighing, and the faraway hum of the wagon train as people went about their daily chores. The clang of a hammer on iron, a vague sound of a man shouting, children screaming, but they were far away and distant, meaning nothing to him. And then he heard Ella's call to Jasper.

She had dressed then, covering that glorious body and when Marrok peered out of the trees he saw her running along the riverbank, back the way she had come.

He closed his eyes, feeling the pulsating hum and burn of his body, yet ashamed of how close he had come to ruining her. A child might have resulted from their union here today in the woods, for Marrok knew well enough that Ella would have let him have his way. He had seen the flush of desire in her eyes and had he pulled her into his arms, not even Jasper's desperate call would have been able to stop the inevitable.

8

Marrok kept to his own camp that night and stayed with his men. But he found himself glancing across the wagon circle to where Ella sat with her own team. He could hear Abe and Wilber laughing and then later Ruby began to sing and Martha and Willard drifted over to join them, leaving Constance to rest in the wagon while her children slept.

But Marrok remained where he was, drinking coffee alone well into the night after his men went to their beds for it was impossible to sleep, not after what Ella had told him. She loved him. But she knew so little about him. And for her sake, Marrok knew she must go on to California with Martha and her family. There she would meet a boy closer to her own age, who would give her what she wanted.

Yet, there it was again, that crawl of something in his belly as he thought of Ella with another man

Marrok threw the dregs of his coffee onto the coals of the fire then stood up to move out into the dark to check his animals. The wagon train began to settle for the night but as people went to their beds, he envied them, for he felt restless and uneasy, as if a storm were coming for which he was utterly unprepared. And for the first time since he left his mother's village as a youth to strike out alone in the world, Marrok felt completely out of his depth.

*

Ella watched him discreetly from her campfire,

seeing him with his men, disappointed he didn't join her. But by staying away, Marrok had made his feelings clear. She had told him she loved him, but he never said he loved her back. And if nothing else, she now knew that his future did not include her.

She watched as he stood up and stepped back into the corral to check on his animals grazing alongside her own. And she suddenly half stood, wanting to go to him despite everything she knew, when Ruby came and sat down beside her. She reached out to take Ella's hand within her own.

"Be careful, my pretty," the girl said softly, pulling her back.

Ella looked at her and Ruby nodded discreetly towards Martha and Willard who sat opposite, laughing with Abe and Wilber. And on the other side of them, sat Clara and Jasper talking quietly.

"I saw Marrok ride off bareback down to the river early this morning," Ruby said, her voice so low that no-one could possibly hear but Ella. "And there's nothing wrong with that, except I saw you walk back from the river with Jasper hours later, your hair wet, dressed in clean clothes. Jasper won't tell me anything, he said he knows nothing, and I believe nothing happened. But when Marrok rode back into camp just a few hours ago, he wasn't himself. And he has an injury to his shoulder which he clearly favors. So let me tell you Ella, as someone who admires you and who cares for you, if I noticed something odd, others have noticed it too. You were gone for hours this morning. And when Clara and Martha asked after you, Jasper said you'd gone visiting. I think that's probably a lie to protect you, so I say again, be careful my lovely."

She glanced towards the corral, where Marrok wandered amongst the animals. "He's a dangerous man, Ella. And there's some folk here who see everything."

"Like you?"

Ruby shrugged. "My life over the past four years has depended on me seeing things. I watch everything and everyone, waiting for my father's thugs to appear, to attack. So yes, I see everything. All I'll say is, go easy Ella. We've still got a few weeks ahead of us before we reach Fort Hall. A reputation can follow a woman until the end of her days."

Ella said very little for the rest of the night. She loved a man she couldn't have, a man who wanted her but didn't love her, and soon they would part ways to live very different lives. Yet Ella wondered how she'd go on without him, because Marrok was as much a part of her life now as anyone she had ever loved and she couldn't bear to think of him not in it.

October 1846

1

The following day the wagon train rolled out on their last push west to Fort Hall. Ella never saw Marrok, as he'd already left when that first bugle call come blasting across camp at 4am. He didn't return for almost a week.

She tried not to think of him, but he filled her thoughts as the wagon train rolled on. She watched for him every day, as the flat prairie lands were left behind and replaced by rolling hills and then high mountainous country. And the only thing which took her mind off him were the hard long days of crossing over mountainous terrain and the nights when Artie called for music after supper, when the fiddles were brought out along with harmonicas and exhausted people found the energy to dance.

It was on one of these nights that Clara and Jasper's growing friendship became something that would last them through many years, becoming a bond of trust and something unbreakable.

Clara arrived back at camp after leaving Ella and Ruby dancing with Abe, Wilber and Moss Weslock, when she found Jasper sitting alone. He'd made a fresh pot of coffee and as she came to sit beside him, he offered her a cup. She noticed Jasper glance at her as she took the mug off him but Clara was well aware of the deep lines around her mouth and eyes and the grey through her hair. She smiled, taking no offence from his gaze.

"Oh Lord, I do feel weary Jasper. I'd dearly love to go to my bed but I ain't got no show of that happenin' with all those fiddles playin' and folks dancin'. I reckon there's enough noise in this here camp tonight to wake the dead."

Jasper smiled. "Where'd you grow up, Miss Clara. You never did speak of it. If you remember, I reckon you's lucky, as I remember nothin' about my early years."

Clara looked at him in surprise. "Nothin' at all?"

"No ma'am. I doan't know if that's because it was real bad or if I got a problem up here," he reached up to touch his head. "All I's remember is bein' with my old mama Violet, except she wasn't my mama at all. I first met her in a slave market, where Ella's daddy bought us together."

Clara tried to hide her shock, for she had thought Jasper a free man.

"Oh, doan't get me wrong," Jasper added, seeing the surprise on her face. "We weren't never treated as slaves. We got to be a part of that family I reckon, once Ella's mama got used to the idea of us livin' there. But I ain't complainin' about my past. The part I remember anyways." He looked at her and smiled. "So where'd you grow up Miss Clara?"

She thought on it a moment, remembering vividly the heat of the big house, the mosquitos in summer, the hard boards of the floor in the bedroom where she slept.

"A place down in Louisiana and if I miss anything at all, it sure ain't the bugs down that way," she paused and looked at him. "I's born on a plantation, finest place you'd ever see Jasper. When I's nothin' more than a child, I's taken out of my mama's arms an' moved into the big house, to be slave to the master's youngest daughter," Clara paused for a moment, before carrying on.

"Her name was Ada Rose an' she was a sweet enough child, just a few years older than me. I slept on a pallet at the bottom of her bed for the next fourteen years, right up 'til she was eighteen, got married an' left for New Orleans. But I done told her, I doan't want to leave, for my mama was still alive, but that sweet child wanted me with her an' that was that. So I left. I was with her in New Orleans for the next twenty years," again Clara paused, but she didn't look at Jasper.

"She died some five years or so ago from river fever, just a month after her husband. Her only child, a girl they called Esther 'though I never did take to that name, had moved to New York to live with her husband years before. When Ada Rose died, Esther came back to New Orleans to sell the house an' pay off the servants, includin' me. She said she had no use for me in New York an' she doan't want her husband's family knowin' her mama had slaves. So I's sent out into the street with the few dollars in my pocket she gave me, but with no mind of where to go or what to do. I got no schoolin'. I'd been slave to one woman since I was four years old an' now I was nearly forty. I called myself the forgotten slave."

"What'd you do?" Jasper asked in dismay.

"Found work on one of the paddle steamers on the Mississippi River. Just cleanin'. Mostly moppin' up folks' sick when they didn't take too kindly to river crossing," she shook her head.

"One day I's walkin' around St Louis, askin' folks if they were lookin' for a cook or cleaner, for

I reckon I could do both well enough, when a saloon took me on. I's there more'n five years. But that man done wore me to the bone. But I stayed, for I got no better offer. An' where else a tired old black woman goin' to go, heading for her forties," she paused again, and this time she did look at Jasper.

"That's where I met Miss Ruby, in that saloon. She did what I done. Walked in an' asked for a job. But I'll tell you now Jasper, I do fret some over what's ahead for me with Miss Ruby, for she ain't a girl to stay put for long. She's a child that needs constant movement, constant change, but I ain't like that. I like to settle."

"Well, I reckon you should talk to Marrok. He's lookin' for folk to help him set up his ranch. If Miss Ella decide she doan't want me, I's going to work for him. He might need a cook. Or a cleaner. You go on and ask him, Miss Clara. It can't hurt none to ask. All he can say is no. But I's hopin' he'll say yes."

Clara looked at him, loving him for his concern, but not loving him like the other way. Not like her mistress' husband liked to love her.

*

The night before Marrok rode back into camp, Elmer Weslock collapsed and died. The day after that, Moss asked Ruby to marry him.

Elmer's health had deteriorated over the past four months and with the hard physical work of looking after the wagon and oxen, he often struggled to breathe. When he collapsed while walking alongside the wagon one warm autumn day less than three weeks out from Fort Hall, everyone grieved for him, with Nell and Moss burying him by the side of the trail.

The following day, after Ella invited Nell and Moss to join her and her team for supper, Moss took Ruby aside and proposed to her. Ruby declined, doing it as gently as possible, but Moss was devastated.

Ruby assured Ella he'd get over it. "It's grief that made him do it," she said. "Once he meets the right girl, he'll understand this was the right decision. I could never make him happy."

Meanwhile Abe and Wilber continued to court the two sisters from South Carolina, even as Ella watched with a growing sense of unease.

She wished the brothers would just stop and ask themselves if this was what they wanted. She had a feeling that if Abe and Wilber let this drag on for much longer, the girls' father was likely to come looking for them with a shotgun.

2

Marrok stood under a pine and looked out across the densely forested hills. He couldn't see the wagon train from here as it was another two days away from reaching these hills, but it would come.

He had spent the past two days with the Blackfeet and listened as they talked of going to war.

Now he stood up in the hills, looking back towards their village and wondered if Artie's wagon train would make it through, even though the Blackfeet had given him their word they wouldn't attack.

Marrok had no reason to doubt them, but he also knew this tribe were at the end of their fuse and all someone had to do to stir things up, was light it.

He mounted his horse and headed out, back towards the wagon train.

*

He caught several wild hares in traps the following evening and roasted them on spits above a fire, sharing them with two old French fur trappers he'd found camped on a river.

The men were in their seventies and had spent most of their lives in the wild trapping furs. Like Marrok's grandfather and father, it was likely they would also die in the wild.

"Just come back from looking at another new trading post that's opened up, way in the north," the eldest of the pair said, a man by the name of Richaud. "Mostly trading with Indians for now, but likely that will change as more settlers come through.

He spoke in French, because despite knowing several Indian dialects, he knew little English.

"Man who built it reckons there'll be more of them in the years ahead," said the other man, who went by the name of Gysbert. "Getting so a man can't travel too far these days without coming upon a trading post or fort. Although can't say I mind too much, not when we can get supplies without travelling all the way back to St Louis, or up to Lower Canada. But makes a man lazy."

"You trapping much?" Marrok asked.

"Sure, of course," said Gysbert. "But no-one wants fur anymore. The market for fancy hats has died away in Europe so there's no money in it for us, not like there was. But we still trade furs with the trading posts, just don't get as much for them. Enough to buy what we want, so we got no complaints, not at our age."

"We heard some fool say not too long ago that one day there'll be trading posts from one end of the country to the other, but can't see it myself," said Richaud. "Clearly he's never seen how big this country is, not like us. We've been travelling the length and breathe of it for some sixty odd years, since we was boys, so no, I can't see such a thing ever happening."

"You hear anything about the Indians talking war?" Marrok asked.

The two men nodded and looked at him.

"They been talking war for a few years now, but they like to trade as well," Richaud said. "But those folks got a lot to lose with those settlers coming through," he shook his head. "Glad I don't have to see that war when it comes," he glanced over at Marrok and shrugged. "But what do I know? I've been up here in the wild for so long, can't quite remember who owns this darn country anymore."

He spat in the fire, then took a long drink of water from an old, stained waterskin. "First, it was the Indians. Then it was the French and Spanish. Last time I looked, it was the Americans. So just wait a while and I reckon it'll go back to the Indians."

Marrok laughed and moved to cut some meat off the spit.

3

He made it back to the wagon train as it was pulling into camp beside a lake two days later. Mountains now towered around them, the days long and hard as animals and wagons negotiated narrow passes. Ella saw him ride in, a lone figure coming out of the forested hills in the north, a man dressed in buckskin yet wearing a wide brimmed hat.

But Marrok wasn't thinking about Ella, not then. All his thoughts were on meeting up with Artie as soon as he could and tell him about the Blackfeet. As he left his horse to his men to be brushed down and watered, he wondered if the people on the wagon train should be warned. But that might cause more problems. Besides, the Blackfeet had given their word they wouldn't attack.

Ella saw him hurry across to the wagon master and as the men huddled together and talked, she took Abe and Wilber with her down to the lake to fill buckets with fresh water, to pour into their water barrels on the side of the wagon. But as they climbed a slight rise, before making their way on down through the pine trees to the water's edge, they stopped and stared in awe as the view opened up before them.

The lake was at least a mile wide, yet beyond it, through the trees, they could see a mountain range that seemed to rise to meet the heavens, their peaks covered in thick virgin snow with vast evergreen forests sweeping away as far as the eye could see.

"Lord above," said Wilber. "We got to get the wagons through more of those mountains."

Ella remembered what Marrok had said about the Rockies all those months ago when they were travelling to Independence from St Louis.

If we don't get through before winter we won't make it, because we'll never find enough to feed the animals. And once the animals are gone, there's no hope of getting through the deep drifts of snow that'll fall up there. Only a log cabin, or a teepee, and a fire will keep us warm, but certainly not a wagon. People would freeze to death in the bitter cold

Abe put his hands on his hips and shook his head. "Not sure I want to go over any more mountains. And I'm not liking this cold at night. How much colder can it get, do you reckon?"

"Can't imagine," Wilber said. "But if you're thinking on marrying one of them gals and joining her family in Oregon, you'd better get prepared for the cold."

"Well it sure ain't warm up here like it is in St Louis or Tennessee," Abe grumbled.

They turned as a group of men came towards them through the trees and Ella recognized his voice before she saw him. Marrok stopped to greet them, allowing his men to go on without him.

"Look at that view, why don't you," Abe said, nodding towards the mountains. "It's something, I grant you that, yet how's a man meant to get wagons across that range? It's hard enough now."

Marrok smiled. "If everyone takes it slowly, you'll get over without any trouble."

"But you won't be heading that way, will you?" Wilber asked.

Marrok shook his head. "No, but I'll have enough mountains of my own to cross as I head north."

He excused himself then and walked off, but as Ella and the brothers made their way down to the water, as Ella gathered her skirts about her, Marrok glanced back and thought that she belonged out here in the woods. She was born to live on the land.

She turned suddenly as though aware he watched her and grinned, before hurrying after Abe and Wilber. Marrok grunted, a deep primal sound of desire, then he turned to follow his men.

*

That evening Artie called a meeting. "You all keep close to the wagons now, until we reach Fort Hall. Don't go riding out, or leaving without telling folk where you're going because we're in Blackfoot country now and they don't take kindly to us traipsing through their lands. So keep your eyes about you as I don't want no trouble."

After the meeting, Marrok and Artie were walking through camp when they stopped to accept a coffee from Willard.

Ella was sitting with Martha, keeping the children occupied, as Constance lay down in the back of the wagon, feeling restless and uncomfortable, wishing her pregnancy over.

"She's past envying those women who've already given birth," Martha said. "All she wants now is for it to be over and she has a healthy babe in her arms. But I hope she don't give birth until we reach Fort Hall. It's too hard on a woman with a newborn out here on the trail."

As Marrok and Artie accepted a coffee from Ella, Willard asked them about their plans. "What will you do after you leave us in Fort Hall?"

"Breed horses and do some trading with the Hudson Bay Company," said Artie. "I'd like to think my days as wagon master are almost over."

"Will you ranch up by the Willamette Valley? I've heard a lot of folks talking about it," Martha asked.

Marrok shook his head. "Further north of Willamette. Closer to the Canadian border."

"Well, I guess it'll be cold up there in winter," Willard said. "And that's alright if you like the cold, but I'm looking for a warm place to settle and California seems to have it. I've heard oranges grow as big as my fist out there and they have fresh air blowing in off the ocean where you can taste the salt. I can't tell you how much I'm looking forward to seeing it for myself."

They talked some more of what lay ahead for each of them, then Artie made his excuses to leave. When Marrok got up to go a little while later, Ella also made her excuses, so she could walk back with him. As they made their way through that darkening camp, she asked how he came to find his land.

"When Artie and I finished last year's wagon train he invited me north to meet the Chinook, his wife's people. We went out hunting one day and as we came out of the woods, there it was, a wide fertile valley spread out below us like some kind of paradise. A ring of mountains circle it, with a wide deep river running through its center and forests sweeping across the mountain foothills. I've never seen so many herds of deer. The wolves run in such big packs you can hear them howling to each other across mountain ranges at night," he paused and smiled.

"We stayed there that night and when we woke the next morning, Artie and I both knew we wanted to live there. We talked about it for days, until deciding we could breed horses and sell them on to settlers or the Hudson Bay Company. But all that land belongs to the Chinook people so after talking on it, they agreed we could settle there as long as we trade with them. Which is why my wagons are full of supplies. Good quality blankets, the best guns and tools I could buy, as well as clothes and cooking utensils," he paused and looked at her, seeing the excitement on her face as she listened, leaning towards him.

Marrok suddenly remembered that kiss they had shared in St Louis. She'd left him bruised after that kiss and he knew he hadn't yet healed from it. But suddenly, as if a curtain had lifted before him, Marrok saw her there in that valley, living with him, helping him build his new life. He knew she loved the mountains because she often woke early to watch the sun rise over those distant peaks, and at night she waited for the moon to appear over that shadowy jagged skyline.

"Don't stop now, Marrok. I want to hear more!" she scolded him, unaware of his thoughts.

Yet Marrok felt torn in half, knowing she would love his valley, but he could never take her away from her family. If she went to Oregon with him, Ella would never again see Martha, nor Willard and Constance and the children.

"Please?" she said, taking his hand and pulling him down by the fire. "I want to hear it all!"

Marrok sat cross-legged on the grass, longing to tell her of his plans yet also unwilling to share it, in case he lost it. But as he looked at her, seeing the wonder and curiosity on her face as she waited to hear more, Marrok couldn't help himself and began to talk of it.

"Our biggest problem will be getting the wagons over rough country, so we can either sell them in Fort Hall or dismantle them and take them overland by horse and travois." He turned to look out into the dark night. "I've thought of that valley every day since I left it more than a year ago and every day I can't wait to get back. The water in the river is crystal clear Ella and so sweet you'll wonder at its source. The woods are so vast you could spend your life in them and never meet their end. We've seen eagles with wing spans as long as I am tall, herds of bison along with deer, wild mountain cats and grizzlies. A man will never go hungry up there, nor want for shelter, for there's hides aplenty to make a teepee or wood to build cabins."

He paused and turned as Ruby appeared out of the dark along with Abe and Wilber. The three of them looked in a somber mood, but Ella knew they'd been helping Nell and Moss go through Elmer's belongings. The brothers said goodnight and went to their beds, but Ruby joined Marrok and Ella by the fire.

"Lord, that was hard. Poor Nell. She doesn't know what she'll do. She doesn't want to be a burden on Moss but everything's changed since Elmer died. She's talking about getting some sort of job once they reached California, to help Moss out."

Marrok had heard about Elmer's sudden death from Artie. "Give them both time," he said, feeling sad for the Weslock family as he'd liked Elmer. "It's been a shock for both of them but I think Moss will do the right thing by Nell. Everyone can see how close they are," he said, then stood up, excusing himself. "I must away before I fall asleep here by the fire. I'll see you both in the morning."

Ella was disappointed he left and as she watched him walk away, she heard Ruby mutter something beside her.

"What is it?" Ella asked, turning back to look at the younger woman in surprise.

"Ella honey, we need to talk," Ruby said, her voice low and soft. "You see, I'm feeling rather foolish that I interfered in whatever this thing is between you and Marrok. I want to apologize for it, as I believe I was wrong. I can see the way you look at each other when you're alone, as if no-one else exists in the world," she paused, aware of the shock on her friend's face.

"What I'm trying to say is, you must follow your own path, Ella. You're old enough to know what it is you want. Don't listen to me or Martha or anyone else because we have our own lives to live. We know what we want. Martha will continue on to California and live out the rest of her days with her son's family. I'll go on to sing in one of the big halls in San Francisco. But what about you Ella? What do you want?"

Ella glanced back towards Marrok's camp and

Ruby smiled as she saw the longing on her friend's face. "Honey, I think you know what you want. Yet you believe you must go west with Martha, just as Marrok no doubt thinks he can't drag you north to live a life in the wilderness when you have a family here. But know this Ella, once we reach Fort Hall, Marrok will head north and the chance of either of you making a decision will be lost forever."

Ella said nothing, but suddenly remembered a conversation she'd overheard between Martha and Willard a few days ago which quickly became heated, for both of them were strong characters.

For the first time, she wondered if she'd be happy living with them, because that was what she was heading for. Did she really want to help Constance and Martha run a household with four children? Or did she want to use what little money she had left and start out on her own? She had no idea what she would do. Perhaps buy a bit of land for Billy and Bear to run on, grow some vegetables, find work doing something in the nearest town.

"Once I reach California," Ruby continued, interrupting her thoughts. "I'll be heading off to follow my own dream, whether Clara decides to come with me or not. I hope she does. But you be careful you don't leave your dream behind in Fort Hall." She reached over to hug Ella before leaving her alone to go to her bed.

4

Clara was already asleep when Ella crawled into their shelter. She quickly undressed to her shift and crawled under the blankets but lay awake, thinking on Ruby's words, until she couldn't help herself and reached out to pull aside the shelter's flap so she could look out towards Marrok's camp.

He was sitting alone, his own men gone to bed like everyone else, except for the men on guard. He seemed deep in thought as he stared into the flames, chewing on a piece of willow, the same fiber he'd used to make her dreamcatcher, when he surprised Ella by glancing over towards her camp. She saw him shake his shoulders, as though eager to relieve the tension there, before he went to his wagon, reached for a blanket and strode off into the dark, towards the lake.

She thought back over his words, spoken in St Louis after their kiss and again beside that river of death, when he'd told her he wasn't the marrying kind. Those words had hurt her, but at least she knew the truth and she would rather have his truth than lies. She wasn't a girl who could live on false hope or waste her life on a man who wouldn't commit, listening to his lies while the best years of her life drifted away.

But did she want to leave him at Fort Hall without ever knowing what it was like to be with him? To be with a man like that? She'd had a taste of it back in St Louis and in truth, she wanted more.

Clara turned over in her bed and snored softly. She seemed able to sleep through anything, as some mornings Ella had had to shake the older woman to wake her. Perhaps living in a saloon in St Louis for more than five years had taught her to close off to everything.

Ella knew Marrok was going down to the lake to bathe, but the memory of him standing half naked in his wet buckskin pants sent a fire storm through her body. It was a desire unknown to her and its fierceness was so powerful, it was as though she were gripped with a madness she couldn't control and Ella could think of nothing but being with him.

So without thinking of the consequences, tired of doing what was expected of her, she pushed aside her blankets, grabbed one off the bed, grabbed her dress and crept outside. She didn't bother with her boots, nor did she bother putting the dress on because she didn't want to chance waking Clara, or Ruby sleeping above her in the wagon.

It was utterly still, everyone abed except for the men standing guard. She saw a man coming her way and she stepped back into the shadows. She hardly breathed as he passed her by. Then he was gone.

She took off, keeping to the shadows of the wagons before racing towards the cover of the trees surrounding the lake.

Ella knew she faced Marrok's wrath, because he'd asked her not to go out alone. Yet here she was stepping out into the night, wearing nothing but her shift.

She stopped under a stand of pine and listened. For a moment she was met with only silence, then she heard the distant sound of water splashing. She walked barefoot through the trees, thinking of nothing but the desire to be with him. And then she saw him, the wispy clouds blown away by a soft breeze, allowing the waxy moonlight to reveal the shadow of a man swimming about a quarter mile out from the bank.

She watched him, aware that no other man in the wagon train would do such a thing at this hour of the night, but at least she was confident they were alone. She hurried on down to the water's edge, feeling the soft prick of pine needles beneath her bare feet.

5

Marrok heard someone coming through the trees, the sound of bracken being trod on and he moved fast, pushing himself through the water as silently as he could, reaching the bank where he'd left his weapons.

He ran at a low crouch towards his clothes, reached for his knife then sprinted behind a tree, watching as the shadow came to stand at the water's edge, not ten feet from where he stood.

He stared incredulous for a moment then uttered a soft oath of astonishment, for even in the faint glow of moonlight he would recognize her anywhere. He stepped out from behind the trees, buck naked, but he knew Ella saw him only in shadow, as he saw her.

"Ella?" he called softly, bewildered by her coming here, yet as a man, he knew. Yet he hardly dared believe it.

She turned to him and despite the pale glow of the moon, she was well aware of his nakedness. She could hardly breathe with the want of him, the need to touch him.

"What are you doing here?" he asked, his voice nothing more than a whisper.

"You know why," she said, her own voice low as she stepped towards him. "I don't want to live with regrets, Marrok. Oh, I know full well you don't want me, not like I want you, but I no longer care about that. I willing to take whatever I can from you, before you leave my life forever," she stepped closer to him, aware of Marrok's absolute stillness.

"I want you to love me. I want you to be the

first, rather than some young man Martha pushes me to marry in California. I want to always have the memory of you, of us, like this."

Marrok stood in silence, unable to argue with her anymore. He was done battling this struggle against her.

Ella stepped closer and put a hand on his chest, holding it there, feeling the dull steady thud of the beat of his heart.

But this wasn't like St Louis, where she'd reached out and grabbed at his shirt to stop herself falling.

This was intent. This was the touch of a woman who felt desire.

She moved her hand, running it slowly down his naked muscular belly, her touch as light as a feather, feeling the hardness of his body, the slight indentation of his belly button and then she went further and heard his sharp intake of breath.

"We have a whole night ahead of us Marrok. Please don't waste it," she begged.

6

She lay atop him, her naked body warming him. But Marrok didn't need warming. She kissed him again, softly now, not like before, not like the hot heated thing that had been between them.

Marrok felt every inch of her along every inch of himself, even as his hands reached down to caress her thighs, as her hands caressed his shoulders and chest and her lips teased him.

"Do you have regrets?" he asked, his voice low and deep.

Ella pulled back a little to look down at him, then shook her head. "Never! For how could I be sorry for what we just shared?" she asked, her own voice husky, her body aching where he had been, yet she couldn't move away from him if she tried, such was her love for him.

Marrok took a deep shuddering breathe before rolling over so she lay beneath him. Ella bought her leg up so it rested over his and closed her eyes with pleasure as he kissed her again, before his lips moved to her neck, her shoulder and then her breast. Ella felt his sex rise again where he lay on her belly, but he was in no hurry. And she knew she could lie like this forever with him.

He reached for her hand and held it in his own, leaning back to look at her. The moonlight shared enough light for her to admire his rugged beauty, his hard body that had given her such pleasure, and pain. He brought her hand to his lips and kissed it, a gentle caress, yet Ella knew how fierce and demanding that mouth could be as it claimed her own, along with the rest of her.

"There's something about you Ella that drives

me to the point of not knowing my own mind. I've never known it with another woman and I do believe you have the power to destroy me. I think I've known it since that kiss we shared in St Louis. Like the flame destroys the moth, so you could destroy me."

"Well, you may think of yourself as a moth if you prefer Marrok Gauvain, all I know is that I'm in love with you. And even though we only have tonight I don't care. I shall carry this memory with me for the rest of my days," she looked up at him and smiled, reaching up to trace the outline of his lips with her finger. "Shall I tell you now that every day is torture for me when you ride out, when I don't know where you are or if you're safe. I understand that's your choice and the way you live your life, but I can't rest easy until you're back in camp, until I know you're safe and I can watch you and hear you and pretend you're in love with me, as I am with you."

She saw him smile and he let go of her hand to trace his fingers over her body. She felt that now familiar rush of pleasure at his touch and moved her other leg up and away from him, so he lay between them. He looked at her, his voice husky and low.

"Don't tempt me Ella, for I'm well aware this is your first time."

"I don't care. I want this night to last forever. I'm not afraid of anything."

"Oh, I know that well enough," he said, moving his large frame gently off her so he could kiss her belly. So she moved her legs around him, caressing him with them, driving him to that other place where he'd lost control, when she'd pulled off her shift, even as he'd tried to still her.

But Ella would not be stilled. And when she'd stood there naked before him, her hands reaching for him, Marrok had lost all thought of what might come of this night and taken her in his arms.

As he lay above her now, smelling her sweet scent and feeling the hot warmth of her beneath his hands, he knew he'd wanted this from the moment he'd seen her riding Bear across the fields in that wedding dress back at the ranch, the gown billowing behind her, as though she didn't give a damn.

"Yet what is a man to do after a night like this?" he asked, kissing her. "How am I meant to go on? I can't bear to think of you heading off to California, knowing I might never see you again. Nor can I bear to think of any other man having this. And what if there's a child tonight?" He sat up then and Ella moved to sit before him, yet unable to be apart from her, he lifted her so she sat on his thighs, her legs wrapped around him. Again, he felt the heat of her against him.

"I shall deal with that if it happens," she said, taking his face in her hands and kissing him gently, her lips soft against his cheek, his mouth. "Women have dealt with such things for centuries. But know this, Marrok Gauvain. I would keep your child. I wouldn't allow others to raise our babe. And whether a boy or girl, they'll likely want to be in the wild, just like you, just like your father and grandfather and the men and women of your mother's people and I could never deny our child that."

Marrok looked at her in the moonlight, his dark eyes holding her own and suddenly he felt that curtain lift again and knew that this was destiny. Her being with him tonight wasn't wrong, it was fate, it was meant to be. He'd felt it, that sense of destiny, back at the ranch when he'd asked her to come west with them. He'd known it when he put his own schedule on hold for almost a month, to help her, to make sure she travelled with him. He just hadn't had a name for it, until now. This young woman who owned so much courage, who wasn't afraid of anything, was his soul mate.

"Then marry me Ella. Come with me to Oregon. Help me build a new life in that valley I spoke of, alongside Artie and the Chinook. Bring Jasper and Clara if they want to come. I think Clara already understands that Ruby will move on one day, leaving her alone, but she won't be alone with us. Abe and Wilber can join us if they want, as some of the men in my team have decided to come with me, but Artie and I will need all the help we can get to build cabins and corrals."

Ella wrapped her arms about his neck, yet her thoughts were of Martha and saying goodbye forever. It would break her heart, but if she had to choose between Martha and Marrok, there was only one choice to make.

"Yes," she nodded, kissing him. "Yes, I'll come to Oregon with you."

7

The next few weeks couldn't come fast enough for most people on that wagon train, as Fort Hall loomed in the distance. But none more so, than Ella and Marrok. They had decided to wait and get married there, which Artie had suggested, because Marrok had to ride out again for a few days and Artie didn't want his head full of Ella.

"It's less than three weeks away and you'll be gone for most of it. Let the girl marry in Fort Hall where she'll have all the luxury the trading post can offer."

Marrok finally saw the sense in it and Ella reluctantly agreed, but as he rode off, as she kissed him goodbye, all she wanted now was for this journey to be over so they could start their lives together.

Most people on the wagon train were shocked by the upcoming nuptials, including Constance and Willard, as they hadn't noticed the blossoming romance between Marrok and Ella.

Jasper cried when Ella told him she was going to marry Marrok. "Oh Lord, I's so glad Miss Ella. I wanted to go with him real bad and work his land and breed horses. Now we can take Billy and Bear with us."

Martha and Ruby weren't shocked by the romance, but they were devastated to learn that Ella had agreed to marry Marrok and follow him into the wild. Both women had presumed if there was to be a marriage, Marrok would follow Ella to California.

Martha tried to talk Ella out of it, but soon realized she was wasting her breath.

"I can't live without him Aunt," Ella said. "He's my life. He's everything to me. I'll only be half alive if I'm not with him."

Martha wiped the tears from her eyes. "I tried to stop it so many times, because I saw the attraction between the two of you from the moment you met. Remember that day back at the ranch, when you burst into the kitchen and Marrok almost pushed the table over getting to his feet? It happened right then, this thing between you two and like I said, I've done my best to squash it, but love will find its way," she paused to wipe her eyes again. "Well, I'll miss you girl, but you know that already I hope. Anyways, you've got your own life to lead and it's not for me to hold you back, but I think your mama and daddy would be pleased. Marrok's a good man and I know you'll be happy with him."

Ruby found it impossible to believe that Ella would choose to live in the wild, in a wagon, until Marrok could build her a cabin.

"I had thoughts of him following you to California! Not the other way around!" Ruby said in astonishment. "But there's no getting around how you feel about each other. I can only hope that one day I'll find someone as worthy of me, as Marrok is of you." She paused to reach out and hug her friend. "Do you know, we both escaped west by wagon train and look what you found. I hope I'm lucky enough to find my happiness."

Clara was thrilled to join Ella and Marrok in Oregon, even though Ella thought the deep friendship that Clara now shared with Jasper might be another reason for it.

"I know it'll be hard, I got no doubts 'bout that," Clara said to Ella when they spoke of it one evening. "Mr Marrok an' Jasper done tol' me how hard it'll be, livin' like this for months until a cabin gets built an' havin' Indians for neighbors. But I don't care 'bout none of that. I's just want to get settled. I just want to have a home."

"Me too, Clara," Ella said softly. "Together we'll create a family up in the north, you and me and Marrok and Jasper. Along with Marrok's men, and Artie and his wife and her family. We'll certainly never be alone, that's for sure."

*

The night before they arrived in Fort Hall, men brought out their fiddles and harmonicas after supper and people got up to dance. While Ella stood off to one side watching Ruby dance with Moss, Artie approached her. Marrok had been gone for days, scouting the country ahead, but he'd meet them in Fort Hall on the morrow.

"I know you'll make Marrok happy," Artie said softly, so no-one could overhear them. "He's a very private man, I'll tell you that now, but not once in all the years I've known him have I ever seen him this happy. He never lets his guard down to anyone, certainly not a stranger, but he did with you," he paused to watch the people dancing, then turned back to Ella, his hair and beard trimmed for their arrival in Fort Hall, ready for the handover of his wagon train to the two new wagon masters.

"Over the years I've seen a lot of women drawn to Marrok, but he gave none of them so much as a glance, until he met you. And forgive me if I'm speaking out of turn Ella, as I'm not entirely sure Marrok would thank me for it, but I'm pleased as hell that you're coming to Oregon with us. I think my wife and her people will love you."

Ella reached up to kiss him on the check, then Artie smiled and walked away, back towards his own team and to celebrate his last night driving a wagon train west.

Fort Hall
October 1846

1

The Shoshone Indians called it the Snake River and on a patch of cleared land above that long winding river which travelled all the way to the distant Columbia, stood Fort Hall. Built on Shoshone and Bannock land, these tribes traded with the fort, along with fur trappers who worked the rivers in this territory for the Hudson Bay company in the north.

The team of seven muleskinners who had talked to Marrok and Artie just over a month ago had long since delivered their supplies. The shelves within the trading post were stocked with goods and as everyone purchased what they needed before they headed out, either to California or north to the Willamette Valley in Oregon, Marrok and Ella made plans to wed.

He'd arrived at Fort Hall the previous night and taken the time to wash, shave and change into clean clothes. He'd also cleaned and brushed down the woolen pants and calico shirt he'd purchased in St Louis to take Ella out to dinner, because he planned to marry her in those clothes.

When the wagons rolled into Fort Hall, Ella had seen him sitting on horseback watching for her wagon. She ran to him as he dismounted and as the wagons moved into their circles and unharnessed animals so they could graze, they made plans to marry.

Martha wanted Ella to wear her mother's wedding band, for as her aunt said. "It ain't proper if you ain't got a ring on your finger."

Fort Hall didn't sell anything like wedding bands and Ella didn't like the thought of wearing her mother's wedding ring, so chose the ring she'd found at the ranch instead, which fitted her perfectly and which she thought might have belonged to one of her grandmothers.

Martha still felt uneasy about this marriage and tried to persuade Ella to wait a few more days to make sure this was what she wanted, but Ella assured her she had no plans to change her mind. She didn't want to be anywhere else but by Marrok's side. She was prepared to live in the back of a wagon for the rest of her life if it meant they could be together.

"Well, if that's your mind made up, all that's left to say is I wish you the very best, just as your mama and daddy would have done," Martha said, reaching out to take Ella in her arms.

"They would be so proud of you, just like I'm proud of you and I think you'll do just fine up north. Just remember not to dwell on the hard times when they come and they will come, because everyone has them. Just think on what you and Marrok share, because that kind of love can get you through anything. And try and send me a letter if you can, send it to a hotel in San Francisco, if they have such a place, even if it takes a while to reach me, just to let me know you're alright. One day I'll get it, I don't know how, but someone might know where we are."

Ella brushed away her tears and took her aunt's hands in her own. "I'll miss you so much. You've been a mother to me for more than half my life and you know I'll think of you every day. And I promise that somehow, I'll send you that letter, I'll find a way."

Martha wiped away her own tears. "Well, you know I'll be alright. I've got Willard back and I'll have four grandbabies to take care of. They'll run me off my feet, but I wouldn't have it any other way." She smiled as she looked at the radiant girl standing before her. "I might be losing you to the wilds of Oregon, but I'd rather it be this way and know you're happy, then you be trapped and living a life of misery on a ranch back home."

"I know Aunt," Ella said softly. "Ruby and I both had a lucky escape thanks to Marrok. And I wouldn't change what's happened for the world."

2

The morning of the wedding, Ruby used her precious soap supplies so Ella could bathe, using a large bucket and lots of hot water which Clara boiled for her.

After helping Ella dry her hair, Ruby curled it, using her own pins and weaving strips of satin ribbon through the curls.

Clara found wildflowers in a meadow behind the Fort, where she'd gone with Clarissa and Eleanor earlier that morning and now they gently pushed the small, scented flowers amongst the pins and satin ribbons before Clara used what was left to make a small bouquet.

When Martha appeared at the back of Ella's wagon not long before the wedding, she stumbled from the weight she was carrying.

Clara and Ruby rushed to help her climb up into the wagon and then Martha was unwrapping a blanket which held a large bundle.

Ella gasped in shock as she stared at the stunning wedding dress Jebediah Crawley had purchased, hoping to wed her.

"When you and Marrok rode over to talk to Jebediah, I sponged all the mud splatter out of it best I could. I patched the silk and lace gloves months ago, when I had a spare moment, hoping you wouldn't see. I couldn't bear to throw anything away."

"I didn't know," Ella whispered. "I didn't know you'd kept it and brought it all this way west."

"I couldn't leave it behind. I couldn't let Jebediah have it, knowing you'd worn it, knowing the sort of man he was. The thought of it made my stomach crawl, so better for me to wash the mud out best I could and bring it with me. I never thought to see you in it. I didn't really know what I'd do with it to be honest, but if you want to wear it, I guess that'll be your choice."

"But Marrok's seen me in this dress. When I was out riding Bear across the fields and again in the kitchen. Won't that mean bad luck for us?"

"It's only bad luck if you want to believe it. Now, let's get you dressed and put some rouge on your cheeks and lips. There's a tall handsome man waiting for you out there. I wouldn't keep him waiting if I were you."

Ella had never felt more beautiful. Her hands were trembling within the gloves as she climbed down out of the wagon, as she saw all those people who had come all that way west from Independence looking up at her, standing in a circle before Artie.

Then Ella saw Marrok. He stood tall and proud and handsome in the clothes he'd worn to take her to dinner in St Louis, his coal dark eyes looking at her with such love and longing she couldn't wait to go to him.

When it came time for her to repeat her vows after Artie, it seemed as if the world faded away, as if there were no-one else there but her and Marrok.

She heard Artie's words, and then her own, followed by Marrok's vows. As Ella said *I do*, she knew without any doubt that this was where she was meant to be and she suddenly understood why her father hadn't left her sole beneficiary of the ranch.

Quentin knew she would have worked until that

ranch broke her, as it did him.

By leaving a half share to his brother, a man he knew to be a wastrel, he knew Ella would have no choice but to move on, to stand on her own two feet and seek out a new life for herself.

He hadn't done it because his mind was half gone with the disease that was eating him alive, he had done it because he loved her. Yet what that decision must have cost him!

Ella felt herself trembling with emotion as she thought of Quentin. He would have loved Marrok, as would her mother and it had all started by taking a chance, of having the courage to step into the unknown and heading west by wagon train.

*

To celebrate the ceremony, the women on the wagon train each gave a little of their limited supplies so that cakes and fresh bread could be made.

Some of the men went out hunting with Marrok and Artie, while others dug a fire pit on which to roast the butchered deer meat when it was brought in.

When the fiddlers started playing and everyone clapped and cheered, encouraging Marrok and Ella to get up and dance, Ella knew she'd never heard Marrok laugh so much as he laughed that day.

Along with the food, which wasn't a feast by any means as no-one had the money or supplies for it, a young man on the wagon train eager to start his own brewery in California, where he'd been told the grapes grew as big as plums, supplied a few stone jars he had of elderberry and berry punch.

When Ella and Marrok finally snuck away to one of his wagons, which he'd purposely left under a grove of trees some way from the others, Ella was grateful for the privacy on their first night together.

Later, when she fell asleep in his arms, she couldn't imagine there being anything better in the world, than this.

3

The night after their wedding, Constance went into labor and in the early hours of the morning was safely delivered of another boy. Martha helped deliver him, along with the two midwives who had travelled west with them.

Abe and Wilber declined Marrok's offer to join him in Oregon. They also declined the offer to join the family from South Carolina in the Willamette Valley. Instead, they joined Moss and Nell Weslock's team, along with Ruby, with the aim of going on to California, which had been their dream from the very beginning.

Ella felt some guilt about leaving half her team stranded at Fort Hall, although they didn't seem to mind too much.

"I've got to get to California somehow," Ruby said to her. "Now that my ride with you is over, I'm happy enough to travel with Nell and Moss. They're good decent folk and you know me Ella, I'm always ready for a challenge."

Moss couldn't have expected a better outcome, despite being well aware that Ruby didn't feel the same way about him, as he did her.

"I don't mind so much anymore, I've got over my disappointment," he said to her one night when they sat down together. "All I know is that I've been struggling since Pa died, working the oxen and the wagon alone, so I'll be mighty grateful for Abe and Wilber's help. And we all know Ma has found life hard on the trail since he died, so I think you'll be good for her. You'll take her mind off her grief."

Ruby was grateful he said this, because they

both knew there was little hope of romance between them. But she liked his relationship with his grandparents, she'd liked the way he'd called Elmer 'pa' and his grandmother 'ma', even though she never asked him why.

When Moss made Ella a decent offer to buy her wagon and oxen, it was Marrok who persuaded her to sell them.

"We've got six wagons between me and Artie. We don't really need another, or more oxen, and we'll likely have to dismantle the wagons to get though the mountain passes anyway. We could use them as shelters for everyone coming north with us, but I'd rather trade some of our oxen for teepees as they'll be warmer in the winter months ahead. So go make your sale Ella but keep the money in your pocket. One day you might have something to spend it on, just for yourself. It'll remind you of your parents and the ranch and this journey west by wagon train and how we met."

Moss was delighted with the sale, which gave him two good wagons and twelve oxen to start up the ranch he hoped to buy in California. It also meant Ruby could remain sleeping in Ella's wagon as their paying passenger.

4

Four days after Ella and Marrok were married, Joe Bracedon was sworn in as the new wagon master, responsible for taking the wagon train on to California. They were scheduled to roll out at 6am the following morning. Miller Minson was sworn in as the wagon master who'd take the rest of the settlers on up to the Willamette Valley. They planned to roll out just after the bigger wagon train, bound for California. When the first bugle call came at 4am, Ella, Marrok, Artie and all their teams got up to wave the settlers off and say goodbye.

"Don't fret about me, my lovely," Ruby said, hugging her. "You know I'm different to you. I wish with all my heart I could settle down and find a good man like your Marrok, but you know I'll never settle down. So please be happy for me? I'll think of you often, for how could I ever forget you, or Marrok, or Clara and what the three of you did for me. If you think of me at all, think of me standing on stage in a big concert hall, being paid to sing!"

Ella wiped away her tears and turned to say farewell to Martha, Constance and Willard, as their girls watched on, upset that Ella was leaving. Their only consolation was that Ruby was staying and they had a new baby brother to fuss over.

But Martha couldn't stop her tears. "I can't believe I'm losing you. It don't seem right somehow."

It was then that Constance stepped forward, just out of bed after giving birth five days earlier. She put an arm around her mother-in-law's shoulders and gently pulled Martha away. "We'll do just fine,

Ella," she said. "You go on and live a good life. We know you'll be happy, because anyone just has to see you with Marrok to understand no other man would do for you."

Willard hugged Ella goodbye. "Martha mentioned you'll try and send us word. I'll look forward to receiving that letter."

When the second bugle call came at 6am, as everyone made ready to leave, Ella felt her heart lurch with grief, knowing this would be the last time she saw Martha, or any of them. With one last hug goodbye, Martha climbed up to sit beside Willard on the buckboard and as the wagon rolled out, as they waved farewell, Martha wiped away her tears.

"I love you, darling girl! Be happy, Ella!" she cried and then she was gone, the wagon passed by.

Constance and the three older children sat at the back of Willard's other wagon, with the new baby in Constance's arms. "Take care Ella!" Constance called as they waved goodbye, the two girls upset as they called farewell.

Then the two wagons which belonged to Moss and Nell were coming towards her. Abe and Wilber walked at the head of each team of oxen, with Moss sitting on the backboard of his wagon, and Nell and Ruby on the other. Ella watched as her father's wagon came slowly towards her, along with the team of oxen she'd purchased with Marrok in St Louis. She felt a mix of emotions on seeing that wagon and team. When she saw it was Nell who held the reins that had once belonged to her father, not Jasper, she heard the sob in her throat. And then Ruby was waving goodbye to her, from where she sat beside Nell on the buckboard.

"Don't worry about me, Ella! You know I'll be just fine!" the girl called. "Once I get to San Francisco, a whole new life awaits! I love you!" She reached over and put an arm around Nell's shoulders, as Clara ran beside the wagon, calling goodbye.

"You take care of yourself, girl!" she yelled to Ruby. "You go on an' find someone to hold durin' the worst of storms!"

"I'll miss you Clara!" Ruby cried. "I love you! I love you for taking care of me!"

And then they were gone, as other wagons rolled up behind them, blocking them from sight. Ella openly sobbed now as she watched them go, the dust rising behind them as Marrok held her close and then the smaller wagon train was heading out, on its way to the Willamette Valley. But as Ella leaned into the strength of Marrok, she was aware of his tension and knew he was also eager to ride on out.

When the last of the wagons had gone, they were alone with the few people who lived at the trading post. The large group of Bannock and Shoshone had left the day before, riding out at dawn to head back into the mountains, back to their own valleys.

"Are we ready?" Artie called.

Marrok nodded. "Let's go," he said and as everyone headed back to their wagons, their oxen harnessed and ready to go, Marrok turned to Ella.

"Are you alright?"

She nodded and smiled at him, wiping away the last of her tears as Artie climbed aboard his wagon.

But before he flicked the reins to lead the wagons forward, he raised his arm. *"Wagons ho!"* he yelled.

Ella mounted Billy, then looked over at Jasper who was sitting astride Bear. Jasper wasn't a natural rider, mainly because of his legs, but he'd ride the old horse at a walk, leaving Clara to sit on the buckboard beside one of Marrok's men who'd driven that wagon all the way west. Ella glanced over at Clara and the older woman smiled at her. They were the only women accompanying twenty-two men north, along with six wagons and thirty-six oxen.

Ella turned as Marrok rode up beside her, reaching between their horses to take her hand. And one final time, Ella glanced back towards the wagons heading for California, too small to make out now as the last of them moved between a forest of pine way in the distance.

She felt that loss again, then turned to look at the man sitting astride his horse beside her, holding her hand. And she knew, without any doubts whatsoever, that this was where she was meant to be, right here, with him. Whatever lay ahead, the good and the bad, Ella knew in her heart that Marrok would always be there for her. She smiled and raised his hand, bringing it to her lips to kiss it. "Let's go Marrok. It's a long ride to Oregon."

Epilogue

April 1849

Ella reached for a shawl and draped it around her shoulders, before covering the infant in her arms to keep him warm as she walked silently towards the bedroom door. Before she closed it behind her, she glanced back at Marrok. He lay abed, in shadows, fast asleep, as it wasn't yet dawn. But Ella had no desire to wake him. He looked so peaceful lying there and she couldn't help but think that in the years since they'd married at Fort Hall, he'd barely changed. A few more lines around his eyes, but that was all. He was still fit and lean and she loved him as much, if not more, than she did when they married. The passion was still there, but since she'd had the babe they now shared a deeper, stronger bond.

She shut the door quietly behind her, the moccasins on her feet keeping her warm as she stepped into the main room of the cabin, moving across to the hearth to stoke the hot coals before adding several logs of wood, shivering a little in the coolness of the early morning. Even though it was April and the beginning of spring, it was still cold up here in the high country.

She walked across to the window and opened one of the wooden shutters to look out at the mountains which surrounded them, as the sky slowly turned to grey in the pre-dawn light. This was her favorite time of the day, watching the sun rise, for soon the colors of pink and gold would come, turning the darkness of the night sky above the mountains into something breathtaking.

The babe squirmed in her arms and Ella closed the shutter to keep the heat in the room before opening the front door and stepping out onto the porch. As she pulled the door shut behind her, she glanced at the two smaller cabins built just beyond this two-room cabin she shared with Marrok. One of them belonged to Clara, the other to Jasper. Smoke drifted from both, as well as the half dozen cabins built up in the woods where the six men who had stayed on to work for Marrok lived, four of them with their Chinook wives.

Ella squinted in the early morning light as she looked over towards the river, as it wound its way between the trees that lined its banks, the branches of the cottonwoods and birches now bare from winter. Way on the other side of the river she could see the drift of smoke coming from the two-room cabin where Artie lived with his Chinook wife and beyond them, the cabins where ranch hands lived with their wives and young families.

She turned as the mares ready to foal walked restlessly in the corral, which Marrok had built near the house. Beyond them, way out across the valley, the rest of the herd grazed on open land. These were Marrok's horses. Some of them he'd brought west with him, others had been bred with the hardy mustangs the Chinook preferred. On the other side of the house, the oxen that Marrok had brought west with him from Independence, grazed within large corrals.

Ella smiled as she looked out over the ranch. She'd loved it from the moment she'd first laid eyes on it, for it was as beautiful, as vast, as fertile as

Marrok had described. Some thirty miles wide by some forty miles long with a wide shallow river running through the center of it, Artie and Marrok had each claimed a side of the river for themselves.

They traded with the Chinook for everything they couldn't grow or hunt themselves, but once a year they did a seven-week round trip to Fort Vancouver to buy supplies of flour, coffee, sugar, salt and salted bacon. Tomorrow morning Marrok and Artie would leave with several of their men to do that annual trip again, but this year they hoped to return with a few pigs so they could breed from them and make their own salted bacon, as well as a few milking cows and chickens. They had put the order in last year, knowing the stock would have to come across from Hudson Bay or up from California. But now that Ella had the babe, her need for fresh milk was urgent, as her own milk wouldn't last much longer. Besides, she longed for the chance to make cheese and butter.

She usually went with the men to Fort Vancouver, but this year she didn't have the energy, not with a four-month-old child.

Jasper had also declined Marrok's invitation this year, even though he always went with him to Fort Vancouver. But Ella was glad to have him stay back, along with Clara and a few ranch hands to help her while the men were away.

But Ella knew there was another reason why Jasper didn't go with Marrok. She knew, just like everyone else, that Jasper's knees and hips pained him now, more than he let on. When the Chinook came to visit, Jasper always welcomed them, as they brought him herbs to help with his joint pain. But despite the bone aching cold of these high mountain winters, Ella knew Jasper would never change the life he had here, to the life he'd left behind in St Louis, or the warmer climate there.

Nor would Clara change a thing. She'd told Ella once that she'd found a deep peace living in these mountains and had even declined several offers of marriage from men who worked on the ranch. She liked her life just the way it was, having her cabin all to herself, spending her days with Ella and the babe.

Ella suddenly thought of the letter she'd written to Martha. She must remember to give it to Marrok on the morrow, for it had taken her over a year to write. Marrok had promised to give it to the captain of any ship docked in Vancouver Bay heading for California, with instructions to leave the letter at some respectable establishment. Ella didn't know if Martha would ever receive it, but it gave her pleasure knowing she'd sent it.

She'd written to Martha of her joy in Marrok and her son, of building their cabins and settling down, of her pride in her vegetable plot of corn and squash, the seeds given to her by the Chinook. She wrote of the wild blueberry patch she'd found up in the woods behind the house, of Clara making pies with those berries, reminding Ella of the blueberries they'd found on that wagon trail all those years ago. She also wrote of their first winter spent with the Chinook, sheltering in teepees against the bitter cold, of having to dismantle their wagons so the oxen could carry them over the mountains with the help of travois the men had built, before finally reaching this valley in the spring of 1847.

That was two years ago, yet it felt like an age, for their lives had changed so much. Ella could still remember how isolated she had found it, living out here in the wild, but once the men built the cabins and the ranch hands settled down and had families of their own, everything changed. And the Chinook were always here, ready to trade, setting up their teepees close to the river, offering a share of their hunt while everyone gathered around their open fires. Soon enough the salmon would come, filling the rivers, and everyone would feast on them.

Ella sometimes thought of her father's ranch, along with those three graves on the hill behind the house. She couldn't imagine living there now, and when she bothered to dwell on her lucky escape from Jebediah Crawley, she still felt her belly crawl with disgust for him and her uncle.

One thing she wished for but knew she could never have, was for her parents to have met Marrok and her son. But she never said it aloud, never wanting Marrok to know how much she missed them. Nor did she speak of her longing for the muggy summer heat of St Louis on those bitterly cold days of winter, when temperatures plunged below freezing.

But she wouldn't change anything. And she wouldn't leave here, not for anything in the world.

She smiled, taking a deep breath of the cold fresh morning air, aware of the scents of damp grass and herbs and horses, remembering the hard times along with the good. The baby whimpered and she held him close to her body's warmth against the chill of the day, when the door opened behind her. She turned as Marrok stepped out to join them, a blanket around his shoulders and as he bent to kiss her, he moved to wrap the blanket around the three of them, enveloping them in a hug, pulling them close.

She would miss him during the seven weeks he'd be gone, but he'd be back by summer. She couldn't wait and as the babe whimpered in her arms again, Marrok moved to take him, holding the child to his heart, whispering to him in his Ojibwe dialect. Ella understood the words, for she knew some of them now, along with some Chinook. She leaned into Marrok, looking up into his strong, handsome face and whispered the same words back to him. "I love you."

The following in an excerpt from Ruby, the second and last book in the *escape west by wagon train* series. Because it's an excerpt, it might change a little in the final book:

Ruby paused as she climbed the hill to look down over the town below and the ocean beyond. The sea birds flew on the hot thermal air currents, those same salty breezes blowing in from offshore sweeping around Ruby, making her feel alive, as if she too could fly away on them, like those gulls.

She turned to glance up towards the trees above her and knew the sooner she reached the shelter of them the better, for she could feel her pale skin burn in this heat. So she lifted her skirts and pushed herself onward, her hat falling about her shoulders, leaving her face flushed with the excursion of the climb and the heat of the day.

When she reached the trees she sank down in the long grass beneath them, grateful to be in the shade and in an effort to cool down, she pulled her skirts up above her knees before taking off her boots. She closed her eyes in bliss as she leaned back against a tree, grateful not only for the silence, but for that blessed cool breeze.

She saw them less than an hour later, after she'd feasted on the bread and cold roast beef and cheese she'd brought with her. Two men, one older than the other, far below, climbing towards her.

Ruby pulled on her boots and swept her skirts down before pushing herself to her feet, annoyed at being disturbed.

But she also felt a tremor of fear.

She was all alone up here and there was

nowhere for her to go. Nor anywhere to hide. And before she reached for her jacket and the small pistol hidden in the pocket, she pulled her bonnet on, pulling the ribbons tight, making sure every bit of her fiery red hair was covered.

If you liked Ella's story, check out Ruby, the second and last book in the series.

And if you want more, you'll find everything you need to know about Sadie here www.sadieconall.com including free previews on all her books as well as excerpts. You can join up for her newsletter, find links to her Goodreads page, along with Facebook and Twitter and if you want to contact her personally by email, go here sadieconallauthor@gmail.com

Made in the USA
Monee, IL
15 September 2021